The Traitor

The Traitor

JØRN LIER HORST

Translated by Anne Bruce

MICHAEL JOSEPH

PENGUIN MICHAEL JOSEPH

London Borough of Enfield	
91200000825292	
Askews & Holts	28-Nov-2024
AF CRI	
ENOAKW	

Published in Great Britian by Penguin Michael Joseph, 2024
First published in Norway by Bonnier Norsk Forlag as *Forræderen*, 2022

001

Copyright © Jørn Lier Horst, 2024
English translation copyright © Anne Bruce, 2024

The moral right of the author has been asserted

Penguin Random House values and supports copyright.
Copyright fuels creativity, encourages diverse voices, promotes freedom
of expression and supports a vibrant culture. Thank you for purchasing
an authorized edition of this book and for respecting intellectual property
laws by not reproducing, scanning or distributing any part of it by any
means without permission. You are supporting authors and enabling
Penguin Random House to continue to publish books for everyone.
No part of this book may be used or reproduced in any manner for the
purpose of training artificial intelligence technologies or systems. In accordance
with Article 4(3) of the DSM Directive 2019/790, Penguin Random House
expressly reserves this work from the text and data mining exception.

Set in 13.5/16pt Garamond MT
Typeset by Falcon Oast Graphic Art Ltd
Printed and bound in Great Britain by Clays Ltd, Elcograf S.p.A.

The authorized representative in the EEA is Penguin Random House Ireland,
Morrison Chambers, 32 Nassau Street, Dublin D02 YH68

A CIP catalogue record for this book is available from the British Library

HARDBACK ISBN: 978–0–241–53388–8
TRADE PAPERBACK ISBN: 978–0–241–53389–5

www.greenpenguin.co.uk

Penguin Random House is committed to a
sustainable future for our business, our readers
and our planet. This book is made from Forest
Stewardship Council® certified paper.

1

As blue lights flashed in his mirror just before the motorway exit, William Wisting slowed down. Through the rain-spattered rear window, outlines were blurred in the darkness. The emergency vehicle, a fire engine, approached at speed and a sheet of water splashed the side of his car as it passed.

Nils Hammer looked up from the passenger seat. He cleared his throat but said nothing.

The fire engine turned off towards Larvik. Behind them another emergency vehicle hurtled into view. Wisting kept his speed down to let them pass. Yet another fire engine, followed by two ambulances. Wet autumn leaves swirled up from the asphalt in their wake.

As Wisting switched off the car radio, he caught sight of the dashboard clock: 23.42.

Hammer sat up to open the glove compartment and took out the handheld police radio. They got through mid-message, a Bravo patrol being instructed to drive south. '*Roger that*,' the handset rasped.

They both remained seated in silence, expecting new messages to give some clue about what had happened. 'A traffic accident,' Hammer suggested. 'A serious one, I'd guess.'

Wisting fixed his eyes on the black, sodden road surface. Visibility was poor. The windscreen wipers streaked across the glass, but rain still obscured the blue lights ahead of them and they soon disappeared. His pulse rate always raced at even a glimpse of blue lights.

'Nothing for us,' Hammer added. 'We'd better stick to bicycle thefts.'

That was the most serious incident to occur while they had been at a seminar. Two Romanians had been stopped with a lorryload of stolen bikes.

Hammer still sat, radio in hand. Neither man spoke a word. They both knew that if the Bravo patrol had been directed south, it was likely that something serious had taken place, something that would also require investigative input.

Yet another emergency vehicle caught up with them. Now Wisting slowed right down and drew close to the crash barrier while an oncoming taxi moved aside. As the fire service control unit barrelled past, the side draught rocked the car.

'9-8, 9-8, 9-8. This is 1-1.'

Wisting shot a glance at Hammer and set off in pursuit of the fire tender. 9-8 was a seldom used, urgent response call to all units.

'*Reports from Møllebakken state that at least four houses have been swept away by the landslide. Request the first unit on-site to notify us immediately. Available resources check in on channel two. Over and out from 1-1.*'

Swearing under his breath, Hammer changed radio channel.

'1-1. This is unmarked Fox patrol on channel two,' he called in, and gave their names. 'We're three minutes away, just behind the fire service control unit.'

Wisting activated the blue lights on the radiator grille. Suddenly rain bombarded them with coloured needles.

Møllebakken was situated in a residential area approximately midway between Larvik and Stavern. The houses were located on a slight slope down to the fjord. He found it difficult to imagine an extensive landslide striking there.

The operator allocated them the call sign Fox 4-1.

'The lead officer at the accident site is on channel five.'

'Channel five, roger, over and out,' Hammer acknowledged.

He switched channel. Messages were already ricocheting in all directions from the emergency services. These were instructions about a secure meeting place, descriptions of the extent of the landslide, discussions on safety perimeters and the erection of floodlights.

'Hermod lives in Møllebakken,' Hammer piped up. 'Right down by the water.'

'Sissel's father?' Wisting asked.

He heard Hammer lick his lips, as if he felt the need to moisten his mouth before answering. 'We were there for dinner on Sunday,' he said, nodding. 'On 7 October. It would have been her mother's seventieth birthday.'

Wisting concentrated on driving but found his mind straying to whether he knew anyone who lived there. The only person he could think of was an art dealer whose name he could not recall.

'Do we have any gear with us?' he asked.

Hammer twisted round in his seat, peering into the back of the estate car before confirming that they had.

Most service vehicles were provided with a box of equipment in the boot, mainly in case of assistance being required at road accidents. It contained first-aid items, warning lights, flashlights, a casting line, a few tools, a fire extinguisher and some woollen blankets.

Hammer responded on hearing the officer in charge at the accident site use their call sign.

'*Estimated time of arrival?*' he asked.

Wisting glanced again at the clock on the dash: 23.47.

'Less than two minutes,' Hammer replied.

'*Roger. Your assignment is to set up an ambulance control point on the eastern flank and establish a reception area for the dead and injured.*'

As Hammer accepted these instructions, Wisting reflected on the turn of phrase. 'Ambulance control point' and 'reception area' were operative expressions he had once learned but had never needed to put into practice.

He turned off from the main road. The electricity was out and the surrounding houses lay in darkness. Wisting followed suit when the fire service command vehicle ahead of them braked. A few hundred metres in front, blue lights lit up the black night sky.

The fire engine continued straight on. Wisting turned left, down towards the sea, and switched his headlights to full beam as the slanting rain sprayed up from the asphalt. They passed a man carrying a torch, running in the same direction as their car. An elderly woman stood in a doorway with a blanket draped over her shoulders, her eyes following them.

An ambulance had parked across the road ahead. A group of people had gathered on one side, three men and two women, as well as the paramedics.

Wisting drove on to the hard shoulder, grabbing his jacket from the back seat as he stepped out. Above the roar of rain and wind, he could hear scattered shouts.

Some of the spectators moved aside to let them through. Wisting zipped his jacket as he walked through the huddle. Only a few metres further on, the asphalt had completely ruptured and there was a wide gap of around sixty metres.

Wisting took a couple of steps towards the precipitous edge of the crater. Hammer, hard on his heels with two flashlights, handed him one. The landslide appeared to have followed a natural cleft in the rocky hillside, dragging with it everything located between the two flanks. Where they stood was solid ground and he dared to venture a little further forward, out on to a small ridge to the right of the road. The flashlight beams failed to reach all the way down, but he could see earth, stones, clay and what remained of buildings. Smashed roofs and walls. Buried cars. Spilling down through it all, the trajectory of a fast-flowing stream.

Fifty metres above, to their right, light flooded down from the mast on a fire engine roof. In the spotlight, the extent of the catastrophe became clearer. There must have been more than four houses involved, perhaps as many as ten. Affecting about forty people, then, if all the houses had been occupied.

Hammer clung to a tree as he stooped forward towards the edge. 'Hermod's house is still standing,' he yelled with obvious but restrained relief.

Wisting looked in the direction his colleague was pointing and realized he meant a house on the opposite side of the affected area, almost down on the shoreline. The fire engine's floodlight did not reach that far, but they could see that some of the debris from the landslide had stopped at the wall of the house.

Hammer drew back from the edge. The strident wail of sirens from several emergency vehicles rose and fell as they approached. Wisting noticed a faint movement down in the crater, just to their right, and aimed his flashlight. A dog was scrambling on to the undercarriage of an overturned car, its wheels in the air. No other signs of life were to be seen.

2

One of the houses nearest the landslide was a two-storey detached building with a double garage and extensive courtyard. Wisting bowed his head against the foul weather and rushed back to the huddle of neighbours gathered beside the ambulance.

'Who lives there?' he asked, pointing at the house.

A man, soaked to the skin, identified himself.

'We need a reception point,' Wisting said. 'Could you open your garage and clear space inside?'

The man seemed pleased to be given something to do. He answered with a brief nod of the head before darting off.

Hammer gave location details over the radio, reporting that they were in the process of setting things up.

The garage door opened manually from inside. The householder drove out in a Tesla and was helped by neighbours to push out the jet ski on a trailer that occupied the other space.

Wisting and Hammer dashed under cover. Two more ambulances drove up. They turned in the street and parked, ready for duty. The surrounding area shimmered with the blue lights in the torrential rain.

Messages proliferated on the radio transmitter. It sounded as if two survivors were being airlifted out slightly further up in the disaster area, while messages were relayed about fresh, minor landslips. One message was repeated regarding a safety zone of a hundred metres for the land not situated on bedrock, and responses ticked in about the locations that had been successfully evacuated.

Wisting took up position in the garage doorway and noticed something going on in the neighbouring garden – two men supporting a woman. Barefoot, she was wearing only a T-shirt and briefs and was covered from head to toe in mud and muck. A large, bleeding gash was visible on her right thigh and she was shrieking hysterically, struggling to free herself. The paramedics rushed forward. Wisting stepped out into the rain again. The woman was screaming a name, Helene, repeating it over and over before she collapsed on the ground.

'This is Ellen Trane,' said one of the men who had brought her.

A neighbour, Wisting understood. He seemed confused. He began to say something more but had to start over again as he gasped for breath. 'She managed to haul herself up,' he finally said, 'but her daughter's still down there. Helene.'

'Where?' Wisting asked.

The man pointed.

'You'll have to show me exactly,' Wisting told him. 'Wait a minute.' He headed to the police car and returned with the casting rope.

'Call it in,' he instructed Hammer.

Two men accompanied him to the crater. They forced their way through a thuja hedge and emerged into a garden. A children's playhouse teetered on the very edge of the landslip, partly overhanging the drop.

They moved on, crossing the next property, treading carefully as far as the edge. Only one of the men carried a pocket torch and he directed the beam downwards.

'Helene!' he shouted.

Leaning forward, Wisting used his own flashlight but could see nothing but a muddy mass of earth, clay, bushes, trees and debris.

'A bit further up,' the man said.

They continued to follow the landslide perimeter, the floodlight mast on the fire engine casting only long shadows. They searched with their torches and watched the beams criss-cross in the darkness.

'There!' the man called out.

His torch beam flickered around what must have been a garage door, fifteen metres below. Clods of earth loosened from the edge as Wisting inched forward. He spotted the head of a fair-haired child who was sitting in a puddle, clutching what was left of a grey cellar wall.

'Helene!' the man shouted.

Her answer did not reach up to them. The girl tried to turn to face them, but she was unable to twist all the way round.

The man cupped his hands on his mouth and shouted, louder, 'We're coming!' before turning back to Wisting.

Both men expected Wisting to take action. 'The water's rising around her,' one of them said.

Wisting looked down. Rainwater was pouring in from all sides and collecting in the hollow where the girl was trapped. The rescue crew with the necessary equipment would not arrive in time.

'OK,' he said, though he did not really know where to begin.

A wire-mesh fence hung over the edge, dangling above the crater. The closest fence post was located a metre away on the lawn. Wisting checked it out, rocking the post back and forth. It was fixed into a block of cement and held firm.

Handing his flashlight to one of the men, he wrapped the rope diagonally across his chest. Some of the edge gave way when he ventured on to it. He sat down quickly and grabbed hold of the squares on the wire-mesh fence. The crater wall sloped steeply downwards, with torn electricity cables and severed sewage pipes protruding from the waterlogged earth.

Behind him, his two companions called out encouragement to the girl down below as Wisting launched himself out, planting his feet on the earth wall while clinging to the fence to distribute his weight.

He was wearing a pair of lace-up shoes made of synthetic leather, a birthday present from Line two or three years earlier. The soles were worn and slippery and he could see that one of the laces was untied.

He climbed on, struggling to use the fence and gain a foothold. The toes of his shoes were too broad to insert into the netting holes, but at each of the fence posts he was able to stop for a breather.

A pain shot through his right hand. He had gripped a steel peg projecting from a joint in the fence. Blood trickled from his hand, but he clenched his fist a couple of times and moved on.

The fence did not reach all the way down, however. He had to let go to cover the final two metres. He slid down the earth wall and set both feet firmly into the soft mud. He had only one shoe on when he pulled his feet out.

The two men above him used their torches to provide him with light. The girl was ten metres away. Wisting lumbered forward, skirting around something that looked like a garden table as well as a large mattress.

All of a sudden, from the other side of the crater, loud

yells echoed. Wisting stopped in his tracks. He looked up and heard a resounding crack. A house perched on the edge was now tipping over. It was left hanging for a moment or two before the ground disappeared from under it.

The earth shook around him as the house slid out, crushing everything below. The walls parted and tore asunder, sheet by sheet. The roof flattened out, gliding down towards the sea before settling on the shore.

The men above him shouted reassurance to the girl, who still lay wedged beside the wall. 'It's OK! He's right behind you!'

Wisting toiled onwards and eventually reached the girl. The water was now up to her shoulders.

He trudged around her, raising her head and rousing her. Small and slight, she might have been about seven or eight years old. Her skin was cold and her lips were pale blue.

'I'm here now,' he said, addressing her by name. 'I'll set you free.'

He fumbled beneath the water and took hold of something lying on top of her. He managed to yank it off and throw it aside. A bicycle.

She was still trapped, however, her lower body buried in mud.

'Your mum's doing fine,' he went on. 'She's reached safety.'

He circled her again, this time taking hold under her arms and attempting to pull her out. She yelled in pain but remained equally stuck.

Wisting moved around again, feeling his way along her legs, scrabbling down into the mass of mud. His hands encountered planks of wood, stones and twisted metal. He cleared it all away and arrived at something that felt like a metal pipe clamped against her left leg.

The men on the edge shouted out, anxious to know what was going on. Wisting did not answer. He used all his strength to lift the girl. As he raised her, he had to wrench the metal pipe aside to free the girl's foot.

The exertion drained all his energy. He was unsure whether he had succeeded.

'We'll try again,' he said, as much to himself as to the girl lying there.

He gripped her again, under her armpits. This time it was surprisingly easy to drag her free, even though the girl gave a heartrending cry of pain.

Wisting dragged her out of the water and halfway on to the mattress beside them. She was barefoot and had an open wound in her right ankle, with part of the bone projecting from the cut.

Wisting gazed across at the wire-mesh fence. 'Now we have to get you up and out of here,' he said, despite having no idea how to go about it.

Several more people had arrived at the crater's edge. One was lowering a metal ladder, and Wisting grabbed hold. It reached only halfway up but would be of some help.

He carried the young girl across and tugged the rescue rope over his head as he shouted to the others, explaining how he planned to tackle it: he would throw the rope up to them and fasten the other end below her arms. Then the helpers above would have to haul her up along the ladder.

He made an attempt at casting the line but realized that would not work. He would have to climb up with it. He heard shouts as a garden hose was thrown down. That would do the trick.

He wrapped the rubber hose around the girl, twice

around her upper body, before tying a knot and pulling it tight.

The little girl whimpered, fighting for breath, but Wisting paid no heed. He dragged her with him to the ladder and braced her back against it. Then he signalled that the others could begin to heave.

Wisting positioned himself underneath to steady the ladder. The first stage went smoothly. The girl slid along the rungs. Once she reached the spot where the ladder could not reach, progress slowed. Wisting feared the rubber hose would tear, but in the end they managed to flip her over the edge to safety.

Adrenaline had sustained him. Only now did Wisting feel how cold he was and that his right hand was throbbing with pain. He stood gathering his strength before gripping the ladder. He heard shouts from above and, glancing up, saw that the nearest bystanders were pointing further into the crater. Wheeling around, he scanned the site. The dog he had spotted earlier limped towards him.

Wisting brought the ladder down again. The dog came right up to him and nuzzled his leg. Wisting crouched down and scratched behind the mutt's ear, offering him some words of comfort.

The dog was medium-sized and of indeterminate breed. He lifted him up and felt his weight. Maybe ten kilos. Not too heavy to carry with him, but tricky to manipulate up the steep wall of mud. He would need to put it inside something.

He set the dog down and staggered across to the mattress that still lay half buried in earth and clay. A sheet was draped across it. As he disentangled it, he saw that the dog had followed him. He carried it by the shoulders back to the mud wall, where he moved it on to the sheet. The dog thrashed about as Wisting folded it over him and tied it up like a sack.

The bystanders now understood his intentions and sent down the garden hose again. Wisting secured it tightly and gave a sign when he was ready so that they could hoist up the bundle. Once the dog had been saved, he began to scale the ladder himself. It wobbled as he neared the top, but he continued and clambered on, crossing to the wire-mesh fence. Although his legs were shaking, he managed to grope forward to catch hold of it. His arms were aching, but he hauled himself up, holding so tightly that his fingers blanched. When he neared the summit, two pairs of arms grabbed him and heaved him over the edge.

Wisting collapsed on the ground, rolling on to his back, and lay there, relishing the rain on his face.

3

By three o'clock in the morning, they had gained some perspective and control. Evacuation of the houses in closest proximity had been completed and the scale of the landslide was not as rapacious as Wisting had initially feared. No fatalities were reported and no casualties still awaited transport.

He had changed into clothes from his travel bag and also been loaned boots and a thick jumper by the owner of the house where they had set up the reception centre.

Equipment was unloaded. Small petrol-driven generators provided electricity and light. At a camping table, Wisting stood perusing a map of the residential area. A total of eleven dwellings had been demolished in the landslip, each circled in red pen.

The first report had reached the emergency call centre at 23.36. Most of the residents were in bed when the landslide struck, but they had managed to escape, some in nothing but their nightclothes.

The landslip had first formed a deep fissure through the hillside. The nearest buildings had toppled and were left horizontal before the earth was gouged out and they slithered down. This had given the occupants time to leave their homes.

Lists of names and addresses from the population register showed that thirty-two people had been affected, and they had also traced two visitors. Eighteen of these were recorded as having minor injuries and six were in a serious condition, though their injuries were not life threatening. Seven were reported to be unscathed, and one married couple had called in to say they had not been at home. This meant they had one person still unaccounted for, and in addition there was the uncertain factor of whether there had been pedestrians in the vicinity.

The missing person was a twenty-eight-year-old man who lived on his own in a basement apartment. August Tandberg. The radio reported that his parents had arrived and were at the operations centre just beyond the northern perimeter.

Wisting ran through the lists with Hammer one more time to be certain of the numbers before an update was relayed to the media.

The police radio sat at one corner of the camping table. Activity continued at a frenetic pace. One of the rescue helicopters announced a result from the thermal imaging camera for the third time. Previously they had found a cage of rabbits and a wood-burning stove still emitting heat.

Wisting moved out from the garage doorway. The helicopter was hovering above the lower part of the landslip area, lighting up a house that lay on its side with three walls still intact as well as parts of the roof. Another helicopter shone a diagonal light down to the same spot. Two rescue workers were lowered down.

Hammer fetched binoculars. He watched closely for a while before handing them to Wisting. The rescue workers were searching behind piled-up layers of rubble. A number of messages were broadcast on the radio. The background noise of rotor blades made it difficult to decipher what was said. The messages were continually repeated and confirmed that they had found an unconscious victim, a woman.

Wisting returned to the camping table and checked the lists. He saw seventeen females noted there, but all had been crossed off.

The two helicopters changed places and a bundle of equipment was dropped. A short time later, the jarring noise of a power saw filled the air. Then everything went quiet and a radio request was made for a basket stretcher.

The first helicopter returned and lowered the basket. It hung in the air for a couple of minutes before the injured woman was raised with one of the rescue crew and flown out.

The doctor on-site made preparations as the helicopter approached in the air above them and lowered the line. Paramedics took hold of the stretcher. Wisting waited until the helicopter had flown off before he strode forward. The woman was around thirty and had dark hair. She had an open cranial fracture. Hammer allocated her the serial number F-14. The fourteenth woman to be removed from the landslide. Wisting managed to take a photo of her before she was hooked up to a respirator. Her heart rate and blood pressure were low and her body temperature was measured at thirty-three degrees Celsius.

A heating pad slid aside as she was transferred to another stretcher to be transported by ambulance. She was completely naked and her bedraggled body was covered in cuts.

The ambulance drove off and Wisting added her to the list as unknown, with a brief description. Being unclothed indicated that she had been indoors when the landslide hit, but this did not tally with the lists in his possession. All the female residents had been accounted for.

The helicopter had turned back to a spot slightly above

where the woman had been found. Another two rescue workers were set down. Wisting fixed the binoculars to his eyes. He could see them clearing an area littered with a jumble of broken planks.

'They're talking about another find,' said Hammer, who was listening to the radio reports.

It took some time before they received confirmation that the report referred to a man discovered in the depths of the rubble created by the landslip. Unconscious, but alive.

While they waited it stopped raining, but the sky and surroundings were no brighter as a result. After half an hour or so, it was reported that they had succeeded in freeing him and required another basket stretcher.

A team stood by to receive the casualty. Wisting and Hammer moved forward as soon as the helicopter line was detached. Hammer held out his mobile with the photos they had been sent of August Tandberg. Although the man on the stretcher was smeared with blood and muck, they could see that this was the right person.

He was barefoot and had no clothing on his upper torso, wearing only a pair of trousers. They were buttoned at the waist but the zip was undone and the belt unfastened, as if he had been throwing on some clothes when the disaster struck.

Hammer listed him as M-12. The doctor seemed concerned about a large swelling in his abdomen, but apart from that he had no major visible injuries. Before he was taken away, Wisting snapped a photograph to be sent to whoever had contact with his family.

The discovery of the last missing person did not lead to any immediate reduction in the rescue efforts. The helicopters continued to circle for some time above the landslip crater even though all the missing victims had been found, but they eventually abandoned the search as their fuel supplies began to run out.

At four thirty Wisting gave instructions to wind down the reception point and meet up at the operations centre.

The accident site headquarters was housed in a marquee on a football pitch provided by Civil Defence. The press crew had gathered in the same area. No one paid any attention to Wisting and Hammer when they entered.

Within the walls of the tent, the temperature was welcomingly warm. The police chief stood in a group side by side with the heads of the various rescue services. Until the last missing person had been found, she had been directing personnel from within police headquarters. The local mayor was also present. Soon they would face the press, and the chief of police required a status report. The officer in charge ran through the main points in the sequence of events and a list of the operatives who had participated in the rescue efforts. Wisting provided a verbal update and explained that all residents and visitors were accounted for. The coordinator from the health service gave an account of the varying degrees of injury. No one had been admitted with life-threatening injuries.

'Any news of the fourteenth woman?' Wisting asked.

The paramedic shook his head.

'She's being kept unconscious due to her head injury,' he said. 'Her identity's still unknown.'

The police chief shot a glance at the accident coordinator.

'We've no reports of any missing persons,' he said.

A discussion followed about how to handle this at the press conference. Wisting drew back. His work was over for now.

4

Wisting managed a couple of hours' sleep before he had to report for duty. The washing machine had just completed its cycle with his grimy clothes when he entered the bathroom. He hung them up and phoned the station to say he would be at his desk in an hour's time. He had showered before bed and now made do with splashing his face with cold water. The stubble on his cheeks chafed as he dried his face.

As the water had loosened the plaster on his right hand, he tore it off, cleaned the wound and applied a new one.

It was now almost 8 a.m. He switched on the TV in the living room to watch the morning news for the latest updates.

He heard a noise at the front door. Line called out a greeting and came inside with Amalie. On the screen, live footage from the landslip area was being broadcast. The grey morning light showed how extensive the damage was. Wisting looked down at his granddaughter, who had her schoolbag on her back.

'We've talked about it,' Line assured him. 'We just watched the news together.'

Wisting smiled. 'Our houses are solid,' he said. 'They're built on rock. Your school too. And the police station.'

The police chief appeared onscreen. These images were a couple of hours old. She used Wisting's formulation to state that all residents and visitors had been accounted for. The unidentified woman was not mentioned.

'See if you can find something nice in Grandpa's drawer,' Line said, sending her daughter into the kitchen.

They heard the bottom drawer being pulled out.

'Thea lives out there,' Line told him. 'From high school.' This was one of her best friends from high-school graduation.

'Not in that precise location,' Wisting told her with a nod at the overhead footage on the TV screen. 'She's not on the lists.'

His daughter gave him a meaningful look. 'Have you been at work, then?' she asked.

'It happened while Hammer and I were on our way home last night,' he replied. 'We were sent out there.'

'My goodness,' was all Line could say. 'Has anyone else we know been affected?'

Wisting shook his head. 'Not that I know of, but of course Gunnar Helner lives there.'

'The art swindler,' Line said with a smile. 'That's right.'

She had written about him when she worked at the *VG* newspaper. A story about shambolic accounts, customers who had not received their dues, as well as sales of fake paintings and trade in artworks stolen from Jews during the Second World War.

'He was one of the residents who emerged unscathed,' Wisting told her. 'But his house is gone. There's probably a lot of irreplaceable art down there in the rubble.'

He saw that this had sparked her interest. It was an unusual story among all the others that would come to be told in the aftermath of the catastrophe. A few years earlier, Line had moved from news coverage to making documentary films. These were long-term projects in which much of her work could be done from her home office, but from time to time it also demanded a lot of travel.

Amalie returned with a packet of biscuits. 'Take two,' Line said.

Wisting crouched down, lifted her up and deposited her in the armchair. 'Have you learned any more letters?' he asked.

'I know them all,' Amalie answered proudly.

Wisting got her to read the name on the packet of biscuits. 'O-R-E-O.'

Clapping his hands, he took a biscuit for himself. 'Soon you'll be able to read me a whole book,' he said.

Amalie laughed.

'Can you take her on Saturday?' Line asked him. 'I'm going out.'

'Oh, yes?'

Line gave a sigh of resignation. 'Just with a few friends,' she said.

Wisting drilled a finger into Amalie's side. 'Of course she can come here,' he said.

'And stay overnight?'

'All night long,' Wisting reassured her.

On the news, journalists were clamouring for answers on blame and responsibility. The mayor was besieged with questions about the cause of the landslip and replied that it was far too early to comment.

'It's been raining for a week,' Line commented. 'That has to have something to do with it.'

Wisting lifted Amalie down on to the floor.

'Will you be doing more work on it?' Line asked, nodding towards the screen.

'Not out at the site, anyway,' Wisting replied, as he accompanied Line and Amalie into the hallway. 'But all these cases end up as admin work, and something unexpected always turns up.'

5

The site coordinator had moved into the large conference room on the second floor of the police station and had called a meeting for 9 a.m. Wisting entered his own office and cancelled a number of scheduled meetings before heading to the office at the end of the corridor where Maren Dokken was located. She was not yet thirty years old but was one of the investigators he valued most. Thorough and conscientious, she was a keen worker.

'Many appointments today?' he asked her.

'Two,' she replied.

Wisting nodded thoughtfully. 'I'd like you to assume responsibility for the investigation into the landslide,' he said.

Maren glanced at the bundle of case files on her desk.

'You'll be released from everything else for the first few weeks,' Wisting assured her.

'I've never taken on anything like it before,' Maren said.

'You won't be on your own, and most of the work will be done by specialists,' Wisting said. 'Geologists and folk from the Water and Energy Directorate. They'll find the cause, and then it's a matter of how far the disaster could have been avoided. What judgements were made during the planning process and the construction stage, that sort of thing. I need someone who's good at gathering and organizing information. The rest will be up to the police prosecutor.'

Wisting's eyes strayed to the clock. 'If you're ready, we can go up to the meeting.'

With a smile, Maren got to her feet and picked up her pen and notebook.

It was still a few minutes to nine and the leaders of several agencies in the district stood chatting with the coordinators of the various rescue services. Some were drinking coffee and others talking on their phones.

Ada Worren had taken charge of operations for the police. In her mid-thirties, she belonged to the new generation of colleagues more interested in furthering their own career plans than their actual job performance. She had seated herself at the head of the table along with a superintendent on the police chief's staff, who was engrossed in something on a computer screen.

Wisting stepped behind the nearest seat and stood with his hand on the back of the chair. 'Maren Dokken will take part as an investigator,' he said.

The superintendent looked from Wisting to Maren and back again. 'You're not participating yourself?' he asked.

'Not this time,' Wisting answered.

He took a step back and let Maren sit down before leaving to return to his department. Nils Hammer was on his way to his office. He looked exhausted, with heavy eyelids, and his jacket hung awkwardly on his slumped shoulders.

'How's Sissel's father doing?' Wisting asked.

'His house is within the evacuation zone,' Hammer replied. 'He's living with us in the meantime.'

'You didn't need to come in,' Wisting said. 'Go home and look after them.'

'Who's taking the case?' Hammer asked.

'Maren,' Wisting said.

Hammer nodded. 'That's good,' he said. 'Any news on that last woman? Number fourteen?'

Wisting shook his head.

Hammer adjusted his jacket. 'Are you sure you don't need me?' he asked.

'Not today,' Wisting assured him.

Hammer pointed through the doorway to his desk. 'Then I'll stay for just an hour or so.'

'See you tomorrow,' Wisting said, setting off for his own office.

The entire police station was affected by what had happened the previous night. Wisting's task was to try to maintain business as usual. Now and again he checked the online newspapers. Personal stories and experiences from the landslip were now highlighted. Wisting recognized names and faces. Reading what they had gone through made a strong impression on him. In some cases, it had been sheer chance and a matter of seconds that had decided whether or not they escaped with their lives.

Towards the end of the day, Maren appeared. 'I'm going out to see it for myself,' she said.

Leaning back in his chair, Wisting turned to face the window. Following another downpour, there was now only a fine drizzle.

'Can I come with you?' he asked.

'Of course,' Maren replied.

Grabbing his jacket, he followed her down to the garage in the basement.

'Has anyone been bold enough to express an opinion on what happened?' he asked.

'The local authority had a crew on their way out when it struck,' Maren told him. 'The lower road was flooded at

Stavernsveien. The culvert must have been blocked and so the water was obstructed. The golf course on the upper side had been transformed into a lake. Millions of litres of water were bearing down. Before the municipal engineers got there, the road gave way. It became a tidal wave that tore the earth away on its way down to the fjord.'

'A blocked drain, in other words,' Wisting summarized.

'Minor things can have major consequences,' Maren commented.

The road leading to the crater was busy with traffic. Vehicles were parked at the verges on either side of the road, and they had to ease their way forward.

First Maren was keen to see the perimeter of the landslide, where the road had collapsed. Wisting raised two fingers in greeting to the police officer seated in a car at the outermost barrier. At the inner barrier, Maren drove straight up, leaving the bonnet tucked beneath the police tape.

A member of the Civil Defence force met them on the other side. 'Don't go too close,' he warned them.

They stood a few metres from the edge, where the asphalt was ripped asunder. On the other side, they saw a camera team. Between them, a stretch of almost sixty metres of road was missing.

In the ravine, a fast-flowing stream of water cascaded down. Clods of earth were still breaking off from the edges, slithering down to the bottom, where they were swept away by the water.

The landslide had followed the land formation, turning slightly to the right. They could make out the water about three hundred metres further down, but from where they stood they did not have a full overview of the damage.

The first section had been deciduous forest, below which people had lived as if in an amphitheatre, around the cove and beach below. Less than a hundred metres above them, the traffic travelled to and from Stavern. All they could hear was the hum from the road. Last night it had been closed, but in the early hours of the morning it had been checked and declared safe.

'There was a smaller landslip out in Helgeroa in the eighties,' Wisting said. 'I was driving a patrol car in those days. It destroyed a barn and a few pigs were killed, but no one was injured. The sequence of events was something similar. An inadequate conduit became blocked and the water banked up. In the end the road gave way, like a dam bursting. Nothing on the other side could withstand it.'

Maren nodded her head. 'By the way, the last woman to be rescued was called Jorunn Sand,' she said. 'Her husband reported her missing this morning.'

'What was she doing here?' Wisting asked.

'No idea,' Maren answered. 'Her husband thought she was at work.'

'Where would that be?'

'Home nursing care.'

Wisting looked at her. The light rain shone like dewdrops on her hair.

'Does the community nursing service have clients in the area?' he asked.

'No,' Maren replied. 'Anyway, she wasn't at work. She had called in sick earlier in the day.'

'Is she awake?'

'I don't think so.'

They returned to the car. Maren reversed out, turned in the roadway and drove up to the crater from a different angle. Wisting directed her towards the spot where he and Hammer had set up a reception centre the night before. No one was guarding the inner barrier, so Wisting got out and raised the plastic tape so that Maren could drive under it.

They parked in front of the double garage. The courtyard was strewn with litter left by the paramedics.

Neither of them spoke a word. The car doors slammed. All they could hear was the cry of seagulls.

Maren walked uphill, tugging her jacket shut. Wisting brought binoculars from the car and stood beside her.

A flock of seagulls circled above the crater while others fought over food scraps and other titbits they had come across.

Wisting told her about the rescue efforts. Maren borrowed the binoculars as he pointed out the spot where he had saved the girl and where the helicopter had found the last two survivors.

A man was walking along the verge on the other side of the landslip.

'That's a private individual,' Maren said. 'He's very far inside the barriers.'

Wisting reclaimed the binoculars and adjusted the focus. 'It's Gunnar Helner,' he said.

'Do you know him?'

'He lived here,' Wisting explained. 'His house was located around that area.' He pointed to a site further up the crater. 'I once took part in a search there,' he went on. 'Found some paintings in his basement.'

'That he had stolen?' Maren asked.

'He'd received stolen goods, yes,' Wisting replied, handing back the binoculars. 'Gunnar Helner has always been involved in buying and selling paintings and other artworks, but he's never paid too much attention to where the pictures or objects come from. He had a large collection in his house. That's probably what he's looking for now.'

The man on the other side noticed them at this point and moved back from the perimeter of the landslide. At the same time, the intensity of the rain increased.

'Shall we go?' Wisting asked.

Maren remained standing there, binoculars in hand, but did not say anything.

'What is it?' Wisting asked.

'I don't know,' Maren answered, handing him the binoculars. 'Look to the left of that red wall.'

She pointed in the direction she indicated. Wisting understood and lifted the binoculars to his eyes. The distance, as the crow flies, was no more than a hundred metres. Everything zoomed into focus.

'What am I looking for?' he asked.

'A training shoe,' Maren replied. 'Lying with the sole in the air. I think there's a leg underneath it.'

Wisting located the shoe. Beneath, what could be a trouser leg disappeared down into the mud. Dirty jeans.

'It must be something else,' Wisting said. 'Last night, they searched the area in minute detail with thermal imaging cameras.'

Wiping the rain from his eyes, he stepped ten metres or so to the side in an attempt to take a look from a slightly different angle.

'It could be a display mannequin or something,' Maren suggested.

'Or something,' Wisting repeated. 'I think we'd better find out.'

Once back in the car, he rang the accident coordinator and managed to speak to Ada Worren.

'We've spotted something,' he said after explaining where they were. 'There might be a dead body in the lower part of the landslide area.'

'How could that be?' Worren asked. 'No one's missing. All the residents are accounted for.'

Wisting gave a more detailed description of what they had seen. 'I think we should check it out,' he said. 'The easiest way would be to send in a drone to take a closer look.'

There was silence at the other end.

'We should do it before it grows dark,' Wisting added.

'I'll send out a drone and a pilot,' Worren said.

The conversation ended with no parting pleasantries. Wisting cradled the phone in his lap. By now, the rain was hammering on the roof of the car and windscreen. When Maren started the engine, the wipers swept rhythmically across the glass.

'We'll wait here,' Wisting said.

6

The van with the drone was on the scene half an hour later. While they waited, the wind had picked up, but not enough to cause navigation problems.

Maren gave directions to the approximate area. Wisting stood in the background, watching the images on the screen. The drone buzzed like a huge, angry insect when it descended into the crater.

There was still movement in the mass of earth. The water flowing through the landslip kept finding new routes, carving its way forward and creating new landslides. Down by the sea, containment booms had been installed to hold back the flotsam. A vessel from the coastguard service kept watch.

The training shoe was in the same place. The images were clear and sharp. The pilot zoomed in and let the sole of the shoe fill the entire screen before turning the drone round to the other side.

The shoelaces were tied. The drone was raised and pulled back just as the camera angle tilted. The blue jeans fabric on the leg came into view. It had ridden up a little and, between the trouser and the shoe, there was a gap where they could see a sock and a hairy human leg.

The drone pilot swore. 'I think you're right,' he said.

'It's still too dangerous to go down there to check it out properly,' the other operator commented.

The drone was left hovering in mid-air as Wisting produced his phone. 'Can you relay these images?' he asked.

Nodding, the drone pilot opened a screen menu. Wisting waited until the file had been transferred before calling Ada Worren.

'We need helicopter support,' he said after outlining their conclusions.

'Wait a second,' Worren said.

Wisting understood she was examining the images while he was kept on hold. Nearly two minutes ticked by before she came back to him.

'You'll get a Sea King,' she said. 'The rescue centre estimates they'll be with you in around half an hour. Both an ambulance and a doctor have been requisitioned.'

Wisting passed on the message to the others. The drone was recalled and Wisting and Maren returned to their car to wait.

'It's been less than twenty-four hours since the landslide,' Maren pointed out. 'This must be someone who hasn't yet been reported missing. Maybe someone who lives along there and was out for a walk that evening or something like that.'

'All the same, it's not good,' Wisting said. 'We should have expressed some reservations in our statement. The police chief said that everyone had been rescued from the landslip and everyone was accounted for.'

The ambulance appeared ten minutes later. Five minutes after that, the doctor's vehicle turned up. Behind that, a patrol car arrived with Ada Worren in the passenger seat. Wisting switched the police radio to the shared rescue service channel but remained in the car. When Maren activated the windscreen wipers, Wisting leaned forward and stared up at the sky. After a short spell of silence, he caught sight of the helicopter, approaching from the south-east with its lights flashing. Immediately after that, they heard an announcement on the radio.

'*Larvik police, Larvik police. This is Saver 4-0.*'

Ada Worren responded and gave the exact coordinates from the drone images.

Wisting and Maren left their car. The pulsating noise of the rotors blasted them, along with the rain and the wind. The other teams came to join them as the helicopter executed a flypast at low altitude.

'*No result on the thermal imaging,*' the crew reported.

'How quickly does body temperature drop?' Maren asked.

Wisting glanced at his watch. Almost 3 p.m.

'It's been no more than fifteen hours since the landslide struck,' he said, looking at the doctor.

'A lot of factors come into play,' the medic replied. 'Weight, air temperature and environment, but it shouldn't be anywhere under twenty-five degrees as yet.'

Wisting hunched his shoulders. He estimated the air temperature to be somewhere around ten degrees Celsius, slightly above the norm for October. A dead body would still produce a significant result on a thermal imaging camera.

'Maybe it's a display mannequin,' Maren suggested again.

'Let's hope so,' Wisting answered.

The police radio crackled. '*We have visual observation,*' the helicopter pilot announced. '*Going down.*'

As the side hatch on the helicopter slid up, a rescue worker attached himself to the winch rope and was lowered down. He swayed like a pendulum until he tentatively planted his feet on the ground.

Wisting used the binoculars and saw he had landed in the right spot. He tossed aside twigs and planks before striding forward to investigate the discovery. Then it looked as if he was reporting something in the headset microphone on his helmet. At once, the message was relayed from the helicopter: '*Confirmed find of corpse.*'

'*Roger*,' Ada Worren replied.

Maren had not caught the exchange.

'Dead body found,' Worren clarified.

Wisting passed the binoculars so that Maren could see more clearly.

Another rescue worker was lowered, carrying two spades. Even without the binoculars, Wisting could watch them digging out the body. Shovelling through earth and mud, tossing wreckage aside.

Then the stretcher was lowered and the corpse transferred to it. One of the rescuers accompanied the stretcher as it was manoeuvred across to the waiting police officers. He detached the stretcher and unclipped his harness before the helicopter wheeled round to pick up his colleague.

It was a man's body. In his mid-thirties. His head was swollen and discoloured and the cadaver was grimy and grubby. He had longish hair and was wearing jeans, a turtleneck sweater and a waterproof jacket. A large gash was visible in his lower jaw and he had grazes and scratches on his forehead and nose as well as a deep gouge in the flesh of his left cheek.

Stepping forward, the medic crouched down and carried out a routine check for vital signs before declaring the man dead.

'He should be autopsied,' he said as he stood up again. 'Rigor mortis has left the body so he's probably been dead for more than forty-eight hours.'

'Before the landslide hit?' Ada Worren asked.

The doctor shrugged. 'That's my conclusion, at least.'

'Can you say anything about when he died?' Wisting asked.

'That'll be up to the pathologist,' the doctor answered. 'But the external injuries, such as the lesion on his cheek, look as if they were inflicted post-mortem. There's no sign of bleeding and they most likely occurred during the landslide.'

The helicopter flying overhead seemed to be intending to land on the football pitch.

Wisting took a few photographs of the dead man before asking the paramedics for a pair of latex gloves. Tugging them on, he checked the dead man's pockets but found them empty. The man wore no watch or rings. The skin on his hands was deeply lined and pale flakes had sloughed off.

Ada Worren fetched a body bag from the patrol car. She unfolded it on the ground and explained how she wanted the others to help her lift the body across. Wisting stood at the man's head and took hold of his upper right arm.

'On the count of three,' Worren said.

Wisting placed his hand behind the man's head to support it. They raised him and laid him down carefully.

Worren pulled the zip up from the foot end.

'Wait a minute,' Wisting said.

He turned the head to one side. The hair was tangled, smeared with mud and muck. Wisting separated the strands. At the top of his neck, the man had a wound, a small cavity that one of his fingers had slipped into when he had cradled the head.

The rain pattered on the hard plastic sheet encasing the body and had already gathered in the hollow between the man's legs.

For a second Wisting considered asking the doctor to look at what he had found, but instead he signalled to Ada Worren that she could close the bag. Wisting had seen similar injuries before. It was a gunshot entry wound.

7

It was dark outside when Wisting closed the conference room door. He had assembled the personnel he needed. Everyone around the table knew that this impromptu meeting related to the corpse now designated M-13, but only Maren Dokken was familiar with the background.

Benjamin Fjeld was one of the detectives called in. He had worked in the department previously but had then moved to Oslo with a girlfriend. Now their relationship was over and he had applied to return. The five years he had spent as an investigator in the capital had given him a wealth of knowledge and experience and, what's more, he was as enthusiastic as always.

Espen Mortensen had been drafted from the crime scene investigation section and Nils Hammer had returned from home, looking more rested and refreshed.

Police prosecutor Christine Thiis would have legal responsibility for the murder investigation Wisting was to lead. In addition to the officers who would form part of the investigation group, Wisting had asked police chief Agnes Kiil to attend, along with her communications adviser, prior to a planned meeting with the team in charge of the accident investigation on the floor above.

'Why wasn't he found earlier?' Kiil demanded. 'The search shouldn't have been abandoned until we were absolutely certain.'

Wisting put his hands before him and spread all his

fingers on the tabletop. 'We don't know who this man is,' he said. 'But he's not a victim of the landslide.'

The police chief cocked her head as Wisting gave an account of the information from the doctor who had estimated the length of time since the man died.

'The cause of death won't be established until the autopsy tomorrow morning, but on-site observations suggest he was shot,' he concluded.

The chief of police asked him to repeat what he knew one more time. Wisting displayed images on the large screen, of both the discovery site and the dead body as he ran through the report again.

Mortensen was keen to have more information on the injuries mentioned.

'I spotted an entry wound at the back of his head with an exit wound through the jaw,' Wisting stated.

The police chief turned to the comms adviser. 'How do we communicate that?' she asked.

The adviser's neck had taken on a distinct red flush. 'That's really up to the investigation leader,' he said, glancing at Wisting.

'We have to convey the factual circumstances,' Wisting replied. 'What's most crucial is that we find out who the man is.'

'Give me something in writing,' the police chief instructed, 'and I'll include it in the press briefing at 7 p.m.' She got to her feet and left the room with her adviser.

Nils Hammer reached across the table. 'Where does he come from?' he asked, glancing at the big screen. 'How did he end up slap bang in the middle of the landslip?'

Now that the chief of police had left the room, the meeting changed character, becoming more of an investigation.

Wisting clicked on a new image, this time a map of the landslide area, the same one he had used on the night of the disaster. Now the affected properties and houses had been shaded red.

'It's unlikely the body was dumped there after the landslide,' he said. 'He must have been in the upper section of the neighbourhood when the landslip struck.'

Mortensen spoke up. 'What do we know about the earth and rubble in the spot where he was found?' he asked.

Wisting returned to one of the earlier photographs. 'Red timber cladding,' Wisting answered. 'That's the most specific thing. At first light I'll get the crime scene technicians down into the crater.'

'Do we know how many red houses we're talking about down there?' Benjamin Fjeld asked.

Wisting shook his head. 'We need a survey and a background check of every individual resident,' he said, returning to the shaded overview image.

Each of these houses could have been a crime scene that had been destroyed in the landslide.

'I'll do that,' Benjamin volunteered, jotting this down.

'Is there no one reported missing?' Christine Thiis asked. 'Maybe somewhere else in the country?'

'No one who matches M-13,' Wisting replied.

He addressed himself to Mortensen again. 'The body is at the hospital here in Larvik,' he said. 'It will be transported to Forensics early tomorrow morning. I'd like you to secure fingerprints before that.'

Mortensen nodded.

'What about the naked woman?' Maren asked. 'Could there be a connection?'

Wisting checked the time. 'Make sure we're informed

as soon as she regains consciousness,' he said. 'We have to persuade her to talk.'

They continued around the conference table, lobbing hypotheses back and forth. This was how an investigation took shape. Once they had all expressed their thoughts and opinions, Wisting pushed back his chair and stood up.

'Let's get cracking,' he said. 'We're already at least forty-eight hours behind in relation to the time of the murder.'

He headed straight to his office and wrote a few notes for the police chief regarding what he wanted her to say. Then he shrugged on his jacket and made his way to Maren's office.

'Do you have a list of where the residents have been housed?' he asked.

Maren flipped the image on her computer screen. 'Most of them are staying with family or friends,' she said. 'The rest are being put up in a local hotel. Who do you have in mind?'

'The art dealer,' Wisting replied. 'Gunnar Helner.'

Maren ran her eyes down the list. 'He's at the Grand Hotel,' she answered. 'Room 302.'

'Thanks,' Wisting responded. 'I'll start there.'

8

In the hotel lobby, Wisting met journalists on their way out. Reporters, cameramen and photographers who had installed themselves alongside the evacuees. The clock above the reception desk showed the time as past six thirty. Less than half an hour until the police chief planned to update the press, and then the discovery of the body would be public knowledge.

Wisting climbed the stairs to the second floor and knocked at room 302: no reply. He put his ear to the door and listened but could not pick up anything.

Gunnar Helner was a name he had placed at the top of his own personal list. It would be interesting to talk to him before the instigation of a murder inquiry became common knowledge. He had tried to call him but had been unable to reach him by phone. Probably his mobile had disappeared in the landslide.

An elderly couple passed him and descended the stairs. Wisting knocked again, a bit harder this time, but still to no avail.

He returned to reception to leave a message and was just about to speak to the woman behind the counter when Gunnar Helner walked in with a dressing on his forehead. His boots were mucky and his trouser legs stiff with dried mud.

Wisting strode forward to greet him. Helner nodded in recognition. They were both the same age, but Helner had not grown up in Larvik and hadn't moved to the town until he was an adult. They only knew each other from the previous case Wisting had investigated.

'How are you doing?' Wisting asked him.

Gunnar Helner shrugged. 'What can I say?' he replied.

'Have you got time for a chat?' Wisting asked.

Helner, appearing exhausted and worried, launched into a dismissive response, but then seemed to change his mind. 'Have you eaten?' he asked.

Wisting realized how hungry he was and gratefully accepted the idea of keeping the art dealer company over a meal.

They secured a table at the far end of the restaurant. Wisting could not remember what length of sentence Helner had received as a result of his arrest for receiving stolen goods. The court case had ended in a decision that most of the custodial period should be conditional, but he had certainly spent a few months behind bars.

Helner ordered a bottle of wine before the waiter made himself scarce. Wisting requested some Farris mineral water.

'What happened?' he asked once they were alone together.

'I was sitting reading,' Helner began. 'I could hear the rain drumming on the windowpanes.'

He looked out into the dining room, as if he felt the need to collect his thoughts and impressions before he went on.

'There was a strange swishing sound from outside,' he said, 'like a great gust of wind. It grew into a rumbling noise, like a fierce thunderstorm. The whole house began to shake and creak at the joints.'

He paused again, grabbing the menu with one hand, but did not look at it.

'I sprang to my feet,' he continued. 'Pictures were falling off the walls. The wallpaper had an enormous tear, all the way across the entire wall. Windows flew open and glass showered all over the place. I was making my way to the door when the power went off. Everywhere was plunged into darkness, and at the same time it felt as if the entire house had been wrenched free and tipped over, almost like a boat listing. I had to hold on to the doorframe. Loose objects shot out from all the shelves and cupboards. The bookcase and other furniture toppled over and slid down into an enormous crack that had opened up in the floor. Then it seemed to grind to a halt, and all of a sudden I was standing in the rain. Half of the house had gone. The part where I stood was teetering on the edge of the landslide.'

The waiter reappeared and asked Helner to taste the wine before filling his glass.

They both ordered meat dishes without examining the menu very closely.

'How did you escape?' Wisting asked.

'I fought my way to the door, but couldn't open it,' Helner told him. 'I clambered out a window and legged it – without looking back. By the time dawn came, the rest of the house was gone too.'

Wisting told Helner about the part he had played during that night but omitted the drama involving the young girl he had rescued.

'How long had you lived there?' he asked.

'Nearly twenty-three years,' Helner replied.

'Have you lost much?'

'I keep most of my valuables at my business address,' Helner answered. 'But all my own personal possessions, they're gone.'

He met Wisting's eye and dragged one corner of his mouth into a reluctant smile.

'You've been in my house,' he said. 'I had a considerable collection. Paintings and other works of art, antiquarian first editions and unique copies with dedications. All of it well documented and insured, but the loss is considerable, all the same.'

Wisting nodded. 'I saw you walking at the edge of the crater today,' he said. 'Inside the barriers.'

Helner looked down. 'It was a distressing sight,' he said. 'Worse than the TV pictures suggested.' He raised his eyes again. 'What plans do you have for the area?' he asked. 'Will people be able to get any of their possessions back?'

'It's too early to say,' Wisting told him. 'And depends entirely on how safe it is to move around inside the crater. It's still raining, of course, and a lot has already been washed into the sea.'

Their food was served and they ate for a while in silence.

'Twenty-three years,' Wisting repeated. 'Do you know your neighbours well?'

'Not particularly,' Helner replied. 'Mostly the ones who've been there longest.'

'A good neighbourhood?' Wisting asked, with his mouth full of food.

'Yes,' Helner answered, without adding any further details.

'Any arguments between neighbours or other local conflicts?' Wisting added as he chewed. 'Loud music or noisy parties?'

'No more than any other place,' Helner replied.

Wisting went on fishing for information about the locale, but the impression he had already gleaned from computer printouts about age profiles, gender division and income levels remained unchanged. Nothing stood out.

'You're asking questions as if one of us there was to blame for the landslip,' Helner commented as he put down his cutlery.

Wisting glanced at his watch. It was nearly half past eight. The news was out.

'A dead body was found in the crater,' he said, wiping his mouth.

Helner looked at him. Nothing but amazement could be seen on his face.

'Who was that, then?' he asked. 'They said everyone made it out.'

Wisting inclined forward slightly. 'We're investigating it as a murder,' he said. 'The medic said he's been dead for at least forty-eight hours.'

Gunnar Helner sat with his mouth open for a moment or two before he was able to say anything. 'Who was he?' he asked again.

'No one who lived in the area,' Wisting answered. 'That's practically the only thing we know.'

The waiter arrived to clear their plates. 'Dessert?' he asked.

Wisting shook his head as he passed the question to Helner. 'No, thanks,' he replied. 'Just the bill.'

'He could have been killed some time around the start of the week,' Wisting went on. 'Did anything happen in the locality that you might be able to connect to that?'

Leaning back in his chair, Gunnar Helner shook his head.

'Any strangers or unusual vehicles?' Wisting suggested.

'I was away until Sunday,' Helner replied. 'In Paris. Got

home that evening. On Monday I left early for the gallery and was there until late. Same on Tuesday.'

Something occurred to him. 'I have a few cameras around the house,' he said. 'They're lost now, of course, but the footage is stored externally at the supplier's. I have the same system installed at my business address. They're fitted with activity sensors. One of them records traffic in front of the house. I can get hold of the footage, if it's of interest to you.'

'Yes, please,' Wisting replied.

When the waiter returned with the bill, Helner covered it with his hand.

'This probably means you'll be doing more detailed searches in the crater itself?' he asked. 'That you'll be looking for a murder weapon and other clues?'

'We have to assess the possibilities,' Wisting answered.

Helner seemed to be holding something back, before he appeared to make up his mind. 'There's one thing you could maybe look out for,' he said, drawing the bill towards him. 'Something I think may be of interest to you and your team.'

'What do you have in mind?' Wisting asked.

'I can't go into details,' Helner replied. 'Not yet. But I had a green fireproof safe. A slim, metal container, a metre and a half in length. I'd like you to let me know if you come across it.'

'What's inside?' Wisting asked.

Helner shook his head. 'Not now,' he said. 'But if you do find it, you'll get the whole story.'

He turned aside and thrust his hand into the pocket of his jacket, which was draped over the back of the chair.

'I managed to bring this with me when the house

vanished,' he said, holding out a key fob. He displayed each of the keys in turn. 'This one's the house key . . . the car key . . . the shop . . .' The fourth key was more solid and had a row of little teeth. 'And this one's for the safe,' he rounded off.

Wisting nodded as Helner gave him a crooked smile. 'Call me if you find the container and I'll come with the key.'

9

Just before midnight, Wisting rounded up the investigators. Twenty-four hours had elapsed since the landslide and five since they had last met around the conference table. Nothing had happened to drive the case forward. The police chief's appeal for information and tip-offs had not led to anything. The dead man's fingerprints had been obtained and run through records with no result. The statement given by the naked woman rescued from the landslip suggested she had nothing to do with the case.

'She was in a relationship with August Tandberg, M-12, and had phoned in sick to spend the night with him in his apartment,' Maren explained.

As it was late, they agreed to call it a day. They all needed to catch some sleep if they were to be able to think clearly again.

Line had sent him a text message while he was at the dinner table with the art dealer. She had probably seen the news but wondered if he would drop in to her place for a bite to eat after work. He replied that he had already eaten but would call in, though it might be late.

He parked his car outside his house and walked down to hers. The rain had eased off but surface water was streaming along the verges and gurgling in the ditches and drains.

The door was unlocked. He tiptoed in to avoid waking Amalie but could hear sounds from the living room. Amalie sat on the settee beside Line, hair tousled and cheeks flushed.

'Hi!' Wisting said in a soft voice. 'Are you wide awake?' He ran his hand over her back.

'She just woke up,' Line whispered. 'I think she had a bad dream.'

Wisting sat down beside them on the settee. Amalie laid her head on her mother's lap, twisting round, eyes blinking.

Line pointed to a blanket on the arm of a chair and Wisting tucked it round his granddaughter.

'So a dead body was found?' Line said.

Wisting glanced at Amalie. Her eyes had slid shut and she was breathing peacefully. All the same, he chose his words carefully as he told Line about the dead man whose body had been recovered.

Line posed the same questions that had already been aired by the investigative team. He had not always been able to speak to her so openly. When she worked as a news reporter, there had been greater restrictions on what he could share with her. He still withheld some things, but it was sometimes helpful to talk about the key fundamentals. Generally the only difference between what was relayed at a press conference and what he told his daughter was that he could add his own feelings and impressions.

'Maybe he's not Norwegian,' Line suggested.

He admitted she had a point. East European and Albanian networks were behind much of Norway's serious crime, but this man's appearance did not suggest that.

They sat for half an hour or so before Wisting finally got to his feet. He hoisted Amalie up from Line's lap and carried her solicitously to her bedroom. In a deep sleep, she did not even notice when the bright ceiling light flicked on.

He had trouble setting her down and unravelling the blanket, but in the end managed to place her little head on the pillow. He did not know where her button nose came from, but she must have gotten the curls and hair colour from her American father. The blue eyes and long lashes were undoubtedly inherited from Line, while her golden skin was a combination of the two.

He lingered for a moment, thinking of the girl he had saved from the landslip before switching off the light and closing the door.

Line stood in the living room with her arms crossed. 'Are you still OK for Saturday?' she asked.

Wisting had forgotten he had agreed to look after Amalie. 'When are you going out?' he asked.

'We're meeting up at seven, but I don't need to be there before eight.'

'Seven's fine,' Wisting assured her.

'Are you sure?'

'It's one of the advantages of being the boss,' Wisting told her with a smile. 'I get to decide when the workday is over.'

She returned his smile.

'But I might not see you tomorrow,' he said. 'The first day's always the most hectic.'

Line accompanied him to the door. 'We'll manage,' she said.

10

The back yard at the police station was deserted when he drove in. Only the bicycle thieves' Romanian lorry was parked there, taking up three spaces. Wisting left his car close to the staff entrance and hurried inside to find shelter. At this time of day, the patrol section officers were usually sitting writing reports on the events of the night, but the ground floor was also unoccupied. They must still be out on shift, perhaps assigned to guard duties at the landslide.

He trudged upstairs to his office, where he fired up the programs on his computer. No messages.

It was always frustrating when nothing happened at the start of a new case. This time they had unusually little to go on. Even though it was still early stages, he already felt anxious that they would never find a solution.

The initial reports about the actual landslide had been completed. He read them on the screen to check the geologists' findings. Media outlets had already cited climate change and increasingly mild, wet and wild weather as the cause. The professionals also pointed to record rainfall but were more dispassionate in their commentary. They suggested blockage of water channels, inadvertent damming and sudden penetration as the triggers.

Wisting was looking for a description of how the landslip mass had moved, whether the geological calculations contained anything to suggest how the dead body had been propelled through the mud. In other cases he had employed engineers from the Marine Research Institute to calculate how a body had drifted in ocean currents. The geologists' report included nothing similar, but he made a note of their names so he could ask them if it might be possible to undertake such calculations.

The police station began to fill up. First cleaners, then office staff and finally detectives. The corridors were buzzing with activity. Phones were ringing. The photocopier began to churn.

Gathering his notes, Wisting headed to the conference room. Empty pizza boxes and discarded coffee cups were left from the previous evening, and he cleared these away before the others arrived.

The morning meeting was soon over and done with.

They spent most time on Benjamin Fjeld's survey of the affected residents and their backgrounds. This included how long they had lived in the area, their employment and financial details and any criminal convictions or fines. The presentation was not yet complete, but there was little to suggest that any explanation for the discovery of the cadaver would be found among the landslide victims.

'Could we publicize his photograph?' Christine Thiis asked.

He understood the impetus for her question. They were all impatient.

'It might be an idea to show it to the residents,' Wisting said. 'But we should wait until we get photos once he's been cleaned and the injuries are camouflaged.'

Turning to face Mortensen, he asked the crime scene expert to ensure the fingerprints were sent out through Interpol.

Maren Dokken gave a brief account of the geologists' findings and the possibilities of undertaking forensic work down in the landslide crater. 'At present it's not advisable,' she rounded off.

Fresh ideas that had surfaced overnight were shared around the table, but these brought them no further forward and in the end they agreed to meet up again when the post-mortem report was available.

A beautifully wrapped bouquet of flowers lay on his desk when he got back. Although his name was written on a yellow Post-it note, there was no mention of the sender.

Picking up the bouquet, he carried it out into the corridor and along to the administration office to ask Bjørg Karin.

'Do you know anything about this?'

She glanced at the flowers. 'They were delivered downstairs to the duty desk,' she told him. 'There's probably a card inside.'

He retraced his steps to his office to unwrap the flowers, a large bunch of white roses. Tucked between the blooms he found a handwritten card, signed Karen Trane. He had to read what she had written to learn that this was the grandmother of the girl he had rescued from the landslip.

He pictured in his mind the overview Benjamin Fjeld had drawn up. The house was situated approximately in the centre of the landslip. Ellen Trane had been alone with her daughter while her husband worked in the North Sea. On the card she had written that all three would like to meet him.

Wisting stuffed the card in between the flowers again and placed the bouquet on one corner of his desk. The stalks were packed in moist paper and the blooms would survive for a few hours.

For the next hour he waited impatiently to hear details from the autopsy. Forensic examinations always provided something specific to work on. He was pleased that the task had been allocated to Mogens Poulsen – the Danish pathologist was one of the most experienced they had, always considered and thoughtful in his deliberations.

Just before eleven, he received an email from the investigator in the ID section at Kripos, the National Criminal Investigation Service, who had taken part in the postmortem. He had attached a selection of photographs and a videoconference link. Wisting asked Hammer and Mortensen to join him before logging on from the conference room. While they waited, they perused the photos, the most interesting of which was the last one taken, after the corpse had been undressed and cleaned. The head had suffered changes in death and taken on a bluish-black discoloration, but the rest of the body was relatively pale. The images showed several tattoos on the upper arm and chest, as well as an irregular surgical scar on his stomach. That gave them something to work on.

As soon as the video was hooked up, the Kripos investigator came straight to the point and told them they had no evidence of the man's identity, going on to detail the routine securing of trace samples from the clothes and body. Mogens Poulsen listened, keeping track in the paperwork. The camera in the other conference room was located high on the wall, and they were looking down at his scalp through his sparse, unkempt hair.

'The cause of death is as presumed,' he said when it was his turn to speak. 'A shot to the head with the entry wound through the occipital bone. The path of the gunshot goes through the pineal gland, severs the pons and exits through the mouth and jaw. Death occurred more or less instantly.'

'We're talking about a contact shot,' the Kripos

investigator added. 'The bullet travelled through the body. Measurements show it's a nine millimetre.'

The pathologist took over: 'So we're dealing with a man of North European origin. Six foot one in height, blue eyes, blond hair. Age around thirty-five.'

Wisting's phone buzzed. The call was from the duty officer on the ground floor. Dismissing it, he switched to silent mode.

'Can you say anything about the time of death?' he asked.

'Some time has elapsed, so there are a number of factors that make it uncertain,' he replied. 'There are still a few biochemical tests to do, but based on the classic signs of death, I'd estimate late on Saturday night.'

'The landslide struck on Wednesday,' Hammer commented. 'It's Friday today.'

Wisting jotted down a few notes. They were almost a week behind.

'Many of the external injuries were inflicted after death,' Poulsen continued. 'They're consistent with him being hurled around in the landslide. What may be of relevance are the wounds on his forehead and the back of his neck. We see signs of bleeding there, so they occurred just before, immediately after, or in connection with his death.'

Wisting's phone was now vibrating on the table, but he ignored it.

The Kripos investigator glanced up at them from the other side of the video link. 'Those are grazes, really,' he said by way of explanation. 'What's interesting about them is we've found traces of cement in them.'

'Cement?' Mortensen echoed.

'Enough for us to analyse it for additives,' the investigator confirmed.

'Like from a concrete floor?' Hammer suggested.

'It might be significant if you find a possible crime scene,' the man from the ID section agreed, nodding.

'But you'll most likely also find large quantities of blood there,' Mogens Poulsen added. 'The dead man lost a massive amount of blood.' He turned to his own computer screen. 'You've seen the photos?' he asked.

Wisting confirmed this.

'There is a great deal to suggest that the body had been lying head down and he lost a lot of blood through those wounds there,' Poulsen explained. 'This correlates with the internal collection of blood around the chest and head that took place after blood circulation ceased.'

'He was lying upside down in the landslide,' Hammer pointed out.

Mogens Poulsen pondered this. 'But this had already happened in the first twenty-four hours,' he said. 'Long before the landslip struck.'

There was a knock at the door behind them and Wisting turned around. A young uniformed police officer stood in the doorway. He scanned the room until his eyes landed on Wisting.

'A woman is asking for you down in reception,' he said.

Glancing at his phone, Wisting realized this must be important since one of the officers on duty had been sent up to him.

'She's Swedish,' the young officer added. 'She thinks the man who was found in the landslide could be her boyfriend.'

11

The other waiting members of the public focused on Wisting when he emerged into the reception area. The Swedish woman stood by the exit. She looked as if she was desperate to flee, but she took a step forward when the duty officer accompanying Wisting pointed her out. The sensors on the sliding doors registered movement and glided open behind her.

Wisting moved forward and introduced himself.

'Nina Lundblad,' the woman reciprocated, her voice barely audible.

Before they had a chance to say anything further, they were interrupted. An older man approached. 'Excuse me,' he said, looking straight at Wisting.

Although the man's face was familiar, at first glance he could not place him.

'I was wondering if you'd found my bike,' the man continued. 'I didn't notice it was gone until today and haven't reported it yet. It's an e-bike, and I thought it might have been among the ones the Romanians had in that impounded lorry.'

Wisting remembered him now as one of Line's teachers from junior high school.

'Rikhard will be able to help you with that,' Wisting said, handing him over to the young officer by his side.

Although the man thanked him, he did not seem entirely satisfied. Wisting shook the Swedish woman's hand and apologized for the interruption.

'Good of you to come,' he said. 'We'll go up to my office.'

He led the way up the stairwell. In the corridor, he bumped into Maren Dokken and invited her to join them.

Wisting shifted the bouquet of flowers from the desk to the top of a storage unit and closed the door behind them. They sat down, Maren seated at the computer screen and Wisting and the Swedish visitor on the easy chairs.

'Would you like something to drink?' Wisting asked. 'Water, coffee or anything?'

Nina Lundblad moved her head almost imperceptibly from side to side.

'What's your boyfriend's name?' Wisting asked her.

'Mats Beckman,' she answered.

Wisting heard Maren tapping on the keyboard, noting the information.

Mats Beckman sounded like a very ordinary Swedish name.

'How old is he?'

'Twenty-six.'

'And your name is Nina Lundblad?' he asked, gesturing in the direction of Maren at the computer. 'Could we have your date of birth and address?'

She was twenty-seven and gave an address in Stockholm.

'Is Mats also from Stockholm?'

'Yes, but we don't live together.'

'What makes you think it's Mats we've found?' Wisting went on.

'Do you have a photo of him?' Nina asked. 'I can bear to see it – I just need to know.'

'I don't have one here,' Wisting replied, deflecting the question. 'When was the last time you spoke to him?'

'Last weekend,' she answered. 'On Saturday, early evening. We spoke or sent messages to each other every day, but since Saturday I've not heard a word. Yesterday I jumped into my car and drove here.'

'What was Mats doing in Norway?'

'Working on an IT project.'

'For a company?'

Nina Lundblad shifted in her seat, twisting to one side. 'Along with a few friends,' she replied. 'He didn't tell me very much about it.'

'What friends?'

'I don't know. He didn't say much about them.'

'But he was living here in Larvik while he was working?'

She nodded. 'He came here two months ago.'

'Have you visited him here?'

'No. He went home as often as he could.'

'Do you know whereabouts in Larvik he was staying?'

'No.'

Maren cut into the conversation. 'William?' she said.

Glancing across at her, he understood she wanted to show him something on the screen.

'When was he home last?' he asked, getting to his feet.

'A month ago, but we didn't meet up in Stockholm. We went to Gothenburg. His aunt has a holiday house there.'

Wisting moved to stand beside Maren. On the screen, she had a picture of a man who resembled the murder victim. It was a photo from the criminal records of the Swedish police, followed by a few words stating that Mats Beckman was wanted for murder.

Wisting shot a glance at the woman in the easy chair. 'Just a second,' he said, clicking into the further details.

Mats Beckman was charged with the murder of a sixty-eight-year-old man in a district outside Stockholm city centre. There was scarcely any other information about the case. The murder victim was named as Sture Segelby. The date of the crime was more than six months earlier. Any sightings were to be reported to the national headquarters of the Swedish police.

He returned to his seat. 'We require some basic information about him,' he said as he resumed his seat.

Nina Lundblad provided her boyfriend's date of birth and phone number.

'Have you spoken to his family?'

'He didn't have many relatives. I got hold of his sister's number, but she didn't even know he was in Norway. They hadn't spoken in a long time. His father's an alcoholic and lives in Spain. His mother is ill. I think she lives in a mental institution.'

She provided their names. 'I haven't been able to contact his aunt,' she added.

'How long have you been in a relationship?' Wisting went on.

'We got to know each other about a year ago.' She looked across at Maren. 'Does it say something about him there?' she asked, indicating the computer screen. 'Has he done something wrong?'

'What makes you think that?' Wisting asked.

'He'd just been released from jail when I met him,' Nina replied.

'What was he inside for?'

'It was something to do with the internet, some kind of fraud. When I didn't hear from him, I thought he'd been arrested again. I tried to phone, but no one would tell me anything. First of all I drove to the holiday house in Gothenburg in the hope that he might be there, and then I came here.'

'What type of car does he drive?'
'A Volvo estate.'
'His own?'
'I think so.'
'Norwegian or Swedish plates?'
'Swedish.'
'Do you remember the reg number?'
'No.'
'Colour?'
'Black.'
'Model?'
'V60, I think.'
'New or old?'
'Six or seven years old, maybe.'

'Did he have friends or acquaintances in Norway? Has he mentioned any names?'

She shook her head. 'He wasn't the sort of guy who talked a lot,' she replied. 'At least, not about other people.'

Maren now spoke: 'Is he on Facebook or any other social media?'

'No. He doesn't like that kind of thing, and of course it's not allowed in prison.'

'Do you have any photos of him?'

Nina took out her mobile and found one her boyfriend had taken of himself. He was sitting at a pavement café with his sunglasses pushed up on his forehead, raising his glass to the camera in a toast while he took the selfie. Wisting recognized the street behind him and realized it had been taken outside the Golden Peace in Stavern. The foliage on the trees in the background was changing colour, so the picture could not have been taken much more than a month ago.

He knew the woman who owned the restaurant. They

could show the photo to someone who worked there. Mats Beckman might have been a regular customer. If they were lucky, they would recognize him and say something about who had been in his company there.

'Do you have more?' he asked.

She showed him another two, the second of which had been taken indoors. In the background there was a grey settee, a coffee table with a cola bottle, a wall covered in green wallpaper and a window with a large tree outside.

'Could you send us these?' Wisting asked. 'All the photos you have of him in Norway?'

'All of them?'

'We might well find out where he's been, or where he's been living,' Wisting explained.

Maren gave instructions about how to transfer the photographs and she complied immediately.

'Do you think it's him?' Nina asked.

'I'll certainly find out,' Wisting assured her.

'Will that take long?'

Wisting checked the time. They should have a response from the Swedish fingerprint register within a few hours, but he made no promises.

'Where are you staying while you're here?' he asked her.

'I haven't organized anything yet,' she replied.

He looked at Maren.

'I'll come down with you,' she said as she stood up. 'We have some rooms at our disposal in the hotel.'

Wisting was left sitting there on his own. At last, this was the break they needed.

12

Almost two hours had elapsed since Nina Lundblad had left the police station, and forty-five minutes since Mortensen had sent the prints to Sweden. A message might come in at any minute. The computer system took only seconds to find matching points, following which the prints had to be manually compared before an ID report could be written.

Maren Dokken appeared at the door. 'Heard anything?' she asked.

'Not yet,' Wisting answered. 'Did you manage to get her a room?'

'It all went smoothly, thanks,' Maren confirmed.

She lingered at the door as if she wanted to say something else. 'I don't think she's told us everything,' she said.

'What do you think she knows?'

'Well, I think if I had a boyfriend I didn't see very often and who was secretive about what he was doing, I'd be a bit more inquisitive,' Maren said. 'Snooped around a little, tried to see who he was phoning or sending messages to. Asked for some names. That kind of thing.'

'She knows he belonged to criminal circles,' Wisting said. 'That means you don't ask too many questions. What you don't know won't hurt you.'

Maren seemed far from convinced.

Wisting rose from his seat. 'By all means follow it up,' he said. 'Maybe she needs some time to mellow.'

She nodded and left. Wisting paid a visit to the toilet while he mulled things over.

As soon as they knew for certain the identity of the murder victim, they would have a direction to follow in the investigation. Gradually, as a picture emerged of what kind of person he was, it would be easier to work out a sequence of events and an underlying cause.

Leaving the cubicle, he washed his hands and splashed his face with cold water. He gazed at his face in the mirror as he dried his hands. A grey, pale complexion and deep furrows at the corners of his mouth, eyes and nose. He would soon be sixty, but felt he looked older. He could have retired three years ago and should really do so now, but the recent reorganization and police reforms had changed the pension age and given him the opportunity to work for seven more years. He had grabbed that with both hands.

His phone buzzed as he turned away, Mortensen calling.

'Identity confirmed,' he said.

'Mats Beckman, then,' Wisting said, just to be sure this was the right name.

Mortensen read out the date of birth as a final form of verification. 'I've given you as the contact person,' he added.

Wisting did not plan to wait until the Swedes made contact. He rushed back to his office and dialled the number provided in connection with the missing person report.

A woman answered. Wisting leafed through to a blank page in his notebook as he explained who he was. 'It has to do with a red notice on a Swedish citizen,' he said, providing the name and ID number.

'Wait a moment,' the woman replied.

She asked him to repeat the details. It sounded as if she

was finding it difficult to locate the particulars on the computer, but finally she tracked down the case.

'Have you come across him, then?' she asked.

'He was found dead here yesterday,' Wisting answered. 'We've launched a murder investigation.'

'I see,' the woman said. 'Any arrests or suspects?'

'No,' Wisting replied. 'I'd like to speak to the investigator in charge of the case you've brought against him.'

It took a few more minutes before the woman identified a name. 'Jan Serner,' she told him, reading out the phone number.

They agreed on certain formalities to do with the official reporting of the death before Wisting could make the second call. He introduced himself again once he was speaking to the Swedish detective.

Jan Serner was a man who listened more than he talked. Wisting explained about the landslide, about the identification and about Nina Lundblad. Serner refrained from interrupting with questions or comments.

'We're keen to know whether the murder might be related to the reason you've issued a wanted notice, or if there's any kind of threat against him,' Wisting rounded off.

'I'll have to come back to that,' Serner replied.

'We're in the initial stages of our investigation and have zilch to go on,' Wisting said. 'Anything you can contribute would be of interest to us. Right now we don't know much more than his name.'

'What did his girlfriend tell you?' Serner asked.

'Very little,' Wisting answered. 'Nothing we can work on, anyway.'

'Could she not tell you anything about why he was in Norway?' he asked.

'I don't think she even knew he was a wanted man,'

Wisting said. 'It would be useful for us to access his history with the Swedish police.'

'That would have to be cleared with the prosecution service,' Serner replied. 'They'd need a formal application.'

'Of course,' Wisting replied. 'I'd just like to be one step ahead of the formalities.'

'Let's start with me receiving a report of the discovery, with confirmed identity and a statement from the pathologist, and then I'll get back to you.'

Wisting had made contact in order to receive information, not to share it. He promised to send the material Jan Serner had requested but tried all the same to persuade him to be a bit more forthcoming.

'Do you have information that he belonged to a particular criminal fraternity?' he asked.

The answer was probably only a few keystrokes away on the computer Serner was sitting at, but he made no effort to assist. 'If you send me a list of questions, I'll get someone to collate all the relevant information,' he said.

Wisting's mobile phone had buzzed twice while he was speaking to the Swedish investigator. Both calls were from the police chief's communications adviser. A text message asked him to get in touch.

Wisting considered waiting until he had dealt with the paperwork but decided to return the call.

'They're saying the body's been identified,' the adviser said. 'Could you give Kiil an update before she attends the press conference?'

'When's the press conference?' Wisting asked.

'Four o'clock,' the adviser replied. 'The murder's the main focus in the media, so it's possible she'll want you with her.'

Wisting was keen to inform the other investigators

before talking to the police chief or letting the press know. 'When will you be here?' he asked.

'In an hour,' the adviser answered.

They agreed that the chief of police should report to his office when she arrived.

Wisting snapped his notebook shut and got to his feet. On the way along the corridor, he gathered all the investigators present in the station at a meeting in the conference room. Nils Hammer, Maren Dokken, Benjamin Fjeld and Espen Mortensen. There were so few of them, they filled only the lower end of the conference table.

'We have a name, but at the moment we know very little about him other than that he's wanted for murder in Sweden,' Wisting said by way of introduction. 'Before we go home today, I want to know where he was living in Norway and what he was doing here.'

He turned to face Mortensen. 'Have the photos from his girlfriend given us anything?'

'They were taken on an iPhone,' he replied. 'I'd hoped there would be coordinates in the raw data, but he can't have activated the location function on his phone.'

'That's not so strange, if he was on the run,' Hammer commented.

'I'll go on working on the photos,' Mortensen continued. 'Try to find any content that might be of help to us.'

Wisting now turned to Benjamin Fjeld. 'I'd like you to show his photos to the evacuated residents. If he lived in the area, someone might know him.'

'What about going public?' Hammer asked.

'I'll discuss that with the chief,' Wisting answered. 'But we have to let his girlfriend and family know first. She'll also have to sanction use of the images.'

'I'll see to that,' Maren said, making a note.

Wisting ploughed on: 'Time's beginning to run away from us. We're already on day six. CCTV footage will have to be secured before it's deleted. Hammer?'

The burly investigator in the seat beside him nodded his head.

'Anything else?' Wisting asked.

The room was silent. Hammer drummed his fingers on the table. Wisting waited for a few more seconds before pushing his chair out to indicate that the meeting was over.

13

The rain had soaked the police chief's hair in the short distance from the car to the station. She sat down and raked her fingers through her wet locks.

'Why won't the Swedes share any information with us?' she asked.

'It's in the pipeline,' Wisting told her. 'The guy in charge of the investigation's a stickler for formalities. It has to get legal clearance first.'

'Is there anything I can do to hurry things along?'

'Christine Thiis is handling that,' Wisting assured her.

'We need to make this public as soon as possible,' the chief of police commented.

Wisting nodded. He had tactical reasons for publicizing Mats Beckman's name and photograph. It could lead to interesting tip-offs and disclosures. As far as Agnes Kiil was concerned, it was a matter of correcting the unfortunate statements she had made earlier. The previous day she had appeared in front of the press corps and told them that everyone who had been in the landslide area was accounted for. It would assist the optics if she could now say that the man they had found was a wanted man, a Swedish citizen hiding from justice in Norway.

'We've informed his sister in Sweden and the girlfriend who turned up here,' Wisting said.

'His sister's given as next of kin?'

'Strictly speaking, it's the parents, but she'll pass on the news.'

Agnes Kiil patted her hair again.

The communications adviser had sat in silence. Now he spoke up. 'I suggest that Kiil first gives a brief update on the landslide,' he said. 'The status of the injured, what's being worked on now, and that the emergency team is being wound down. Then she should go on to say that the dead body has been identified and introduce you as the officer in charge of the murder investigation. Then you can deal with the details and say whatever else you want to say.'

They continued to discuss the wording of the statement and the practical aspects of transmitting the photograph.

Wisting was not fond of press conferences. Over the years his nervousness had dissipated and the actual articulation of information was no longer problematic for him. It was simply a case of presenting the central facts and elements that were significant for the investigation. What he disliked, however, were the questions that followed, which were usually naïve or speculative. Both kinds were difficult to answer, and the journalists seldom received the responses they were after. It seemed as if a news story was not enough in itself and they expected something sensational. And if there was nothing sensational in the story itself, they tended to turn their attention to the police and write instead about faults and discrepancies in the investigation.

The press conference was to be held in the spacious conference room on the second floor. The text Wisting was to deliver filled less than a single A4 sheet. He tucked it into his notebook and followed the police chief.

'William!'

Nils Hammer came running after him along the corridor. Wisting stopped. The police chief stood waiting.

'Mortensen thinks he's discovered where Beckman may have been living,' Hammer told him.

'Where?'

'On the eastern side of the Larvik fjord, diagonally across, a spot you can just make out beside the cranes at the container port.'

He held out an enlarged section of the living-room window in one of Mats Beckman's selfies. It was a bad printout, but in one corner of the window, Wisting could discern parts of a crane. With a pinch of magnanimity, he could also pick out the huge grain silos further back.

'Probably an apartment in Holmejordet,' Hammer went on. 'We're on our way out there to try to pin it down.'

Wisting glanced across at the police chief and then back at Hammer. 'Give me half an hour, and I'll be there with you.'

14

Hammer and Mortensen were waiting in their car. Wisting drove up beside them and lowered the side window. When the rain slanted into the car, he raised it again to avoid getting drenched.

'Over there,' Hammer said, pointing at the address they had figured out.

Wisting loosened his seatbelt.

It was a grey-painted apartment with drawn curtains at the end of a terrace. The wind whipped through a thuja hedge facing the street. Wisting twisted round in his seat to squint out at the other side of the fjord. Behind a misty veil of rain he could make out the container port. The angle looked accurate.

'No name on the door or mailbox,' Hammer continued. 'No addressed post.'

Wisting glanced across at the apartment again. 'Who's the owner?' he asked.

'A property company in Sandefjord,' Mortensen replied. 'Some guy's on his way with the key. All they could say for the moment was that it's been rented out to a Swedish firm since the beginning of August.'

'Two months, then,' Wisting worked out.

'He should be here soon,' Hammer said.

'What does it say in the population register?' Wisting asked.

'No listing.'

'Have you spoken to the neighbours?'

Mortensen leaned forward a little in the passenger seat. 'The two nearest ones,' he answered. 'Both thought a man lived there on his own, but no one had any contact with him. They didn't even know whether he spoke Swedish.'

'What about a vehicle?' Wisting asked, scanning the area again.

'There's a shared car park,' Hammer said, nodding to the other side of the street. 'One person we talked to thought a Swedish-registered Volvo had been parked there, but it's not there now.'

'It could be somewhere in the landslide,' Mortensen broke in.

Wisting pictured the vehicles he had seen flung around amid the mud and rubble. 'I'll get Maren to scour the footage from the helicopters,' he said. 'Or else we can send out a drone to do another search.'

A car drove around the corner, slowing down as it approached. 'I think that'll be him,' Hammer said.

Wisting inched forward to avoid impeding the driver and the new arrival drew up behind him. Watching in his rear-view mirror, Wisting waited until Hammer gave a signal.

All four dashed under the eaves at the entrance to shelter from the torrential rain.

The man from the rental company inserted the key in the lock. 'His name is Mats Backman,' he said, turning round.

'Backman,' Wisting repeated. 'Are you sure? Not Beckman?'

The landlord shrugged. 'It says Backman in my papers.'

'Who pays the rent?' Mortensen asked.

'An IT company in Stockholm. Datakonsult AB.' He opened the door for them. They saw a pair of shoes on the floor of the porch and a grey rain jacket on a peg.

'Thanks,' Hammer said. 'You can wait in the car.'

Once Mortensen had handed out latex gloves and foot protectors, Wisting led the way. The air inside was remarkably dry, as if suffused with some kind of synthetic material.

The hallway opened on to a living room. From somewhere further inside they could hear a low, buzzing noise, reminiscent of an old TV left on after the final broadcast.

Wisting looked in through the first door on the left. The bathroom. His eyes quickly checked the room. Dirty clothes on the floor in front of a washing machine, a shower cubicle with bottles of shampoo, a glass and toothbrush by the basin, an electric shaver. Nothing out of the ordinary. Across from this was the bedroom. A double bed with a quilt, unmade. A bedside table with a clock radio and phone charger. A pair of socks lying on the floor.

Hammer shouted from the next room and Wisting moved to stand in the doorway. Two walls were lined with aluminium shelving and computer servers, lights flashing and cooling fans humming. On a desk by the window there was a monitor with mouse and keyboard.

'A server farm,' Mortensen commented. 'A bit over the top for work in a consultancy firm.'

Hammer walked up to one of the computer towers. Cables connected each component to the next.

'What the hell is he doing here?' he asked. 'Porn?'

Wisting approached the desk and nudged the computer mouse. The screen sprang to life but demanded a username and password.

He cleared his throat. The dry air in the room made his throat contract. 'We'll have to summon the computer technicians,' he said.

The desk drawer lay half open. Wisting pulled it out and

found several cables, a couple of screwdrivers and bundles of technical manuals for various items of computer equipment.

Mortensen had looked up the firm that paid the rent on the property. 'There are a lot of IT companies that offer consultancy services, but only one called Datakonsult AB,' he said, glancing up from his phone. 'According to the Swedish register of companies, it was set up three months ago, but it doesn't have a webpage.'

'A computer company without a webpage?' Hammer mused.

'Does it say anything about what they do?' Wisting asked.

Mortensen shook his head. 'There aren't even any contact details provided.'

Wisting lingered for a while in the IT room before moving on to the living room. He recognized the furnishings from the photograph, but all the same moved to the window and pulled the curtains aside. Outside, it was growing dark, but he could see the twinkle of lights from the container port.

The living room had an adjacent kitchenette and there was scarcely space for anything other than a settee in front of the TV and a dining table. An empty plate and glass had been left out. On the coffee table in front of the settee, he saw a Swedish comic book and a tin of snuff as well as two remote controls.

On the kitchen worktop, several empty bottles were lined up against the wall, but otherwise it was tidy.

'One thing's for sure,' Mortensen said. He stood in the middle of the room, surveying his surroundings. 'This isn't a crime scene. He was killed elsewhere.'

Hammer responded with a grunt as Wisting opened the fridge. The contents were scant – a pack of cold meat approaching its sell-by date, and little else to help draw a timeline.

'I should get my camera before we do anything else,' Mortensen said, heading for the door.

After the initial once-over, it was important to search for clues. They would have to open drawers and cupboards, rummage through pockets and down the back of settee cushions. A note with a name could propel them forward, a receipt could tell them where Beckman had been, a phone number could suggest who his contacts were. They did not really know what they were looking for, but they would understand once they found it.

Wisting returned to the bedroom. Bedside-table drawers were always interesting. He found a blister pack of throat pastilles, a tube of moisturizer, a nasal spray and a ballpoint pen.

His phone buzzed. It was the chief of police. 'The Swedes want a meeting,' she said. 'Jan Serner's coming here.'

'Good,' was Wisting's immediate reply.

He shifted the phone to his other ear to lift the bedclothes. The police chief told him that the Swedish police prosecutor had contacted her. 'She's coming too, as well as someone from NOA, their national operations department.'

Wisting dropped the quilt and crossed to the window. 'They're coming here? All of them?' He moved the curtain to one side, peering through the reflected contours of his face out into the darkness.

'They're arriving from Stockholm by helicopter,' the police chief told him. 'They'll be here in two hours.'

Wisting saw the frown on his reflection. Something had put a rocket under the Swedish police.

15

He heard the helicopter before he caught sight of it. The low-frequency thrum pulsed on the office window as the enormous machine flew in from the east at low height, lights flashing. It circled above the fjord before tilting to one side and veering back, hovering in the air above the harbour while the ground crew guided it down.

Wisting headed to the conference room, leaving the door open behind him. A tray of buttered bread rolls had been laid out, along with drinks of various kinds. The chief of police sat at the head of the table on what was usually Wisting's seat.

'They just landed,' he said.

Her response was a nod of the head.

He had recruited Maren, Nils, Espen and Benjamin from his own staff, and so six chairs remained unoccupied around the table. He was unsure whether that would be enough.

A door slammed in the distance, followed by footsteps along the deserted corridor. Wisting put his head around the door. One of the officers from the patrol section was escorting a plain-clothes policeman with *Kripos* printed on the ID tag dangling from his neck.

He held out his hand. 'Josef Helland, Organized Crime.'

Wisting shook his hand and glanced across at the police chief. She gave no sign she had been aware that the Norwegian section for organized crime would also be taking part.

As the Kripos investigator took a seat at the table, Nils Hammer removed a wad of snuff from beneath his top lip and asked, 'What are you doing here?'

'Let's wait for our Swedish colleagues,' Helland replied.

Hammer dropped the used snuff on the lid of the tin and closed it with a peremptory click.

Five minutes later, their Swedish guests arrived, two male and one female. The woman spoke first and introduced herself as police prosecutor Ann-Mari Walin. 'Thanks for meeting us as early as this evening,' she said, hanging her jacket over one of the empty chair backs.

Jan Serner, a physically powerful man with dark wavy hair and a well-trimmed beard, gave Wisting a brief nod as they introduced themselves. The other man's name was Ralf Falk and he worked in the same department.

The Swedish police lawyer placed a folder in front of her on the table and turned to speak to Agnes Kiil. 'What progress have you made in the inquiry?' she asked.

Kiil passed the question on to Wisting. 'I think it's best if you first tell us what this is all about,' he said.

'OK, then,' Walin said. 'I'll let the head of the investigation, Jan Serner, explain.'

Serner had set down a laptop in front of him and he focused on the screen, as if his notes were written there. 'Let me first inform you that it's absolutely crucial that what is divulged at this meeting does not spread any further without our say-so,' he began. 'My colleagues and I work at the intelligence service in the operations section of the Swedish police, and it could be damaging to third parties if any information from here leaks out.'

Serner and his colleagues exchanged looks.

'Good,' he said, when no objections were forthcoming.

'I myself have not been on this case for longer than a fortnight, but almost a year ago we launched Operation Aurum. That's Latin for gold. The trigger for this operation was what we call the Malmgren Affair in Sweden. It's also been covered in the Norwegian media.'

As his gaze swivelled around the table, he received a number of confirmatory nods.

'Christer Malmgren is a third-generation goldsmith, responsible for the largest volume of sales of gold items in Sweden,' Serner went on. 'In November last year, his daughter was abducted. He emptied his business of practically all its goods and handed them over in exchange for his daughter's life.'

He gave a short account of how the twelve-year-old girl had been drugged with gas introduced through her bedroom window before they broke in. They left instructions on her bed and an article about the white slave trade as a warning about what would happen if he didn't cough up.

'Much of the jewellery was marketable, but we believe most of it was melted down to be used as a means of payment in the narcotics trade,' Serner continued. 'The stock was extensive in advance of Christmas sales. It was reported that there was gold of various carats, with a total of more than sixteen kilos. The retail value of the jewellery was almost 40 million kroner, whereas as raw material, molten metal, it would be about eight.'

Eight million, Wisting mused. Not a huge profit for a crime with a severe maximum sentence. Invested in the narcotics market, however, it would provide earnings well in excess of the original value of the jewellery.

'His daughter was found seven hours after the handover, unconscious by the side of a road in Huddinge. She'd been awake for periods of time while held captive but could not tell us much more than that she'd been held in a lorry and that there were two perpetrators who spoke to her in English.'

'A tiger kidnapping,' Hammer commented.

Serner agreed with the terminology. This was a phenomenon they had seen little of in Norway, but it involved family members of key individuals with access to considerable fortunes being abducted to force the relative to bleed a business of cash or other valuables. The nickname was given because the procedure was compared to a tiger's method of following its prey to learn its weaknesses before pouncing.

Serner's computer screen had darkened and he fired it up again with a single keystroke before ploughing on.

'Early this summer we had a similar attack, this time aimed at the owner of a web-based goldsmiths, where individuals can send in old, unwanted items of jewellery and be paid by weight or carat. His spouse was abducted in the same way. Instead of complying with their demands, he went to the police. The case has not been made public, but the investigation has led nowhere and his wife is still missing.'

The gravity of the situation hung like a heavy weight around the table.

Wisting spoke up. 'Where does Mats Beckman come into the picture?'

Jan Serner smacked his lips before answering. 'Mats Beckman was working for us.'

'What do you mean?' Hammer demanded. 'In what sense?'

'We've used him before, in other cases,' Serner replied. 'He's experienced and has produced results.'

'An infiltrator?' Hammer asked.

'From a technical point of view, he's employed and paid by the police,' Serner said.

'Via Datakonsult AB,' Mortensen commented.

Hammer did not allow Serner to answer. 'Let me check that I've understood this correctly,' he said. 'You've let a wanted killer go free so that you can use him as an infiltrator?'

Serner passed on the question: 'Ann-Mari?'

The Swedish police prosecutor shifted in her seat, seeming disconcerted. 'He's not a murder suspect as such,' she replied. 'That was part of the back story we provided for Beckman to make his story plausible. These tiger attacks are carefully planned and carried out by well-organized criminals. To ensure the success of an infiltrator, we had to rely on rock-solid preventative measures that would be watertight if Beckman's cover story were ever checked, for example through police channels.'

'The story we used is not a murder case as such,' Serner interjected. 'Sture Segelby's death was investigated but decreed an accidental fall. That conclusion will remain. He was chosen because he has no family or other close relatives.'

'Following the unsuccessful case this summer, we received intelligence that the criminals involved are looking for new targets,' the police prosecutor added, as if she needed to explain that desperate situations demand desperate measures.

Wisting could see Hammer was troubled. He was finding it difficult to sit still.

'So you had an infiltrator on assignment in Norway, who's now been liquidated?'

Serner glanced at the Kripos investigator. 'We've been

following him closely with personnel in Norway and daily reports,' he assured them. 'The incident occurred after he'd signed out for some time off. The last report we received was that he was packing to go to his undercover house in Gothenburg to spend time with his girlfriend.'

'"The incident,"' Hammer mimicked, shaking his head. 'Did you have any other security measures in place that would set off the alarm klaxons? Tracking device on his car, or some arrangement to let you know something was wrong?'

'Not on his car, but we always had the opportunity to track his mobile.'

'But didn't you do that?'

Serner failed to reply. 'However, the car has a hidden, voice-activated recording system,' he said instead.

'Sound and image?'

'Only sound.'

Hammer stretched forward. 'Where are the recordings?'

'In the car.'

'Only there?' Hammer shook his head. 'They send direct pictures from the space station to Earth, but it didn't occur to you that it might be a good idea to rig up a link to the vehicle?'

'That was considered, but it would have increased the risk of our operator being unmasked,' Serner answered. 'The gang we're talking about have access to advanced signal detectors and have used them in the past.'

Hammer slumped back heavily into his seat.

'His apartment is equipped differently,' Serner went on. 'There, the signals are camouflaged by the computer traffic in the server room.'

He searched for something on his laptop and turned the

screen to face them. 'This is footage of Beckman leaving the apartment on Saturday, 6 October at 21.37.'

Wisting leaned forward. The concealed camera must be located in the alarm system in the porch. The images showed Mats Beckman donning his jacket and shoes before heading out, followed by the sound of a door shutting behind him.

Serner pivoted the computer again. 'Two minutes later, the signals from his mobile disappear,' he added.

Outside, the wind must have changed direction. Sheets of rain battered the windowpane.

'Why did you send him to Norway?' Wisting asked.

Serner referred to his colleague: 'Ralf, maybe you'd like to take over now?'

His younger colleague had a military haircut and a gaunt face with prominent jaw muscles.

'Ralf Falk was Beckman's handler,' Serner added before he handed over.

'The investigation of the Malmgren case led to well-known circles in Sundbyberg previously involved in robberies from security vans and, later, credit card frauds, when the cash trade dwindled.'

He opened his folder and took out two sheets of paper. 'Our intelligence suggests that these two were at the centre of the planning and execution of the crime.'

He spread the sheets around the table, displaying a picture of a bald man in his forties and a similar man of the same age who sported a thick, dark beard. The first one looked Swedish but the other one looked as if he came from somewhere in south-eastern Europe, or perhaps Iran, Iraq or Turkey.

'Gillis Haack and Elton Khan,' the Swedish detective

informed them. 'This summer they travelled together to Ankara while Elton's cousin came to Norway.'

He produced another photograph, this one also of a man from south-east Europe, with broader shoulders and a bull neck.

'Dogan Bulut has been living in Stavern since then, in a basement apartment in Solstad.'

Nils Hammer rolled his eyes and groaned loudly. Ralf Falk ignored him.

'We have reason to believe that Bulut also played a part in the planning of the Malmgren case. Our intention with placing an informant here was to get close to him and then the two others.'

'Did you achieve anything?' Wisting asked.

Jan Serner now took up the thread. 'He quickly established contact with Bulut,' he replied. 'That seemed entirely natural. They were two Swedish speakers in the same small town who got talking. They'd both been inside and they shared acquaintances as well as interests and problems in common.'

'What kind of problems?'

'The flow of cash in Europe, especially in the Nordic countries, has been reduced,' Serner explained. 'Less money in circulation creates problems for people who operate inside the black economy. Some of them avoid it by going back to using precious metals as a means of payment.'

'Gold,' Wisting concluded.

Serner nodded. 'Other characters have adopted digital currency, such as bitcoin,' he continued. 'Mats Beckman had experience and knowledge of encrypted currency transactions that might prove of interest to our suspects.'

Espen Mortensen broke in. 'The computer room in the apartment,' he said. 'It must be a bitcoin mine.'

'That's part of the operation,' Serner confirmed.

Hammer did not appear to grasp what they were talking about.

'Bitcoin mining,' Mortensen explained. 'He's mining for bitcoin, using computer power to extract digital currency.'

Wisting felt increasingly anxious as he began to appreciate what was really going on. 'You believe they're planning a new attack, here in Norway?' he said, glancing at the guy from Kripos.

Serner let the prosecutor answer this time.

'There's every reason to believe that's why Bulut is in Norway,' Walin agreed.

'Do you know the intended target?'

She shook her head. 'Beckman's assignment was to find out, but we do suspect that something was imminent.'

'What makes you think that?'

Now Serner answered: 'Gillis Haack and Elton Khan left Turkey ten days ago. They flew to Amsterdam and have most likely travelled north by car.'

'Are you tracking them?'

'Not since they arrived in Europe.'

Hammer spluttered in dissatisfaction.

'What about Bulut?' Wisting asked. 'Do you know where he is now?'

Josef Helland now spoke for the first time. 'What we know is that his mobile phone is at home.'

'You're monitoring his communications, then?'

'Of course,' Helland answered. 'But it's given us very little information. All communication among the three suspects takes place on encrypted phones with a separate operating system. So we have no chance of picking up conversations and data transfers or even locating their position.'

'They communicate with their victims in the same way,' Serner added. 'They leave a phone that can't be traced.'

'I have a surveillance team that arrived here in Larvik at the same time as me,' the Kripos investigator said. 'They're keeping close watch on the apartment now.'

He looked down at his laptop, flipped open in front of him. 'Nothing to report so far.'

Wisting sat up in his chair and reached forward. 'What are your thoughts on what has happened?' he asked. 'Is it the case that the infiltrator was exposed, or could he have been running some sort of scam on the side that landed him in trouble?'

'It's too early to say,' Serner said.

'It's obvious his cover was blown, though,' Hammer said. 'The question is how.'

Jan Serner gazed down at his computer screen. 'That's something we can come back to,' he said.

The police chief glanced at Wisting, as if requesting a signal to speak. Wisting gave her a nod.

'Thanks for the report,' she said, making eye contact with each of the speakers in turn before she went on: 'We find ourselves in a challenging situation. The conduct of the police may have cost a human life. This investigation will be led from here by William Wisting and I expect full disclosure and cooperation from everyone involved.'

16

The police chief tugged the neck of her uniform jacket and cleared her throat, as if she wanted to say something further about the responsibility she had invested in him.

'Keep me posted,' was what she made do with before moving out to the car park.

The rain fell like threads in the headlight beam when she started the ignition. Wisting hovered in the doorway until she had driven off.

On the map there was a kilometre and a half as the crow flies between the spot where Mats Beckman had been found and his apartment. A drive would take four or five minutes. Locating his car could be crucial to the progress of the investigation.

The door slid to and closed with a click. Wisting took the stairs up to the department and headed along the corridor to Maren Dokken's office.

'Seen anything so far?' he asked, standing behind her.

She shook her head without taking her eyes off the onscreen footage. The silent helicopter images drew his thoughts back to the night of the landslip. The camera had followed the cone of light beneath the helicopter, searching systematically through the crater for victims.

The searchlight hovered above a pile of rubble consisting of planks sticking out in all directions before moving on to a settee and a bunk bed. A car appeared in the picture, lying on its side, half buried in mud and clay. It was difficult to see what colour it was, but it did not look like a Volvo.

'A Nissan Leaf,' Maren suggested. Wisting agreed.

'How many hours of footage are there?' he asked.

'About twelve from the night,' Maren replied. 'In addition, we have the drone footage the geologists recorded the next day. Benjamin is going through that now.'

Wisting stood for a few minutes longer before moving on.

The Swedish police prosecutor had checked into the hotel, while Josef Helland from Kripos and the two Swedish detectives were still at the station. They had been allocated one of the smaller meeting rooms and had rigged up some semblance of a shared office. A computer screen in the centre of the table showed Dogan Bulut's entrance door.

'It's taken from a vehicle we parked right across the street,' Helland explained.

The camera lens was angled through a rain-spattered windscreen, distorting the picture, but they would catch sight of anyone leaving the building.

'Has there been any movement?' Wisting asked.

'Not a thing,' Helland answered. 'The surveillance team are of the opinion that his car hasn't been used in a while.'

A raindrop trickled across the video image as Wisting watched. 'What sort of contact have you reported between Bulut and Beckman?' he asked. 'Has he been in that apartment?'

'Bulut has been at Beckman's place on only one occasion,' Serner said.

'Do you have footage of that?'

'Yes.'

'Could I take a look?'

The Swedish policeman logged into a computer system to retrieve the pictures. Bulut and Beckman were standing in the computer room. They heard Beckman explain how impossible it was to trace encrypted transactions.

'But this can't be used as proof of contact between them,' Serner said. 'Not at the stage we're at now.'

Wisting continued to watch the recording. Bulut seemed primarily focused on how bitcoin could be exchanged for normal currency and withdrawn in cash.

'How long ago is this?' Wisting asked, pointing at the screen.

Serner checked the date. 'The first of October,' he replied. 'Eleven days ago.'

Onscreen, the two men moved towards the door. Bulut cast one final glance into the room before moving out into the hallway and turning right towards the living room. Beckman closed the door behind them.

'In the living room they talk about how cryptocurrency can be used for extortion purposes,' Serner continued. 'Nothing specific is said, but you can listen if you like.'

Wisting shook his head. 'Let me see the footage from the computer room again,' he said.

Serner restarted the recording. Wisting fished out his mobile and called Mortensen. 'I'm in the meeting room beside the canteen,' he said. 'Could you come up here?'

Two minutes later his colleague was in the room. 'What's it about?' he asked.

Wisting pointed at the screen and asked Serner to spool forward to the end, when the two men exited the room.

'Stop there,' he said as Bulut turned to take one last look at the bitcoin mine.

The image froze.

'Wind forward slowly.'

The onscreen image crept on one frame at a time until Wisting called a halt.

'There,' Wisting said, pointing at Bulut, who had placed his hand on the doorjamb on his way out.

Mortensen nodded, as if he had already understood.

'I want you to go to the apartment and find those fingerprints,' he said. 'That will furnish us with a reason to ask questions. It's already been six days since the murder. Tomorrow we'll haul him in for interview.'

Jan Serner was about to protest but had no chance to speak before Wisting left the room.

17

At some point during Wisting's drive home, the rain had cleared up. The wiper blades scraped several times across the dry windscreen before he noticed. He switched them off and turned into the front courtyard of his house.

The wind had also eased off. Somewhere in the darkness, water was dripping, probably the roof gutter, but apart from that it was remarkably quiet.

A note from Line lay on the kitchen worktop. She had scribbled: *Food in the fridge*. Sometimes she let herself in, bringing some leftover food when he was working too late to drop in on her.

He shot a grateful glance out of the kitchen window, down to her house, before opening the fridge door.

A portion of lasagne sat on the bottom shelf. He pierced the plastic film and popped it into the microwave. While the plate rotated, it dawned on him that tomorrow he had promised to have his granddaughter stay overnight, a promise he was reluctant to break.

While he ate, he rattled through his messages and emails. Gunnar Helner had sent him a link to the CCTV footage from his home and he reciprocated with a brief reply thanking him for the recording. In light of what had emerged during that day, he had little faith that it would contain anything of relevance to the case. Nevertheless he clicked on the last segment of footage to see if the landslide had been caught on film.

The camera was in night mode. The entrance and the street outside were shown in various shades of grey. The image shook, since the camera must have been activated by the tremors, before the camera tilted backwards and slanted up at the dark sky. Seconds later, everything went black, probably because either the power or the internet connection had been severed.

Throughout the day he had also been approached by other people. He had worked as a police officer in the same town for nearly forty years and in that time had formed many relationships. When the police made statements to the media asking for information, some chose to make personal contact with him. Most of these tip-offs concerned sightings of Swedish men. None looked interesting at first glance. He sent them on to the tip-off hotline to be filed along with all the other reports.

However, one email was different. It was from a joiner who employed former convicts in order to guide them on to the right path. Tobias Mehl. Most of Wisting's contact with him had been in connection with thefts from a construction site. It was difficult to shake off the suspicion that one of Mehl's employees might be involved and it had created an unpleasant atmosphere in the firm as a whole. Wisting had followed a tip-off that led to the stolen tools being recovered from a lorry making its way aboard a ferry to Sweden.

He checked the missed calls on his mobile and saw that Tobias Mehl had also tried to phone him in the course of the evening. In his email he wrote that it was in connection with something that might have nothing to do with the case, but ten years earlier he had taken on a job in the house belonging to Gunnar Helner, the art dealer, and it had consumed his thoughts for a long time afterwards. Wisting could return his call if he wanted more information.

By now it was almost half past one in the morning. Although Wisting's curiosity was piqued, he could not phone at this hour. It would have to wait. Now, he needed some shut-eye.

18

The weather was still fine when Wisting left for work but, overnight, grey haar had spread across the land, swirling around the car as he drove.

He chose a different route into town from the one he usually took and drove past the block where Dogan Bulut rented the basement apartment. A man with a dog crossed the street in front of him, giving him a natural reason to slow down. Wisting spotted the car filming the entrance and glanced up at the building, where the curtains were still drawn. A Swedish-registered BMW was parked a few metres from the door. Fallen leaves from nearby trees had settled on the roof.

Despite no expectations of detecting anything, he was keen to familiarize himself with the area.

His plan for the day was to haul Bulut in for a witness interview on the grounds that he was the only person they knew Mats Beckman had been in contact with in Larvik. In a preliminary conversation he would withhold the information that Beckman was a Swedish police infiltrator but instead emphasize that he was wanted for murder. This would be an interview in which he would have to adjust his approach as he went along, listening to what Bulut had to say and following whatever direction the conversation took. The most important aspect would be that while Wisting held him at the station, they could covertly search his apartment and install surveillance equipment. Wisting had no faith that the interview itself would yield results, but discovering the associates Bulut contacted afterwards and what they talked about would probably provide some impetus to drive the inquiry forward.

Before they had left the previous evening, Wisting had called a morning meeting for 9 a.m. This gave everyone involved some time to prepare and check any new information they had received in the course of the night.

The conference room began to fill up as early as quarter to. At five to nine everyone had arrived and there was no point in waiting.

Wisting began with the technical aspects and gave Mortensen the floor.

'I found fingerprints on the doorframe in Beckman's apartment, just as indicated in the film footage,' he said. 'Forensics in Stockholm have confirmed they belong to Dogan Bulut.'

Mortensen took a swig of his coffee but signalled that he had not finished.

'We've found something else that might be more suitable to use in the interview,' he went on. 'The log from the Swedish police operation shows that there were seven public meetings between Beckman and Bulut, from the first time they bumped into each other in the supermarket.'

Wisting nodded. This had been a pre-arranged encounter, when Beckman had ended up behind Bulut at the checkout with a six-pack of beer. During the conversation, Beckman had begun to drop hints that he had money problems and was interested in taking part in a plan in which they could make use of his knowledge of cryptocurrency. Bulut had been far from dismissive.

'The last time they met was nine days ago,' Mortensen

continued. 'It's logged that one of the things they did was to walk through the storage yard at the marina in Stavern, deep in conversation.'

He took another drink of coffee before exchanging the cup for an iPad.

'I know the chairman of the yacht club,' Mortensen explained. 'They have CCTV there. At first he was sceptical, since the footage should really have been deleted, but anyway, we now have pictures of the two of them together.'

He displayed a still image of the two men, one holding out his arms as if explaining something to his companion. Beckman and Bulut.

'We'll go out and pick him up as soon as we've finished here,' Wisting said, moving on. 'What do we have on Mats Beckman's car?'

'Nothing,' Hammer replied. He had updated information from the toll stations. 'All patrols have been alerted, and they're keeping their eyes peeled,' he added. 'But it may well be lying wrecked somewhere in the rubble.'

'Not on the surface, though,' Maren Dokken broke in. 'I've been through all the helicopter footage.'

'We'll have to consider issuing a public appeal,' Wisting commented.

He riffled through to a blank page in his notebook before addressing the Swedes. 'Do you have any news for us?'

'Not at the moment,' Jan Serner answered. The other two simply shook their heads.

Wisting encouraged everyone around the table to say a few words before winding up the meeting. No progress was to be found here. They would have to move out into the field.

19

Wisting slipped the bulletproof vest over his head and deployed the Velcro strip, pulling it taut at the side to hug his body. Hammer did likewise. They had no idea what awaited them when they rang Dogan Bulut's doorbell.

'What do we do if he's unwilling to come in for interview?' Hammer asked. 'What if he flatly refuses? Or if he isn't home?'

Wisting struggled into his sweater. 'Then we're no further forward,' he replied.

They went downstairs to the car. Unaccustomed to wearing protective vests, they found it difficult to get into the vehicle and sit comfortably.

Hammer drove. Josef Helland announced over the radio that the forensics team needed more time to prepare the bugging equipment they intended to install.

'I have to buy some snuff anyway,' Hammer said, pulling up in front of a grocery store. 'We can wait here until they're ready.'

He parked and stepped out. 'Do you want anything?' he asked as he opened the door.

'No, thanks.'

The door slammed. Wisting lowered the window on his side for some fresh air. The fog still drifted around them, carrying a raw tang of the salt sea.

Taking out his mobile, he checked his email and scrolled down to the message from the joiner with information about Gunnar Helner.

His thumb slid across the screen to find the number. He

cast a glance at the shop while the phone rang out. A man passed by, pushing a trolley loaded with empty bottles.

Tobias Mehl was out of breath when he answered. 'It probably has nothing to do with the discovery of the body,' he said in a rush. 'But of course, Gunnar Helner's house was destroyed in the landslide and it brought to mind a special job I once did for him.'

'What kind of job?'

Mehl lowered his voice. 'He wanted me to build a secret compartment in the basement,' he replied. 'He had a lot of valuable art and other items and probably wanted a secure place to store them, in case of burglary or fire.'

'And you made one?'

'Yes, at the same time as renovating the basement. I imagined he wanted a double wall or something like that, but he wanted it inserted in the basement floor.'

'In the floor?' Wisting asked.

'There was a lot of work involved, you know,' Mehl continued. 'I had to drill down into the cement and create a recess, but it worked out really well. In the end the compartment was flush with the rest of the floor. Impossible to spot it.'

Wisting thought of the time when he had visited on an official search, around eight years ago. They had found stolen paintings but had not discovered any recess in the basement floor.

'When was this?' he asked.

'At least ten years ago,' Mehl replied.

'Whereabouts on the floor?' Wisting asked.

'In the middle of the room. I expect he put some furniture on top of it. Probably a rug as well.'

Hammer emerged from the shop, tossing a tin of snuff in the air and deftly catching it.

'I see,' Wisting said.

'What I thought unusual was that there can't have been space for any paintings in that secret compartment,' Mehl continued. 'At least nothing of any great size.'

'Why was that?' Wisting asked.

Someone shouted for Mehl in the background, but he asked them to wait.

'The space was custom-made,' he said. 'Two metres in length, sixty centimetres wide and sixty centimetres deep. He wouldn't have room for any paintings down there, but a human body would be a perfect fit.'

Hammer clambered in and looked at Wisting, who shook his head to signal that there was no news.

'As I said,' Mehl went on, 'it probably has nothing to do with the case. He most likely wanted to put other valuables down there. But when a body turned up in the landslide I thought I should mention it.'

'Thanks very much,' Wisting said. 'Interesting to hear about it, all the same.'

The police radio crackled into life again. Helland was calling. Hammer grabbed the microphone but waited to answer until Wisting had rung off.

'*Ready for action*,' Helland announced.

'Roger,' Hammer responded as he started the car. 'Switching to the open channel.'

Wisting turned on the transmitter in his jacket pocket and inserted an earplug.

'Testing, one, two, three,' he said in the direction of the microphone on his lapel.

Flipping open the snuff tin as he drove, Hammer picked out a wad and placed it under his lip.

They passed a side street where a patrol was positioned

in case Bulut tried to flee or some other emergency arose.

Wisting pointed out the house. They would have to park in the street.

'You do the talking,' Hammer said as they got out.

Wisting adjusted his earplug while approaching the entrance. A damp pall of cold fog settled on his face.

'*Abort,*' he heard in his ear. '*Abort, abort, abort.*'

He looked at Hammer, who nodded, having heard the same message.

'Aborting,' he confirmed.

They did a quick about-turn and returned to their vehicle. Hammer fired up the engine.

'What's going on?' Wisting demanded.

'*A situation has arisen,*' Helland replied.

Wisting realized he would not be given any further explanation over the radio.

'OK,' he said. 'We're coming in.'

20

Wisting snatched off his microphone and threw the transmitter down on the table. 'What on earth happened?' he asked.

The Swedes deferred to the Kripos investigator. 'There's been another abduction,' Josef Helland said.

'In Norway?' Wisting asked, since Helland was the one who had imparted the news.

'In Skien,' Helland said. 'Obvious similarities with the first abduction in Sweden. The kidnapping victim is Nanette Kranz, and she's married to the owner of EdelKranz. The biggest producer and seller of precious metals in Scandinavia.'

Wisting removed his sweater. Skien, the largest of the six local authorities in Grenland district, was located just over half an hour away.

'When did this happen?' he asked, loosening the constricting protective vest.

'Wednesday evening,' Helland replied.

'The night the landslide occurred,' Hammer pointed out.

'That's more than forty-eight hours ago,' Wisting said.

'The proprietor is Niklas Kranz,' Helland began to elaborate. 'He was on a business trip to Estonia and should have been home on Thursday but postponed his journey back by one day. He didn't return until around 4 p.m. yesterday and found a message from the kidnappers. He spent all evening and all night figuring out what to do. Three hours ago, he contacted the police.'

Hammer sat down, still wearing his protective vest, though Wisting had jettisoned his. 'Has he been in touch with them?' he asked.

Helland shook his head. 'But moving against Bulut could have endangered the victim,' he said. 'We had to call things off.'

'Have they made any demands?' Wisting asked.

'An encrypted phone was left with a message saying he had twenty-four hours to obtain sixty kilos of gold.'

'Is he willing to pay, or even able to?'

'No idea,' Helland answered. 'I only learned of this half an hour ago, and at that point I don't think the police over there had done much more than take a statement and call in some investigators.'

'Do they have anything to go on?' Wisting asked.

'No information on that,' Helland replied.

Hammer stood up again. 'We have to go there,' he said. 'Find out what's actually happening.'

'We can't,' Wisting said, glancing at the Swedish detectives. 'If these people are as professional and organized as you describe, they'll be keeping both Kranz and the police under observation. We can't risk them seeing us barge in there along with Kripos and the NOA.'

Josef Helland must have had the same thought. 'I've requested a video meeting,' he said. 'Just need to give them a specific time.'

Wisting looked at his watch. 'Twelve noon,' he suggested. It was just before that.

'Let's do it on the big screen downstairs,' Hammer said.

Wisting stared down at the tabletop and spent a few minutes plotting the new information on a timeline. The Swedish infiltrator had been exposed and killed on Saturday evening. Nanette Kranz was kidnapped four days later. It was risky, but the planning must have been so far advanced that they could not turn back. If not for the landslide, the abduction could have been implemented and the gold taken out of the country long before Mats Beckman was found.

Lifting his eyes, he eyeballed Jan Serner. 'This is what you've been waiting for,' he said. 'Another abduction.'

'This is what we'd feared,' Serner confirmed. 'That's why we placed the infiltrator here, in the hope of gaining some insight into their plans. In order to prevent something like this.'

'Do you have any new information about the others in that network?' Wisting asked. 'Gillis Haack and Elton Khan?'

'Nothing,' Serner admitted.

'But this means they're in Norway, doesn't it?' Hammer said. 'Bulut has been here for months, preparing for an abduction. The other two must have joined him here now to carry it out.'

Wisting rose to his feet. They were now facing an entirely new situation. The whole premise of the investigation had shifted.

'Let's hear what they have to say in Skien,' he said.

21

The investigator on the video screen had a stain on her sweater, just above her left breast. Wisting recognized her as they had worked together on other cases. Pia Gusfre. She had small children at home, he knew. Maybe she hadn't had time, or even thought, to change when she had been called out and given charge of the investigation.

Gusfre was sitting on her own in a conference room. Wisting spoke to her as if she were in the room with them, glancing at her image on the screen instead of the camera. He made a round of introductions before asking her to provide an account of the investigation.

'We've only just got started here,' Gusfre said. 'Your information has given us a completely different jumping-off point from where we began. For a few hours we suspected that the whole abduction had been staged.'

Wisting understood what she meant. In the case that had suddenly landed on Gusfre and her colleagues, it would be quite natural to consider the possibility of the husband somehow being involved.

'Niklas Kranz contacted one of our police prosecutors just before 9 a.m. this morning,' she went on. 'They know each other personally. He passed on the news.'

The empty room she sat in lent her voice an eerie echo.

'Kranz had been on a business trip abroad since Tuesday,' she continued. 'When he came home yesterday afternoon, the house was deserted. He found a package in the mailbox that contained a brief message and a mobile phone.'

She leaned across the keyboard in front of her and shared a photograph with them, a computer printout with a square font covering four lines of text. The message was written in English and stated succinctly that the sender had taken Kranz's wife and demanded her weight in gold for her safe return. In twenty-four hours, the kidnapper would make contact by phone with further instructions. *No police* was the stipulation on the last line.

'The same formulation as in the Malmgren Affair,' Jan Serner commented. 'It's not public knowledge that the kidnappers demanded the daughter's weight in gold. All Malmgren managed to gather in was just over sixteen kilos. The kidnappers decided to make do with that.'

Pia Gusfre switched the picture to show the encrypted phone. It was a make that Wisting had never seen before, but Serner nodded in recognition.

'Produced in the Czech Republic,' he said.

'We assume the kidnappers have kept an eye on the house and seen when Niklas Kranz came home,' Gusfre continued. 'The twenty-four-hour deadline had already expired when he brought in the post. Ten minutes later, he received a new message.'

She showed a picture of the mobile screen: *24 hours from now.*

Underneath, they saw that it had been read at 16.11 the previous day.

'The phone looks as if it's linked to a foreign subscription,' Gusfre added.

'How was she abducted?' Helland asked.

Pia Gusfre was back on the screen.

'We found her car an hour ago,' she replied, 'parked outside a sports centre in Falkum. We're waiting for data from the on-board computer to find out when it was left there, but according to the husband, she exercises there every Wednesday evening. We assume she was taken around then. The car was parked beyond CCTV coverage, but we're working on collecting footage from the surrounding area.'

'What's the husband's attitude to the demand?' Wisting asked.

'He's able to pay, but I don't think he's willing,' Gusfre answered.

Wisting let her explain.

'EdelKranz was established at the start of the twentieth century. Niklas Kranz is the fifth generation of owners. His father developed the firm to become a leading supplier of precious metals to gold and silver manufacturers throughout northern Europe. They have a workshop and production department here in Skien, but branches in six other countries. Last year the turnover was almost a billion kroner.'

Hammer gave a loud whistle.

'They don't only produce jewellery,' Gusfre went on. 'But also sell gold and silver for investment purposes, as an alternative to funds or shares.'

'But you say he's not willing to pay up?' Helland asked.

'He claims that kind of volume is not easily accessible, but it may be an ulterior argument,' Gusfre replied. 'The people behind this have obviously put a lot of work into planning and preparation, but they clearly haven't cottoned on to the fact that Nanette and Niklas Kranz were in the process of separating. That was one of our reasons for suspecting him. A divorce would cost him far more than the kidnappers are charging.'

Wisting looked at the time again. The new deadline

would expire in less than four hours. 'Why did he delay alerting the police?' he asked.

'He wasn't sure what to do,' Gusfre replied. 'According to him, his initial idea was to comply with their demands without involving the police. But after ruminating on it for a while, he decided to get in touch.'

'What are you doing now?'

'We haven't agreed on a plan of action, but we're banking on buying ourselves some time,' Gusfre said. 'I hope we can enter into dialogue with the kidnappers and negotiate our way to a settlement.'

'Where is Niklas Kranz now?'

'At home. We have two officers with him.'

'Who got in unnoticed, I trust?'

'Hopefully,' Gusfre replied, explaining how they had both entered via the back garden while Niklas Kranz was sent out to the mailbox as a diversionary manoeuvre.

The video call then switched around, and now Pia Gusfre was the one asking the questions. Jan Serner and Josef Helland were required to give an account of their investigation.

'So you knew something like this was going to happen,' Pia Gusfre summarized. 'Was Niklas Kranz a target you considered?' The question was directed at Josef Helland from Kripos. 'Since there had been earlier demands for payment in gold, I mean,' Gusfre added.

'He was on our list,' Helland confirmed.

Gusfre refrained from criticism. There would be time for re-evaluation later.

After the meeting, Wisting felt the need for a breath of fresh air. He headed for the terrace outside the canteen. The fog had lifted, but the weather was still bleak and it threatened to rain again at any time.

The railings were wet. He wiped them with his hand and stood looking out over the town.

They had not spoken of Nanette Kranz except to say she had been abducted. No one had given a thought to how she was, whether she was confined to a cellar, tethered to a bed or tied to a chair.

He took out his phone and looked up her details. Her name sounded Italian to him. Her appearance suggested southern Europe too – dark hair and a suntanned complexion.

The door behind him opened and Jan Serner appeared, shaking a cigarette out of a packet. 'We have to access Bulut's apartment,' he said as he inserted it between his lips.

Nodding, Wisting showed him the photo of Nanette Kranz. He doubted whether she would be in Bulut's basement apartment, but one of his tasks must have been to identify a location where they could hold her captive and where all the conspirators could remain in hiding. There could be clues within his apartment to suggest where this place might be.

'We're trying to locate the landlord,' he said, returning his phone to his pocket.

According to the surveillance log, the whole family in the apartment above had left by 9 a.m. Both children had been wearing sports attire and were probably heading for a handball or football match.

Jan Serner lit his cigarette and took a deep drag. 'I'd really given up,' he said, gazing at the cloud of smoke he blew out. 'But this case . . .' He shook his head.

'Why isn't it possible to track the use of the encrypted phone?' Wisting asked. 'I mean, we're sitting here with one side of the communications channel, aren't we?'

'Because the other party is communicating via a server from a provider that doesn't cooperate with public authorities,' Serner answered. 'Most likely there's not even a phone at the other end, just a computer that routes all traffic through tunnels of fictional networks.'

Wisting always had a craving to understand but had almost given up when it came to advanced computer technology.

'What about the SIM card in the phone they left?' he asked. 'Isn't it possible to trace where that was bought?'

'In the Malmgren case, it was a Dutch pay-as-you-go card,' Serner replied. 'Bought in a kiosk in the east end of Amsterdam six months in advance. We got no further than that.'

Stooping forward, Wisting gazed down into the back yard. The Romanian lorry that had been towed in was still parked adjacent to the neighbouring building.

Even among bicycle thieves, there had been developments. From using bolt cutters, they had moved on to battery-operated angle-grinders in order to defeat the most advanced cycle locks. It was understandable. When it came to the sophisticated technology used by certain criminal gangs, Wisting had eventually grown accustomed to accepting this was how things were, without having to know exactly how it was engineered.

The terrace door opened again, this time to reveal Maren Dokken. 'We've found the guy who rents out Bulut's apartment,' she said. 'They're at a handball tournament in the Stavern Sports Complex.'

Wisting gave her a nod. 'I'll drive out there.'

'Do you want me to come with you?' Maren asked.

Jan Serner pinched his cigarette between thumb and forefinger. 'I'm coming too,' he said, tossing the butt over the railings.

22

A female volunteer in the kiosk, standing at the back cooking waffles, was pointed out to Wisting. When she heard the police wanted to speak to her, she pulled out the waffle-iron plug and came out.

'It's to do with Dogan Bulut,' Wisting told her.

The woman's hand went straight to her mouth. 'Oh my God,' she groaned. 'We talked about that . . . was it him?'

Wisting realized she was referring to the news coverage about the Swedish man found murdered in the landslide debris. Before he had a chance to clear up the misunderstanding, she shouted to a man walking by with a bag of rubbish.

'Einar!'

Loud cheering reached them from the crowd inside the hall as the man approached.

'The police,' the woman explained. 'It's about Bulut.'

'When did you last see or hear from him?' Wisting asked.

'It's been very quiet down there for a long time now,' she answered.

'Last weekend,' the man said firmly. 'Saturday.'

His wife agreed. 'About four o'clock,' she decided. 'He was doing something in the car when we arrived.'

'The car's still parked there,' Serner pointed out.

The couple nodded but could not come up with any explanation for where Bulut might have gone without transport.

'If it wasn't for the car, I'd have thought he'd gone home to Sweden for a visit,' the woman said.

'We'd like to take a look inside his apartment,' Wisting said.

'Of course,' the man replied. 'I can come with you. Give me two minutes.'

He disappeared with the bag of rubbish while Wisting and Serner went outside to wait. A visiting team were sheltering under the eaves, jumping on the spot and tossing the ball to one another. When one of the balls bounced in their direction, Wisting picked it up and lobbed it back.

'Do you have kids?' he asked Serner.

Serner was lighting a cigarette. 'A daughter,' he replied, without volunteering her name or age.

'I have to make a call,' Wisting excused himself. He rang Line and could hear music in the background when she answered.

'I'm sorry,' he said. 'This case has become more complicated than I'd anticipated. I know I said I'd take Amalie tonight, but I'm not going to manage that.'

He had been looking forward to it – just the two of them, snuggling up on the settee. Amalie was in the habit of falling asleep there, in the crook of his arm.

'I understand,' Line replied. 'I'll work something out. I'll get Sandra to come here and I'll just leave a bit earlier.'

Sandra was a teenager who had babysat a few evenings earlier.

'Are you sure?' Wisting asked.

'It'll be fine,' Line assured him.

Both houseowners came out and Wisting wrapped up the conversation.

'Shall we drive ahead, or . . . ?' the man asked.

'Just one thing before we leave,' Wisting said. 'The name of the Swedish guy we found in the landslide was Mats Beckman.'

The couple facing him seemed bewildered.

'He and Dogan Bulut have been in contact while they were both living here,' Wisting went on.

The woman tilted her head. 'What does that mean?' she asked. 'I thought . . . do you suspect Dogan of something?'

A brief silence hung between them. Wisting allowed it to confirm the woman's assumption but went on to explain that they were in the initial stages of a complex inquiry that demanded discretion.

'Is there any way we can enter the apartment unobserved?' he asked.

The two householders exchanged glances. 'There's a door to his apartment from our basement,' the man responded. 'We can let you in that way.'

'That's preferable,' Wisting said. 'Is it possible for us to drive only one car?'

He glanced at the vehicle he had arrived in. It did not take much to work out that it was an unmarked police car.

'You can have a lift with us,' the man offered.

Wisting nodded his thanks and collected a bag of equipment from his car. Serner stubbed out his cigarette, but some of the smoke accompanied him into the back seat.

The drive took no more than ten minutes. Serner checked the surveillance log as they approached. 'No movement,' he reported.

The man drove the car up as close to the entrance as possible. Wisting waited with Serner until the couple had let themselves in, and then they crossed over to the house in only a few steps.

'It's down here,' the man said, pointing at a staircase leading from the hallway.

'One thing first,' Wisting said. He put the bag of equipment on the floor and removed the contents. 'This is a thermal imaging camera,' he explained. 'We'd like to skim your floors to see if there's anybody inside the apartment.'

Neither said anything, and they merely watched with interest as Wisting used the equipment. The camera did not work well from a distance and through insulated external walls but did function adequately through internal floors.

As Wisting paced back and forth, the camera screen showed various shades of blue, purple and green. Nothing to suggest heat or indicate any human presence.

'OK,' he said. 'Now we're ready.'

The basement staircase creaked under the weight of the three men. A freezer blocked the door of the rented section. Serner helped the houseowner to push it aside before unlocking the door.

Wisting stepped in first, walking swiftly from room to room to obtain an overview. The apartment was simply furnished, probably with only what was provided in the rental. It comprised a living room with kitchenette, one bedroom, a bathroom, a storage cupboard and a hallway. They divided the rooms between them and Wisting took the bathroom, cupboard, bedroom and hallway, while Jan Serner conducted a search of the living room and the kitchen.

Everything seemed sterile and impersonal. They found no information on the person who lived there, no indication of what he did for a living. On one bedside table Wisting saw a Swedish edition of a glossy history magazine. It had been issued that summer and appeared to be a special edition on one of Hitler's special units and a battle on New

Year's Eve, 1944. A few clothes were stored in a wardrobe, while some were still in a travel bag on the floor. All these items were black, except for a pair of white sports socks.

There was an array of toiletries in the bathroom. A toothbrush in a tumbler, a deodorant and shaving gear, all suggesting that Dogan Bulut would return at any moment.

Serner called out from the kitchenette. He pointed beneath one of the drawers he had pulled out. Wisting crouched down and saw an envelope taped to it.

He used his mobile to take some photos while Serner ripped it off. Several pieces of tape criss-crossed it, as if the envelope had been repeatedly taken out and hidden again.

The flap was tucked in and had been slit open. A few banknotes slid out when Serner laid it on the worktop. Norwegian 500- and 200-kroner notes. Almost 20,000 kroner in total when they counted them.

'We need to get Helland's technicians in here to install some surveillance gear before he comes back,' Wisting said.

Serner replaced the money in the envelope. The tape loosened when he tried to stick it back in place, but the roll of tape was in the adjacent drawer. He tore off a strip and managed to put the envelope back exactly as it had been.

'What about his car?' Serner asked. 'The key's inside the microwave.' He motioned towards one end of the worktop.

'I can check,' Wisting said.

Letting himself out, he shot a glance at the parked surveillance vehicle he knew was filming him before unlocking the BMW and squeezing into the passenger seat. The rain drummed on the car roof as he rummaged through the glove compartment, door pockets and centre console, without finding anything of significance. Discarded hot dog wrappers and empty bottles littered the footwell, as well as two parking tickets. They were from two different streets in the town centre and both were a few weeks old. Wisting photographed them and put them back.

A black leather jacket lay on the rear seat. He checked the pockets, finding only a used napkin and a packet of throat pastilles. He scanned the street before stepping out and skirting round to the back of the car. He spotted an indentation in the middle of the boot lid. Wisting slipped his fingers underneath and located the opening mechanism. He found a hockey stick, a large roll of plastic, a pair of rubber gloves and a few tools. Lifting the rubber mat, he peered into the spare wheel well, but nothing was concealed there.

A car drove past, the tyres hissing on the wet road surface. Wisting took a photo of the boot contents before closing the lid again and scurrying back indoors.

'Nothing there,' he said, returning the key to its hiding place.

'Are we finished, then?' Serner asked.

Wisting took one last look around the living room. A few empty beer bottles were strewn across the coffee table in front of the TV, beside a bowl of peanuts. On a corner unit he saw two more copies of the same history magazine as in the bedroom, alongside a ballpoint pen. He walked across and picked up one of the magazines. This one was about Egyptian treasures. He leafed through a few pages before turning it round. On the back page, he caught sight of something written in the margin. The handwriting was difficult to read, but it looked like an address. A street name and number that must have been scribbled in haste. Duedalsveien 23 or something similar.

'We might have something here,' he said, drawing Serner's attention to it.

Serner cast a glance at the magazine. It was obvious to Wisting that he recognized the address.

'Duedalsvägen,' he said. 'They must have been following him. That's where Mats Beckman spent his time off. The undercover apartment outside Gothenburg.'

Wisting took a photo of the magazine before putting it back. 'Let's get out of here,' he said.

23

Wisting slumped into his office chair, unwrapping a filled baguette he had bought en route.

The police top brass had decided that the two cases should be investigated in parallel. Pia Gusfre was to lead the kidnapping case in Grenland, while Wisting had responsibility for the murder inquiry. With one condition – there should be a free flow of information between the two.

This investigation was different from most cases Wisting had been in charge of previously. They already knew who was behind it all. In a way, they were in possession of the answers, but had to gather evidence to reach a solution. At the same time, there was a limit to what they could do as long as there was an active hostage situation.

The Swedes had transferred digital files on the three suspects: Gillis Haack, Elton Khan and Dogan Bulut. Internally, within the investigative group, they were referred to only as the Tigers.

Wisting read as he ate. It was always useful to know your opponents.

Gillis Haack appeared to be the leader. His childhood in Stockholm had been chaotic, involving countless moves and changes of school, and he had begun thieving as a teenager. He stole cars and committed housebreaking crimes, buying and selling everything from counterfeit money to guns. At the age of seventeen he had been given his first prison sentence. At around the same time, his parents had divorced. His mother was Swedish, but his father was from the Netherlands. Gillis moved with him to a small town just outside Amsterdam, apparently mainly to dodge the jail sentence. For a number of years he had worked on one of his uncle's fishing boats, but he was arrested when he docked in Gothenburg with eight hundred kilos of hash onboard. That case had earned him the nickname Skipper.

In the Swedish prison, he had made contact with a robbery gang and was later found guilty of three armoured transport heists. Halfway through his sentence, he had forced his way out of jail by taking a prison guard hostage. He had been on the run for a year before being arrested in a strip club in Amsterdam.

After his next lengthy prison stretch, he remained in Sweden, where he tried his hand in the restaurant trade and was subsequently given more jail time for false accounting practices and other financial crimes. In a final comment he was described as a bitter, tough and determined criminal who was after money, power and respect but who had never attained any of these things.

Elton Khan was part of the robbery gang Gillis Haack had got to know in prison. His parents were Kurdish refugees who had come to Sweden in the late eighties. As a teenager, Khan had applied to join the military and was signed up as an officer cadet. At the end of his term of service, he was refused admission to the follow-on officer training and applied instead to the French Foreign Legion, where he underwent a trial period before returning to Sweden to work in his parents' greengrocer's shop. At a local gym he eventually became linked to a criminal milieu that enlisted him in a gang of robbers dubbed the Dillstad Boys by the media.

Dogan Bulut was described as a fixer. He and Elton Khan were cousins. Bulut's parents had arrived in Sweden a year after the Khans, but the two boys were the same age. While Khan had applied to the army, Bulut had embarked on the study of economics, but was expelled after being caught cheating in exams. Instead he became a guard at a security firm, eventually obtaining a driver's job with armoured transport vehicles. When his cousin's gang of robbers was arrested, he was convicted of collusion and collaboration, having made use of his inside knowledge.

The time was approaching when the kidnappers had arranged to make contact with Niklas Kranz. Christine Thiis and Nils Hammer passed by in the corridor on their way to the conference room. Wisting brushed off a few crumbs and tossed the baguette wrapper in the bin before lifting his notebook and following them.

In the conference room, a video link had been set up with Kranz's house, a simple arrangement with a handheld mobile phone.

Niklas Kranz, restless and with legs sprawled wide, was seated on a settee in front of a coffee table. Wisting positioned himself behind Ralf Falk. The Swedish police prosecutor stood beside him. There were still a few minutes left before the extended deadline of twenty-four hours ran out.

An investigator entered the video, carrying a metal case around the size of a shoebox.

'What's that?' Christine Thiis asked.

'A signal-blocking shield,' Josef Helland explained. 'The microphone in the phone may be open, allowing the kidnappers to hear what's being said in the room.'

The detective opened the lid of the case and took out the encrypted phone.

Wisting kept his eyes on the screen. Niklas Kranz grabbed a glass of water. His foot moved fitfully under the table. As he drank, he shot a quick glance at the camera before looking away and putting down his glass.

Time passed slowly. Wisting crossed his arms. Helland checked his watch.

'One minute past,' he commented.

Jan Serner shifted anxiously in his seat. Outside, it had started to rain, steady drops that hit the window ledge with increasing intensity.

Niklas Kranz raked his fingers through his hair and looked up at the camera again. He had dark eyes, cropped dark hair and facial stubble. It seemed as if he was about to say something when a shrill ringtone punctured the silence.

The investigator holding the camera stepped a bit closer. The phone on the table lit up. The camera zoomed in on the display, showing a call from an insignificant series of numbers, symbols and letters.

Niklas Kranz squinted at the detective beside him, received a nod and tapped the phone.

'Hello?' he said.

'*Mr Niklas Kranz?*' It was a computer speaking, in a calm and friendly female voice.

'Yes,' Kranz replied.

'*What was the name of Nanette's white cat?*' the voice asked in English.

Wisting shifted his weight to his right foot. This was some kind of control question, intended both to reassure the kidnappers that they were really talking to Niklas Kranz, and at the same time let him understand that they were holding his wife.

'Katitzi,' Niklas answered without a second thought.

Then came another question. *'Where did you go on your first holiday together?'*

'To Crete,' Kranz replied, but then grew uncertain. 'Or, no, to Italy. Rome and Naples.'

This answer was obviously accepted. *'Have you obtained what we requested?'* was the next question.

Kranz swallowed hard. The investigator pointed to a sheet of paper on which various alternative responses had been written in advance.

'Who am I talking to?' he asked.

No reply was forthcoming. Niklas Kranz bent over the phone on the table.

'Hello?'

'Have you obtained what we requested?' the computer voice repeated.

Kranz had another response pointed out to him. 'I need to know she is OK first,' he insisted.

A few seconds' silence.

'In English, please,' the computer voice intoned.

Kranz reiterated his answer in English, but the kidnappers ignored him.

'Have you obtained what we requested?'

Kranz looked down at the sheet of paper with the prepared responses, gave the detective a quizzical look and received a nod in confirmation.

'It's not so easy,' he began to answer in Norwegian, but quickly changed to English. 'I don't have access to such large quantities.'

It appeared that the kidnappers, too, had prepared their responses. *'Weight on 10 October was 60.3 kilos.'*

'It's just not possible,' Kranz replied. 'Not at such short notice.'

This time it took longer before an answer came. '*We can remove an arm,*' the female voice offered in a matter-of-fact tone. '*Would fifty-five kilos make it easier for you?*'

Wisting shifted his weight to the other foot again. The Swedish prosecutor beside him was breathing in fits and starts. The scene on the screen in front of them seemed surreal. The very fact of it being shown on video made it feel as if he was watching a film.

Kranz had got to his feet. 'No, no,' he protested, grabbing the phone. 'I just need some time.'

'*Time is money.*'

'What do you mean?'

'*Time will cost you.*'

'I'm not making this up,' Kranz said. 'All I want is for this to be over and done with.'

'*Everything is up to you. When do you want it to be over?*'

'As fast as possible.'

The computer voice repeated, '*When do you want it to be over?*'

The investigator on the settee slid a sheet of paper across.

'It's the weekend,' Kranz argued. 'I need until Monday, maybe even Tuesday.'

He looked up at the camera, as if seeking confirmation that he was doing the right thing. Dragging things out was the whole purpose of the conversation. In twenty-four or forty-eight hours, everything could look completely different.

'*Don't think Nanette will like that,*' was the answer that came.

Kranz slammed one hand down on the table. 'I can't do anything else,' he said.

Silence followed again.

'*You have eighteen hours,*' was the answer they heard now. '*Contact us if you manage it before that.*'

And then the connection was severed.

Kranz scratched his head. 'Christ,' he said, clearly stressed out. 'Bloody hell.'

His voice sounded even more jittery than when he had been talking to the kidnappers. It was trembling. His whole body began to shake.

'You did well,' the detective by his side reassured him.

The camera was focused on the floor and the transmission cut before Pia Gusfre's face appeared on the screen. She was sitting in the police station in Skien, having watched the broadcast with her team.

No words were spoken. Wisting understood that the others were waiting for him to break the silence.

He looked at the time and calculated forward by eighteen hours. 'Quarter past ten tomorrow morning, then,' he said, searching for words that might inject some optimism into the case.

The sound of a phone ringing was broadcast via the large screen, but it was quickly switched off.

'Our advantage is that they don't know we're gathered here,' Wisting continued. 'They're not certain of what we know and how we're cooperating.'

He glanced from the screen to Josef Helland from Kripos and on to Jan Serner from the national unit of the Swedish police force.

'We'll make use of that,' he added.

'Cooperation is all very well, but we've nothing to go on,' Hammer objected.

'We have Dogan Bulut,' Wisting said. 'A previously convicted Swedish citizen who has been in touch with our murder victim.'

His gaze locked on Mortensen's eyes. 'His fingerprints

were found in the victim's home and we have video footage of them together.'

Mortensen nodded. 'In addition, he's gone into hiding following the murder,' he pointed out.

'If this were a normal investigation, and we had no knowledge of the kidnapping and the rest of the background, we'd have gone public with his details,' Wisting went on.

There were a few nodding heads around the table, both in the room with him and onscreen.

'Media interest is still huge,' Christine Thiis said. She had responsibility for the legal aspects of the case and was also the conduit for press inquiries.

'Tip-offs from the public might not only lead us to him, but also to the location where they're holding Nanette Kranz,' Wisting summarized.

'Have you announced a press conference?' Pia Gusfre asked.

'I've promised a debrief at 9 p.m.,' the police prosecutor answered. 'If we announce that we'll also reveal details of a wanted person, we'll get wide coverage.'

'Any comment?' Wisting asked, scanning the faces around the table.

Jan Serner and the other members of the Swedish group seemed unconvinced, but they said nothing.

'Then that's how we'll tackle it,' Wisting said, pulling out his chair.

24

The photograph of Dogan Bulut was shown on the TV news and throughout the online newspapers, both in Norway and Sweden. After an hour or so, more than thirty tip-offs had come in, fewer than Wisting had anticipated. They had also decided to publish the registration number and pictures of the car he drove but had chosen to focus on him as a person of interest, since they were well aware of the whereabouts of the vehicle.

Hammer and Fjeld were tasked with sorting through the calls, organizing them and checking out whatever seemed most relevant. At present they had not yet reported back.

The computer screen flickered, as if there was a bad connection somewhere. Wisting stood up, crossed to the window and phoned Line. 'Hi,' he said. 'Did you work something out for Amalie?'

'Yes, it's fine,' his daughter replied. 'Sandra's here. It'll be popcorn and the Disney Channel and then she can go to bed with the iPad.'

Wisting stared through his own reflection, out into the darkness and the rain. 'I can pay Sandra,' he offered.

'Not at all, it's perfectly OK. She's staying here until one o'clock. I'll be home by then.'

'Maybe I can pick you up,' Wisting suggested. 'Then drive her home afterwards.'

She laughed. 'She only lives two hundred metres along the street!'

'Give me a call when you're ready to go home, then,' Wisting said. 'Maybe I'll be free.'

Line did not bother to answer that.

'I saw the photo of the Turkish guy you're looking for,' she said. The echo made it sound as if she was in the bathroom. 'You said on TV you believe he's still in Norway. Why's that? After all, it's been a week since the murder.'

'He's Swedish,' Wisting corrected her. 'Turkish background.'

'Why do you think he's still in Norway, though?' Line asked. 'He'd only been living here for a few months. I'd have legged it as fast as I could.'

'We don't share everything with journalists,' was Wisting's terse response.

Line picked up on his tone. 'I'm not a journalist any more,' she said jokingly. 'At least, not a news reporter.'

Wisting put his finger on the windowpane and followed a bead of water as it trickled down.

'Have a nice time tonight, then,' he said.

'I'll take a taxi home,' Line told him. 'You need to sleep. You looked exhausted on TV.'

Wisting laughed this off, but he could feel the physical toll the case was already taking on him. He had lost a lot of sleep.

The hours ticked by without any incoming information to move the case forward, and midnight came and went. Wisting knew everyone needed a few hours' rest. Soon they would be busy again.

He was last to leave the police station. Outside, the rain continued relentlessly. He took a deep breath of cold air down into his lungs as he trudged across the car park.

25

Wisting was rudely woken by shouts. There was someone outside. The ear-splitting noise of banging and kicking at the front door ricocheted through the house.

He sprang up, glancing at the clock as he pulled on his trousers: 05.23.

On his way to the door he realized it was Line. She collapsed into his arms when he opened up but struggled free as he tried to embrace her. All she was wearing was a T-shirt and briefs. He grabbed hold of her again and held her upright. The very worst thoughts of what had happened to her raced through his head.

'What's wrong?'

Rainwater streamed from her hair, down on to her face. Her hand was clutching a scrap of paper.

'Amalie!' she sobbed.

A knot of nerves tightened in his chest, constricting his breathing. Wisting pushed his daughter away and moved out on to the steps. His bare feet trod on water while he squinted down at Line's house. The door was wide open. He looked back at Line but did not wait for an explanation as he broke into a run.

'No!' she shrieked after him.

Wisting did not stop. He stormed into the house, sliding barefoot across the floor, and had to put his hand on the doorframe for support while rounding the corner into the kitchen and then the living room. On his way towards the child's bedroom, he knocked into something that crashed to the floor.

The door was open and the light switched on. He plunged in, terrified of what he would find.

The room was empty. Wisting was left standing in the middle, walking around in circles to verify that his granddaughter was not there. The quilt had fallen halfway to the floor and a soft toy lay on the pillow.

Calling out his granddaughter's name, he dashed out into Line's bedroom. She was not there either.

'Amalie!'

Nor was she in the bathroom.

Line was standing in the living room when he came out again.

'She's gone!' she managed to say before her voice broke. 'They've taken her.'

She held out her hand, showing him the piece of paper.

Wisting approached her, adrenaline still flooding through his body, making his hands tremble as he took the note.

It was crumpled and sodden with rain. The ink on the words had run, but the brief message was easy to read. Three lines in English.

We have your daughter.
Get your father. He must answer when the phone rings.
Do not speak to anyone else.

Wisting struggled to read it one more time, but simply could not. His brain was suffering from a lack of oxygen. The letters danced before his eyes. He tried to utter something, but his mouth was completely dry. A logical part of him was striving to understand what this was all about, but it was hard for him to gather his thoughts. Pulling Line towards him, he held her close. He could feel her shudder and shake as he groped for something to say. Something reassuring, some words of comfort.

'The phone,' he said, with a gulp. 'My phone's at home.'

She pushed back from his embrace. Struggling to breathe, she found it difficult to speak.

Wisting did not let go completely but gripped her arms and gazed at her, trying to make eye contact.

A ringtone caught their attention. A phone buzzing, somewhere close by.

'Answer it,' Line told him.

Wisting followed the sound. It came from Amalie's room, where he caught sight of the phone on the window ledge with the display illuminated.

'Answer it,' Line repeated behind his back.

It was cold after lying in front of the half-open window. He cradled it in his hand as it continued to buzz. It was an encrypted computer call, showing a combination of letters and numbers.

His thumb landed on the green answer icon, but he delayed saying anything until he had flicked on the loudspeaker function.

'This is William Wisting,' he said, his voice not as steady as he would have liked.

Behind him, Line moved forward.

'*Chief Inspector William Wisting?*' an AI voice asked in English.

It was the same friendly female voice that had spoken to Niklas Kranz.

Changing to English, Wisting replied: 'Yes, it's me.'

'*Grandfather William Wisting?*' the voice asked.

Line gave a sob, but Wisting stared straight ahead, out into the darkness, picturing the person he was talking to somewhere out there staring back at him.

'That's also me,' he replied, grasping Line's hand.

'*Ingrid Amalie Wisting is in safe hands with us, as long as you do as we say.*'

'What do you want?' Wisting asked.

'*First of all, neither you nor the child's mother must speak to anyone else about this. Do not involve anyone else.*'

Wisting and Line exchanged glances.

'*And secondly,*' the computer-generated voice went on, '*you must be totally honest with us.*'

'OK,' Wisting answered. 'What else?'

'*Totally honest,*' the voice repeated. '*Is that understood?*'

'That's understood.'

'*Excellent. Can you then say whether or not you have spoken to Mr Jan Serner?*'

The question was sudden and unexpected, but Wisting's response was unhesitating: 'Yes.'

'*Is Mr Jan Serner in Norway?*' was the next question.

Line looked at him, her expression betraying her lack of comprehension.

'Yes,' Wisting replied. 'Can we talk about Amalie?'

'*She is asleep.*'

Wisting turned his back to the window. 'What do you want?' he demanded.

'*This is most of all a matter of what we do not want,*' the voice responded.

'I don't understand,' Wisting said.

The computer voice went on to explain, in the same unruffled tone: '*We do not want any investigation of Mats Beckman's death.*'

'You know that's not just up to me,' Wisting replied.

'*You have to make sure no evidence is found.*'

Wisting shut his eyes. Undoubtedly, he would be able to sabotage the inquiry. That would not be a problem. The difficulty would be that this would drag out the investigation. He could not let Amalie remain in the kidnappers' violent clutches for an indefinite period of time.

'There is no evidence,' he said.

'*But a wanted person notice has been issued,*' the voice insisted.

Wisting's hand tightened around Line's.

'It's really not within my power to withdraw that,' he said. 'But it's based on a slim suspicion, and I can make sure it comes to nothing.'

He had no idea how he would manage that. The video footage of Bulut and Beckman at the marina was something he could probably delete, but the fingerprint in Beckman's home would be more problematic. However, neither of these proved anything.

'*Thanks,*' was the immediate response.

There was a moment's silence before the voice continued: '*In six hours, you will receive a message with login details for our computer server. You must upload all the documents in the Mats Beckman case.*'

The onscreen clock on the encrypted phone showed the time as 05.38. Wisting calculated forward.

'*All the documents,*' the voice reiterated.

Wisting steered his thoughts away from the practical and factual consequences this would involve. 'I understand,' was all he said.

'One final question,' the AI voice said.

'Yes?'

'*How much does Nanette Kranz weigh?*'

Wisting released Line's hand and ran his fingers through his hair. This was a control question. They wanted to know if Niklas Kranz had contacted the police. If he revealed that, it would put the hostage's life in danger.

'What did you say?' he asked, to gain some time.

'*You have to be totally honest,*' the voice said, in an echo of the earlier comment. '*Totally honest, is that understood?*'

'Yes,' Wisting replied.

'*How much does Nanette Kranz weigh?*' the voice asked again.

'Sixty point three kilos,' Wisting answered.

There was a lengthy silence before the line was cut.

26

Staggering across the floor, Line collapsed on to Amalie's bed and hugged one of the pillows, clutching it to her chest.

Wisting closed the window and drew the curtains before dropping the phone into his pocket and helping Line to her feet.

'We can't stay in here,' he said, taking the pillow from her. 'We have to leave everything undisturbed.'

He led her out into the living room, requiring all his strength to hold her upright.

'You have to do it,' she said. Tears and snot were running down her face. 'You have to give them what they want, do what they say.'

'I will, I promise,' Wisting replied. 'All of it. We'll get Amalie back.'

She thumped his chest with her clenched fist. 'You know who they are,' Line cried. 'This is your fault. You know them. This is because of your job.'

He did not flinch from the blows. When they lost impact, he drew her towards him again and held her tight. 'It'll be all right,' he whispered.

They stood motionless for a while. Wisting felt the panic still coursing through his daughter's body. She was shaking uncontrollably and now and again gasped for breath.

He led her to the settee and sat her down there before finding a blanket to cover her. He was reluctant to leave. Instead he sat down by her side.

'Listen to me,' he said, gripping her hand. 'If we're to do this, I'm going to have to go soon.'

He saw her summon all her strength to regain control.

'You're going to have to stay here on your own,' he said.

Line sat bolt upright, took a deep breath and gritted her teeth.

'Will you be OK?' Wisting asked.

She nodded, now breathing more easily, and used the back of her hand to wipe her nose. 'Who were they talking about?' she asked. 'What was that about the woman who weighed sixty kilos?'

Wisting looked down at the floor, searching for where to begin. Two toy figures lay there, male and female characters from a children's TV programme.

'Say something,' Line begged.

He had met countless people in crisis and sorrow, and knew that information was vital, no matter how brutal the truth might be.

He started with the body in the landslide. While he talked, he noticed her composure grow. The tears stopped. She sat up and listened intently. No interruptions, but she did ask questions.

'You're shivering,' she said when he was done, handing him the blanket.

Wisting draped it over his shoulders while she left to get dressed. Woollen socks, pyjama trousers and a thick sweater.

'Tell me what you're thinking,' she said, flopping down on the settee again.

'I'm thinking of doing what they ask,' Wisting replied.

'That could cost you your job,' Line told him.

The blanket slid off one shoulder and he yanked it up again. She was right, but that meant nothing.

'We don't need to think so far ahead,' he said. 'But you must be prepared for this to take time. They're probably going to use me until they receive the gold for Nanette Kranz and flee the country.'

'Are we going to get Amalie back?' Line asked.

'I'm sure of that,' Wisting replied.

'How can you be so certain?'

'They're depending on it,' Wisting told her. 'They'll need my protection once this is over, and the only reason I'm going to help them is the threat that this could happen again.'

Line sat with her feet tucked under. 'So they get away with what they've done?' she asked. 'And Amalie will never be safe despite it all?'

'A lot can happen before that,' Wisting said. 'First we have to bring her home.'

He rose to his feet. 'I'll go home and get ready and then I'll be back,' he said. 'We can eat breakfast together before I go to work.'

Food was probably the last thing on their minds, but she nodded and accompanied him to the door.

The neighbouring houses were still shrouded in darkness. The front door of his house was still ajar. He locked it behind him and headed for the bathroom, where his trousers had been left lying in a heap on the floor. Steam belched as water from the shower poured down his back and shoulders. He leaned his head into the spray and stood thinking of what he should have done differently, how he could have handled things in a more professional manner. His alternative was to let the chief of police and a restricted group know so that they could set up some double-dealing in which they released information without detriment to the investigation at the same time as using their contact with the kidnappers to track them down. He decided this was a risk he was unwilling to take. In the Swedish Malmgren case, the kidnappers had been given what they demanded and released the daughter after a few hours. Not until Amalie reached safety would he pursue the perpetrators.

He turned his face into the spray and felt the jets of water on his skin.

One thing was sure, he thought. The men who had done this would not escape punishment.

27

A cleaner let herself in just as Wisting stepped out of his car. She held the door open for him and made a comment about the rain soon easing off. Usually he would exchange a few words with her, but now he merely gave her a brief nod and continued along the corridor and up the stairs. He should have spoken to her, he thought later. Behaved exactly as normal and conformed to custom.

The criminal investigation department was in darkness. He switched on the light and followed his usual routines, activating the computer, turning on the coffee machine and checking the shelf for post in the photocopier room before taking a seat and opening the case management program.

Everything so far undertaken in the investigation into Mats Beckman's murder had been documented. The system contained all the reports and interview records, all the forensics tests carried out and all the personal details. In addition, documents and other background information shared by the Swedish investigators had been logged. In the course of the few days the inquiry had been active, enough material had been produced to fill several ring binders.

Line had given him a memory stick. He fished it out of his trouser pocket and inserted it into the machine.

The operation itself was simple. It only took a few keystrokes for all the information to be collected into a single PDF document. This was the same function used when a copy of the case files had to be sent to a defence lawyer.

He would leave behind an electronic trace in the system and each individual page would be marked with his ID number. This was mainly a security measure incorporated in order to prevent leaks to the media. Nils Hammer kept his passwords in a note under his desk blotter. Wisting could have logged in with his colleague's ID to conceal his tracks, but he refused to risk involving anyone else in any way whatsoever.

The wait cursor rotated in the centre of the screen once he had completed the task and the LED activity light on the memory stick lit up. No error messages appeared.

Unconsciously, he had been holding his breath while the computer toiled. His chin trembled as he breathed out.

He checked that the assembled file had transferred to the memory stick, but he left it attached. The kidnappers had demanded all the documents in the Mats Beckman case. There were other records elsewhere. The surveillance log and everything connected to their undercover investigation methods were logged in a different system. Although Kripos had set up the intelligence project, Wisting had been given access to that data. All contact between Mats Beckman and Dogan Bulut could be surmised from that, including what Beckman had reported back to his Swedish handler. All of the tapped phone conversations had been transcribed and all computer communication had been listed. This was information at a level very few in the police force were cleared to access. He could get away with not delivering that to the kidnappers, at least in the initial stages, but at the same time the contents would not be directly damaging to the investigation. Mats Beckman had already been exposed and eliminated. The surveillance of communications had revealed only mundane conversations. It uncovered the three people on whom both the Norwegian and Swedish inquiries were focused, but that would hardly come as a surprise to them. And if he failed to secure all the contents at this early point, it could delay the process of Amalie's return. At the same time, the material was likely to make them feel safe. It showed that the police had no idea of their location. Moreover, it would be to his benefit to demonstrate goodwill towards them.

He felt a pulse throb rhythmically in his neck as his heart rate accelerated. With a fleeting glance at the door, he cocked his head and listened. When he heard no sound, he copied the strictly confidential documents across to the memory stick.

The tip-offs were stored in a third system. These had increased in number to fifty-five, but were still fewer than Wisting had expected. After the detectives had headed home for the night, the dedicated phone line had been transferred to the switchboard, where the operators had recorded three calls. The first two of these had been added to the series of mistaken sightings. A man thought that Dogan Bulut was working in a car wash in Horten, while another was sure he had spotted him at a shopping centre in Sandefjord a few weeks previously. The third call had been phoned in less than an hour ago. This man said he had met Dogan Bulut in an industrial area between Skien and Porsgrunn. The caller bought up goods from bankrupt estates and stored them in a warehouse there. The guy he thought was Dogan Bulut had been sneaking around and the caller had approached him. He had spoken Swedish and claimed he was looking for somewhere to have an exhaust system repaired. The caller had given him directions to a workshop in the vicinity but had considered the man's behaviour to be so suspicious that he had made a note of his car number plate, a Swedish-registered BMW.

Wisting recognized the number but had to double-check. It was indeed the BMW parked outside Bulut's basement apartment.

The caller's sighting had been on Thursday, 4 October, ten days ago.

On the noticeboard in front of him, a drawing Amalie had given him before summer was pinned up. It was a Norwegian flag and a figure dressed in blue clothes and a black hat. The figure was Wisting himself. She had drawn it at nursery after he had visited in uniform to rehearse marching in the children's National Day parade on 17 May.

His eyes welled up with tears. He blinked them away, leaning forward to the computer screen and reading through the tip-off again. This was the most specific information they had received, the closest indication of the possible location of a hideout. Also the most damaging. He could not risk a patrol car being sent there, but neither could he let the kidnappers know that the police were in possession of information that might put them on their trail. That would cause them to panic and act irrationally.

There was only one option.

Wisting used his phone to photograph the screen and then clicked on the icon to delete this entire snippet of information. The system asked if he was sure. Hesitating slightly, he got to his feet and moved to the door to listen in case any of the other investigators had arrived and had the opportunity to read through the tip-offs. Nils Hammer was usually one of the earliest arrivals, but his office door was shut. The whole corridor was silent.

He returned to his seat and confirmed his intention to

delete the file selected. He gathered the other tip-offs in a single document and copied them to the memory stick. When the wait cursor switched off, he snatched the stick and shoved it into the depths of his pocket. He sat for a while waiting for his pulse rate to slow before standing up and walking to the photocopy room to fetch a spiral-bound, lined writing pad.

He had always kept a logbook when working on major cases. He noted the time and key words for what he had done and the choices he had made. This helped him remember everything he knew about the cases he worked on, but also what he still needed to find out.

Now it would be more important than ever. Later, when he had to assume responsibility for what he had done, it would be easier to explain and defend his actions if he could rely on the notes he had written at the time.

He spent ten minutes writing a summary of the night in question and the conversation with the kidnappers, and then listed the documents he had copied and prepared for transfer.

He heard a door open somewhere in the department. Wisting closed the writing pad and locked it in the top drawer of his desk. His armpits were sweaty and the roots of his hair were burning. He rose from his chair and headed to the toilet. Noticing a glimmer of perspiration on his upper lip, he splashed cold water on his face and dried it with rough paper from the wall dispenser.

There was only one way out of this, he thought, meeting his eye in the mirror. Straight ahead, all the way through.

28

The investigative team assembled in the large conference room, arriving with notebooks, laptops and coffee cups. Wisting greeted each of them in turn as they sat down at the table.

Hammer sat diagonally opposite him. 'Are you feeling ill?' he asked.

Wisting avoided his gaze. 'I didn't sleep too well,' he replied, busying himself with his pen.

'You look as if you're coming down with a cold,' Hammer told him. 'All those hours in the rain on the night of the landslide, it was bound to happen.'

'Maybe so,' Wisting agreed. Slowly, he rubbed his face with his hand, as if to verify this.

'You mustn't fall ill now,' Hammer went on. 'We need you.'

Clutching his pen, Wisting concentrated on the notes in the book in front of him. 'I'll be fine,' he assured him, focusing on underlining a few random words.

Pia Gusfre and the main investigators in Skien appeared on the big screen at the end of the room, seated around a table like Wisting and his colleagues.

The Swedish police prosecutor was last in the room. Apologizing, she sat down beside Jan Serner. Wisting moved to the door and closed it before opening the meeting.

'Let's begin with the wanted notice for Dogan Bulut,' he said, asking Hammer to provide a list of the tip-offs.

'We've received a few calls about possible sightings here

in Larvik in the days prior to the murder, but nothing to tell us where he is now or who he's with,' Hammer summarized. 'I'd like to suggest we bring in his car, take some photos and use those to supplement the appeal.'

'Is that really a good idea?' Wisting asked. 'The house-owners told us it hasn't been used for more than a week.'

'Dogan Bulut has been in Norway to plan the attack on Nanette Kranz,' Hammer replied. 'His assignment was to find a place where they could hold her captive. All the locations where the vehicle has been sighted will be of interest to us.'

Wisting could not argue against that. Instead he addressed himself to Pia Gusfre on the screen.

'Any news from your end?' he asked.

'We've had two investigators at Niklas Kranz's house all night,' she told him. 'He's most concerned about the financial loss and the future of his company. We've had our legal team go through his insurance contracts. Their conclusion is that he's not covered for a situation such as this.'

The Swedish prosecutor spoke up before Wisting had a chance to say anything. 'Has he been informed about the outcome in our two cases?' she asked.

Gusfre confirmed this.

'So he knows these people are deadly serious?' Ann-Mari Walin continued. 'That the only hope of his wife surviving is for him to pay up?'

'That may not be the only hope,' Hammer corrected her. 'This could have an investigative solution. We still have time and opportunity to locate them.'

The leader of the Swedish investigation fixed her eyes on him. 'Such a solution doesn't appear to be imminent,' she said. 'I say this because it's the reality. Niklas Kranz is the one who will have to live with the consequences of this.

By not paying, he'll forever feel partly responsible for his wife's murder. He might not think that way right now, but this should be a major consideration in terms of the advice given to him by the police.'

Wisting leaned forward. Everything would draw to a faster conclusion if Niklas Kranz paid up.

'It would also have advantages from an investigative point of view,' he said. 'Her survival would give us something to work on, and with the safe return of the hostage, we'd have more scope to hunt down the people behind it all.'

'But he doesn't possess what they're asking for,' Gusfre interrupted. 'He says his holdings in Norway are somewhere between eighteen and twenty kilos – he'll have to import the rest from branches in other countries, and that will take time.'

'Can we be sure they'll have smooth transit through customs, in that case?' Wisting asked.

He now made eye contact with Josef Helland. Kripos had responsibility for international aspects of the case.

'We can get it in as an authorized delivery,' he said, nodding. 'It won't take any longer than the actual transport time.'

Wisting glanced up at the screen again. 'Have we initiated such a process?' he asked.

'We're waiting,' Gusfre replied. 'The kidnappers have said they'll be in touch again at quarter past ten. These are ideas we'll propose to them as part of our tactic of drawing things out.'

'Have you analysed the previous conversation?' Wisting asked.

'There's not much to gain from it,' Gusfre answered. 'Our technicians believe they're communicating directly from a computer, so there's no background noise. They type in the text and play it via a computer-generated voice. It's been identified as the software developed by Microsoft and installed in all machines with their operating system.'

'What about the language?' Hammer asked.

'The sentences are short and fragmented. It's difficult to interpret much from that, but in some instances the word order suggests that English is not their mother tongue. Those who've listened closely to it think a translation program may have been used, that they've typed in some text in a foreign language that is translated into English and then read out.'

The remainder of the conversation around the conference table was far from productive. Wisting should have drawn it to a close, but he had started to dwell on thoughts that unsettled him. They did not know for certain how Mats Beckman had been unmasked, but one simple explanation came to mind. Someone had fingered him.

The Swedish investigation had been breathing down their necks. They had come down hard on the criminal fraternity in Stockholm and ended up with three names: Gillis Haack, Elton Khan and Dogan Bulut. Their most effective method of keeping themselves safe would have been to gain access to the police investigation material.

Wisting took these thoughts to their logical conclusion. Someone in the Swedish police must have fallen victim to the same ploy as he had and shared information with the gangsters. They had already been betrayed.

Placing his palms on the table, he looked first at Ralf Falk, then Jan Serner and finally Ann-Mari Walin.

One of them, he thought. Someone at this table.

29

Wisting closed the office door. He needed some thinking time on his own. The kidnappers had asked if Jan Serner was in Norway but had not followed up with any further questions. They already had inside information and knew he was here. The question was simply a test to see if Wisting was being honest with them.

Serner, Falk and Walin were the three most central figures in the Swedish investigation. They were the ones who had given the Malmgren Affair a face in the media, just as Wisting had done in Norway. If the kidnappers were to target anyone in charge of the investigation, it would be most expedient to pick one of them.

He wrote down their names on a blank page in his notebook and drew three columns. Falk was the one who had been least forthcoming, remaining in the background, keeping a watching brief. Maybe he was always withdrawn, or perhaps he had his reasons. Serner had been dismissive on the phone when Wisting had spoken to him initially, but he had become more accommodating. In Bulut's apartment he had overlooked the address scribbled on the back of the magazine in the living room. Walin had mostly remained at the hotel and only participated in the formal meetings. This morning she had argued strongly that Niklas Kranz should be encouraged to meet the kidnappers' demands.

There was no reason to direct suspicion towards any single one of them. No matter who it was, their betrayal was even greater than his and had cost Mats Beckman his life.

When someone knocked at the door, Wisting snapped his notebook shut and called out: 'Come in!'

It was Maren. She stole a glance at the bouquet of flowers, still lying on the shelf, but passed no comment.

'I can't get hold of Nina Lundblad,' she said. 'She's not answering her phone, so I called in at the hotel just before our meeting. She wasn't there.'

Wisting sat up. 'Could she have got cold feet for any reason?' he asked.

Maren shrugged. 'Possibly,' she replied. 'I checked her out. She has a few convictions herself, including for drugs offences. That could be the reason for keeping her distance, but at the same time, she was Mats Beckman's girlfriend.'

Wisting gave her a searching look. His thoughts had been elsewhere. He had failed to consider that Nina Lundblad might be in danger.

'She didn't know anything about what he was actually up to,' Wisting told her.

'We don't know whether she told us everything, though,' Maren objected.

Wisting did not like the situation that had arisen. Nina Lundblad had understood that her boyfriend was involved in criminal activities. She came from a criminal background herself and knew the rules of the game. It would not be so strange if she had withheld something from the police at their initial encounter.

'It may be nothing,' Maren went on. 'I just wanted to let you know.'

'Let's wait and see,' Wisting said. 'Ask the hotel to inform us if she turns up. She should be told about her boyfriend's true status.'

'I've already asked them to,' Maren said. She left the room, shutting the door carefully behind her. Wisting picked up the phone and called Line.

'Any news?' she asked.

'No, sorry.'

He was not keen to share his suspicions about the Swedish group with her. The tip-off about Bulut's car being spotted in an industrial area was not something he was keen to divulge over the phone either.

'I arranged what we needed,' he said in a rush. 'I'll come home to see you later.'

'Can't you come now?'

'We're waiting for the kidnappers to ring Niklas Kranz. I have to see to that first.' He looked at the time. 'It won't be long now.'

'Is he going to pay?' Line asked.

'We're not certain they'll call him,' he replied. 'They now know he's contacted the police. I revealed that to them. They may have pulled back.'

'What will happen to Nanette Kranz, then?' Line asked.

Wisting had no answer to that. 'But they've invested a lot of work in it,' he said instead. 'They've gone to great lengths and the rewards could be considerable. And as long as they've got me under their thumb, I think they'll keep going.'

'It'll all be done and dusted if he just pays up? Won't it?'

Wisting was reluctant to promise too much. The kidnappers would probably want to be out of the country before they released the hostages.

'Let's hope so,' he said.

'Tell me the truth,' Line pleaded. 'Is it going to be all right?'

'We're doing everything they've asked of us,' Wisting replied. 'There's no reason for things not to go well. The Malmgren case went well.'

He heard his daughter relax a little, enough for him to round off the conversation. As for himself, he was not so sure. Much could still go wrong.

30

It was five past ten. The broadcast from Niklas Kranz's living room was live. Both police officers who had spent the night with him were on camera. The images looked as if they were being relayed from a computer at the opposite end of the room.

Wisting was seated with Hammer, Helland and the Swedish representatives. Serner seemed restless and sat sketching abstract matchstick figures on a sheet of paper while they waited. The case was clearly stressing him out – he had admitted as much when they had been waiting outside the handball stadium for the couple who rented the basement apartment to Bulut. It had even caused him to start smoking again.

'Have you spoken to the folks back home today?' Wisting asked.

Serner glanced up from the paper, seemingly oblivious to the question.

'Have you talked to your family today?' Wisting asked again. 'You mentioned you had a daughter.'

'Not today,' Serner replied. 'They're well used to me being on the road.'

'How old is she?'

'Soon be nine.'

Wisting was tempted to say something about his granddaughter, but resisted. Instead he looked across at Ann-Mari Walin.

'Do you have children?'

'They're grown up,' she answered.

'Grandchildren?'

She gave him a stiff smile. It was difficult to see if this was because the question insinuated something about her age, or whether there was something else.

'One,' she replied.

'Me too,' Wisting said.

He was keen to say more, but spotted movement on the big screen. One of the detectives left the room and returned with the case in which they stored the encrypted phone. Wisting slipped his hand into his pocket, gripping the phone he had been given to avoid any risk of the microphone divulging something.

Niklas Kranz had the phone placed in front of him. He got to his feet and paced back and forth across the floor.

'Can't I tell them I no longer care about her?' he asked. 'That we're getting divorced. They have to understand I can't spend a pile of dosh on a woman who's been unfaithful to me. They have to let her go.'

Neither of the officers seemed to know what to say to this.

'His name's David Berg,' Kranz went on. 'He has money too. Owns a car dealership, selling Porsches and Jaguars. They can have his name. Phone number and address into the bargain. Maybe he'll pay for her.'

The detective who had brought the phone returned it to the case. 'They're calling in three minutes,' he said in an undertone. 'We've agreed on what you're to say. I don't recommend departing from that.'

Kranz ignored him. 'I can tell them I hate her,' he said.

The Swedish prosecutor sat bolt upright in her chair. 'We can't let him do that,' she said, glancing at Wisting.

Hammer told her to hush. 'We can't do anything from this end,' he pointed out.

On the screen, Kranz was gesticulating wildly. 'Or I can just refuse to answer the phone,' he said. 'I can drop out of this, and they can do whatever the hell they want with her.'

One of the detectives looked at his watch as the other stood up. 'I realize this is a trial for you,' he said. 'You've gained respect by the way you've dealt with this so far, but now I think we should just stick with the script: talk to them, persuade them to reduce their demands so you can emerge from this in a reasonable fashion, with your head held high.'

Kranz turned his back on him, moving out of camera shot. Some time elapsed before they heard the muffled sound of a phone signal.

The investigator looked at the case, allowing the phone to ring one more time before he removed it.

Wisting did not like the situation.

The fourth ringtone died out. 'Niklas?' the onscreen investigator asked. 'You have to take the call. Say whatever you like. But you must answer it.'

Kranz appeared in the frame again. He sat down and reached for the phone.

'Yes?'

'*Mr Niklas Kranz?*'

The same calm female voice.

'Yes.'

'*Are you ready to deliver?*'

Kranz glanced at the investigator and received a nod in response.

'I have nine kilos,' he said.

Wisting was unsure how the investigators in Skien had arrived at this figure, but it was unrealistic to think they would accept such a small amount. The kidnappers were caught in a situation in which they had to be prepared for life as fugitives, dependent on finance to give them freedom to operate.

'*Why?*' the voice asked.

'It's the wrong time,' Kranz replied. 'I have limited holdings here in Norway. If I'm to obtain more, it will have to be imported. That takes time. Probably a week to double the quantity.'

Silence ensued.

'Hello?' Kranz said as the hiatus continued.

'*Wait,*' the voice told him.

More time passed, and then they played back what Kranz had said the previous day: '*It's the weekend. I need until Monday, maybe even Tuesday.*'

'That was to check it all out,' Kranz said. 'I've already managed to do that.'

'*You are disappointing us,*' the voice went on. '*You are disappointing Nanette.*'

'You can have those nine kilos today,' Kranz countered. 'Just tell me where to deliver it.'

'*Unacceptable,*' was the response. '*Be ready when we phone at five o'clock.*'

Then the caller rang off.

The detective on the screen leaned over the phone as if to assure himself that the conversation was finished. 'That was good,' he said. 'That was one of the scenarios we anticipated.'

'It solves nothing,' Kranz said.

'They get a few hours to think it over,' the investigator said. 'You have to remember they're also keen to have this settled as soon as possible.'

The broadcast ended and Pia Gusfre appeared on the screen.

'No progress,' Hammer summed up.

The conversation had lasted less than a minute. Wisting's top lip was perspiring. In an hour and a half, it would be his turn to hear from the kidnappers.

'You ought to take steps to import gold from abroad,' Walin said.

'He's opposed to that,' Gusfre replied. 'And as you probably heard, we're balancing on a knife-edge here. However, his accounts show that his gold holdings in Norway are larger than he's admitting. We believe that what he's quoted, eighteen to twenty kilos, is what he's willing to hand over.'

'Then that should be the next offer,' Walin said.

'We do have negotiators in our team here,' Gusfre pointed out.

The Swedish prosecutor realized she had gone too far and averted her eyes from the screen. Wisting concluded the session by arranging a time to link up again.

'I think you may be right,' he said to Hammer as the others were dispersing. 'I could well be coming down with something.'

He got to his feet and used his hand to wipe the sweat from his lip. Hammer watched while inserting another wad of snuff into his mouth.

'I think I might have a temperature,' Wisting added. 'Can you take over here so I can go home for an hour or two? Line has some soothing medicine that might help.'

'That's fine,' Hammer assured him, using his tongue to position the snuff.

Benjamin Fjeld was at the door behind him, phone in hand. 'Beckman's car's been found,' he said. 'A patrol car's just called it in.'

'Where?' Wisting asked.

'Behind an old disused factory, immediately inside the cordon around the landslip area,' Fjeld replied.

He gave directions.

'I'll drive there on my way home,' Wisting said. 'Let Mortensen know. We need to get Forensics out there.'

Hammer followed him out into the corridor. 'Shall we do as I suggested with Bulut's BMW?' he asked. 'Ask the public for sightings?'

Wisting would have preferred not to take any action that would risk rocking the boat but was unable to make any professional objections.

'OK, go ahead,' he said.

31

Two patrol cars were parked at an angle on either side of the Swedish-registered Volvo. The driving rain splashed on the gravel around it.

Wisting pulled his rain jacket hood over his head as he strode forward. A sweater lay beside one of the rear wheels, tucked halfway under the car. A white plastic bag lay just beyond it.

The driver of one of the patrol cars came out. 'It's not locked,' he said.

Wisting walked all the way up to the car but, refraining from opening it, merely peered in through the windows. The glove compartment was open and it looked as if the contents had been dug out and strewn on the floor. Items from a bag were scattered across the back seat – T-shirts, socks and underwear. The floor mats were rumpled and one of the sun visors had been flipped down.

Two vehicles turned into the car park behind him. Espen Mortensen arrived in the forensics van, followed by Jan Serner in a hire car that Kripos had arranged for the Swedish investigators.

Wisting addressed himself to Serner: 'Where's the recording device?'

'Under the driver's seat,' Serner replied.

'Could you check that?' Wisting asked, addressing Mortensen.

'The tow vehicle's on the way,' he answered.

'I'd like to find out as soon as possible,' Wisting told him.

Mortensen made no protest. He headed to his van and returned with a tarpaulin to provide shelter from the rain when he opened the car door. Wisting and Serner took a corner each and got two of the patrol officers to do the same. The rain pattered on the plastic sheet above their heads.

Mortensen had equipped himself with a head torch and latex gloves. He opened the car door and hunkered down. First he felt his way forward with his hand, but then had to crouch right down to take a good look.

'How big is it?' he asked.

'The size of a matchbox,' Serner told him. 'It's probably well hidden.'

Mortensen continued for a few more minutes.

'I think it's gone,' he said. 'I see some loose wires hanging down here, most likely for the seat adjustment and heating. That could mean someone's been here and ripped out whatever they found.'

He stood up and slammed the door. 'I'll dismantle the whole seat, of course, when we take the car into the garage, but I do think it's gone.'

The sound of a large vehicle approaching made Wisting turn round. It was the tow truck.

'The entire car looks as if it's been thoroughly searched,' Mortensen added. 'The glove compartment, centre console and the bag on the back seat. There's a good chance of finding evidence of whoever's done that.'

That thought had already struck Wisting. It bothered him, but he could not think of any excuse for preventing the technical examination. He would have to wait and see what came of it.

They folded up the tarpaulin. Mortensen secured the garment on the ground outside the car as the tow truck reversed into position.

Serner left to wait in the hire car. Wisting remained where he was, scouting around. The open gravel area was about the size of a handball court. It was situated behind a disused woodworking factory that blocked any view from the road. The perimeter lay in darkness, flanked by forest on one side and the mountain's blasted rockface on the other two. Some old roof trusses were stowed beside a rusty waste container, but apart from that the area was deserted. Very convenient for a secret meeting place, suitable for setting a fatal trap.

The tow-truck driver jumped out of his cab, trailing the winch wire behind him. Wisting felt rainwater leaking into his right boot. He moved off to sit in the car with Serner.

'Any news?' Wisting asked, casting a glance at the iPad on the Swede's lap.

Serner shook his head. 'I've got some photos to show how the recorder was attached,' he said, turning the screen towards Wisting.

It was an anonymous black block with a ribbed patch for the microphone. You would have to have known about it, or at least harboured some suspicion, in order to find it.

Wisting trained his eyes forward, out into the rain. 'Where did things go wrong?' he asked. 'How was Mats Beckman exposed?'

Serner put down the iPad. 'We had a meeting with Kripos a fortnight ago, when I was brought into the case,' he said. 'Most likely something slipped up in connection with that. Someone must have followed him.'

'Where was the meeting?'

'At a hotel in Sandvika,' Serner replied. 'He booked and

paid for the room himself. We all arrived separately, Ralf Falk, Josef Helland and I, but we didn't run any counter-intelligence on him. I think Helland arrived in an unmarked Kripos car and my face may well be known to them.'

'Then they must have already had some suspicions, though,' Wisting said.

'Or just felt the need to be sure of him,' Serner commented.

'What was the agenda for the meeting?' Wisting asked.

'It took place the day after Gillis Haack and Elton Khan landed in Amsterdam. It was necessary to have a debrief and provide some clarification.'

In front of them, the Swedish car had been hoisted on to the flat bed of the truck. Serner started the engine and let the wipers sweep across the windscreen.

'You said that was the most likely explanation,' Wisting said. 'What other explanations did you have in mind?'

'His girlfriend,' Serner answered. 'He could have been more indiscreet with her than he was willing to admit to us. She might have passed something on. A rumour could have been started. That's something we need to clear up.'

'We can't get hold of her,' Wisting said.

Serner turned to face him. 'What do you mean?'

'She's not answering her phone and she's not at the hotel.'

While Serner inclined forward across the steering wheel and stared thoughtfully out into the rain, Wisting made an attempt to change the subject. 'Could there be a third possibility?' he asked.

'What are you thinking?' Serner queried.

'A leak from the investigation.'

Serner sat up. 'What makes you think that?' he asked.

'You issued a wanted notice for Mats Beckman, for

murder, as part of his back story,' Wisting replied. 'Walin called it a "preventative measure", in case his story was checked out. The only person who could check out a cover story like that would have been someone in the police with access to the criminal records.'

Serner blew out smoke and his voice took on a jocular tone. 'Well, you know how it is,' he said. 'There have been some unfortunate episodes. Internal information has leaked out. It creates uncertainty, both internally and outside among the criminal fraternity. We investigators fall under suspicion, but as a rule it's through the lawyers that these things come out. Anyway, Walin didn't want to take any chances.'

'I see,' Wisting replied.

Serner fumbled in his pocket for a packet of chewing gum, took a tab and offered one to Wisting.

'No, thanks.'

He wondered if there was anything to read in what Serner had said, or the way he was behaving. It seemed as if something lay below the surface, but the question of leaks was nevertheless a touchy subject that felt uncomfortable to discuss.

The tow truck was ready to leave. Wisting looked at his watch. He still had some time left.

'Follow it,' he told Serner. 'There's something I'd like to show you.'

Serner drove off in pursuit of the truck, round to the other side of the factory building.

The tow truck turned left, out on to the road. It had to wait until a police officer removed the roadblock in order to exit the cordoned area.

'Turn right,' Wisting said.

Serner followed his directions and drove forward to the landslide location. Three metres from where the road ended, he drew to a halt. The rain was hammering on the roof and spraying up from the bonnet.

'I want to show you something,' Wisting said, producing a picture on his mobile phone.

It was an aerial photograph that showed how the area had looked prior to the landslip. The missing stretch of road was about fifty metres in length.

'The pathologist describes massive blood loss from the gunshot wound, as well as internal blood pooling around the chest and head,' Wisting said.

'I haven't had access to the autopsy report yet,' Serner pointed out.

'He also mentions a number of scratches on the scalp with traces of powdered stone and sand, combined with a chemical compound,' Wisting went on.

Serner just stared at him.

'Cement,' Wisting explained. 'There's a lot to suggest that the body had lain head-down somewhere made of cement before the landslide shifted it.'

He enlarged part of the aerial photograph. Although it was fuzzy, it was not too difficult to see that there had been a manhole cover in the middle of the missing stretch of road.

'The overflow from a number of sub-drains and pipes merge under the road,' Wisting told him. 'They're diverted down into a culvert that leads the water beneath the road and out into a stream on the other side.'

He saw that Serner was beginning to grasp his train of thought.

'I think Beckman's body may have been dumped there,' Wisting went on, tapping his finger on the manhole cover in the picture. 'And that his corpse led to the water routes getting clogged and triggering the landslide.'

Serner twisted round in his seat and looked back, towards the spot where they had found the car.

'Interesting,' was all he said.

He sat staring ahead for a while before changing gear and reversing away from the edge of the crater.

'It's only a theory,' Wisting pointed out. 'You don't need to mention it to anyone yet.'

Serner turned the steering wheel, pulled the car over and stopped with the bonnet facing the old factory building. The distance from where the car was found to the manhole cover was no more than one hundred and fifty metres.

Wisting opened the door to transfer to his own car. He had to get a move on.

Mortensen approached them, taking hold of the door as he advanced a slightly different theory. 'He could have been shot here, beside the car somewhere and dumped in the forest that was destroyed by the landslide,' he said, pointing. 'There might still be traces of blood. It should also be possible to find the bullet and cartridge case.'

Wisting nodded. He could only hope that the rain had washed away all the evidence.

'I've requested dogs,' Mortensen added.

Wisting stepped out of the car. His head was throbbing as if he really was coming down with a heavy cold.

32

Line must have seen him arrive. She had unlocked and opened the door by the time he reached the steps. 'You're very late,' were her words of welcome.

'I'll be with you in a minute,' Wisting said, heading into the garden. 'I just want to see for myself how they got in.'

Line slipped her feet into a pair of trainers and accompanied him as he skirted around the house.

The rain had flattened the grass on the lawn, but it was still possible to see prints in front of Amalie's bedroom window, left by someone tramping round. The window vent was open, but there were no signs of damage or evidence that the window had been forced.

'Was the window open?' Wisting asked.

Line shook her head. 'I open it sometimes if it's warm in summer, but otherwise not,' she answered.

He looked at her. The rain showed as dark dots on her sweater. 'And you didn't hear anything?' he asked.

'Not a thing.'

When Wisting pushed the window vent, it slid out again and stopped at the catch that operated the ventilation function.

'When did you get home?' he asked.

'About half past midnight. I took a taxi. Sandra watched the end of something on TV before she left, just for a quarter of an hour or so. I attended to Amalie while she did that and popped in to check on her one last time before I went to bed. It might have been about one o'clock by then.'

'What were you doing up at 5 a.m., when you saw that she was gone?'

'I went to the loo,' Line replied.

'Do you usually get up, or did something wake you?'

'There must have been a noise, I suppose,' Line said.

Wisting nodded. He walked further along the house wall, stopping at the gable end, where he crouched down. The basement window was open a crack. A hole had been drilled in the frame and wood shavings were scattered on the ground.

'That was how they did it in Sweden,' he said. 'In the Malmgren case. They used a hand drill on a window somewhere else in the house. Bored a hole that allowed them to flip up the closing mechanism. Afterwards, one of them made his way to the child's bedroom and used anaesthetic gas while his accomplice waited outside.'

Line gave a loud sob. Wisting could also picture it, a man with a gas mask lifting Amalie from her bed and heaving her out of the window and into a waiting car.

'Let's go inside,' he said.

Their coffee cups were still on the kitchen table and Line's laptop was ready for use. Wisting took out the encrypted phone. He had covered the microphone with tape but put the device in the microwave all the same.

'Is there any news?' Line asked sotto voce.

Wisting was not keen to tell her that one of the Swedish investigators had probably also been subjected to blackmail. Instead he told her that Niklas Kranz had decided to pull out, but that the conversation with the blackmailers had gone according to plan.

The blackmailers had said they would send them a message in six hours' time. That meant 11.38, now imminent.

Wisting removed the encrypted phone and peeled off the strip of tape before sitting down again.

Soon it was one minute past the allotted time, but that meant nothing. They might well have to wait until noon.

Yet another minute passed before the phone emitted a signal.

Stooping forward, they scanned the message together. It was an internet address, a user name and password.

The internet address was meaningless, just a few randomly strung together letters with two as the country code. The user name was William Wisting, while the password was Ingrid Amalie.

The mere sight of that name on the small mobile screen made Line cover her mouth with her hand.

Wisting gave her time to recover. 'Shall we go ahead?' he then asked, glancing at her laptop.

The screen had dimmed and Line brought it back to life.

'I can read it out while you type it in,' Wisting suggested.

He read out three letters at a time and Line repeated them aloud as she keyed them in. The address took them to a page containing nothing but a login field.

As Line continued to type, she was taken to another page, equally lacking in content. *Select file* and *Upload* were the only two choices.

Wisting handed her the memory stick. Line inserted it and completed the upload process, once for each of the three files.

Afterwards he felt drained. Feeble and faint.

They sat for a while in silence, as if waiting for an answer or reaction, but nothing happened.

Line flipped the laptop shut. She was more composed now and somehow seemed energetic.

Wisting replaced the strip of tape and returned the phone to the microwave. 'Come on,' he said, waving his daughter through to the living room with him.

'What is it?' she asked.

'I deleted a tip-off,' he whispered.

'Why did you do that?'

He explained about the man who had noted the reg number of Dogan Bulut's car.

'Do you think she might be there?' Line asked.

'It's a possibility,' Wisting replied. 'But I can't go to find out.'

He glanced into the kitchen. 'If they can listen in with the phone, then they can almost certainly also follow its movements,' he said. 'I can't take it with me in case they're tracking it, but I can't leave it either, in case they make contact again. The drive takes half an hour each way and that's too long for me to be inaccessible.'

Line's eyes widened. 'Do you want me to go?'

'Just to take a look,' Wisting said.

'Now, while it's still light?'

'It's Sunday,' Wisting replied. 'There'll probably be no one else there.'

'OK, then,' she said. It looked as if she was ready to leave at once.

'Wait a minute,' Wisting told her. 'I just want to get something.'

He went out to his car and picked up the thermal imaging camera they had used to penetrate the floor above Dogan Bulut's apartment.

'I checked on the map – there are around twenty buildings there,' he explained on his return. 'If you go all the way up to the exterior walls, you'll be able to see if there's a heat source of any kind inside. Through windows provides even better pictures.'

He explained how the camera worked. 'But if you get no results, it doesn't mean she's not there,' he said. 'She could be in an inner room, in an attic or a basement.'

'OK, then,' Line said again.

Wisting gazed at her, realizing it was a good idea for her to have something to do.

'You must call me if you discover anything,' he insisted. 'Don't do anything without speaking to me, and—'

A noise silenced him. It came from the kitchen. He dashed back in, staring at the microwave oven. The phone was ringing.

33

Wisting leaned against the kitchen worktop with the phone in his hands. 'Yes, hello,' he said, switching to loudspeaker.

Line stood beside him, her hand on his back, as they waited for an answer.

'*What is the problem with Mr Niklas Kranz?*' the voice asked.

Straight to the point. Wisting felt perspiration prickle again on his top lip.

'I'm not in charge of that case,' he replied. 'I'm not familiar with the details.'

The message that followed came quickly and must have been prepared in advance: '*It is in the interests of you and Ingrid Amalie that he follows our instructions. The situation will not be brought to a conclusion until the transaction is completed.*'

The sentences were clumsy and contrived and somehow detached. The analysts who felt that the messages could be relayed through a translation program before being read out were probably correct. The computer voice gave the words an extra chilling character.

'His marriage is breaking up,' Wisting said, repeating what had emerged about his wife's infidelity. 'It's a genuine possibility that he might withdraw from the agreement. You should really accept the offer he has made.'

The response was slow in coming. Wisting put the phone down on the table.

'*Please do not tell us what we should do.*'

'It was just some advice,' Wisting said. 'With the best of intentions.'

Once again, a pause. Line's hand moved to his shoulder and held it tightly.

'*What is the true capability of Mr Kranz?*' the voice asked. Again that impersonal, business-like choice of vocabulary.

Wisting ran his hand over his mouth, wiping his upper lip. He took another few seconds to consider how he should answer. He could not risk saying anything other than what the kidnappers might already know through whatever Swede they were blackmailing. To answer that he did not know was not an alternative either. That would be a lie, easily exposed.

'Around twenty kilos from his holdings in Norway,' he said. 'Ready for delivery today.'

He had to wait for the reply: '*What time is required for transportation and delivery of the remaining goods?*'

'At least twenty-four hours, I'd imagine. Maybe more.'

He added this last comment in the hope that the kidnappers would be unwilling to wait, that they would choose to be content with twenty kilos. Then it could all end sometime this evening or overnight.

He received no response.

The fridge motor kicked in and continued to hum. Wisting raised his eyes and looked out, leaning over the phone again and staring at the screen.

The hostage situation depended on gaining as much as possible out of each contact with the opposition. So far he had only acceded to whatever they asked.

'The documentation has been transferred,' he said, looking across at the laptop. 'What do I receive in return?'

In the silence that followed, he could hear Line's breathing. Shallow and strained.

'*We require similar documentation with reference to Nanette Kranz,*' was the phone's response.

Wisting's eyes moved to the window again. This was a demand he had anticipated and one he could fulfil. From his office desk, he had access to all the material they requested.

'That can be arranged,' he replied. 'You can have it when I see Amalie again.'

The voice allowed no scope for negotiation. '*Send it to the same address by fifteen hundred hours,*' was the simple instruction.

Wisting suppressed a sigh of frustration. In a direct dialogue, he could feel his way forward in conversation, listening to the tone of voice, becoming aware of the adversary's hesitation and finding points where it might be possible to make a breakthrough. This was a situation he recognized from the interview room. Conducting a conversation in this fashion was usually something at which he excelled, but the monotonous computer voice deprived him of every opportunity.

'What happens if I do that?' he asked in an attempt to make them promise to set Amalie free.

'*Nothing will happen to Amalie as long as you comply with our instructions.*'

It was impossible to know whether they had misunderstood the question or if they were simply avoiding it.

'I mean, when will I get to see Amalie again?' Wisting insisted.

'*Make sure that Niklas Kranz honours our demands,*' was the response.

'How will I be able to do that?' Wisting asked.

This was a tactical suggestion, an effort to transfer responsibility into their hands. The question was left unanswered and the conversation was replaced by a continuous beeping tone. The screen showed that the call had lasted two minutes and seven seconds.

Wisting turned to face his daughter, putting his arms around her and holding her close.

'A bit longer,' he said. 'We have to hang on just a little bit longer.'

34

Wisting opened the car door with a forceful push and slammed it shut behind him. He had an urge to do so again to release his restrained anger and frustration, to get rid of some of the tension in his body and alleviate his sense of despair.

He looked up at the police station but saw no one at the windows.

His exhaled breath was quivering. The thought of Amalie brought a stabbing pain to his chest. Where she was, what condition she was in, her fear and terror. If he were to function, these were thoughts he had to squash. The same applied to his niggling doubts about whether he was taking the right course of action.

He entered Nils Hammer's office to let him know he was back. The office, however, was deserted. He moved on to the conference room where Josef Helland from Kripos and the Swedish investigators were installed. Nils Hammer was with them. The atmosphere was tense, as if no one there could envisage any way out of the situation.

'How are you feeling?' Hammer asked.

Wisting gave a dry cough into his armpit to mimic the start of a heavy cold. 'Just the same,' he answered. 'What's the status of the case in Skien?'

Hammer pulled a dejected face. 'No progress,' he said. 'It sounds as if Kranz is having a nervous breakdown. They don't know if he'll be able to contribute anything.'

'They should really speak to a doctor,' Ann-Mari Walin suggested. 'Get him some kind of sedative.'

Although Wisting was not keen to get mixed up in how the Grenland police were handling the case, he expressed his agreement. It was in no one's interest for the conversations to reach an impasse.

'Any news from Stockholm?' he asked.

The circulation by the Norwegians of a wanted notice for Dogan Bulut had provided the Swedish police with an excuse to visit his family and friends in Sweden.

'We've conducted searches in three locations,' Serner told him. 'They haven't found anything to link him to Norway, or the Malmgren Affair, for that matter. No one we've spoken to has had anything to do with him for several months.'

'Could there be more to learn from the criminal fraternity?' Wisting asked. 'Someone gave you the names of Gillis Haack and the other two. Couldn't that be followed up in some way?'

Serner and Falk exchanged glances. 'That source has pulled back,' he replied.

'What does that mean?' Hammer demanded.

'We can't make contact with him,' Falk said.

'Why not?' Hammer insisted. 'Do you know if he's still alive?'

Wisting's interest grew. 'What made him pull back?' he asked. 'Did it have anything to do with the rumours of a leak?'

Serner seemed embarrassed and now exchanged glances with Ann-Mari Walin.

'What leak?' Hammer asked.

'It doesn't have anything to do with this case,' Walin replied.

Falk sat up straight in his seat. 'It might be worthwhile to clarify that there was in fact no actual leak,' he said. 'The claims were investigated and the information that emerged was traced back to documents shared with the defence lawyers in an ongoing case.'

'But the source withdrew because of that?'

Serner shook his head. 'His access to information disappeared when Bulut moved to Norway.'

'Could the source have leaked information back to the kidnappers?' Wisting asked.

Serner rejected this idea.

'At some point they must have realized your investigation had homed in on them,' Wisting continued. 'They've become insecure and uncertain. Something made them suspect Beckman.'

'There doesn't need to have been a particular trigger,' Falk said. 'People in a criminal environment such as this always believe they're being followed and watched. They always take preventative measures, checking and double-checking everything.'

Wisting drew the coffee pot towards him and filled a cup, mainly to give him something to do while he considered what each of the three Swedes had said and how they had said it. If he could discover which of them was being blackmailed, he would be able to find an ally. Someone he could cooperate with through this. The Swedish police prosecutor was the one who had singled herself out most. She was certainly keen to fulfil their demands, but that meant little.

Ralf Falk sat nearest and was the one Wisting had spoken to least.

'Have you been in the national crime unit long?' he asked, sipping his coffee.

'Soon be eight years,' Falk replied.

'As a handler of informants?'

He nodded. Wisting turned halfway round, to face Jan Serner. 'Have you worked together long, worked on other cases together?'

'None like this,' Falk answered.

Wisting did not quite know where he was going with this conversation, but it was important to him to become better acquainted with them in order to understand which one was being blackmailed. Neither of them had any social media presence, incompatible as that was with the professional assignments they were allocated. An online search had not uncovered anything about their family circumstances. All he knew was the little he had gleaned from his conversations with them. Serner was married with one daughter and Walin had grown-up children and one grandchild.

Nils Hammer took out his snuff tin.

'How's Sissel's father doing?' Wisting asked him.

'Fine,' Hammer replied, pushing a portion in place.

'His father-in-law's house was in the landslide area,' Wisting explained for the benefit of the others.

This was an attempt to shift the conversation on to the subject of family, to persuade the Swedish detectives to open up and mention something about their personal background, but it failed to lead anywhere. Wisting sat for a few minutes after the conversation died out before leaving for his own office.

35

'What a shame about these,' Maren said. She had come into the office and picked up the flowers Wisting had been given the day after the landslide. They were still dumped on the shelf beside the door. The petals had shrivelled and faded.

'At least I won't have to find a vase now,' he said.

Maren pushed the withered bouquet further along and crossed her arms. 'I still can't get hold of Nina Lundblad,' she said.

'When did you last speak to her?' Wisting asked.

'The day before yesterday, after the Swedish group arrived. She got confirmation that it was her boyfriend who'd been found in the landslip.'

'How did she take it?'

'Messages like that are always difficult to pass on, as you know,' Maren replied. 'But she was prepared. I sat with her for an hour or so and made sure she had the opportunity to talk to some female friends at home in Sweden. When I left, she was mostly concerned about practical details. About letting his family know and that sort of thing. She wanted to stay here for a few days, until the situation became a bit clearer.'

The expression in her eyes told Wisting she was seriously worried. He checked the time: almost 1 p.m. He had some time to spare and it would be a relief to leave the police station behind and become inaccessible.

'I can come down to the hotel with you,' he said. 'If we

can't locate her, we can ask the hotel to let us into her room.' He got to his feet and grabbed his jacket.

The hotel was situated in Storgata, only a few hundred metres from the police station, but the torrential rain forced them to travel by car.

There was less activity in reception than when Wisting had been there the day after the disaster. Many of the evacuated residents had moved to stay with family and friends, gone to their holiday cabins or had already been allocated replacement accommodation by the local authority.

The lift was empty when it came down and they were the only ones to go inside. 'Third floor,' Maren said as she pressed the button.

Wisting stood at the back, gazing at his reflection beside that of his colleague, who was over thirty years younger. Their eyes met. She was one of the more careful and less inflexible of the investigators. It was not only her age that held her back when she had to form opinions or make decisions. It was a matter of the ability to distinguish between her personal perspective and that of other people. To be able to assess alternative aspects of a case and change her mind in line with new facts. This is what made her a good detective.

The lift doors opened with a grating noise. Maren had been at Nina Lundblad's door before, and she turned left without hesitation, but waited until Wisting stood beside her before knocking on the door.

There was no response.

'Four one four,' Wisting said, mainly to himself. 'I can go down and find out.'

The lift had gone, so he took the stairs and showed the receptionist his police ID.

'We've a Swedish woman staying in room 414,' he said. 'Nina Lundblad. Could you see if she's checked out?'

The receptionist referred to the computer screen. 'No,' he replied. 'She's booked in until Monday, but the reservation's been left open for another three days.'

'Would it be possible for you to give me access?' Wisting asked.

The man removed a key card from a hook behind the desk. 'You can use this,' he said, without making any closer inquiries.

Wisting took the master key back to Maren. It clicked in the lock and a green light flashed.

Wisting pushed the door open, calling out his name, before taking a couple of paces into the room.

Light flooded in through the windows. The bed had been used but remade. A travel bag sat on the floor at the foot end. A soap bag had been left out in the little bathroom and fresh towels hung up.

A folded Swedish newspaper lay on the writing desk. When Wisting opened it out, he froze. His eye had caught sight of a photograph of Jan Serner. The page contained coverage of the Malmgren case, reporting that after almost a year, the police still had no clues about the kidnappers.

Nina Lundblad must have known more than she had said when they met her at the police station.

He scanned the room. Maren was standing in front of the wardrobe. 'The safe's not been used,' she told him.

As Wisting shut the newspaper, he noticed a folded scrap of paper. He drew it out and found it was a printout of an old internet article on the seizure of eight hundred kilos of hash from a fishing boat. *Gillis Haack* was written in one corner.

'Found anything?' Maren asked.

Wisting put the paper back and left the newspaper. 'No,' he answered as he crossed to the window. The glass was spattered with raindrops. He turned his back to the view.

'How did she get here, to Larvik?' he asked.

Maren was on her knees, peering underneath the bed.

'I assume she drove a car,' she replied, glancing up at him. 'We never asked her.'

'Maybe the Swedes will know,' Wisting said.

Scrambling up again, Maren lifted a cable with a mobile charger plugged into a socket above the bedside table.

'She must have taken her phone with her,' she said, looking round. 'Her bag's not here either.'

Wisting moved to the door. 'I'm going to ask if they have CCTV showing when she left,' he said. 'And whether she was with anyone.'

'Do you think she might be in danger?' Maren asked.

'There's no reason for her to be,' Wisting told her. 'No one knows she's here, but Bulut had the address of the hideout where she and Mats used to meet. They may well know of her.'

They took the lift back down to reception, where Wisting placed the key card on the counter. A camera dome was suspended from the ceiling above them.

They should track her phone as well, Wisting thought, but refrained from mentioning it. Maren would probably see to that anyway.

'I have to go back to the place where Beckman's car was found,' he said instead. 'Mortensen has organized a search with sniffer dogs.'

'Just go, then,' Maren said. 'I can walk back. Thanks for coming with me.'

The receptionist turned to them when he was free. Wisting gave Maren a nod as he headed for the rear exit. He turned, saw that Maren was busy and took the stairs instead.

He was wheezing by the time he arrived back at room 414. The door was still open a crack. Stepping inside, he grabbed the newspaper and left again.

Not until he was back in the car did he examine the paper more closely. The article about the Malmgren Affair contained nothing he did not already know. The same applied to the printout relating to the narcotics smuggler who had been given the nickname Skipper. In addition, there was a sheet of paper with the hotel logo between the pages of the newspaper. Nina Lundblad had made a note of foreign names and Swedish phone numbers. Several of these were called Bulut and Haack. Wisting assumed they were relatives of Dogan and Gillis. They had all been crossed out, as if she had phoned round and not received the answers she was looking for.

Wisting refolded the piece of paper, tucked it back between the pages of the newspaper and hid them under the car seat. Then he drove on.

36

Wisting made his way behind the barriers and drove round the old factory building where the Swedish police informant's Volvo had been found. In the middle of the expanse of gravel, a crime scene tent with open walls had been erected. Espen Mortensen stood at a table issuing instructions to two technicians dressed in white overalls. As yet the dog patrol did not appear to have arrived.

Wisting parked and got out of the car. The cold breeze felt fresh on his face.

The two crime scene technicians lifted a ladder and propped it on the side of the waste container at the far edge of the car park while Mortensen poured a hot drink from a thermos flask into a cup. 'Would you like some?' he asked, gesturing towards the flask.

Wisting shook his head.

Returning the thermos to his bag, Mortensen drank as he gazed out across the ground. One of the technicians had climbed up into the waste container to take a photograph of something. The camera flashed repeatedly.

Wisting kicked a stone and watched it roll into a puddle.

The tactical investigation was something he could spin out, but the results of the technical tests would be difficult to keep under wraps.

A few more minutes passed before the dog patrol van turned on to the gravel pitch and drove up to the tent. The dog in the cargo space barked loudly as soon as it stopped. Two women in dark overalls stepped out. The driver moved behind the van to release the dog while her colleague approached Wisting.

'What do you think are the chances?' he asked. 'It's been about a week since the murder.'

'It depends on the amount of blood, but it shouldn't be a problem,' she replied. 'Rain is good; the moisture keeps the scent down on the ground. I'm more concerned about the size of the area. It could wear him out.'

The dog handler approached them with a black Alsatian on a tight leash. It was whining in its eagerness to begin.

'Is any area more likely than elsewhere?' the handler asked.

Wisting explained where the car had been parked and indicated the area down at the edge of the landslide.

The dog handler conferred with her colleague before unclipping the leash and sending the dog out to search. Wisting put his hands behind his back and watched as the large canine set to work. Its tail began to swish to and fro as it circled, moving from side to side across the gravel pitch, appearing to catch a scent before finding something else that seemed more interesting, but without making any significant discovery.

Mortensen produced a metal detector and began to sweep it across the area the dog had already covered. It made continual finds of screws, nuts, bottle caps and similar metallic items.

Without warning, the dog swerved to the edge of the pitch, in between the nearest trees. Its behaviour changed at once – it stopped short, eyes peeled, and suddenly stretched out flat on the ground.

'Find,' was the dog handler's comment.

She approached the dog and handed it a reward. Wisting

and Mortensen walked across to take a look. Down between the blades of grass lay a used condom.

'Can we try again?' Mortensen asked. 'In that direction?' He was pointing to an area that led down to the upper boundary of the gravel pitch. Just as suddenly as before, the dog latched on to a fresh scent, lunging forward before lying down obediently.

There was nothing to be seen, just a puddle and a withered dandelion that had sprung up between the hard-packed stones.

Wisting turned to face the dog handler. 'Are you sure?' he asked.

'The dog is sure,' she answered, with a shrug. 'It could be more semen.'

Mortensen had already crouched down. 'Whatever it is, it's very diluted,' he said.

'Is it possible to test it somehow so that we can get an immediate answer?'

'Absolutely,' Mortensen replied.

He moved to his van and returned with some kind of testing kit containing a spray bottle and a sheet of filter paper. He sprayed the chemicals on the ground where the dog had indicated and drew the moisture up into the paper.

'Positive reaction for blood gives a green result,' he said.

Wisting stared at the paper, but nothing was happening. He turned away and watched the technicians working at the waste container, emptying out the contents without reporting anything of interest.

A minute ticked by before tiny pale green flecks began to appear. One of them grew to the size of a pinkie nail.

Mortensen looked up at Wisting. 'We have a crime scene,' he concluded.

37

A carton of pens fell from the shelf and the contents rolled across the floor, some disappearing under the shelving units that lined the wall. Wisting retrieved the ones he could find and returned them to the box. He was actually looking for a padded envelope.

Maren Dokken appeared at the door of the cramped photocopy room.

'The video footage from the hotel,' she announced. 'Nina Lundblad comes down to breakfast just before nine o'clock. She goes back to her room, but then leaves the hotel at 10.23, to be precise.'

Wisting listened intently, aware there was something more to come.

'Her phone is switched off exactly one hour later, with the last position being on the E18 at Lannerheia, between Larvik and Porsgrunn.'

'Have you received the telecoms data?' Wisting asked.

'Just from the Norwegian telecoms network,' Maren replied. 'I've not found anything significant in the call log, but there's a lot of data traffic. She and her boyfriend used the Signal messaging service for their conversations.'

Wisting went on listening. He refrained from telling her that he was familiar with it. Young people generally felt the need to explain when they spoke to him about new technology.

'It's not like with a phone number,' Maren continued.

'We don't learn who she's been talking to, just that the subscription has been charged for data use.'

'Have you found out whether she came here by car?' Wisting asked.

'Well, she does own a red Audi A3,' Maren answered. 'I'm making a list of toll stations to see where it's been.'

'I think we should issue an internal missing person bulletin,' Wisting said. 'Maybe one of the patrols will come across it somewhere.'

With a nod, she withdrew from the doorway.

Wisting located the padded envelopes and brought a small bundle of them back to his office. As soon as he had closed the door, he took out the encrypted phone. There were no calls or messages and the battery indicator showed more than fifty per cent left.

He slipped the phone into one of the envelopes, sealed it and wrote his name on the outside to make it appear that the contents were personal. Then he called Line.

'How's it going?' he asked.

'Nothing so far,' Line replied. 'But it's taking time. It's a vast area with lots of buildings.'

Wisting logged into his computer.

'Have you uploaded the documents they asked for?' Line asked.

'Not yet,' Wisting answered.

'Why on earth not? It's close to the deadline.' Line's voice was tense. He knew she was stressed.

'I'm doing it right now,' he said, 'as we speak.'

The Skien case files opened up on the screen, with the documents listed in chronological order. The latest report concerned a vehicle, possibly the one in which Nanette Kranz had been abducted.

'Wait a minute,' he told Line as he opened the document.

An analyst had prepared a provisional report. The investigation's initial assumption was that Nanette Kranz had been abducted from the car park outside the sports centre where her car had been found. The analyst surmised that the kidnappers had used a delivery van, probably with a sliding door to facilitate bundling her in. Her gym session ended at 21.30. The analyst had obtained video footage from private and public CCTV on the surrounding roads network, both for the hours before and after in order to survey all the delivery vans that had potentially driven to and from that spot.

The work was extensive. So far, sixty-eight vans had been identified, but the film was either taken from too great a distance or at the wrong angle and the registration numbers had not been caught. The footage then had to be combined with the information from transits through the toll stations around Grenland.

Wisting shifted the phone to his other ear. 'You should be looking for a delivery van,' he said. 'Or a building where it's possible to drive in and out.'

'All the buildings here have vehicle access gates,' Line explained. 'They're mostly warehouses and that sort of thing.'

Wisting inserted the memory stick. 'I see,' he said.

Line told him she would continue as before. 'Call me once you've uploaded the file,' she insisted, before rounding off their conversation.

Wisting gathered the case documents into one large PDF file. He considered editing out the pages that dealt with the delivery van the police were actively tracing, the last document to be included. If he removed it, it would not leave any gap in the sequence of documents, but he would not be able to delete it from the record of contents on the first page. He left it and copied the entire file on to the memory stick.

He had to return to Line's to upload the material. Before he left, he recalled his own case file on the screen. It had expanded by ten or so documents in a matter of only a few hours. His work as leader of the investigation demanded he keep up to date. In order to gain an overview, his task was to review all the information logged and allocate fresh tasks to the investigators.

Most of what was listed in the catalogue of documents appeared to refer to tip-offs that had been dismissed as having led nowhere. He shared out a number of simple, routine but innocuous assignments before opening the padded envelope and checking the display on the encrypted phone. He then dropped in the memory stick and resealed the envelope.

The sense of betrayal of his duty as a police officer, to the public as well as his colleagues, paralysed him momentarily. He was letting down people he had known for a long time. Many of them he thought of as friends. Right now, none of them could depend on him.

The computer screen slipped into sleep mode and he noted the time: 14.33. He would have to leave immediately in order to upload the file before the deadline.

He met no one on his way out and decided not to inform anyone he was leaving the station.

At the intersection with Stavernsveien, he remained stationary when the light changed to green. He failed to notice until the car behind him gave an angry toot. Gripping the steering wheel, he forced himself to concentrate hard on driving.

Line's house was quiet and empty. Her laptop was on the kitchen table with the screen flipped up. Activating it, he repeated the laborious login process before uploading the document file.

There was no confirmation that the file had been received, neither on the screen nor on the encrypted mobile phone.

He took out his own mobile and called Line. 'It's done,' he said.

She thanked him and asked if he had received any response.

'No, but it's only been a couple of minutes,' Wisting replied.

'Maybe you should contact them?' she asked.

Wisting lifted the encrypted phone with his other hand. It operated just like any other smartphone. In the call log, the series of figures and letters they had rung from was listed.

'I can try,' he said, his thumb resting on the number. It rang in the usual way, but no one answered.

'Try to send a message, then,' Line suggested.

Wisting tapped in a short message in English: *The file has been uploaded.*

He sat staring at the screen while he waited for a response. Line remained silent on the other line.

'Have you seen anything of interest?' Wisting asked, as he pressed his thumb against the sticky tape covering the microphone on the encrypted phone. 'Empty pizza cartons or anything like that? After all, they'll need food.'

'No, nothing like that,' Line answered. 'I don't have very many buildings left now. What do we do then?'

Wisting made no reply. He was thinking of another way to solve the case, but it was not something he was happy to share with Line, at least not yet.

The phone in his other hand emitted a signal and the screen lit up: *Received.*

He relayed that to Line. 'What happens now?' she demanded.

'We just have to wait,' Wisting told her. 'They're going to speak to Niklas Kranz again in two hours' time.'

His idea for an alternative escape route from the situation began to take shape, allowing him to be cautiously optimistic for the first time.

'It's going to work out,' he said in a tone that sounded convincing even to him.

38

The steering wheel rattled in his hands as the right front wheel hit a rain-filled pothole. Wisting swung out to the centre of the road and drove slowly up to the roadblock, still guarded by a police patrol. A young officer stepped out of his car to move the traffic barrier when Wisting motioned that he required access.

He drove as close to the edge of the crater as possible and got out of the vehicle with the engine still running. A gust of wind whipped the rain towards his face – pleasantly fresh, but bitterly cold. On the car radio, a melancholy song from the sixties was playing as he slammed the door and moved out to the perimeter.

Above him seagulls were circling with loud, throaty cries. A wide stream tumbled across the foot of the crater, the water continuing to find new routes, digging out clods of earth and triggering new, smaller landslides. Not until the rain eased off and the area dried out would it be safe to venture down there.

He walked into the nearest garden and followed the landslip boundary as far as the fence he had used as an improvised ladder. The breeze tugged at it, making the metal screech.

Earth and pebbles loosened and drizzled down when he moved too close to the edge. Wisting took a step back and stood picking at the plaster on the palm of his hand. The cut he had sustained on his descent into the crater had formed a scab and he pulled off the plaster, crumpled it into a ball and threw it away.

About fifty metres beyond where he stood, a concrete disc protruded from the debris, part of a pipework system, perhaps even the drain where Mats Beckman's corpse had been dumped. It might be worth investigating to confirm that, but this was not an investigative move he intended to make. Not now.

The verandah door on the nearest house was flapping noisily in the wind. Wisting approached and hovered in the doorway, peering inside. An abandoned living room. Two coffee cups on the table in front of the TV set. Closing the door, he made sure it was properly secured.

His car was still idling when Wisting opened the door, but he stood motionless for a moment. He spread his palm on the roof of the vehicle as he surveyed the damage. There was another way out of this situation. Resolutely, he drew his hand across the water pooled on the roof before clambering in. One possibility that was worth trying.

The tyres spun on the wet asphalt before finding a grip. On the car radio, the weather was the topic of discussion. Wisting switched it off.

One of the parking spaces close to the staff entrance in the basement of the police station was free. The corridor inside was deserted. The door to the weapons store was secured by an access card and key and Wisting possessed both of these. His service gun lay in a separate compartment. A 9-mm SIG Sauer pistol with a short barrel and a black rubber stock. Compact and easy to conceal under clothing.

He lifted it out. The magazine lay primed beside it. He checked it was full before clicking it into place.

The overhead ceiling light flashed as Wisting weighed

the pistol in his hand and turned the barrel towards him, staring into the black muzzle. He spotted a speck of black oil on the edge and wiped it away with the little finger of his free hand. Then he slipped the weapon into his jacket pocket and zipped it shut.

The corridor was still deserted when he let himself out.

The others were assembled in the canteen, and Wisting went in to demonstrate his presence in the station.

'You're wet,' Hammer commented. 'Have you been somewhere?'

Wisting ran his hand through his hair. 'Just popped out for a minute,' he replied.

'Did you see Mortensen's message?' Hammer asked.

'No. Anything new?'

'The tech team have found a bullet at the crime scene. The metal detector came up trumps in the area close to where the sniffer dog had marked the bloodstain. A full-metal-jacket lead bullet had drilled several centimetres down into the mud.'

Hammer located the email on his phone and showed him the image of the deformed bullet. 'Nine millimetre, he says,' Hammer went on. 'It's tested positive for blood.'

His mobile buzzed in his pocket before Wisting had a chance to say anything. The one in his right pocket. He fished it out and saw that Maren Dokken was calling. At that same moment, she appeared in the doorway.

'There you are,' she said, her eyes on Wisting. 'Nina Lundblad's car has been found. It's parked on the E18, near Langangen.'

Jan Serner had no idea where that was.

'Approximately halfway between here and Skien,' Hammer told him. 'On the road to Grenland.'

'I'm heading out there now,' Maren announced.

'I'll come with you,' Wisting said. He glanced at the three Swedes, on the lookout for their reactions.

Serner got to his feet. 'Me too,' he said, reaching out for his jacket.

39

Nina Lundblad's car was in a layby on the eastern flank of the two Langangen bridges. A police vehicle, blue lights flashing, was parked to alert other traffic. Maren Dokken drove up behind it.

The wind played a hollow, thrumming tune on the span of the bridge. Scudding in from the south-east, it followed the arm of the fjord and was funnelled through the mountainsides.

The bridge crossed the inner section of the Langangsfjord. Wisting could remember when it was new. Now the concrete was crumbling and the railings were rusty. Soon the new bridge would replace it, further along the valley.

One of the patrol officers approached them, leaving the other behind the wheel. 'It's unlocked,' he said.

Wisting sized up the car. There was no reason to park here, where the road cut through rock. The layby was provided, beside a steep cliff, in case of accident or emergency. There was no access to anywhere from this spot.

'Is the key inside?' Maren asked.

'We haven't looked, just made sure there was no one in the car.'

A steady stream of traffic zipped by on the road beside them, and a heavy goods vehicle passed in the southbound lane. The side draught tugged at their clothes.

This was the road Line had taken to the industrial area outside Skien. The car must have been parked there then.

Wisting strode up and opened the driver's door. Leaning in, he inspected the centre console but found nothing except a pen and a few coins. Maren checked the glove compartment from the other side. She unearthed a few papers there, but nothing that seemed of any interest.

In the door pocket on Wisting's side, there was a pack of wet wipes and a half-empty bottle of water. Above the sun visor, he spotted an old receipt from a McDonald's drive-through somewhere in Sweden.

Wisting shut the door again and surveyed the scene. 'Was this where the phone signal petered out?' he asked, blinking away a few drops of rain.

Maren confirmed this.

'She could have been picked up by another vehicle,' Serner suggested.

The policeman who had greeted them received a message on his radio. Wisting did not catch what was said and watched as the officer turned to face the road. A patrol car drove across the bridge and the officer moved out into the traffic lane, signalling oncoming traffic to stop. The car switched on its blue lights and executed a U-turn to pull up on to the hard shoulder.

'They've found a shoe,' the police officer told them, gesticulating for the traffic flow to resume.

A solitary policeman was seated in the car that had arrived on the scene. He stepped out and pulled on his uniform cap. 'There's a pair of white trainers lying beside the concrete barrier, about sixty metres along the bridge,' he said, pointing.

Wisting could not recall what kind of shoes Nina Lundblad favoured. He glanced across at Maren, who grimaced to show she was not sure either.

'I can stop the traffic to allow you to walk out there and see if they might have something to do with the car or the missing woman.'

'Do that,' Wisting said.

The officer waited for a space between cars and then flicked on the blue lights and parked the patrol car at an angle across one traffic lane.

Maren collected a forensics kit from the car and handed out yellow hi-vis waistcoats to them all before they set off along the road.

They followed the white line for more than thirty metres until they spotted the first shoe, lying on its side, immediately beside the bridge parapet.

'The size suggests a female wearer,' Serner said.

Maren took photos with her mobile phone. The shoe was sodden and soiled with road dust, but might not have been there long. The laces were tied, one end slightly longer than the other.

Passing motorists looked at them inquisitively as Wisting scanned the stretch of road ahead. The other shoe was ten metres further on, beside fragments of black rubber from a car tyre.

He strode towards it. It could originally have been left beside the other shoe but then been dragged forward by the draught from speeding vehicles. A pair of shoes, left neatly side by side. This was something he had encountered before.

'What's your take on it?' Maren asked. 'Did she jump?'

Wisting did not answer immediately. He placed his hands on the parapet and looked over the edge. Beneath them, vegetation sloped down towards the water.

'It seems so,' he said. 'We'll have to go down and see.'

Maren put the shoes in two individual paper bags before they returned to their car.

In order to drive below the bridge, they would have to backtrack and then navigate down through the buildings in Langangen. One of the patrol cars tailed them.

An access road led to the bridge piers. Rainwater had gouged deep channels in the gravel and the car was jolted from side to side.

An old moped, the engine and back wheel missing, lay abandoned in the middle of the turning spot at the end of the track. Maren swung the car around it and stopped with the bonnet facing the way they had come.

Wisting got out. He could hear the noise of the traffic seventy metres overhead. The surrounding area comprised deciduous forest, dark and dense with golden autumn leaves.

'You don't need to come in with me,' said the police officer from the motorway. 'We can investigate and let you know if we find anything.'

'We're staying,' Wisting insisted. 'It's so easy to overlook something.'

They trudged in single file with the two uniformed officers leading the way. From time to time they glanced up at the bridge to be sure they were heading in the right direction. After fifty metres, they spread out in a line, just over two metres apart. Wisting had Maren on his right. He pushed the foliage away from his face and hunkered down beneath the bigger branches.

Maren was the one who found her. At first Wisting could see only a torn shred of fabric dangling from a branch.

She was lying prone, her neck twisted. Her head lay flat on the ground, like a deflated ball. A twig had pierced one cheek and exited through her throat. Her left arm was extended at an unnatural angle, her legs were sprawled to one side and her right arm lay underneath her body. Her clothes were blood-soaked and had hardened into a brittle carapace. Her shoes were missing.

The vegetation must have cushioned the fall but had not prevented instant death.

They huddled around her in a semicircle. A bird screeched hoarsely somewhere nearby and leaves rustled as it took off.

Serner raised his head to the bridge above them. 'She must have jumped,' he said. 'Taken off her shoes, climbed on to the parapet and dived off.'

He gave Wisting a quizzical look but must have sensed his scepticism.

'There's traffic on the motorway twenty-four hours a day,' the Swedish detective continued. 'It would have been too risky to drag her sixty metres across the bridge against her will. Someone would have seen them.'

Wisting could picture a variety of possibilities but refrained from saying so. He looked at his watch. In a few hours it would be dark. He issued a series of brief instructions to the uniformed officers with a view to cordoning off the discovery site before turning to his two colleagues.

'Let's get out of here,' he said, with one final squint up at the bridge.

40

The gun in his pocket clunked on the armrest as Wisting hung his jacket over the chair back. He sat down to check there were no new messages on the encrypted phone before dropping it into the padded envelope.

Some of the despair he had felt since Amalie's kidnap was now receding. It was too early to share anything with Line, but if his assumptions were correct, the solution to the entire situation might be located in the green fireproof container belonging to Gunnar Helner.

He logged on to the media server and the folders containing all the recordings from the landslide – helicopter pictures from the night of the disaster and drone images taken in daylight. Almost thirty hours of footage in total. These were the films Maren Dokken had examined when they were searching for Mats Beckman's car among the debris.

The drone photos were the most useful. The helicopter footage was limited to the area within the floodlight's beam. The camera strafed the same spot for lengthy periods until it had been thoroughly searched, before moving on. The drone had been used the following day to survey the extent of the landslide, the pilot working systematically to cover the whole area.

The first footage file, taken from the upper part of the landslide area, above Gunnar Helner's house, was of no interest. He embarked on the next film and skipped the playback on to an area of more specific interest.

The film glided slowly across the wreckage. Piles of splintered timber, fragments of concrete walls, mangled furniture and fittings. Earth and mud prevented the identification of colours. What looked like a green settee cushion cropped up on the left of the image and slid across the screen. He had to stop the film to examine something more closely – probably a wood-burning stove of green-tinged cast iron.

He was concentrating so hard on the film that he failed to notice Hammer slouching in the doorway.

'Shouldn't we call a meeting?' he asked. 'The original murder victim's girlfriend has now also been found dead. That surely opens up a few possibilities?'

Wisting racked his brain for a stalling tactic. 'For the moment we don't know anything more than what's been logged,' he said. 'Let's get together once the tech guys have something to report.'

'You believe she jumped?' Hammer asked.

Wisting nodded, though he was not really convinced that Nina Lundblad had taken her own life. Considering the present circumstances, a more likely scenario was that she had been bundled into a van, drugged and then held captive. In the middle of the night, when several minutes might elapse between cars crossing the bridge, it would have been a simple matter to stop the van on the road and throw her over the parapet. Leaving her shoes and car nearby to stage a suicide.

Hammer glanced at the computer rather than pursuing the subject. 'Are you looking for the concrete pipe?' he asked, focusing inquisitively on the screen.

'Hm?'

'Jan Serner said you thought Mats Beckman's body could

have been dumped in the drain on the road,' Hammer explained. 'That the blockage in the sewage system triggered the whole landslide.'

'His grazes and scratches contained traces of cement as well as some on his skin,' Wisting reminded him. 'When did you discuss this with Serner?'

'This morning,' Hammer replied. 'Why do you ask?'

Wisting brushed aside his own question. 'It's just that I haven't mentioned it to Maren yet,' he said. 'After all, she's the one tasked with identifying the cause of the landslip.'

'It sounds like a probable theory,' Hammer told him. 'It might be possible to confirm it too, if there's DNA on the interior of the pipes.' He nodded in the direction of the computer screen. 'But first we have to discover where the concrete pipes ended up.'

'I've located one,' Wisting said. 'In the garden below where we were on the night the landslip occurred.'

He swivelled his chair to face Hammer. 'What's your opinion of Serner and the other Swedes?' he asked.

'Why do you ask?'

Wisting gazed over Hammer's shoulder to the corridor beyond.

'Can we trust that they're telling us everything?' he asked, lowering his voice. 'There's to be an inquiry into how the infiltrator was exposed. The guilt may lie with Serner, Falk or Walin. It could be in their interests to withhold facts in order to cover their own mistakes.'

He paused to let this sink in. 'Have you noticed anything of that nature about any of them?' he asked when Hammer failed to respond.

'None of them is particularly communicative,' Hammer answered. 'But it's most likely to be Falk.'

'Why do you think that?'

'If any one of them is following up clues independently, I mean,' Hammer said. 'He was provided with a hire car on the very first day. He's out driving in that right now.'

'Do you know where he is or what he's doing?'

Hammer shook his head. At the same moment, Wisting's mobile buzzed, Line calling.

'I have to take this,' Wisting said.

Hammer moved away from the door. 'I can try to find out,' he said as he left.

Wisting rose from his chair and closed the door behind Hammer before answering his phone.

'I've found a possible place,' Line said.

She was talking disjointedly, and her words came in fits and starts, but Wisting understood that the thermal imaging camera had produced faint results in a building not marked with any company logo, just a sign about premises to let.

'The windows are covered in black plastic on the inside,' she went on to explain. 'It had loosened in one place and I could see in. There's a large cargo container inside a workshop. The positive heat results come from it.'

Wisting felt adrenaline course through his veins. 'Can you get inside?' he asked.

'I could break a window, but the container is locked with bolts and a padlock.'

Wisting glanced at the time. 'Wait outside,' he said. 'I'm on my way.'

'Is it safe for you to do that?' He heard the uncertainty in her voice.

'I'll leave the phone here in my office,' he told her. 'The blackmailers are going to contact Niklas Kranz in half an hour. They'll be preoccupied with that.'

'Hurry, then,' Line begged him.

Wisting placed the padded envelope containing the encrypted phone in a desk drawer.

'Do you see anything else there?' he asked. 'Any signs of human activity?'

'There's a vehicle inside the workshop, hooked up to the container.'

'What kind of vehicle?'

'A grey delivery van.'

'Can you make out the registration number?'

'No. Only an Opel badge on the front, but I can't see the number plate.'

'OK,' Wisting said, heading for the door. 'Stay where you are, then. Don't move.'

41

The other investigators were assembling in the conference room to watch the kidnappers make contact again. Wisting was out of breath when he entered the room. The ventilation system was humming as usual, but the air still felt close and clammy.

His eyes fixed on Hammer's. 'I have to go somewhere,' he said. He touched his hand to his throat. It felt tight and constricted.

'Is something wrong?' Hammer asked.

Wisting shook his head. 'Line was out with friends last night,' he explained. 'Some sort of reunion party. I was meant to drive her and take Amalie to stay the night at my house, but of course I had to work. She arranged a babysitter, but now her car is parked at the home of one of her friends. I said I'd give her a lift.'

It surprised him how easily the lie came to him, spontaneously and fluently, when he had to resort to it. He had learned from the best. Seeing through falsehoods had been his job for decades. Lies that lay close to the truth were the most difficult to uncover.

Hammer nodded sympathetically. He knew how few family members Wisting and his daughter had. There were not many others to ask for help with practical chores. Line's twin brother was stationed overseas. Amalie's father lived in the USA and his career in the FBI meant that, to all intents and purposes, he had been out of the picture even before she was born.

'When will you be back?' Jan Serner asked.

'It'll probably take about an hour,' Wisting replied. He hurried to the door to forestall further questions.

'I have my mobile,' he said to Hammer. 'Keep me posted.'

He met Maren Dokken on his way out and repeated the lie to her.

'They're removing the body from the woods now,' she informed him.

Wisting nodded. Progress had been rapid, but the location where she had been found was not a crime scene. All that was required to be done there was to photograph the corpse.

He was on the point of issuing instructions about the autopsy and further treatment of the discovery site but caught himself. Not because he had no time, but because he could not permit himself to action something that would propel the case forward.

The floors beneath the criminal investigation department were silent when Wisting let himself into the evidence store. The material seized in the case concerning the bicycle thieves who had been arrested earlier in the week lay on a tagged shelf. The bikes were still in the cargo space of the lorry, but the equipment had been labelled and stored.

He lifted the battery-operated angle grinder from the shelf. The motor ran soundlessly when he started it, only a faint hum from the rotating disc blade. The battery indicator showed 32 per cent charge left. It had cut through expensive, secure bicycle locks and would easily deal with the majority of padlocks.

He stuffed the angle grinder into a rucksack stored on an adjacent shelf. Before he left, he also picked up a pair of leather gloves he found on another one.

The cameras in the corridors would have captured his movements, but no one would look at the footage unless something untoward happened. Anyway, Wisting was in and out of the evidence store several times a week, and he intended to return the tool after use.

He slung the bag on to the passenger seat and reversed out of the parking space. It was five minutes past five. It was unlikely that the kidnappers would get in touch with him in the next hour. And by then the whole situation might be resolved.

There was little traffic as he drove. He left the town centre streets without a hitch, turned on to the E18 and floored the accelerator. On the approach to the Langangen bridges, there was a tailback of traffic. Now and then it came to a complete standstill. Wisting realized what was to blame and soon also saw the flashing blue lights up ahead. One traffic lane on the bridge was closed and the vehicles were being manually directed past on a single lane while the crime scene technicians examined the other one.

A police officer in a raincoat raised his arm further and stopped the traffic in his direction.

The technicians would also examine the terrain under the bridge for items Nina Lundblad might have brought down with her in the fall, but it was far from certain that they would look for the active ingredients of narcotics in her blood. Not unless he brought the possibility to their attention.

The tailback began to move. It was highly probable that the traffic controller knew who Wisting was. He drove closely behind the car in front to minimize the risk of being the first car in the queue when the traffic was stopped again.

He slipped by, avoiding the eye of the officer standing there.

The traffic crawled across the bridge. Two men in white overalls were busy at the spot where Nina Lundblad's shoes had been found. It looked as if they were discussing something to do with the parapet.

He cast another glance at them in the rear-view mirror while fishing his mobile out of his pocket. It was strange that the media had not contacted him already.

The traffic now picked up speed, but the queue persisted for the next few kilometres. When he was almost at his destination, he called Line's number.

'Are you far away?' she asked.

'A couple of kilometres,' he replied, requesting directions to a secure spot where they could meet. A few minutes later, she had her arms around his neck. Her hair was soaked with rain.

Wisting heaved the bag containing the cutting tool over his shoulder. Line led the way along the fence to a scrapyard and then on into the industrial area.

'Over there,' she said, pointing to a grey building with graffiti-daubed walls.

They walked all the way forward. It seemed to have been a mechanical workshop. Rusty metal poles were still stored on racks outside. The windows were grimy and covered in black plastic on the inside, just as Line had described. Wisting peered in through a gap, cupping one hand on the glass. He could see the van and the container.

'It's really quiet in there,' Line said.

'Show me the thermal images,' Wisting said.

Line produced the thermal camera and held it up to the wall. The signals were faint, but a couple of red blotches indicated two heat sources. The marks shifted to yellow and green, their shape indeterminate.

Wisting had anticipated clearer images. 'Has there been any movement?' he asked.

'The colours change a little, but they don't move,' Line told him.

Wisting's mobile buzzed in his pocket. When he took it out, he realized it must be a journalist calling.

'How do we get in?' he asked, putting the phone back.

'On the other side,' Line answered.

She took him there. At each corner, the building had signs warning of an alarm system. The enamel had flaked off and they were emblazoned with the logo of a security firm that was no longer in existence.

'I don't think they're in use,' Line said.

If the kidnappers were using the building, they would have some form of surveillance, all the same. In everything else, they had deployed leading-edge technology.

'There,' Line said.

She was pointing at a row of windows set slightly lower into the wall. The pile of concrete blocks on the ground would make it easy for them to climb inside.

'It's a cloakroom,' Line told him.

Wisting studied the window. The hinge was at the top, with a handle in the centre at the bottom.

He pulled off his rucksack, took out the angle grinder and replaced it with a stone.

Line scouted around, pulling her rain jacket over her head.

Wisting threw the bag at the lower corner of the window. The pane cracked. He had to strike it again to gouge out a hole. It made surprisingly little noise.

He wiped away a few shards of glass left on the windowsill, thrust his hand inside and opened the window. Line stood by, ready with a length of wood she had found. She nudged the side security latch and tilted the window outwards.

'You can wait here,' Wisting said, but Line shook her head. They each pulled on a pair of gloves and Wisting entered first before helping Line over the ledge.

They were met by a row of lockers, their doors swung open. Grubby tools were strewn all around. The room stank of sweat and dirt, but they also detected something else, a sweeter smell.

The door led into the spacious workshop they had viewed from outside. The rain was drumming on the sheet-metal roof above their heads. The parked van was registered in Norway and had a dent in one side.

The sickly-sweet smell had become more pronounced. Wisting was beginning to suspect what this was all about.

Line stood in front of the container. She knocked on the metal doors but received no response.

Wisting took out the angle grinder. The padlock seemed secure but manageable. A shower of sparks flew out when he applied the grinder to it. The noise was loud and piercing, but he had sliced through within half a minute.

The steel shackle was now hot. He snatched it from the bolt and let it drop to the floor.

'I don't think she's here,' Wisting warned Line before lifting the latch. The hinges creaked as the door slid open. Damp, sweet-smelling air wafted towards them.

Amalie was not there.

The container was kitted out for the cultivation of cannabis. Two heat lamps were suspended over the lush green plants.

Line remained in the doorway – her body slumped as her head fell forward.

Wisting wrenched out an electric plug, extinguishing the harsh light. 'Let's make ourselves scarce,' he said.

Slinging the rucksack over his shoulder, he put his arm around his daughter and led her away.

42

They drove their cars back to Larvik, Wisting following immediately behind Line. The forensic investigations on the motorway bridge had ended. Undoubtedly, the rain would have washed away all evidence.

As they approached the town centre, Wisting turned up towards the police station while Line continued on in the Stavern direction.

He reached the door of his office without encountering anyone in the corridors. There were no messages or missed calls on the encrypted phone. The battery strength was almost unaltered, but he would have to find a charger cable as his own was incompatible. However, the computer lab was equipped with all standard types. He would be able to find a suitable cable there.

Wisting entered the exact time – 18.23 – into his logbook and wrote a brief summary of his abortive investigations. Afterwards he remained in his seat, pen in hand. The man who thought he had seen Bulut in the Grenland industrial area had not been wrong. The number plate he had jotted down matched Bulut's BMW. He must have had some business there, and Wisting did not believe it had anything to do with replacing a car exhaust.

He had taken a photo of the computer screen before deleting the tip-off. The postcode for the area was listed. Wisting keyed it into the criminal records database and searched for all reported offences from three days prior to three days after Bulut had been seen there. There were only two incidents: one a break-in at a vehicle body shop, in which the only item stolen had been the keys to a newly painted Audi RS6 with provisional number plates. The vehicle had been imported second-hand from Switzerland and had a V10 engine with 734 horsepower.

A getaway car, Wisting thought. He added this discovery to the notepad and locked it away in the drawer once more.

His brain felt sluggish. It was difficult to steer his thoughts away from Amalie and avoid conjuring lurid images of where she was and what peril she was in.

He had not eaten the previous day and left to see if there was any food in the canteen. Not because he was hungry, but because he required nourishment to think clearly.

Some of the discarded pizza boxes he found contained leftovers and he helped himself to a slice with meatballs, chewing it in front of the window. Jan Serner had gone down to the square outside to smoke. Every once in a while he stopped and angled his head back, letting the rain fall on his face, before straightening up and taking another drag of his cigarette.

Wisting took one more pizza slice, crunching into the crust. His thoughts strayed to Gunnar Helner's green fireproof cabinet that might lie buried under several metres of earth, or even have been washed out to sea. However, he refused to give up hope of finding it.

Jan Serner tossed his cigarette on the ground and came back inside. Wisting moved to the kitchen sink and filled a glass with water.

He heard the door open behind him and turned to see Maren. 'Someone mentioned there was some pizza here,' she said.

Wisting pointed at the table as he took a gulp of water. Maren helped herself and quickly devoured a slice.

'Have you seen the report from the hotel room?' she asked.

'What hotel room?' Wisting replied in a forlorn attempt to delay the inevitable.

'Nina Lundblad's room,' Maren explained. 'Mortensen sent two technicians there. They've taken photos and removed her belongings, but there was no newspaper listed.'

Wisting began to feel uncomfortably hot and hoped it did not show on his face.

'Newspaper?' he repeated, taking another gulp of water.

'There was a newspaper on her desk,' Maren said. 'I think it was Swedish but didn't give it much thought until after we'd been there. I wondered whether there was anything special in it, since she must have brought it with her from Sweden and taken it up to her room.'

'Maybe there was something about the landslide,' Wisting suggested.

Maren shook her head. 'The Swedish newspapers hadn't picked that up before she got here,' she said, taking another slice of pizza. 'It's not in any of the photos, either.'

'Maybe a cleaner came in and threw it away,' Wisting said.

'Maybe. I'll have to check. Do you want any more?' She was pointing at the pizza box.

When Wisting shook his head, Maren took the last piece and left the room.

Wisting poured out the rest of the water and stooped over the sink. He felt dizzy and nauseous and stood there until it subsided. Then he straightened up, but took a few more minutes to collect himself before he headed to the conference room, where the Swedish detectives were seated.

Hammer was also present.

A chart with photographs of the three suspects was on the wall behind him. The portrait of Gillis Haack was pinned up in the centre, slightly higher than the others, to indicate his status as leader. There was something secure and self-confident in his gaze, even after he had been arrested and hauled in front of the police photographer.

Lines of connection had been drawn from each of the three men to text boxes containing other names and tiny images, alongside a short explanation of the various relationships.

'Has there been any contact?' Wisting asked.

Hammer nodded. 'They're refusing to give up,' he said. 'Kranz offered them twenty kilos but that was turned down. They seem certain he has access to more and have given him a new deadline of twenty-four hours, until 5 p.m. tomorrow.'

Wisting pulled out a chair but just stood there, clutching the back. 'Is he going to do it?' he asked.

'He hasn't set the ball rolling to gather the gold in yet, but they're working on him, trying to persuade him.'

Serner entered and sat down at the table without saying anything. His hair was wet and he reeked of cigarette smoke.

'A few tip-offs about the BMW have come in,' Hammer went on. 'Some from the Grenland area. That matches what we can figure out from the toll station transits.'

'Anything specific?' Wisting asked.

'We're checking some rental cabins at Norsjø. They'd had a visit from a foreigner in a BMW who spoke Swedish. The same applies to an industrial area near the Porsgrunn river and a campsite at Bamble.'

Although Wisting nodded, he hoped none of this

information would lead anywhere. If the situation were to continue for another twenty-four hours, the kidnappers would demand updated case documents. Everything that was dangerous for them was dangerous for Amalie.

He had to sit down. His thoughts made him feel like a traitor. He *was* a traitor. When this was all over, some individuals would support him and show understanding, but most would claim that he should and could have behaved differently. That he should have trusted his immediate colleagues. Right now he felt he had no other choice but to betray them.

Hammer said something about the BMW possibly having been spotted on CCTV somewhere. Wisting had dropped out of the conversation and had to force himself to focus and get a grip.

'That's the mistake they've made,' he heard Josef Helland say. 'Bulut has been here to arrange things and search for a secure location. If we can track where he's been, then we can find their hideout.'

'The Malmgren daughter was held in a van the whole time,' Ann-Mari Walin reminded them. 'She was driven around until they could release her.'

'Still, they must have some place to operate from,' Hammer said. 'Where they sit with their computer.'

Josef Helland agreed. 'But it doesn't have to be here,' he pointed out. 'In principle, they could be anywhere in the world.'

The discussion moved on to where the kidnappers could be located, but there was no sense of progress, no direction.

Wisting concentrated on listening to the conversation and teased out what the Swedes were saying. How they expressed themselves as well as their arguments and theories. He analysed every single word, watching every movement in his quest for something that might suggest which of the three was also a traitor.

When he got nowhere with this, he entered actively into the exchange of opinions in an effort to elicit something useful.

'We'd have a better starting point if Niklas Kranz refuses to pay up,' he said, 'instead of just waiting. If he pulls out now, we could lay a trap for them. Give the impression he's obtained the gold and arrange a handover. That would offer us a chance to apprehend them.'

For a moment there was silence around the table.

'They've threatened to kill her if he doesn't pay,' Wisting added. 'We'd have nothing to lose in such an operation.'

As far as he was concerned, the stakes would be too high. It would impact Amalie. He would have objected if the suggestion had come from anyone else.

'It's not worth it,' Serner said. 'We'd be the ones with blood on our hands if it goes haywire.'

'This is the best chance we have to stop them,' Wisting continued. 'We're already on the inside and have established dialogue. If they're not stopped, they'll go further. Attack another victim, but this time we won't know where or when.'

Wisting waited for an objection, for someone to lead the discussion in a different direction.

Ralf Falk cleared his throat. 'This is about human life,' he said. 'We shouldn't take any action before we know something about the hostage's situation.'

He spoke slowly, as if carefully weighing every word. 'No matter what happens, we ought to let it pass,' he went on. 'Afterwards, we can gather evidence and go after them.'

Wisting was unable to infer much from what was being said. These observations were rooted in professional expertise but could also have a personal motivation.

'After all, you've been through all this in Sweden,' he said. 'After the Malmgren case they tried again. They failed and carried out their threat to kill the victim and then they continued undeterred. Moved to Norway and attacked again.'

'The difference is we now know who they are,' Serner said. 'We'll find them this time.'

'You've had their names for quite a while, but still no proof in the Malmgren case,' Hammer insisted. 'You haven't subsequently found anything that would nail a conviction.'

A phone buzzed. It was Ann-Mari Walin's mobile. She checked the display and left the room to take the call. Serner busied himself going through his messages. Josef Helland excused himself, saying he had to go to the toilet. The informal discussion around the table ended without reaching any conclusion.

43

Lack of sleep was affecting his ability to concentrate. His head felt heavy and his eyes were smarting. Wisting paused the playback and shut his eyes for a few seconds before opening them again.

The onscreen images showed the same scene. Destroyed homes. The drone flew along the landslide's southern perimeter. A two-storey house had been sliced through. What remained looked like a doll's house, with rooms and floor joists exposed, mostly intact. He peered into a kitchen, where the fridge door lay open, the contents seemingly still in place. In the bedroom, the bed was made, and in the living room a landscape painting still hung on the wall behind the settee.

The camera swivelled round and flew back towards the opposite side, soon approaching the spot where the body had been found. The footage had been recorded in the morning, before the corpse had been discovered and airlifted out. The drone pilots could not have been aware of that – their assignment was to document the damage, and there had been no reason to believe anyone was still in the disaster zone.

Parts of the red-painted wall of a house appeared in the picture, and then he spotted the training shoe. From this angle it looked like all the other debris and was easy to overlook in all the chaos and confusion.

He sat up straight in his chair, following intently on

the screen and struggling to stop thinking of anything other than the green fireproof container. Nevertheless, his thoughts were in turmoil. The responsibility for the murder investigation rested on him. The usual apparatus was in operation – forensic examinations, collection of electronic traces, interviews and handling tip-offs. But there was no progress. Everything ground to a halt with him. The crime scene technicians took it for granted that their discoveries would be included in the main investigation; the officers who contributed observations from door-to-door inquiries anticipated that their reports would be read and actioned; and the analysts counted on him to discuss their test results with the other principal investigators in the case. The chief of police relied on him being the right man for the job. Everyone around him depended on him. All he was doing was to obstruct further progress. It conflicted with everything else he had done in his career, but it was all he could do at present. If the green cabinet contained what he suspected it did, it might provide a way out of the corner into which he had been painted.

The drone camera's lens was smeared with rain and it took time for the image to clear again. Just then, he caught sight of it, or at least something that resembled what he was looking for.

Stopping the film, he rewound a few seconds and played it again at slower speed. Down on the right-hand section of the screen, the corner of a metal cabinet protruded from the mud. A slightly darker green than Wisting had imagined, it looked almost grey. When he froze the image, it grew fuzzy. He had to play the footage again to be certain.

The cabinet lay approximately ten metres diagonally down to the left from the spot where they had found the body. It was probably visible from the assembly location for the injured on the night of the landslide. He played the sequence one more time and used his mobile to film it in order to pinpoint the site. A red kayak lay a little to the left of the image and would act as a marker.

For the first time in ages, he felt hopeful.

When they had moved against Gunnar Helner and seized the stolen paintings, rumours had circulated that he also had *The Three Girls* in his possession. This was the name given to three female portraits by Edvard Munch, said to be the same three women he had painted on a bridge in Åsgårdstrand.

The paintings had a long history. For one thing, holes had been shot in them during the war. In the eighties, they had been stolen from a ship-owner in Fredrikstad. Gunnar Helner's uncle had been suspected of the theft, but had died while the case was being investigated. The paintings had never been recovered.

In the course of the inquiry into receiving stolen goods, it was estimated that the value of the paintings at auction would be around 200 million kroner for each. Sixty kilos of gold were not worth more than about 30 million.

The portraits had been painted on canvas and the measurements matched the height of the cabinet. The actual paintings could have been rolled up and hidden.

If the cabinet contained *The Three Girls*, he could offer them to the kidnappers as an alternative. An exchange.

He was keen to head out for a recce at the landslide crater. His pistol knocked against his thigh when he pulled on his rain jacket. On the way out, he encountered no one who might ask him where he was going. Before he left, he let himself into the equipment store and chose the strongest binoculars he could find, as well as a night-vision telescope.

Yellow leaves from the maple tree on the neighbouring property were plastered on the front windscreen. Wisting pushed them away with the wiper blades before reversing out of his parking space.

Bright lights were visible some distance from the disaster zone. The arm of a mobile crane was angled across the sky and he realized that work he was unaware of must be in progress.

The guard at the roadblock shifted the traffic barrier for him and let him past.

The mobile crane was located on a side road about fifty metres above the rescue site. He heard the revs increase and saw a metal basket being hoisted up with a man aboard. Leaving the binoculars in the car, Wisting made his way through a garden and across a courtyard.

Benjamin Fjeld was in charge of the operation. He was standing at the edge of the crater, relaying instructions. The crane arm was pushed out over the landslide area and the basket beneath began to sway.

Turning to face him, Benjamin lowered the hood of his rain jacket. 'Didn't expect to see you here,' he said.

'I just wanted to take a look,' Wisting told him.

He stretched his neck and gazed down at the drainpipe. Benjamin signalled to the crane driver that the basket was in position.

'We've located three drainpipes that, according to the local authority guys, are of the same diameter as the ones that got blocked and caused the landslip,' he explained. 'We're hauling them all up. I think many of the powers that be will be pleased if we can prove someone dumped something into the drain and the whole disaster was caused by a criminal act.'

The man in the basket was on his way down to the first drainpipe.

'Where are the other two?' Wisting asked.

Benjamin pointed them out, further up the crater. 'They tell us there are nine pipes in total, but the others are probably buried.'

Wisting glanced at his watch. 'Will you get them up this evening?' he asked.

'That's the plan,' Benjamin replied. 'We'll keep going until we're done.'

They stood watching the work as it progressed. The man working below pulled a safety harness behind him out of the basket.

'Do you think it will give us anything to go on?' Wisting asked.

'The forensics team believe we might find traces of Mats Beckman, but not of the guys who dumped him,' Benjamin said.

Wisting stood for a while longer. One end of the drainpipe had to be dug out before the worker managed to attach a chain and prepare it to be lifted out.

'I need to get on,' Wisting said, excusing himself. He returned to his car and picked up the night-vision scope.

The seagulls had settled for the night, but down in the crater, rats and other scavengers were most likely hunting for food.

He zoomed in on the spot where he thought the fireproof cabinet must be located. He could see the kayak sticking up in the air, but not the container.

When he played the footage from his mobile, he could see that there had been some movement in the debris. The rain had washed more of the ground away and caused further minor landslides. The wreckage had tumbled around and shifted. He saw that fragments of a staircase lay in approximately the same place, and the same applied to parts of a settee. The green cabinet could not have moved very far, but he would have to go down there to find it. By night.

44

The condensation was fading on the windscreen. Wisting drove slowly out of the residential area with the fan operating full blast. To his left he could see the first drainpipe dangling from the mobile crane.

He would also need a spade when he returned. And a flashlight.

It would be tricky enough to find the cabinet, but he would also have to open it.

It was too large and heavy for him to hoist out of the crater, so he would have to open it there and then. His original idea had been to use the battery-operated angle grinder, which was still in his car, but it had created more dust than he had anticipated. Also, he was unsure whether the cutting blade would be robust enough to tackle the steel on the fireproof container. There had to be an easier method.

He drove to the hotel on Storgata and sat in the car staring up at the second floor, without quite being able to pick out Gunnar Helner's room. The lights were on in two adjacent windows.

The art dealer's phone number was stored on his mobile. Helner answered almost at once.

'Thanks for the video you sent me,' Wisting said.

'Was it any use?' Helner asked.

'No, but it was worth a try,' Wisting replied. 'I was calling mainly to find out if everything was OK. Are you still staying at the hotel?'

'I've nowhere else to go,' Helner told him. 'Not right now, at least. I'm meeting the insurance company tomorrow. I'll probably get a temporary apartment to begin with.'

'Don't the days drag for you at the hotel?'

'I've mostly been at my office, to be honest.'

Wisting peered up at the windows again. 'Are you there now?' he asked.

'No, I got back a short time ago,' Helner said. 'I'm just going to tidy myself up and then I'm coming down to eat.'

'Maybe I'll see you, then,' Wisting said. 'I have some business to attend to at the hotel.'

'Come and have a meal with me,' Helner suggested.

Wisting thanked him for the invitation. 'But not tonight,' he said.

They rounded off their conversation and Wisting sat looking up at the lights in the two rooms on the second floor.

He called Line while he waited. 'Any news?' she asked.

Wisting regaled her with what had emerged from the last telephone call to Niklas Kranz.

'What does that mean?' Line quizzed him.

'I don't know,' Wisting admitted. 'The kidnappers at least seem determined to push ahead with their demands. They're not budging an inch.'

'Is there anything we can do?' Line asked.

Wisting hesitated. He wanted to say something to give his daughter some hope, but at the same time he did not want to hold out unrealistic expectations.

'I may have come up with something,' he said.

'What's that?' Line asked.

It dawned on him that it would be easier and safer if they both went down into the landslide crater.

'I'll tell you when I get home,' he said.

'When will you be here?' she pressed him.

'That depends on the others,' Wisting answered. 'I can't be first to leave.'

He heard a sharp intake of breath at the other end of the line, as if there was something she was finding difficult to say.

'I thought—' she began, but broke off, unable to continue.

'What's on your mind?' Wisting asked.

Line hesitated. 'I don't know,' she said. 'But we could have sent a message to say that Amalie is ill, that she needs her medicine.'

The light was switched off in one of the two rooms he was watching.

'I still have her inhaler, from those attacks she had,' Line went on.

'That was three years ago,' Wisting pointed out. 'If she's not unwell, then I don't think it will be helpful to tell them anything about that.'

'But what if she really is ill?' Line said. 'Those breathing problems she had were triggered by exertion.'

These were ideas that had not occurred to Wisting. He had been most afraid of later adverse effects and concerned about Amalie and Line receiving support in the aftermath of all this.

'The daughter in the Malmgren case slept practically all the time,' he said. 'She remembered almost nothing of what had happened. Anyway, she's not alone. Nanette Kranz is probably in the same place.'

There was a protracted silence at the other end.

'Just hurry home,' Line finally told him.

The conversation ended. Wisting left his car and crossed to the hotel. The same woman as the previous day was on duty in reception and she recognized him.

'It's about room 414 again,' Wisting said. 'Nina Lundblad. I need access.'

'One of your colleagues was here this morning,' the receptionist said. 'They were given a key.'

'I know,' Wisting lied. 'There's been a bit of a mix-up at our end. I just want to go in for a minute or two. I don't need my own key.'

The woman behind the counter unhooked the master key from the board. Wisting cast a glance towards the restaurant but saw no sign of Helner.

'Thanks very much,' he said when handed the key. 'Just a couple of minutes.'

He took the stairs up to the second floor. An elderly man, waiting for the lift, nodded and smiled. Wisting returned the greeting and headed for room 302, where he knocked on the door.

No response from inside.

The lift arrived. Wisting waited until he was alone in the corridor before producing the master key card.

The electronic lock flashed green and Wisting entered, closing the door behind him before inserting the card in the holder by the door to activate the light.

This was one of the more spacious rooms, with a small sitting area and writing desk. He could see a notebook and some loose sheets of paper beside an empty wine glass. A book and a phone charger lay on the bedside table and there were a few clothes draped over the back of a chair. Wisting felt the pockets, but they were empty.

Gunnar Helner could have his keys with him, of course, as on the last occasion they had met. That was the most likely scenario.

A brown leather case was propped up at the end of the

bed. It looked brand new. Wisting opened it and found several compartments inside, but the contents were only a glasses case, two art books and a few price lists.

He surveyed the room one last time. Only on his way out did he notice the jacket hanging on the inside of the door. The key ring was in the left-hand pocket. For a second he considered unclipping the key to the fireproof cabinet, but instead he grabbed the whole bunch and took them with him.

45

The encrypted phone pulsed on his left thigh. A message had come in. Wisting continued along the corridor without giving away his feelings. Not until he had shut his office door behind him did he take the phone out to read the brief message. *Updated documents by midnight.*

He sank back into his chair. As the demand was not unexpected, he had brought the memory stick with him.

His breath was ragged as he exhaled. He had no means of resistance, no bargaining chips. All he could extract from their communication was information.

He tapped in a message and demanded evidence that Amalie was still alive.

She is safe as long as you do what we ask of you, was the response.

She's ill, Wisting wrote. *Can't cope for long without her medicine.*

No sympathy was to be found in the insistent reply: *Updated documents by midnight.*

No question about what kind of illness or what type of medicine.

Wisting made another attempt, asking for a photograph this time, but no answer came.

The phone in his other pocket buzzed. It was the chief of police.

'The police commissioner has asked for a briefing,' she said. 'I'm having a videoconference with her and the director of public prosecutions in an hour's time. Christine Thiis has kept me updated throughout the day, but I'd like to hear from you direct. Do you have anything new to report?'

'There's not been much progress,' Wisting admitted.

He returned the encrypted phone to the padded envelope and placed it in the desk drawer along with the logbook.

'The investigation is deadlocked as long as the negotiations with the kidnappers are ongoing,' he added.

'Is there any likelihood of a resolution?' the police chief asked.

'At some point it must move towards a conclusion, at least,' Wisting replied. 'I don't know the details of the conversations behind the scenes with Niklas Kranz, but to me it seems as if his motivation is heading in the wrong direction. That he doesn't seem willing to extend himself as far as the kidnappers are demanding. We're preparing a plan for action to be taken when the hostage situation comes to an end. Border controls and international wanted bulletins. That sort of thing. The challenge is that we have no proof. We have three names. One of them has been in contact with the murdered infiltrator, but we can't prove he's behind it. We won't get anywhere with the other two. The Swedes haven't managed to gather any evidence against them. All they have is an anonymous source.'

'We're dependent on catching them with the gold,' the police chief summarized. 'For Kranz to go along with their demands.'

'That would at least give us a better starting point,' Wisting agreed.

They discussed the case for a few more minutes. When they had finished, he checked the encrypted phone again. Still no message.

As he stood with the two phones in front of him, it dawned on him that whichever of the Swedes was communicating with the kidnappers must also have two phones. And the Swedes were together in a conference room, with no opportunity to conceal the encrypted phone as he did.

He put it away again and brought only his own phone with him up to the conference room. Ann-Mari Walin was on her way out. She was in a rush, slinging her bag over her shoulder and dashing towards the stairwell, obviously indignant about something.

'There you are,' Hammer said when Wisting entered.

'What was all that about?' Wisting asked, looking over his shoulder.

'I think the whole situation is problematic for her,' Jan Serner replied. 'She took the loss of Mats Beckman personally, and the hostage situation is developing along negative lines.'

'How so?' Wisting asked.

'Niklas Kranz is turning completely.'

'Completely?'

Helland from Kripos gave an audible sigh. 'There was a full-blown argument half an hour ago. He's threatening to turf the police out of his house.'

Wisting stood motionless beside a chair. 'What's happened?' he asked.

'A technical move has been suggested, fixing a tracker on one of the gold bars.'

'Too risky for him?'

'That's not it,' Helland answered. 'It has a time-controlled transmitter. A tracker won't show results until after the handover, so the risk level is low.'

'So what's the problem?'

'He thinks the authorities should pay up, that the police ought to bear the cost of the ransom if it's being used as an investigative tool.'

'Have any steps been taken to increase the stock of gold?' Wisting asked.

'No,' Helland replied. 'We'll be lucky if he sticks to his offer of twenty kilos.'

Wisting drew out the chair. He sat down and gazed in the direction the Swedish police prosecutor had disappeared.

'I just don't think she's happy to stand on the sidelines,' Serner said. 'She has no authority or function here.'

'She has nothing to do here, really,' Ralf Falk chimed in. 'She should go home.'

The room was filled with a brief oppressive silence.

'But we may have found something interesting,' Hammer said. 'The toll station transits.'

'What have you got?'

'We have Bulut's BMW, but we've looked at the transits before and after him. On one occasion, a delivery van comes right behind him. A Renault Trafic with stolen plates. The same type of vehicle is recorded on a camera in the vicinity of the gym where Nanette Kranz was abducted. Even though the actual number plates weren't caught on film.'

'Where do the plates come from?'

'They were stolen in Skjeberg sometime last weekend.'

'Twenty kilometres from the Swedish border,' Serner pointed out.

'Has a report been logged on this?' Wisting asked.

'What do you mean?'

'Is it listed in the case documents?'

'Yes,' Hammer replied, though he did not appear to understand the import of the question.

Wisting was thinking of the document file he would have to deliver by midnight.

'I'm the only one who's not totally up to date, then,' he said. 'I just had a briefing with the chief, but I wasn't aware of that.'

'It could be a Renault Trafic that was stolen in Eskilstuna three months ago,' Jan Serner said. 'Also, we have a Renault that was stolen in Sundsvall last year, but apart from those, all Swedish vans have been accounted for.'

'We only have one, stolen in Stavanger last year,' Hammer said.

'What are we doing with this information?' Wisting asked.

Hammer grabbed a cup and the pump thermos on the table made a gurgling sound as he tried to fill it.

'We're seeing if there's anything to learn from the theft of the number plates,' Hammer replied. 'Door-to-door inquiries and CCTV in the area. The whole shooting match. The same with the vehicle thefts.'

'Public appeal?'

'Not yet,' Hammer said. 'That would alert them to what we know. The van could provide a chance to approach them on the QT. I don't want to run any risks.'

A phone buzzed. Ralf Falk took it from his trouser pocket, checked the display and stumbled to his feet as he answered the call.

'Falk speaking,' he said, heading towards the window.

Wisting studied his pockets but saw no bulge there. His jacket lay on a chair in the corner and he had a zipped document folder on the table. Both with plenty of space for another phone.

Jan Serner began to pack up his belongings. 'I'm calling it a day,' he said. 'I'll try to have a chat with Ann-Mari at the hotel.'

Wisting glanced at his watch and looked across at Hammer.

'I've a few things to sort out before I go,' his colleague said, taking his half-empty cup with him as he left.

Serner placed his document folder on the table and hovered for a moment, resting his hands on it.

'What would you have done?' he asked, fixing his eyes on Wisting. 'If you were in Niklas Kranz's situation?'

The question was sudden and felt like an accusation. Wisting's pulse began to race and an uncomfortable sensation radiated from his chest to the rest of his body. He had to gather his wits to suppress his physical reaction.

'I no longer have a wife,' he replied. 'Nor do I have millions in the bank.'

'But you have a family,' Serner said. 'What would you have done for them?'

'I think I'd have done everything in my power,' Wisting responded. 'Money's of no importance.'

'What about other values?' Serner pressed him.

'What do you mean?'

'Ethical values,' Serner explained. 'The principles you stand for.'

Wisting tried to read him, to find out whether his words contained an underlying message, but he could not detect anything.

'As I said, I think I'd have done everything in my power,' he answered. 'What about you?'

'Me too,' Serner replied. 'But I think I'd have concentrated on looking forward.'

He picked up the document folder from the table but lingered as if searching for the right form of words.

'There's a time for everything,' he added. 'For vengeance too.'

46

It was after half past ten by the time Wisting got into his car and drove home. Fog had swept in across the land again, leaching the light from the streetlamps.

The short drive offered him welcome respite. Inside the police station, he had to restrain himself, but alone in his car he could give vent to his frantic despair. His eyes filled with tears and he had to blink them away to focus on the road ahead. His breath came in sharp gasps and his entire body was convulsed with violent tremors. He managed to stop that with a loud sob, but he could not get rid of the queasiness beneath his chest.

By the time he parked outside Line's house, he could no longer feel the pangs of desperation. She emerged from the living room to meet him in the kitchen. Amalie had now been gone for seventeen hours. It felt like an eternity. Line had become a different person, a pale shadow of her former self. Shattered and ashen-faced.

Wisting shook his head slowly to indicate that he had no news. They hugged.

'I've . . .' Line began, pushing him away slightly.

Wisting signalled for her to wait. He produced the envelope with the encrypted phone and placed it in the microwave. Line walked ahead of him out into the living room. She had been resting on the settee. Her quilt lay crumpled on the floor beneath the coffee table.

'I've messaged them to say that Amalie needs the inhaler,' Wisting said.

'Have you spoken to them?'

'Yes, not long ago. I need your laptop,' he said.

She brought it and Wisting transferred the updated files.

Line tucked her legs underneath herself on the settee. 'You said you were working on something,' she reminded him.

Wisting nodded as he finished up on the computer. He was unsure where to start. 'There could be another solution,' he said. 'You remember Gunnar Helner?'

Line looked bewildered. 'The art dealer?' she asked.

'When he was arrested, we'd hoped to find *The Three Girls*,' Wisting continued.

'The Munch paintings that vanished?'

Wisting nodded. 'His uncle was suspected of being involved,' he explained. 'He tried to sell the paintings to a private collector in Marseilles but ended up being investigated.'

'I didn't know that,' Line said. 'You didn't mention anything about that when I wrote the article on Helner.'

'The uncle's name was Odd Forsberg,' Wisting told her. 'He died before the police in Fredrikstad could confront him with their suspicions. They entered his house and searched it but found nothing to link him to the case. We didn't find anything when we searched Helner's house either, but unknown to us he had had a secret compartment built in his basement.'

He told her the story he had heard from the tradesman who had constructed the concealed compartment in the floor and about the green fireproof cabinet belonging to Gunnar Helner.

'When Odd Forsberg displayed one of the paintings in

Marseilles, it had been removed from the frame and rolled up,' Wisting went on. 'All three paintings would fit into Helner's fireproof box. They're probably worth more than 600 million kroner.'

Line understood his intentions with the paintings but did not appear entirely able to bring herself to believe that what he was saying could be true. Wisting knew he was clutching at straws, but he had succeeded in convincing himself that this was an opportunity they ought to explore.

'Where else could the paintings be?' he asked. 'It's reasonable to suppose that Gunnar Helner still has them in his possession. His uncle was unmasked when he tried to sell them. How would Helner be able to get shot of them?'

'He could have sold them long ago,' Line said. 'He's operated as an art dealer for forty years and has loads of contacts. And he's bought and sold stolen pictures before now.'

'Gunnar Helner has something special in that cabinet,' Wisting objected. 'He's been searching for it for several days. I've located it. I know where it is, and I have the key.'

He put the bunch of keys down on the table.

Line launched into a string of questions about how he had got hold of the keys, but then a thought struck her. 'What would the kidnappers do with the paintings?' she asked. 'If Helner hasn't managed to sell them, how would the kidnappers make money from them? Gold is much easier to trade.'

'A reward has been offered,' Wisting pointed out. 'An insurance company in London would pay £6 million for the pictures. That's double the value of the gold they're demanding from Kranz.'

'Why hasn't Helner made contact with them if he has the pictures?' Line asked.

'Because his uncle was a suspect,' Wisting replied. 'For all we know, Helner may have been in on it too. He was twenty-five at that time. If he "discovered" the paintings, it would serve to confirm that his uncle had been involved. He would not be entitled to the reward.'

'But the kidnappers can't just turn up with the pictures either,' Line said. 'The insurance company won't pay out the money to just anyone, surely?'

'No, true,' Wisting answered. 'They'll need a respectable middleman.'

Line stared at him.

'I can offer them a better deal,' Wisting added. 'It could solve everything, both for Nanette Kranz and for us.'

He could see a glimmer of hope in his daughter's eyes.

'But first of all we have to go out and find the paintings,' he said. 'If they're there.'

47

The car headlights sliced through the darkness, illuminating the rain-soaked landscape.

The story about the bullet holes had aroused Wisting's curiosity when he had first heard of the stolen paintings. However, the damage had been repaired. When he had seen the photographs of them, there was scarcely any visible trace. The holes had been filled with grout and over-painted at a restoration workshop.

The portraits had been part of Munch's first exhibition in Berlin and were purchased by an art collector from Lübeck. In the thirties they were bought back and returned to Norway to prevent them being destroyed and burned by the Nazis, after Hitler had described them as degenerate art and denounced Edvard Munch. When the war came to Norway, they were hidden on a mountain farm in Ottadalen. The story of the bullet holes was not as dramatic as it might sound at first. They were the result of an accidental shot fired from a hunting rifle in the barn. The bullet had gone through all three paintings stored there, layered one on top of the other. After the war, they had been restored and sold at auction to three different buyers, before ship-owner Ditlef Grundt in Fredrikstad had bought back all three. In the seventies they were almost lost in a fire, but they were rescued from one part of the house, while the ship-owner's son perished in the flames in another part. On the night that Norway won the Melodi Grand Prix in

1985, the paintings were stolen, and since then they had remained missing.

The cordon around the landslide area was still actively guarded. Wisting turned into one of the nearest residential streets and followed it to a turning spot at the end. The closest house was only twenty metres away, but the residents had probably retired for the night and only an exterior light gave off a faint glow in the fog.

Wisting glanced across at his daughter. 'All set?'

She nodded. The cabin light came on when she opened the car door. They stepped out, closing the doors carefully behind them, and scouted around. Everything seemed quiet.

The equipment was in the car boot. Spades, flashlights and a rope, as well as the night-vision scope Wisting had taken from the police station.

They skirted along a garden fence and on through dense forest. The darkness was more impenetrable than Wisting had expected and they had to use their flashlights to grope their way forward, but they made sure to keep them trained low on the ground.

After a couple of minutes they emerged on to a path. Wisting led the way. He switched off his flashlight and let Line's light suffice for them both.

The path ended at an asphalt road. Wisting took a few minutes to work out their location. The electricity had been cut and all he could use to find his bearings was the outline of the surrounding buildings.

'That way,' he said.

They crossed a garden and emerged above the property used as an assembly point on the night the landslide struck.

Soon they were standing at the edge of the crater. Wisting took out the night-vision scope and raised it to his eye. It intensified the existing natural light and he did not take long to pinpoint the red kayak he had used earlier as a landmark.

He gave the scope to Line and explained what she should look for. Once she had oriented herself, he took her with him to the fence he had climbed over the last time he had gone down into the crater. Line had no objections and just seemed eager to make the descent.

The rope he had brought from the equipment store in the police station was an abseiling rope, but he had no climbing harness or any other gear. The rope would provide only support, not security.

He attached it firmly to an apple tree and tossed it out over the perimeter. Then he dropped the spades into the pit.

'I'll go first,' he said, sitting down on the ground. Clumps of earth crumbled away and slithered down.

'Careful, now,' Line warned him.

Wisting used one hand to grab the rope and gripped the wire netting with the other before swinging himself round. As the fence swayed, he could hear metal scraping, but there was nothing to suggest it would not hold.

He wrapped the rope once around his right arm and let it slide through his hand as he clambered down the fence. The ladder that had been sent down to him still lay at the bottom. His feet groped for the top rung and he felt the ladder sink into the soft mud when he put his weight on it.

At the foot, he stepped out on to a broad plank of wood and signalled to Line that it was now her turn.

Having watched how he had accomplished it, she copied his movements easily. When transferring to the ladder, though, she stumbled and lost her footing. Her body swung round and she was left hanging from the rope by one arm.

Wisting was on his way up to help her, but she managed

to turn round and plant her foot on the top rung. 'It's OK,' she whispered.

Wisting stepped aside to make room for her. His boots sank into the mud. He lifted his foot and lurched forward a few steps to avoid getting stuck but lost his balance and fell.

Line tottered towards him and found her footing on some building debris. She helped him up and across to firmer ground.

They used their flashlights only sporadically to mark out their route. They lumbered through smashed brick and stone, ruined furnishings and other effects. All around them, tiny streams spilled and trickled.

The distance they had to cover was about one hundred metres, but each step had to be taken with great care. They used their spades for support, balancing on timber fragments and jumping between them. Everything was slick and slippery. The ground gurgled beneath them. All of a sudden, Wisting made a misstep and his left leg sank to his knee in the mud. He could feel cold sludge run down the inside of his boot.

At first his foot refused to budge, and Line held his hand while he struggled to pull it out. Slowly the mud released its grip and they were able to trudge on.

After half an hour they reached the place where Wisting had spotted the cabinet. He directed his flashlight beam on the area in front of the kayak, sweeping it to the left towards a twisted lamppost and then right towards a still intact flight of stairs. The fireproof container must have become submerged in the debris.

Line pushed the blade of her spade into the earth, and after five attempts it struck metal.

She began to dig. One turn of the spade after another,

through the heavy mush. Wisting held the flashlight, struggling to shield it as much as possible from any onlookers. With every turn of the spade, mud and water slid back and filled the hole.

Wisting put down the flashlight and used his spade to toss the wet clods in a different direction. This helped. Line continued to dig. She cleared away the wreckage by hand and at last was able to confirm that she had found the cabinet. Angled downwards, it appeared to be lying on its side.

They continued to work in tandem, uncovering more and more of the cabinet. Wisting grew hot and could feel perspiration trickle across his back. He straightened up and leaned on his spade.

'We'll have to try to turn it over,' he said.

Line knelt down, took hold of the container with both hands and tried to flip it over, but the cabinet would not shift.

Wisting grasped the flashlight and shone it all around them, finally spotting a long joist. Line was closer to it and managed to take a grip of it. She pressed it down along one side of the container, tilting it and pushing it underneath.

A lamppost lay among the wreckage. Together they succeeded in dragging it across to the cabinet and resting it on the joist so that the length of wood could act as a lever.

When Wisting pressed all his weight on it, the mud gurgled around the container, but he was unable to move it more than a few centimetres.

He tried to delve down at the back of the cabinet to create space for the turning manoeuvre.

All of a sudden, Line switched off the light and pulled him down to the ground. 'There's someone there, up by the houses,' she said.

Wisting whirled around, staring up at the crater's edge. The light from two torches flitted between the buildings, disappearing for a second or two before returning. The beams were being directed at doors and windows on one of the empty houses before moving on to the next one.

'Security guards,' Wisting whispered. 'Keeping an eye on the evacuated properties. Checking there's been no looting.'

They lay there, watching the cones of light. Now and again the beams shifted out to the crater, but they were not bright enough to reach the spot where Wisting and Line now lay sprawled on the ground.

Wisting grew impatient. He straightened up a little and began to dig in the dark, feeling his way forward with the spade and pushing the earth away.

When the lights vanished, Line was keen to try again. She lay on top of the joist and pressed hard. The container began to yield. Wisting moved across, straining all his muscles and pushing with all his might. The joist slid out, but the cabinet had been moved one half-turn, enough to open the door.

Wisting moved forward, running his hand over the metal and wiping dirt away from the lock.

Line held the torch low. 'Do you have the key?' she asked.

He took the keys from his pocket, selecting the right one and inserting it into the lock.

The keyhole was full of mud, preventing him from putting the key more than halfway in. 'It's clogged,' he said. 'We need some water.'

Line played the flashlight beam around them. There were puddles of dirty water everywhere. Moving across to the nearest of these, Wisting kicked off one of his boots and filled it. Hurriedly, he poured the water out and rinsed away the mud, repeating this three times before he tried the key again.

The key grated in the lock as he rotated it. Something clicked into place. Wisting grabbed the handle, turning it clockwise, and heard the bolts retract.

'Open it!' Line said.

Wisting lifted the door up and placed it on its side. Line trained the light on the contents: three long cardboard cylinders with a plastic lid at each end.

Neither of them spoke. Wisting prised off one of the lids and used his fingers to fumble for whatever the cylinder contained. He caught hold of the corner flap of something that felt like parchment and realized it could well be an oil painting. He pulled it carefully towards the opening to let Line see.

'Gently does it,' she warned him.

He showed her one corner before pushing the painting back inside.

'The bin bags,' he requested. Line had brought two black plastic bin bags. She held up one of these while Wisting dropped the three tubes into it, then she drew the other bag over it and tied a knot.

'What about the rest?' Line asked, peering down into the cabinet.

They could see several sealed envelopes in there, a thick document folder secured with an elastic band, a bundle of buff paper and a gun case fashioned from brown leather.

'We'll leave that,' Wisting said.

Closing the cabinet, he locked it and stuffed the bunch of keys into his pocket. Then he picked up the spade and hurled earth and mud until the container was covered again.

'That'll do,' he said. 'Let's go home now.'

48

Wisting reversed the car up to the entrance. Leaving all the equipment in the boot, they brought only the plastic bags with the paintings into the house.

As their outdoor clothes were stiff with dried mud, they wrenched them off in the hallway, dropping them on the floor. Line headed for the bathroom, while Wisting made do with washing his hands at the kitchen sink.

'Do you have gloves?' he asked when she returned.

She took a pair of yellow washing-up gloves from the cupboard under the sink. Wisting carried the cardboard cylinders into the living room and placed them on the settee.

'Draw the curtains,' he said. She did this before returning to help him ease out the first painting.

The roll opened and Wisting spread it out on the floor. The portrait depicted a young woman, a reddish sheen in her hair, wearing a white ankle-length dress. Exactly as he remembered. Down at the left-hand corner, the work was signed with the letters E M.

He ran his hand over the patch where he knew the bullet had gone through and thought he could feel a little bump.

The second picture was of a girl in a red frock and sunhat with a matching-coloured band. On the back of the canvas, the gunshot damage was more obvious. There was a star-shaped tear in the right-hand section of the material.

The girl in the third painting wore a green dress and had a kerchief on her head. The girls in the first two portraits had serious, almost mournful, expressions, but the third had a faint smile on her face.

Wisting put his hands on his hips and stood for a while, studying the paintings. They were evocative but not beautiful. To him, the style seemed simplistic, and it was difficult to imagine that they were worth millions. But other works by Munch were valued at three times that and the paintings in front of him had a special history that would give them appeal to galleries and art collectors.

'What do we do now?' Line asked.

She had mud in her hair and must have scratched her neck while they were down in the crater. It looked like a claw mark running from one ear down to her chest.

'We'll send them a message,' Wisting said. 'To tell them what we have.'

He brought the encrypted phone from the kitchen and sat down with it at the table. The phone operated just like an ordinary smartphone and could send images and read webpages. He found the English title for the three paintings and undertook an online search. The first result was an article with the title 'Munch's Missing Girls' in an English online newspaper. It related the story of the paintings and estimated a value in British pounds. The reward was also mentioned.

He began to phrase a text message, changing and correcting it to ensure its import was as simple and clear as possible. Finally he decided on a single sentence stating that he had a suggestion for a trade-off, and asked them to search for 'Munch's Missing Girls' on the internet.

'That do?' he asked, showing the message to Line.

She nodded and handed the phone back. Wisting let his thumb slide across the screen to press send. After that, he got to his feet and took a photograph of the paintings as they lay stacked one on top of the other, curled up at the edges.

The clock showed 02.47 and he waited a few more minutes before sending the photo and writing that they needed to talk.

Ten minutes passed without an answer. Wisting kept checking the phone. The messages were listed as being sent, but there was nothing to tell him whether they had been delivered or read.

'They might not see it until the morning,' Line said. She rose and began to roll up the paintings. Wisting helped her to feed them back into the tubes.

'What should we do with them?' she asked. 'What if they come here to steal them?'

Wisting snapped the last plastic lid into place. He had not considered that possibility.

'We'll think of something if this drags out,' he said. 'Right now we need to get some sleep. I'll kip on the settee.'

They took turns to use the shower. Line went first.

Brown, muddy water ran over the tiles when Wisting hosed himself down. He borrowed Line's shampoo, rubbing it into his hair and using the contents of the same bottle to scrub the rest of his body.

Line kept watch over the encrypted phone on the coffee table. Before she went to bed, she found a suitable charger cable.

Wisting moved out into the hallway to his bundle of dirty clothes. He picked up his jacket and brought it back into the living room, checking the weight of the gun in the right pocket. Before he lay down, he dragged a chair across to the settee and hung his jacket over the back.

49

His short nap had been restless; he had slipped in and out of fractured thoughts. The quilt was damp and his mouth was dry.

Wisting sat up and checked the encrypted phone. No messages. He rubbed his face with his hands. His skin felt rough and he needed to shave.

The house was silent. He could hear the gutters dripping on the roof outside the living-room window, but it was not raining. His T-shirt lay on the armrest of the settee and he pulled it on before tiptoeing out to the bedroom passageway. He could hear Line stir and knew she was awake.

'Have they answered?' Her voice came out of the darkness.

'No, not yet,' Wisting replied. 'I'm going up to my place to change,' he said. 'But I'll pop in again before I go to work.'

Line said something about making breakfast.

'Coffee will do,' Wisting told her. 'I'll take the phone with me.'

He moved to the hallway and threw on the previous evening's grubby clothes before heading up to his own house, where he shaved, showered again and put on fresh clothes.

Line was sitting at the kitchen table on his return. She poured him a cup of coffee.

'I'll have to let the school know that Amalie won't be coming in today,' she said.

Wisting nodded. Line was cradling her cup in her hands, eyes fixed on the contents. 'You haven't spoken to anyone else about this?' she asked, looking up.

'No.'

She gazed at him. His daughter looked disconsolate. She might need someone to talk to, someone other than him. A doctor or psychologist would have a duty of confidentiality. Although he considered suggesting that, it might all be over in a few hours. It was just a matter of waiting.

'But there's one thing,' he said instead.

'What's that?'

He stood up and put the encrypted phone in the microwave. 'I don't think we're alone in this,' he whispered, to be certain no one could hear them.

Line shot a glance at the microwave. 'What do you mean?' she asked.

'I think one of the Swedish investigators must have fallen victim to the same blackmail methods as us,' Wisting answered. 'That must be how they found out about the infiltrator and his girlfriend. Probably they still have some kind of hold on him, or her.'

He told her about Ann-Mari Walin, Jan Serner and Ralf Falk. It seemed that Line derived some comfort from the notion that others might be in the same situation.

'Who do you think it is?' she asked, pulling her cup towards her. 'Who's the most likely?'

'I know too little about them,' Wisting replied. 'But Jan Serner's the most central player, and the one who seems most stressed out.'

'In what way?'

'There are small signs,' Wisting said. 'He's started smoking again and is tight-lipped, just like me. Says as little as possible to avoid saying something wrong.'

'Is there any way of finding out?' Line asked.

Wisting shrugged. 'Not off the top of my head.'

They might well winkle out a few answers if one of them visited his family in Stockholm, but he had no idea where they lived or even who they were. What is more, they had no time for that.

'I think it would be easier to let him come to me,' Wisting went on.

'What do you mean?'

'Serner's an experienced detective,' Wisting replied. 'He'll think there's a chance that someone in the Norwegian investigative team is being blackmailed. I have a feeling he suspects me.'

'How do you figure that out?'

'He tested me when we were alone together. He asked what I would have done if anyone in my family was abducted like Nanette Kranz has been.'

'How did you respond?'

'I said I would have done whatever it took.'

'And how did he react to that?'

Wisting grew thoughtful. 'Sympathetically, in a way,' he replied. 'But there was something about the look in his eyes and what he said that made me wonder if he was trying to give me some kind of secret message.'

'What did he say?'

'That he agreed. He too would have done whatever it took but would try to look ahead. To believe he would have the opportunity to square things later.'

'Is that how you think of it too?' Line asked.

Wisting looked at her. 'All the time,' he answered. 'That's what keeps me going.'

Closing her eyelids, she nodded, as if she was of similar mind.

A car drove slowly past in the street outside. Wisting stood up. 'I need to get going,' he said.

Line had let go of her cup. Instead she was flexing her fingers. He knew her well and understood there was something she wanted to tell him.

'What is it?' he asked.

She did not have a chance to reply. The phone buzzed.

Wisting moved to the microwave, took out the phone and answered.

'*William Wisting?*' the voice asked.

'It's me.' He put the phone on the kitchen table, hovering above it and placing his hands palm down on either side.

'*Why do you want to give us stolen paintings?*' the voice read out.

The question contained an accusation, for which Wisting was unprepared. It seemed they suspected him of trying to snare them in some kind of trap.

'I'm offering you an alternative form of payment,' he replied. 'It looks as if you won't be able to come to an agreement with Niklas Kranz. You can have these paintings today and bring it all to a speedy conclusion.'

Minutes ticked by before any response was forthcoming.

'*What has changed about Mr Kranz's situation?*'

'All I know is he's done nothing to collect more gold,' Wisting said. 'I don't think he's willing to ruin the family firm for a woman he no longer loves.'

He paused for a moment before adding, 'He's on the verge of a nervous breakdown. It's far from certain he'll be persuaded to speak to you again.'

Line had got to her feet. She now stood with arms folded, staring at the phone.

'*Where did the paintings come from?*' was the next question.

Wisting gave an honest account. 'No one has seen them for more than thirty years,' he concluded.

The answer shot back quickly this time. '*The paintings are worthless to us.*'

'No, no,' Wisting protested. 'There's a reward. Six million British pounds. All you need to do is find a lawyer who'll contact the insurance company for you. You were probably children when they were stolen. No one can accuse you of having been involved.'

This time there was another protracted silence.

'*You will hear from us,*' was the message that finally came. Then the connection was cut.

50

The paintings lay on the back seat. Wisting cast a glance in the rear-view mirror. Line had concealed them under a blanket. Before he left, they had also scrubbed the mud off the seat covers.

He stopped outside the hotel in Storgata and ventured inside. Two men stood with suitcases at the reception desk, waiting to check out. Wisting strode straight past, towards the restaurant and the breakfast buffet. The footage from the time when Nina Lundblad had left the hotel had revealed that there was a blind spot outside the staff door leading into the kitchen. He pulled out Gunnar Helner's keys and let them slide down to the floor, making sure no one saw him.

By the time they had finished serving breakfast, someone would have found them, assumed that a guest or employee had dropped them and handed them in to reception.

His phone buzzed on the way back to his car. His own personal phone this time. The call was from the officer in charge of the central operations switchboard at police headquarters.

'Yes, Wisting here,' he answered.

It was Sverre Brennmo, one of the most dedicated and experienced supervisors, always reassuring to have in command. He had a special ability to create a sense of security and calm in an otherwise chaotic and critical situation.

'Have you got a couple of minutes?' he asked.

Wisting had settled behind the steering wheel. 'Yes.'

'I've just taken over from the night shift,' Brennmo continued. 'A report's been logged that I think might be relevant to the case you're working on.'

The conversation switched to the hands-free set-up as Wisting drove off. 'What have you got?' he asked.

'A vehicle fire in Oklungen, on the border with Telemark,' Brennmo replied. 'It was reported at 04.43 by a passing motorist on the road early for the morning flight.'

'What kind of vehicle?' Wisting asked.

'A Renault Trafic,' Brennmo answered. 'It was well ablaze by the time the report came in. It took a while for the fire service to get there, so there wasn't much left of it by then. It was unregistered, but according to the chassis number we're talking about a van that was stolen in Eskilstuna three months ago. The reports are on their way through the system, but I just wanted to draw your attention to it. Everything to do with Sweden could be of interest regarding the murdered infiltrator.'

'You're right,' Wisting said. 'Where's the van now?'

'Towed in,' Brennmo answered. 'Photos and reports have been logged, but there's not much more to glean from it. A total write-off, completely obliterated by the fire, according to the patrol on the scene.'

Wisting turned into the back yard at the police station. 'Thanks,' he said. 'I'll follow up on that.'

He would have to do this himself, even though he knew it would not lead anywhere. He had given the kidnappers information on the van and only a few hours later they had torched it.

As long as he had been talking on the phone, he had managed to stay calm, but as soon as the call was disconnected, he was overwhelmed with revulsion. A physical reaction to the damage he had caused to the investigation. He thought he could feel the muscle fibres in his chest contract and his breathing grew laboured as he began to hyperventilate. He had to remain seated for a while before letting himself into the police station.

The burnt-out van was the main subject of the morning meeting. Images were shown on the large screen. The van was situated at the end of a road, in front of a barrier. Smoke and steam were still belching from it when the pictures were taken. The heat had caused the black, molten metal to twist and warp. All the doors were open, probably to encourage the spread of the fire. The interior had melted and the seats were nothing but a latticework of steel wires and springs. On the ground in front of the van lay a deformed plastic petrol can.

The number plates had been removed, but the chassis number was impressed on a plate inside the engine cavity. It was legible even in the photograph.

Hammer, frustrated and clearly annoyed, sat back in his chair with his arms crossed in front of him. Now and then he gave a loud sigh or groan.

Jan Serner, busy on his phone, seemed unruffled. Ann-Mari Walin looked as if she had slept badly and her eyes were dull. Her hair was lank and her hands lay motionless on her lap. Ralf Falk watched tensely, occasionally taking notes.

'They torched the van in the Malmgren case as well,' he said. 'At least, a burnt-out delivery van was found in Solna a few hours after the girl was recovered. It was impossible to find traces of her or anyone else inside the van – all evidence had gone up in smoke.'

'Nanette Kranz's DNA was in the back of this van,' Hammer said, pointing to the big screen. 'As well as the perpetrators'. The van could have solved the whole case. Now there's nothing left of it.'

Wisting tried to strike an optimistic note. 'It's a lead,' he said. 'We know what kind of van they used, and they must have made their way to and from the site of the fire. That's something for us to work on.'

'I *have* worked on it,' Hammer told him. 'I've followed the false reg plates through their toll station transits.'

He took control of the images on the big screen and brought up a map. The yellow line of the E18 meandered along the coast from north to south. The toll stations were marked with red dots, sixteen of them in total. Three on the E18, while the remainder were clustered around the neighbouring towns of Porsgrunn and Skien, part of the patchwork of towns in the Grenland region. The co-ordinated financing of new road projects meant that the electronic transit points also became an important investigative tool to chart vehicle movements. However, only the number plates were recorded, with no photos taken of whoever sat behind the wheel.

'Everything suggests that the van was here in Larvik on the day Nina Lundblad disappeared,' Hammer said.

A text box popped up at the transit point on the northbound stretch of the E18. The van had been registered at 10.17 on Saturday morning, around the time Nina Lundblad had left her hotel in Larvik.

'It didn't return in the direction of Grenland until that same night at 03.23,' Hammer went on. 'Immediately behind it was the red Audi belonging to Nina Lundblad. It was left parked beside the bridge.'

The transits were plotted on the map.

'That matches our hypothesis,' Mortensen said. 'There's a fabric impression from gloves in her car. In all probability, someone else drove it and parked there. We anticipate finding traces of anaesthetic gas during the autopsy. She was probably thrown down from the bridge.'

His last words were left hanging in the air.

'Are the stolen plates registered anywhere else?' Wisting eventually asked.

Hammer produced an image of all the toll station transits.

'There are sporadic, scattered transits that don't tell us much,' he elaborated. 'What's of most interest is that the plates aren't registered at toll stations further north or south of the E18. They've remained within that area the entire time.'

With a single keystroke, he displayed a loop that circled around the towns of Larvik, Porsgrunn and Skien. 'Unless they've driven on the side roads,' he added.

The discussion continued around the table, about where within that loop the kidnappers might be staying, and whether there was any chance of finding out what type of vehicle they were now using. Wisting led the meeting on through a summary of the whole case, allowing each of his colleagues to contribute. This was an exchange of views that would not lead to anything specific, but in the present impasse, it was just as much a matter of giving the investigators an opportunity to vent their frustration as moving the case forward.

None of the Swedes had much to say and they met Wisting's eye only sporadically when he looked at them.

Ralf Falk stretched his hands behind his neck to massage a tight muscle, causing him to grimace when he touched a tender spot.

Jan Serner sat with his jaw clamped, his eyes fixed on the window, though he was not really gazing out. Occasionally he picked up a pen, twiddling it between his fingers and then setting it down again.

Ann-Mari Walin blinked a lot – she had long eyelashes that drew Wisting's attention. She kept shifting position and, each time she said something, she stroked her face, as liars habitually do.

All three were probably unaware of the minute signals they were sending out. The problem was that Wisting did not know whether this was their usual behaviour or if the situation they found themselves in was reflected in their body language.

The meeting had lasted three quarters of an hour. Many of the participants had work-related tasks they should be getting on with. Wisting was impatient to check the encrypted phone in the drawer in his office. He now spoke to draw the meeting to a close.

'In eight hours or so, Niklas Kranz's deadline runs out,' he said. 'We'll receive an update from the police over there at noon. Those who can make it are invited to take part in that.'

At last, chairs scraped across the floor as the investigators rose from their seats and left the room.

Serner picked up his pen, put it down again and instead took out a packet of cigarettes and signalled to Falk that he was going out.

Wisting trailed behind him along the corridor. Serner opened the door to the stairwell and disappeared upstairs. He must have found the little platform on the roof that smokers used, where the fans on the ventilation system were situated and the antennae for the radio network were mounted. Wisting went down to his office to check the encrypted phone.

No messages.

He put it back, stepped out into the corridor and ascended two floors. The door leading out to the platform was stiff and had to be given a hard push to open.

Jan Serner stood snugly in a corner with a cigarette in his mouth. He looked up from his mobile phone and gave Wisting a nod.

'I needed a breath of air,' Wisting said by way of excuse.

He walked to the parapet and looked out over the townscape. Thick clouds were scudding in from the south-east. On the fjord, a container ship was sailing into harbour.

The air was cold and raw. Wisting breathed it in and wheeled around. Serner had put his phone in his pocket. He took deep drags of his cigarette and turned away when he exhaled.

'What do you think?' Wisting asked. 'How will they react when they learn that Kranz isn't willing to pay what they demand?'

Serner took another long drag. 'I think it'll work out,' he replied. 'They gave in before, in the Malmgren case, and accepted sixteen kilos.'

'But then they knew there was no more to be had,' Wisting pointed out. 'It's different in this case, and the stakes are so high that they'll need to go to ground completely afterwards. We're talking about two murders.'

'One,' Serner corrected him. 'They don't know we're investigating Nina Lundblad's death as a homicide.'

'They know themselves what they've done,' Wisting insisted. 'Anyway, they have to make sure of sufficient financial gain to allow them to live under the radar for a long time.'

Serner ground out the cigarette on the brick wall, lost in thought, before dropping the butt into an overflowing tin bucket.

'It's not a matter of all or nothing, but of bailing out of this with as much as possible,' he said.

'I'm just not sure they'll give up so easily,' Wisting went on. 'Their brutality scares me. Nina Lundblad's murder shows what they're capable of. What they're willing to do.'

Serner looked past Wisting out towards the town. 'Let's see what today brings,' he said as he moved back inside.

51

The flowers he had received three days earlier still lay on the shelf, completely withered now. Wisting plucked a dead leaf from a stalk and crushed it between his fingers.

Around 170,000 people lived within the circle Nils Hammer had drawn on the map, spread across 2,500 square kilometres. There were skerries, forests and mountains, town centres, urban areas, industries and agricultural sectors. After checking out all the tip-offs to do with sightings of Dogan Bulut, they still had no definite idea of where he and the others might be located.

He sat down to read the most recent documents that had been logged. The only specific detail was a provisional report from Forensics that blood had been found in the concrete pipe hoisted from the landslide crater. The DNA results proving whether it belonged to the murdered police informant would be available within the week.

An hour ticked by. The encrypted phone was in his pocket. He checked it continually, merely to make sure no new message had gone unheard. He interpreted it as a good sign that it was taking so long. His offer would be easy to reject, but accepting it would involve a change of plan and require preparations.

Line was probably waiting equally impatiently. He crossed to the window and messaged her to say there was no news.

Outside, the wind had picked up. He looked straight out

at the crown of the huge maple tree on the neighbouring property. Strong gusts tugged at the branches.

A faint signal, accompanied by a vibration in his trouser pocket, made his pulse race. He took out the phone and saw the screen lit up. *Talk in thirty minutes.*

Adrenaline began to ooze into his bloodstream. Fumbling with the keypad, he had to make corrections and then write the return message over again to say that their text had been received.

Nils Hammer was standing in the doorway, chewing a baguette, when he turned around.

'Is John Bantam back in Norway?' he asked, taking another bite.

Wisting stood lamely with the encrypted phone in his hand. The question slammed into his train of thought.

Hammer finished chewing. 'Bantam, from the FBI,' he said. 'You know, Line . . .'

Wisting could only nod his head. John Bantam was Amalie's father. Seven years earlier, he had been in Larvik when the police in Norway had stumbled upon a lead concerning a wanted American serial killer. Line had covered the story for the *Verdens Gang* newspaper and struck up a relationship with the special agent from the States. Before she knew she was pregnant, he had returned to the USA.

His job made it impossible for him to establish a family in Norway. For a while Wisting had been afraid Line would follow him to Washington, but she and John Bantam had agreed that what had happened between them was not enough to build a long-term relationship. John Bantam had become a distant part of Amalie's life. Line had not had any contact with him for a long time, but when Amalie had grown old enough to ask questions, she had learned about him and he and Line had resumed contact. Amalie's father was not a subject Line liked to discuss, but Wisting understood she had sent him drawings and photographs and that they occasionally chatted online. He should have realized she would confide in him what had happened.

'I've hardly spoken to Line—' Wisting said.

'I think I bumped into him at the Circle K petrol station,' Hammer went on. 'He came out of the toilet and disappeared out to a hire car, talking into a mobile phone with his strong American accent.'

Wisting slipped the encrypted phone back into his pocket.

'I can't be sure it was him,' Hammer said. 'After all, it's been seven years since he was here last, but it looked very like him.' He took another bite of his baguette.

Wisting was lost for words. 'I need to go out for a bit,' he excused himself.

'Is something wrong?' Hammer asked. 'You don't look too good.'

Wisting seized on the question. 'I think I've got a temperature,' he lied.

'Is it more than a cold?' Hammer asked.

'I don't know,' Wisting replied, grabbing his jacket. 'I've managed to get a doctor's appointment. Going to take some blood tests. You'll have to assume responsibility here in the meantime.'

Hammer stepped aside, an expression of concern on his face.

'If you need to, you can go home and rest,' he said. 'I can take care of this case.'

Wisting touched his forehead and realized that he actually was warm. 'I might have to do that,' he said. 'I'll see what the doctor says. There's a videoconference with the police in Grenland in an hour.'

'I'll see to that,' Hammer assured him.

Wisting coughed to give the impression he had a sore throat. 'Will you let the others know?' he croaked.

Hammer nodded. Wisting thanked him as he closed the office door.

'You may not be able to get hold of me by phone while I'm at the doctor's,' he pointed out.

Hammer was chewing down the rest of the baguette. 'No worries,' he said.

Wisting descended the stairs to the basement and moved out to the car park. It was 10.52 when he started the car. The call would come in twenty-three minutes. The drive home to Line went smoothly, with no delays, and eleven minutes still remained when he drew up in front of her house.

A silver Skoda was parked in the driveway, a Hertz sticker on the rear window. John Bantam.

His arrival felt both invasive and a relief. They were no longer entirely alone. Besides, John Bantam was an experienced FBI agent, honest and conscientious with a solid background in police work. He had probably been involved in more high-pressure cases than Wisting and would be able to contribute his expertise and knowledge. At the same time, it meant that Wisting had to relinquish control. With more people involved, the danger of something going wrong would multiply.

They were seated at the kitchen table, Bantam with his back to the door, where Wisting usually sat.

They both stood up, and Bantam turned to face him. Anxiety weighed upon him and clouded his face like a shadow.

Wisting put a finger to his lips before moving to the microwave to stash the phone.

'They're calling in ten minutes,' he said.

Line and Bantam followed him into the living room. He could see that Line had been crying.

'I phoned John,' she said.

'You shouldn't have parked in front of the house,' Wisting told him. 'Everything could fall apart if they find out we've involved anyone else.'

Bantam made no protest. 'I'll move the car,' he said. His voice was thick with emotion, aware as he was of the seriousness of the situation.

Wisting glanced at his watch and answered with only a nod.

Bantam headed for the door.

'Wait,' Wisting said.

Bantam turned around and grasped the hand Wisting had extended. 'It's good to have you here, John.'

'Thanks.'

John Bantam left the room. Line perched on the edge of the settee. 'I was at a loss about what to do,' she said apologetically. 'I needed someone to talk to but didn't imagine for a second that he would come.'

'How much does he know?' Wisting asked.

'He arrived just half an hour before you,' Line explained. 'Direct from the airport. I've told him about the paintings, about everything.'

'What did he say?'

'He seemed relieved, said he thought that could solve everything,' Line replied. 'He was most concerned about how the handover would happen and what the kidnappers wanted.'

Wisting checked the time again. They would soon receive a message.

They heard the door open as John Bantam returned. 'Three houses down,' he said, using his head to indicate the direction in which he had parked the car.

'Good,' Wisting answered.

'Have you examined the phone?' Bantam asked.

Wisting shook his head. 'It's encrypted,' he replied.

'You haven't looked at the SIM card?'

'I haven't been willing to risk anything,' Wisting explained. 'In the Swedish cases, a Dutch pay-as-you-go card was used. They've had experts trying to trace the calls for six months but haven't got anywhere with it.'

Line looked at Bantam. 'Have you come across anything like this before?' she asked. 'Is it possible to trace it?'

'That depends on the operating system,' Bantam answered. 'The CIA have managed to crack a few units, but the most advanced ones are totally resistant. Anyway, I don't have access to that kind of equipment.'

Bantam continued to bombard them with questions about the investigation and the ongoing work at the police station. Wisting brought them both up to speed on the burnt-out van and the apparent deadlock in the negotiations with Niklas Kranz.

Then the phone rang.

52

The phone rang four times before Wisting picked up. The other two had taken up position at the kitchen table. Bantam switched on a mini-recorder and placed it in front of him.

'*We will accept the offer,*' the voice said.

Line gasped and her hand flew to her face.

Wisting leaned over the phone. 'I'm pleased we've reached an agreement,' he said.

'*The handover time will be thirteen hundred hours, and the coordinates will be sent thirty minutes in advance. Come alone.*'

'How—' Wisting wanted to ask how the actual exchange would take place but was interrupted by a replay of the instruction.

'*The handover time will be thirteen hundred hours, and the coordinates will be sent thirty minutes in advance. Come alone,*' the voice repeated.

Then the connection was severed.

The phone lay on the table. It was 11.31. The handover was only an hour and a half away. Wisting had not anticipated this happening until after dark.

He returned the phone to the microwave. The others had gone into the living room.

'One o'clock,' he said, looking at them. It seemed almost too easy.

'Do you have any guarantee they'll fulfil their side of the deal?' Bantam asked, as if reading Wisting's mind.

'There are no guarantees,' Wisting admitted. 'Only hope.'

He turned to face Line. 'They probably won't have Amalie

with them,' he said. 'They'll want to escape first with the paintings secured before they deliver her. In the best-case scenario, we'll be informed of a location to pick her up.'

'Best-case scenario?' Line reiterated.

'The daughter in the Malmgren case was found at the roadside,' Wisting explained.

Line's eyes were shining, brimming with tears, so Wisting dropped the details. It had been seven hours before she was found, drugged and covered in caustic burns from being sprayed with hydrogen peroxide by the kidnappers to destroy any biological evidence.

John Bantam cast a glance at the kitchen. 'We should prepare ourselves as best we can for the situation,' he said in an undertone.

'How can we do that?' Line asked.

'The handover is a meeting point,' he said. 'The kidnappers have to show themselves. That may be the closest we get to them. We should consider the possibility of tracking them.'

Line shook her head emphatically. 'We can't take any risks,' she said. 'We have to do exactly as they say.'

Bantam ran his hand over his mouth and chin, as if reluctant to say more. 'They already have several human lives on their conscience,' he said. 'Both Amalie and Nanette Kranz are eyewitnesses who can lead us directly to them. We run the risk of never hearing anything further from them if we just let them leave with the paintings.'

'What are our options?' Wisting asked.

'Where do you have the paintings?'

'In my car.' Wisting moved to the door. 'What's your thinking?'

'Maybe we can attach some kind of tracker to them.'

'I'll get them.'

Wisting went outside. The wind had brought squalls of rain that slanted towards him, soaking him to the skin and plastering his shirt to his chest.

A car made its way down the street. He waited until it had rounded the corner before taking the paintings from the back seat. The rain made dark stains on the brown cardboard tubes.

The actual paintings could not have trackers attached, but the cylinders they were stored in could be used. The problem was that they had neither time nor the necessary equipment.

He rushed inside again and placed the cardboard tubes on the settee. Line had produced a pair of washing-up gloves and Bantam pulled them on. He picked up one of the cylinders, turning it this way and that before removing the plastic lid from one end.

'Do you have any gear with you?' Wisting asked.

'Not really,' Bantam replied.

He extracted one of the paintings and placed it on the floor, where it partially unrolled. The girl with the sunhat and the red silk ribbon.

Bantam was more interested in the tube that had contained it. The stiff cardboard was almost one centimetre thick and the opening around the size of a clenched fist. He held it up and peered inside before inserting his hand. The rim reached to the middle of his forearm. He withdrew it and set aside the cylinder.

'I have this,' he said, unfastening his wristwatch, a black sports type with a rubber strap and flat dial. 'It has built-in GPS, and I can use a phone app to follow it.'

Wisting was doubtful. To enable any kind of tracking, they would have to use something smaller.

Bantam unhooked the strap and stood holding the watch face in the palm of his hand. 'We can tape it securely inside the tube,' he said. 'The painting can be pushed in and out without it being noticed.'

'Can't they pick up the signals?' Line asked.

'If they have the right equipment,' Bantam answered. 'But I think they'll fulfil their part of the bargain even if they find it. They'll know it's an amateurish attempt, not something the police are involved in.'

Wisting saw that Line was unhappy with the suggestion. 'It's risky all the same,' she objected.

'They won't want to hold the hostages any longer than necessary,' Bantam said. 'It doesn't benefit them to inflict any injury on them either.'

'Dad, what do you think?' Line asked.

Wisting took the watch from Bantam's hand. It did not weigh much, as most of it was made of plastic. Including the case.

'How long will the battery last?'

Bantam checked his phone. 'Almost sixteen hours,' he replied.

'Let's see how it looks,' Wisting said, turning to his daughter. 'Do you have sticky tape?'

She went out to the hallway and returned with a broad roll of tape and a small carpet knife. 'We can try to carve a notch in the cardboard,' she said, 'so that it won't be so lumpy.'

Bantam agreed this was a good idea.

As the one with the slimmest arms, Line was to undertake the task. She broke off the knife blade and sat with the cardboard tube in her lap.

'Try to make it as far inside as possible,' Wisting told her.

Line peered into the cylinder, mainly working blind, and scraped off small slivers of cardboard. Laboriously, she shaved off several layers.

'Let's try that,' she said after a while.

Wisting handed her the watch. It was nearly noon by now. At the police station, Hammer and the others would soon receive an update from the investigators in Grenland and discover what position Niklas Kranz had adopted.

Line pushed the watch inside the tube. It dropped into the groove she had fashioned.

Bantam tore off a strip of tape and handed it to her. She managed to coax it down into the cylinder, securing the watch and smoothing out the tape.

Wisting took the tube from her once she had finished. He could spot the unevenness, but the result was better than expected.

'We can make it less obvious,' Line said. 'Camouflage it, in a sense.'

'How do we do that?'

'Tape on something else,' Line suggested.

She disappeared into the hallway again and this time returned with a plastic container filled with screws and nails.

'We can attach a few nails inside each opening,' she said. 'If they start examining them, they'll think they're part of the packaging.'

Wisting nodded in agreement. Line vanished again and returned with a roll of grey paper. She cut off a suitable length, picked out some panel pins and wrapped them in the paper. Then she taped the package a few centimetres inside the tube. It looked no different from the watch that was attached further inside.

However, Line was not yet totally satisfied. 'The tape looks too new,' she said.

She fetched sandpaper from a store cupboard in the basement and rubbed it carefully over the lengths of tape, but still was not entirely happy with the result. She brought out the vacuum cleaner, took out the bag and tore it open. Then she rubbed the dust over the tape and around the rim of the cylinder.

'That'll do the trick,' Bantam said.

They prepared the other two cylinders in the same way. Wisting could see that the task ignited enthusiasm in Line and her eyes had taken on an eager glint.

'Are you happy with that?' Wisting asked.

His daughter nodded. She rolled up the last painting, threaded it into the tube and snapped the lid on the end. 'What time is it?' she asked.

Time had passed while they had been busy. Only a quarter of an hour now remained until the instructions about the handover location.

53

The message was prompt. At 12.30 on the dot, the display lit up with a series of numbers, running over two lines.

'The coordinates,' Wisting commented.

Line flipped open her laptop and turned the screen around.

Bantam gave them both a quizzical look.

'It's just outside town,' Line said. 'Ten minutes from here.'

Wisting wrote back to say the message had been received before placing the encrypted phone out of earshot and returning to the computer.

The handover location was a public transport hub, established at the time the new motorway was built. Both local buses and express buses from Oslo en route to Grenland stopped there. In addition there was a vast car park for commuters. From here, the road network extended in all directions, and it would be difficult to cover them all with the intention of locating vehicles to follow the getaway car. Also, it was an exposed spot, with no buildings or surveillance cameras. The location seemed carefully chosen, perhaps originally with the idea of using it for the handover of gold from Niklas Kranz.

'They'll most likely arrive in a black Audi,' Wisting said, telling them about the car stolen from the industrial area where he and Line had searched for Amalie.

'Registration number?' Bantam asked.

'Probably stolen plates,' was Wisting's response.

Line pointed out a residential area on the map. 'We could wait somewhere here,' she suggested, making eye contact with Bantam.

Wisting nodded. As the crow flies, the distance was six to seven hundred metres from the handover location. A safe distance, but also close enough if intervention became necessary.

All of a sudden, time dragged. They were thinking aloud and picturing how the meeting and the handover should be conducted. Bantam introduced a fresh possibility: 'There are three paintings . . .' he began. 'We could hold back one of them until they've freed Amalie. As a guarantee that she's left unharmed and to speed up her release. They'll still have the upper hand, with one hostage remaining.'

Wisting understood his train of thought. This was the main principle in all hostage negotiations. Demand something in return. Gain a little for giving a little. But he saw from Line's face that this suggestion complicated things for her. Wisting was not comfortable with the idea either. There were only a few minutes until it would be time to leave. Changing plan and arrangements at the last minute was seldom a good idea and would involve a heightened risk for Amalie.

'That's a possibility,' he said.

'Can't we just do as they ask?' Line said.

'We haven't discussed terms with them,' Wisting pointed out. 'Just received a message about the handover spot, with no further instructions.'

'It wouldn't hurt to make the suggestion,' Bantam said. 'Just to hear how they react.'

Without arriving at any decision, it was left up to Wisting the next time the kidnappers made contact.

'We need to go,' Line said.

Wisting tucked the three cardboard tubes under his arm. The cylinder with the sports watch was marked with a nick in the cardboard.

The torrential rain was cold and remorseless, leaving puddles in front of the house and rivers gushing down the street.

The car was unlocked. He put the paintings on the back seat and covered them with the blanket before settling behind the wheel. The radio blared as soon as he started the engine. A song heavy with bass notes and drums. Wisting switched it off and glanced in the mirror. Line and Bantam had agreed to wait a couple of minutes before following in the hire car. They planned to rendezvous and wait together until the appointed time.

On the main road, he swung out behind a lorry and followed closely behind. Its rear wheels flung dirty rainwater on to his windscreen.

He dropped back a little and looked in the mirror again. In the heavy rain it was difficult to see if anyone was following him. He dismissed the thought as paranoid. There was no reason for the kidnappers to be on his tail. On arrival in the area Line had pointed out on the map, he nevertheless drove around the block several times to ensure no one was behind him.

He stopped beside a group of collection containers for used clothes. Line and Bantam drove up and transferred to his car to make final preparations. Line wedged her father's phone between the back and headrest of the passenger seat and rang her own phone to set up a video call, so that she and Bantam could watch and listen as the situation progressed. She had stuck a fresh strip of tape over the encrypted phone's microphone, but also given Wisting her wireless ear buds to be completely certain that the kidnappers could not listen in on them.

'Seven minutes to go,' Bantam said.

Wisting nodded. Line gave him a hug before leaving the car and slamming the door shut. The rain plastered her hair to her head and streamed down her face.

Two children in rainwear, with school satchels on their backs, crossed the street. Wisting waited until they reached the opposite kerb before driving off. He manoeuvred out of the residential area on to Brunlanesveien and down to Farriseidet.

'The watch is working.' Line spoke into his ear, the code phrase to verify that they were tracking the movements of the paintings.

A bus drove out from one of the bus stops just as Wisting turned in. It moved to the left and continued in the direction of Oslo.

At the car park, there were rows of cars, and Wisting drove slowly along the ranks to capture all the number plates on the film Line was recording.

All the vehicles were empty, and the same applied to the bus shelters.

'No one here,' he said into the ether.

'What about the blue delivery van?' Line asked.

Wisting drove round again. At the beginning of one row, an old Volkswagen Caddy was parked, with rusty wheel rims and rear mudguards. It had a sliding door on the right-hand side. The cargo space had no windows. Inside the windscreen, a toll chip was attached, and an air freshener dangled from the mirror, but apart from that there was nothing significant to note.

From where he sat, Wisting had no chance of checking the registration number.

He drove to the end of the car park and reversed the car into one of the empty spaces but rested his hands on the steering wheel.

It was 12.56.

His breathing was ragged.

He had no clear picture in his mind's eye of what was about to happen, but probably he would receive a message telling him to leave the paintings and depart.

A minute passed by. Wisting was watching every car that drove past up on the main road.

'Do you see anything?' Line asked in his ear.

Wisting was about to say no when a grey estate car turned off the main road. 'There's a car approaching,' he said.

'We see it,' Line told him.

There was one solitary person in the vehicle. Rain and light on the windscreen made it impossible to make out anything more.

The car stopped, idling, with the windscreen wipers streaking across the glass.

Wisting looked down at the encrypted phone on the seat beside him. He fired it up to check whether he had missed a message, but there were no texts.

The onscreen clock changed from 12.58 to 12.59.

'What's he doing?' Line asked.

'He's just sitting there,' Wisting replied.

No one else in sight.

Another bus drove along, slipping slowly into the terminal and stopping in front of one of the shelters. Both doors slid open. Two women emerged from the rear and the driver came out to open one of the luggage holds.

The driver's door on the waiting estate car swung open. A young man stepped out to meet the younger woman. He took her bag and gave her a brief hug before they both darted through the rain. The other passenger was handed her case and trundled it across to one of the parked cars. The bus drove on. The young couple moved out immediately behind it. The other woman put her case on the back seat of her car and drove off.

It was now 13.01.

Wisting picked up the phone and keyed in a message: *I'm in position.*

No answer came.

Line and Bantam were deep in discussion in the other car. Bantam felt there was no reason to be worried, that the kidnappers were merely waiting to show themselves, that they were probably watching from a distance to make sure Wisting was on his own.

Another minute ticked past.

Wisting shifted restlessly, peering out through the windows in every direction. A steady stream of cars passed on the road above. In front of him, a seagull landed on the asphalt, using its beak to peck at some rubbish before flapping its wings and flying off again.

The phone buzzed. His own this time.

He leaned forward to focus on the screen beside the headrest. Nils Hammer. This most likely meant there had been some kind of development in the case: something had happened. But it would have to wait.

Hammer gave up after six rings, and the video image of Line and John filled the screen again.

It was now five past one. Wisting considered sending another message, but then a text ticked in: *Change of location. E18, northbound lane. Exit 44 in seven minutes.*

Wisting read it aloud as he set off in the car. 'They've changed the handover spot,' he said.

'That's not surprising,' Bantam said. 'A sudden shift will reveal whether you've planned an ambush or aren't alone.'

'Where is exit 44?' Line asked.

Wisting was unsure. 'It can't be far away,' he said. 'I've only got seven minutes.'

He pulled out on to the slip road leading to the E18, checking the mirror to see if anyone was following him. All he could see through the rain was blurred headlights.

'We're moving slowly in the same direction,' Bantam told him.

Wisting did not answer. He moved out behind a lorry and hung there for a few minutes until the left lane was free and he was able to overtake.

He took two minutes to drive through the motorway tunnel under Bøkeskogen. On the opposite side, exit 45 was flagged up. For a moment he was afraid he had come the wrong way, but then it dawned on him that the exits were numbered in descending order towards Oslo.

'The next one,' he said aloud as he passed.

The rain had pooled in the tyre tracks on the road. His speed made the car shake on the asphalt surface.

After a few kilometres, another sign appeared. Exit 44. He slowed down and turned off.

'I'm here,' he said.

'We see that,' Line reminded him.

The exit road ended at a roundabout. Wisting drove slowly on to it, circled three quarters of the way round and crossed the bridge leading to the roundabout on the other side of the motorway. Then he drove back and manoeuvred on to the hard shoulder, leaving him parked with his bonnet facing the intersection.

It was now 13.12. The message about the location change had been received at 13.05. He had taken exactly seven minutes.

'There's nobody here,' he said.

'No new message?' Line asked.

'No.'

He tapped in another message: *There now.*

Several cars drove by in both directions. There were banks of earth with wildlife fences on either side. On the opposite section of the motorway, he could see a petrol station. A number of cars were parked facing him, but if the kidnappers were there, they would have exposed themselves to the cameras at the station.

'We're driving past,' Line said in his ear. 'We'll turn at the next exit.'

At that moment, the mobile vibrated in his hand. *Postponed*, was all it said.

Wisting swore.

'What is it?' Line asked.

'They've put it off,' Wisting told her.

'That could have been a test,' Bantam said. 'To make them feel secure about the situation.'

'We've done everything they asked,' Wisting said. 'There's no reason for them to call it off.'

'They may want to wait until dark to go ahead, all the same,' Bantam said.

'Can you phone them?' Line asked.

'I can try,' Wisting replied.

He located the call log and tried to ring the combination of numbers and letters on which he had been contacted. There was a lengthy silence before a series of rhythmical tones were heard, indicating he could not get through.

Line sighed. Wisting keyed in a message: *How long?*

The answer took a while. *Undecided*, was the response that finally came.

'What do we do now?' Line asked.

'We'll just have to wait,' Wisting replied.

His own phone buzzed again. He released it from its temporary anchor below the headrest and balanced it on his knee. On the screen he could see Line and John Bantam, heads together in the front seats of the hire car, both peering into the camera lens.

'It's Hammer again,' he said. 'I'll have to take it.'

He put Line on hold and answered.

'Sorry to disturb you,' Hammer began. 'But there's been a development you should know about. A suspicious death. We think it may be one of ours.'

Wisting struggled to understand. 'What do you mean by "one of ours"?'

'Dogan Bulut or Elton Khan,' Hammer answered. 'At least, it's a dark-skinned male. The message came in just over an hour ago. The location is a small lake beside the inland road leading to Porsgrunn, less than a kilometre from the spot where the burnt-out van was found. He's probably been there since last night.'

Wisting checked his mirrors before pulling out on to the road. 'Cause of death?' he asked.

'The circumstances are unclear,' Hammer replied. 'According to the caller, his face has been destroyed.'

'Destroyed?' Wisting repeated.

'That was what he said,' Hammer answered. 'I don't know any more than that. The technicians have just arrived but haven't reported back as yet.'

The rain was pummelling the windscreen. Wisting ramped up the wiper speed as he moved out into the stream of southbound traffic.

'I'm on my way there,' he said, his grip tight on the steering wheel. 'Then I'm coming in.'

54

A string of cars was parked along the narrow road. Wisting drove up behind the last of these. Other traffic was being directed past.

The water level in the small lake was unusually high, submerging the tree trunks that lined the shore. Twenty more centimetres and the road would have flooded.

The stretch of road was blocked off, police crime scene tape twisting in the wind. Wisting stood for a moment to take in the scene. Three white-clad forensics technicians were huddled under a tent with open walls, and a fourth was crouched at the water's edge, picking at the ground. A rowing boat with oars lay in the reeds nearby and directly opposite a white tarpaulin was spread on the ground, the contours of a body outlined beneath it.

Maren Dokken and Espen Mortensen sat in the front seats of a car, both turning halfway round to face a man in the back seat who was pointing and explaining something. Mortensen stepped out when he caught sight of Wisting.

'The man who found him,' Mortensen said with a nod in the direction of the car. 'First of all he drove past sometime around 9 a.m. and saw something floating on the lake. When he drove by again at noon, it had drifted closer to shore, and he realized it must be a human body, so he took one of the boats from the north end and rowed out.'

They moved into the shelter of the tent. The rain was drumming on the roof.

'I was told the face had been destroyed,' Wisting said.

'Severe burns,' Mortensen explained.

Wisting accompanied one of the other technicians to the tarpaulin. They held one corner each and lifted it.

The corpse lay on its back, arms drawn up to the chest. The face was horribly disfigured by fire, covered in blisters and black, scorched folds of skin. The lips had contracted into tight strips beneath two gaping nostrils. Strands of hair hung in loose tendrils.

Wisting covered his nose and mouth with his forearm to shield himself from the stink of burnt human flesh.

The man must have been wearing a jacket made of highly flammable material. Only a few twisted rags remained. Part of the stomach had been exposed and it was swollen, with a bluish tinge.

The fabric of the black gloves on his hands had blistered badly, but his trousers and legs were unscathed. His feet were encased in lace-up leather boots.

Wisting gave the technician a nod to signal that he had seen enough. They gently replaced the tarpaulin before heading back to the tent to shelter from the rain.

'What do you think, Espen?' Wisting asked.

'I expect it's connected to what happened last night,' Mortensen replied. 'The torched van was found on a side road, just a few hundred metres north of here.'

He pointed out the direction.

'Something went wrong,' he continued. 'One of them has spilled flammable liquid on himself, been set on fire and badly burned by the flames. The others have taken him in their vehicle and stopped here by the lake to cool him down.'

A car door slammed. Maren Dokken joined them in the tent.

'When can we get an ID on him?' she asked, her gaze fixed on the tarpaulin at the waterside.

'If it's urgent, we can make an attempt now,' Mortensen replied. 'Try to obtain a fingerprint.'

He conferred with one of the other technicians and they settled on who would do this before venturing out into the rain again. Maren helped by holding the tarpaulin aloft. One of the white-suited technicians, equipped with mask and gloves, raised the cadaver's stiff right arm and jiggled a pair of guillotine scissors in under the glove. Then he made an incision along the palm and across to one of the fingertips. The fabric was easy to hack through, but it was no easy task to remove the glove from the hand. He had to snip repeatedly before it detached, leaving shreds hanging from the dark skin.

Mortensen was standing by with a mobile fingerprint reader. He chose the index finger, pressing it against the glass surface and activating the scanner. A red light slid back and forth.

The result appeared on a small screen. 'Dogan Bulut,' he announced.

No one spoke. A gust of wind caught the tarpaulin and Maren Dokken had to step back to regain her balance.

The technician slipped a plastic bag over the bare hand.

'He has third-degree burns on his face, but those injuries were not fatal in themselves,' Mortensen said before the tarpaulin was drawn over the body again. 'He might even have been conscious.'

'What are you trying to tell me?' Wisting asked.

Mortensen began to pack up his equipment. 'It would not surprise me if they find water in his lungs during the post-mortem,' he replied.

'Drowning?'

Mortensen shrugged. 'What else could they do with him?' he asked. 'He was wanted in connection with murder. They couldn't drive him to a doctor or a hospital. The simplest thing would be to leave him behind.'

'To die?' Maren Dokken asked.

A timber lorry drove past on the road. Mortensen moved his head slowly from side to side.

'I think they satisfied themselves that he was dead before they left,' he said. 'Dogan Bulut is the only one we can pin anything on. Our investigation stops at him. He's the link to the others. If he can't talk, then we have nothing.'

Wisting wiped the rain from his face. He had nothing to add to Mortensen's comments. This hypothesis was entirely in tune with the cynicism they had already witnessed.

It seemed the others were waiting for him to say something. They were accustomed to seeing him display both initiative and resolve, refusing to allow himself to be distracted in complex and demanding situations.

'Have you found any forensic evidence?' he asked.

'Not so far,' Mortensen said. 'Any footprints and tyre tracks in the gravel have been washed away by the rain. In theory, we may find something on his body. If we assume they've had close contact, then there could be transfer of hair or skin particles from the others, but I'm not optimistic. He's been through fire and water.'

'I see,' Wisting replied.

He was unsure what impact Dogan Bulut's death would have on the current situation. If anything, it should make the kidnappers more intent on winding up the whole business.

'They're now one less,' Maren commented. 'Maybe that

will make it easier for them to accept a reduced offer. Fewer of them to share out the proceeds.'

Mortensen glanced at his watch. 'We might well know in a few hours,' he said. 'The deadline is five o'clock, and they're going to phone again.'

Maren addressed herself to Wisting: 'Can you give me a lift again?'

She turned to Mortensen: 'I expect you'll be here for a while yet?'

The forensics technician nodded.

Wisting still had the paintings on the rear seat of his car but could not think of an excuse to refuse Maren a lift into town.

'Of course,' was all he said.

A photographer had turned up at the barrier, with one camera slung over his shoulder and another in use. He snapped a few pictures of Wisting as he took off his jacket and threw it down on the back seat.

'We're roughly in the centre of Hammer's circle,' Maren commented as he started the ignition.

Wisting turned the steering wheel and executed a U-turn on the road. He was at a loss for something to say and merely looked at her. The eagerness in her eyes made his chest contract again. Withholding information from her made him feel like a fraud. Maren was one of the people who would stand by him when this was all over and done with. She would understand his lies and why he had gone behind everyone's back, but at the same time she would feel betrayed. Nothing would be the same afterwards.

Maren continued to share her thoughts on the case. She was preoccupied with what would happen if Niklas Kranz turned down all their demands.

'In a way, everything will be easier for us,' she said. 'We can go public with the whole case and declare Gillis Haack and Elton Khan to be wanted men.'

Wisting wished he could say he agreed, but instead only cleared his throat in embarrassment. Publicizing their names would be the next step for the officers in charge of the case in Grenland, but that would be the worst thing that could happen. It would apply pressure to the surviving kidnappers, making them desperate and reckless.

'We ought to wait until Nanette Kranz has been found, one way or the other,' he said.

'That could be too late,' Maren objected. 'It's in the hours after their demand has been rejected that we have the best chance of locating them and finding Nanette alive.'

'The problem is that we don't have anything to link them to the case,' Wisting told her. 'It's as Mortensen said: everything stops at Dogan Bulut. We don't have any legal basis for issuing a public wanted notice.'

'But the Swedes have connected them to Dogan Bulut,' Maren said.

'They have no proof, only rumours from snitches who will never stand up in court and say what they've heard.'

Strictly speaking, he was arguing against his better judgement. An open investigation would be easier to handle, and declaring Gillis Haack and Elton Khan wanted men would be a crucial part of that. The most interesting aspect to emerge from a discussion about further investigation would be that it could draw out and unmask the Swedish traitor. He or she would be the only one to support his argument.

They drove into the back yard at the police station.

'How are you feeling?' Maren asked. 'Hammer said you'd been at the doctor's. You look a bit . . . worn out.'

'I'm fine,' he replied, stopping at the staff entrance. 'I have to leave again, need to call in at the pharmacy and pick up some medicine.'

Maren jumped out of the car and Wisting drove on, home to Line.

55

There was something monotonous about the rain. Grey, sad and miserable, like the rest of his existence.

Wisting looked at the dashboard clock: 14.53.

He counted the hours since Amalie had been taken – almost thirty-four. The situation was exhausting, but he was not worn out in the usual way. It was not due to lack of sleep or nourishment, but to being prisoner of his own inadequacy.

He drove up in front of Line's house. The bike Amalie had been given last summer lay beneath one of the old fruit trees in the garden. Dead leaves had swirled up and collected beside it in a heap.

The house seemed empty when he walked in.

'Line?'

She called out a reply from the basement, where she had her workstation. Wisting stowed the encrypted phone in the microwave and went down to her. Line got to her feet, but Bantam remained seated, a laptop on his knee.

'Have you heard anything more from them?' Line demanded.

Wisting shook his head and explained in English about Dogan Bulut.

'This can't be why they postponed things, though,' Line argued. 'That happened last night.'

'It's not easy to know anything,' Wisting said. 'They're going to contact Niklas Kranz again in two hours. That will be critical for what's to happen afterwards.'

He took one pace forward to peer at her computer screen. A document with scattered text and several photos was displayed. It was the first time she had applied herself to anything since Amalie's abduction.

'What are you working on?' he asked.

'I'm trying to gather information on the Swedish investigators,' Line told him.

Ann-Mari Walin was a lawyer, not an investigator, but Wisting did not bother correcting her.

'I've had some help from a Swedish journalist I've worked with before. Micke Larson. There's some information in text archives and internal records.'

'And?' Wisting prompted.

'Not much to learn from it, really,' Line replied. 'Ralf Falk has no children of his own, but he lives with a woman who has an eight-year-old daughter from a previous relationship.'

'A bonus daughter,' Wisting commented. 'Who's the real father?'

'I don't know, but his partner also works in the police.'

Line flopped down into her chair and scrolled up to a picture of Ann-Mari Walin, taken at a press conference.

'Walin has two sons and one grandchild aged five,' she went on. 'A boy called Roy. Her daughter-in-law posted a few photos of him from a holiday in Spain three weeks ago, and she also published photos of herself and some friends from a birthday party on Friday. Everything looked normal.'

She continued to scroll.

'Serner is married and has a daughter who's nine, Isabelle,' she pressed on. 'He was married once before, but had no children then.'

'Have you found out anything more about the daughter?' Wisting asked.

'No, but Micke owes me a favour. I can get him to check, pay a visit to the family home in Stockholm.'

'Have you said anything about why you're interested?'

Line shook her head. 'He won't ask any questions. Will I ask him to do it?'

Wisting felt doubtful. He was unaccustomed to being indecisive, but the situation demanded that he weigh up risk versus gain differently from the norm. He did not like the idea of involving an outsider, but on the other hand he failed to see how it could hurt.

'If he can be discreet,' he replied.

They had spoken in English to avoid excluding John Bantam. He had not taken part in the conversation but listened while writing on his laptop.

'John might be able to find out something,' Line said. 'He has a friend in the CIA.'

Wisting glanced at the FBI agent.

'It's worth a try,' Bantam said. 'The CIA has access to a system that keeps track of card transactions.'

'In Norway?' Wisting asked.

'In the entire world,' Bantam answered. 'Mastercard, Visa, Amex . . . they're American companies operating internationally.'

'That presumes they don't just deal in cash but also use a credit card,' Line said. She and Bantam had obviously discussed this. 'One that must be in the name of a completely different person,' she added.

'We know Gillis Haack and Elton Khan have been in Turkey,' Bantam pointed out. 'They travelled from Ankara to Amsterdam and probably on by car through Germany and Denmark prior to Norway. Maybe they were also in Sweden. What we're looking for is a credit card that was used in two or more of these countries at the time we know Gillis Haack and Elton Khan were there. It's like looking for a needle in a haystack, without being sure it even actually exists, but the CIA have been successful with similar cross-matching in Europe before now. There's less flow of cash here than in the States. Certain goods and services are impossible to buy without a credit card. Air travel, for instance.'

'What do we learn from it if we find a card?' Wisting asked. 'Can we find out where it was last used?'

'Yes,' Bantam answered. 'It could help us narrow the circle, but it might also give us other opportunities too. We could receive an alert in real time whenever the card is next used.'

Wisting looked down at the laptop on Bantam's knee. It felt surreal for the CIA to play a role in the case and for sweet little Amalie to be involved in anything like this.

'When will you have a response?' he asked.

'It might take hours or even days,' Bantam replied. 'It depends entirely on how much data is produced in the automatic searches. After that, it's a matter of organizing it all, and it's far from certain that our case will receive priority.'

'Keep me posted,' Wisting requested. He checked the time and headed for the stairs. 'I'm going back to the police station to find out what's going on there.'

He rested his hand for a second on the banister before leaving. It felt as if they were closing in on something now, that this would soon be over.

56

Inside the police station, there was an expectant mood that Wisting recognized. A compressed, charged atmosphere that usually spread among the investigators when they were all aware of entering a crucial period.

Hammer's voice reached out into the corridor. Wisting stood in the doorway, mainly to let him know that he was back.

'Wait,' Hammer said into his phone. 'Wisting's here. I'll put you on loudspeaker.' He set the phone down on the desk. 'It's Mortensen,' he explained.

Taking one step into the room, Wisting thrust his hand in his pocket and fumbled to check the tape was secure on the encrypted phone.

'It's to do with Dogan Bulut,' Mortensen said. 'The autopsy won't be until tomorrow morning, so we decided to conduct a superficial examination here at the hospital before he's sent on. Going through his pockets and suchlike to try to come up with something that would tell us about their hideout or his accomplices.'

'Did you find anything?' Hammer asked.

'The only definitive thing was a snuff box in his right trouser pocket, but we found something interesting when we took off his boots.'

'What was that?'

'He was wearing a pair of knitted woollen socks,' Mortensen told them. 'In the threads of the left sock, we found a long, dark strand of hair, slightly wavy. It measured around thirty centimetres. The length doesn't match any of the other suspects or Nanette Kranz.'

Amalie – the thought struck Wisting like a hammer blow. He felt his pulse reverberate in his neck. Long, stray hairs were always left behind when she had paid a visit. Line sometimes teased him, accusing him of having a woman around when she came across them.

'I've just sent some images by email,' Mortensen added.

Hammer clicked into his inbox and opened the message. Wisting walked forward and inclined his head towards the screen. The sock was mottled grey and seemed mass-produced. It was dirty and showed a few dark stains. The hair had become entangled in the shabby threads of yarn.

'It's fallen off at the root,' Mortensen went on. 'So the follicle is intact. In a few days, we may have a DNA profile.'

In another picture, the hair was extended to its full length on a sheet of grey paper beside a measuring tape.

Hair grew around one centimetre per month, Wisting mused. The hair in the photograph had started to grow when Amalie was five.

'There's reason to believe that whoever the hair belongs to was in the same room where Dogan Bulut was walking around in his stockinged feet,' Mortensen said. 'If we find that person, then he or she could tell us a great deal about where Bulut was and what he'd been up to these past few days.'

Hammer leaned over the phone. 'Any chance of hurrying that DNA analysis along?' he asked.

'We're completing the paperwork and driving the sample in now,' Mortensen answered. 'The lab is familiar with the case we're working on and they're holding people in reserve. They'll start work on it this evening, but these analyses take time. It's unrealistic to imagine we'll get a result before Wednesday morning.'

'We'll put the Swedes on to it in the meantime,' Hammer said. 'They'll have to check who in his orbit has long, wavy hair, both male and female.'

Wisting nodded in acknowledgement, well aware that this work would not take them any closer to a breakthrough.

'What are the dark stains?' he asked, pointing at the computer screen, even though Mortensen could not see him.

'Some kind of synthetic material,' the forensics technician replied. 'We're analysing that too, but it's something he's trodden on. My guess would be drops of oil.'

'What does that suggest?' Hammer asked. 'An industrial location?'

'Or a garage or basement,' Mortensen said.

They discussed the discoveries further and made arrangements for the practical aspects of report writing and document handling before the conversation was wound up.

At half past four the investigators assembled in the spacious conference room for an update on the abduction case.

Hammer was having trouble with the video connection to Grenland.

'Niklas Kranz has asked to speak to a criminal lawyer,' he clarified as he waited for a response from the computer program. 'He called Sigurd Henden this morning.'

Someone in the room gasped when they heard the lawyer's name. Although he was smart and principled, he was a cool customer, not open to pragmatic solutions.

'Henden went to his house and is still there now,' Mortensen added.

The onscreen image flickered before Pia Gusfre's face appeared.

Hammer led the meeting on their side. Wisting sat slumped in the nearest chair.

'I was just explaining that Henden is now involved,' Hammer said.

Pia Gusfre nodded. 'In many ways it's easier to deal with him than with Niklas Kranz,' she said. 'Kranz doesn't always know what he wants and our advice is not necessarily intended to look after his interests.'

'What's the current status?'

'Henden claims his client is faced with an unreasonable ultimatum that's impossible to fulfil,' Gusfre answered. 'So he believes he should respond as all Western governments do: refuse to deal with terrorists. His advice, therefore, is that Kranz should turn down their demands and leave it to the police to solve the case in the best way possible.'

Jan Serner reached across the table. 'Does that mean he wants to renege on his offer of twenty kilos of gold?'

'That's not clear,' Gusfre replied.

'But he has obtained the gold?' Hammer pressed her.

Gusfre nodded. 'Twenty kilos of rolled gold, divided into one hundred and thirty manufactured bars. It was brought to his home before the lawyer arrived on the scene.'

She moved a cup on the table in front of her but did not drink from it.

'They've said they're willing to listen when the kidnappers phone but are prepared to refuse all their demands,' she rounded off.

'We should consider how we're going to handle that,' Josef Helland said. 'What we do next.' The Kripos investigator had mainly remained quiet until then. Now he stretched heavily across the table.

'The question really is what are the kidnappers going

to do,' Hammer said, turning to face the two Swedish investigators.

'That's not so easy to answer,' Serner said. 'But we know how things went in spring when nothing was paid. There was no further contact after their demands were turned down. The woman is still missing and there are no grounds to believe she's still alive.'

'What are our chances of rescuing Nanette Kranz if the negotiations fall through?' Hammer asked.

Pia Gusfre now spoke up. 'We've made it clear to Kranz and his lawyer that if he decides not to pay up, we'll issue a public wanted notice for Gillis Haack and Elton Khan,' she said. 'They've been made to understand that at that moment the suspects will start to remove all evidence, including elimination of the hostage.'

Wisting's eyes strayed to Jan Serner, waiting for him to speak up and make some comment, but he just sat expectantly. Ralf Falk's gaze was fixed on the big screen, his jaw muscles working. Ann-Mari Walin jotted down some notes on a sheet of paper without looking up.

'However, we've instructed Kranz to take part in the next conversation so that we can buy some time before they clock that he's in cahoots with the police,' Gusfre continued. 'The time window is extremely narrow, but hopefully they won't do anything drastic before the missing person notice is issued.'

Wisting glanced at Maren Dokken. He had his counter-arguments ready but was afraid he would not get anywhere with them.

'Let *us* make their names public,' Hammer suggested before Wisting had a chance to speak. 'For murder or conspiracy to murder Mats Beckman and Nina Lundblad. We'll obtain the same response from the public, but without revealing the kidnapping. They may well believe they still have a chance to reach a settlement.'

Wisting felt his muscles and nerve endings tense throughout his body. The instructions from the guys who had abducted Amalie had been clear. Mats Beckman's murder must not be investigated.

Josef Helland approved the suggestion. 'That could give us extra room to manoeuvre,' he said.

'Issuing that kind of wanted notice requires charges to be drawn up,' Wisting pointed out, darting a glance at the police prosecutor. 'We have no proof that Gillis Haack and Elton Khan are involved.'

'We have nothing to link them to the kidnapping either,' Helland said, 'but criminal procedures are of secondary consideration. Of prime importance is saving Nanette Kranz's life.'

'We publicized Dogan Bulut's name,' Wisting argued. 'That didn't lead us to her.'

Josef Helland threw out his arms in exasperation. 'Do you have a better suggestion?' he spluttered.

Wisting was nonplussed and Christine Thiis intervened. 'There's more reason to issue a notice in connection with Dogan Bulut's death,' she said. 'At least that can be defended in accordance with the Criminal Procedure Act. There's a well-established, direct link between him and the other two.'

Josef Helland shrugged, as if it were all the same to him.

'It would have the same effect in the media,' Nils Hammer pointed out. 'Maybe even greater. The circumstances are more unusual.'

'Do we have time to get that done?' Pia Gusfre asked.

'We'll set up a press conference now,' Hammer said. He shot a glance at Wisting but saw he was less than enthusiastic.

'I can draft a proposal,' Helland said, flipping his laptop open.

Christine Thiis pushed back her chair. 'I'll clear it with the boss,' she said.

Wisting wanted to leave the room with her but hung back. He felt that all eyes were on him. That he had said something offensive and exposed an ignorance not expected of him. His discomfort meant he could not quite manage to rejoin the conversation around the table.

Hammer led the discussion and gave Jan Serner the floor. The Swedish investigator directed his gaze at the camera above the screen displaying Pia Gusfre's face.

'What preparations have you made in case they do accept the twenty kilos?' he asked.

'Then the case will shift to a different phase,' she answered. 'Most likely, instructions will come in about the place and time of the handover, just like in the Malmgren case. We've prepared Niklas Kranz for that and equipped his car with surveillance and a GPS tracker so that we can follow him from a distance. In addition, we have a surveillance team ready and the helicopter service has been alerted and is on standby.'

'Have you thought of tracking the gold itself?' Serner asked. 'There was some talk of inserting a tracker into one of the gold bars.'

'It proved impossible,' Gusfre replied. 'But a time-activated transmitter has been attached to one of the bags. The idea is to program it to begin transmission one hour after the agreed handover time. If they have signal detectors, they'll have used them before that.'

Serner nodded and made a note of something, as if these were vital details. His questions were entirely relevant, but the information was also crucial for a traitor to elicit.

The discussion moved on with various contributions and developed into an informal chat in which they were all able to air their views, including random thoughts.

The time was fast approaching for fresh contact between Niklas Kranz and the kidnappers. Hammer made preparations to hook up the camera in Kranz's living room to a separate screen. The conversation dwindled and died out.

Wisting folded his hands. He thought he could feel it in his bones: some kind of premonition that what was about to happen would be quite different from what anyone in the room expected.

57

Three men appeared in the picture – one investigator, Niklas Kranz and his lawyer. Kranz sat in a chair with his head bowed. His lawyer sat on the settee, while the police officer stood by his side. The encrypted phone lay on the table in front of them.

Wisting picked up a ballpoint pen and let it slide through his fingers. There were still a few minutes until 5 p.m.

'Do we have sound?' Helland asked.

Grabbing the remote control, Hammer increased the volume until they heard a constant hum.

The investigator on the screen moved halfway out of shot before coming back and clearing his throat.

Hammer turned down the volume again as Kranz looked up and fixed his gaze on his lawyer, Henden.

'I think you'll have to do the talking,' he said. His eyes were swollen and red-rimmed. His lawyer nodded. It seemed to be an option they had already discussed and agreed.

'I'll make myself known and can take over if there's any bargaining to be done or if it gets difficult in any way,' he said.

It looked as if the investigator present was minded to protest, but the lawyer beat him to it: 'These negotiations have gone on for far too long without any progress,' he said. 'The other party must understand that Kranz has sought professional advice. I can't imagine it'll make any difference to the threat level. Anyway, all the conversations I take part in are protected by the duty of confidentiality implicit in my relationship with my client. I'll make that clear to them.'

His tone was arrogant, almost hostile.

The investigator made no comment and simply exchanged glances with his colleague operating the camera.

The unpleasant atmosphere in the room infected the audience. On the smaller screen, Pia Gusfre shifted in her seat. She looked down at a sheaf of papers and seemed concerned on behalf of her investigator colleague.

The ensuing silence grew oppressive. Wisting closed his eyes in an effort to gather his thoughts. The kidnappers must have received the message that Kranz had twenty kilos of gold ready. This was information that had come from Grenland while Wisting was with Line and Bantam, information that the Swedes had also picked up. The handover of the paintings had been postponed in anticipation of this being clarified. They wanted to have their cake and eat it too.

He opened his eyes again and turned them on Jan Serner. The Swedish detective was staring at the big screen with a remarkably tense expression that was difficult to read. Ralf Falk sat with his elbows on the table and his hands clasped in front of his mouth. Quiet and expectant. Ann-Mari Walin hugged a glass of water and alternated between focusing on that and the screen.

Henden wore an oversized watch he glanced at from time to time. Wisting was watching the clock on the wall. One minute past.

'What do we do if they don't get in touch?' Ann-Mari Walin asked. 'Do we have a plan B?'

She received no answer. Yet another minute ticked by before the phone rang.

Wisting leaned forward and watched Henden on the screen do the same. Niklas Kranz gave the others a questioning look and the investigator nodded in response.

The phone rang one more time before Kranz reached forward. He left the phone there but used one hand to steady it as he answered with the other.

'Hello,' he said. 'Niklas Kranz here.'

'*You are listening to a pre-recorded message,*' a computer voice announced. A few clicks were heard before the almost clinically clean background noise was replaced by a constant buzz.

'*Hi, Niklas, it's me. Nanette.*'

Kranz gave a start when he heard his wife speak. The voice sounded anxious. Faint and choked with tears, but at the same time somehow jittery.

'*It's been five days, and I'm still here.*' She cleared her throat. '*It's the fifteenth of October, at 4 p.m. The headline news on the VG website is about a woman who was saved from a flood in Oppland.*'

Hammer turned up the volume. They could hear Nanette Kranz take a deep breath.

'*They're saying that you're refusing to pay up,*' she continued, with a sob. '*Please . . . don't let me die! I . . .*'

The words were lost in convulsive weeping that developed into lengthy, heart-rending moans.

Kranz had his head in his hands. 'Nanette!' he shouted, as if in an attempt to calm her down.

'She can't hear you,' his lawyer told him. 'It's a recording.'

The plaintive sounds changed to distraught gasps. '*They tell me . . .*' Nanette began to speak again but had to struggle for breath before she regained control of her voice.

'*They can accept twenty kilos,*' she managed to say. '*But it has to happen this evening. Please . . .*'

Her voice again broke down into incoherent sobs, and then the recording ended.

Kranz rose to his feet. 'Christ,' he groaned, covering his mouth with his hand.

His lawyer raised his hand towards him to signal for quiet.

'*You have heard a pre-recorded message,*' the computer voice intoned. '*The recording will be made public and shared with the media if you let your wife die.*'

Then the phone line was cut.

Kranz turned away as his lawyer stood up and put his hand on his client's shoulder.

'We're moving towards a solution,' he said. 'They've accepted our offer. It may all be done and dusted sometime this evening.'

Wisting watched as Kranz's shoulders shuddered. The few half-choked words he uttered did not reach him.

Around the conference table, people shifted uncomfortably, but no one said anything.

An abrupt message alert caused Henden to wheel round towards the encrypted phone. Kranz did not appear to have heard it.

Henden glanced at the investigator, who responded with a nod. He picked up the phone and read the message.

'They want to know if we have a deal,' he said.

Niklas Kranz took some time to collect himself. He stood with his eyes shut, breathing through his open mouth.

'It's your decision,' the lawyer said, touching his hand to his shoulder again. 'But this case could damage you far more than the loss of 20 million kroner. Purely from a reputational point of view.'

Kranz shrugged his lawyer's hand away. 'We'll do it,' he said. 'We have a deal.'

Sigurd Henden handed him the phone, but Kranz shook his head. 'You answer,' he said.

Henden keyed in the letters as he repeated the content: *Yes. We have a deal.*

In the silence that followed, Wisting watched the reactions around him. Ann-Mari Walin seemed relieved, as did Serner. Ralf Falk's expression was more strained, as if it was too early or even wrong to think a deal implied any kind of resolution.

Wisting himself had mixed feelings. He had pictured a simpler, quicker resolution of the impasse with the paintings, but now, if nothing else, a major step closer to a conclusion had been taken. At the same time, the stakes had been raised. Nanette Kranz had been awake and conscious. The very fact she had been instructed to read out a message meant she had close contact with the kidnappers. She must have spoken to them, maybe even seen them face to face. That made her a threat.

Nils Hammer put down his pen, having taken a few notes. Maybe some of the same thoughts had occurred to him.

Still no one in the conference room spoke a single word.

Another message alert was heard. The kidnappers had answered. Henden squinted at the phone in his hand.

Get ready, he read aloud. *Instructions will be given at 21.00.*

58

Wisting left the conference room before the others. On the way to his office, he checked the encrypted phone. He no longer dared to walk around without it.

No messages.

Line had tried to ring once on his other phone. He waited until he was back in his office and had shut the door behind him before returning the call.

Outside, it had grown dark, he noticed.

'Any news?' Line asked.

He told her about the most recent development. 'The handover will take place sometime this evening,' he said.

'But you haven't heard anything more?'

'Not yet, but we're getting closer to a resolution.'

Line held back and asked instead: 'Do you think it was wrong of me to phone him?'

Wisting understood she was reluctant to use his name, as she was in his company.

'You mean John?' he asked.

'I'm afraid it'll be too much for Amalie,' Line went on. 'First what she's been through, and then all of a sudden her father is here. I haven't prepared her for any of this. He's a stranger as far as she's concerned.'

'No need to worry about that,' Wisting told her. 'Amalie will need something else to focus on when she comes home, something positive in her life. Then it will be good to have him here. Not only as a diversion for Amalie, but also for you.'

Line seemed somewhat reassured, perhaps mainly because his assumption had been that Amalie would come home safely.

'Can she sleep in bed with me for the first few nights, or would that be the wrong thing to do?' she asked.

'Her room is a crime scene,' Wisting replied. 'She can't spend any time there to begin with. It would be best if you both stay at my place for a few days.'

He heard Line take a few short, stuttering breaths. 'Is that necessary?' she asked. 'Does there have to be an investigation? Interviews and a court case. Does she have to go through all that?'

'We'll take things one at a time,' Wisting answered. 'There's going to be—' The encrypted phone in his pocket vibrated. 'Wait,' he said. 'I've got a message.' He brought out the phone.

'What are they saying?'

Wisting glanced at the door before reading it. 'They're demanding more case documents,' he told her. 'Everything logged up to and including seven o'clock this evening.'

He looked at the clock on the right-hand corner of the display. Just over an hour to go.

'What about Amalie?' Line asked.

'They haven't said anything.'

'Ask them!'

He began to tap in a message, writing that he had to know what was to happen with Amalie, but he grew uncertain about his choice of words and turn of phrase. Using first names was an important aspect of forming relationships in negotiations, but using Amalie's name did not feel right.

Must know what is to happen afterwards. Can't have any more postponements, he wrote.

That was suitably to the point and avoided being overly compliant.

He read it aloud to Line as he pressed the taped microphone on the encrypted phone. She must have had her phone on loudspeaker. This time it was Bantam who answered: 'Good.'

He sent the message. Time passed. The screen on the encrypted phone dimmed.

'Do you have the memory stick there?' Line asked.

'Yes,' Wisting replied, but he felt for it in his pocket all the same.

'Are you coming home to upload it?'

'Yes. Hammer has practically taken charge of things here, but I should be back by nine o'clock. That's when the new instructions about the gold will come.'

The encrypted phone lit up again. *Instructions will follow.*

Wisting sighed. 'We'll just have to wait,' he said.

Behind him, there was a knock at the door. Nils Hammer opened it before Wisting had time to say anything. He waved him in.

'I'll speak to you later,' he said into the phone before hanging up.

Hammer hovered in the doorway. 'The police chief is coming later to be here for the handover,' he said.

Wisting shuffled some papers on his desk and covered the encrypted phone. 'You've kept her up to speed?' he asked.

Hammer nodded. 'Will you be here tonight too?' he asked. 'The whole time?'

'I expect so,' Wisting replied. He touched his forehead

as he cleared his throat. 'But I want you to remain in charge,' he added. 'It'll be Grenland and Pia Gusfre who lead the operation, but you'll have to follow up from this end.'

He stood up and moved to the door, as if planning to leave the room. 'How are things at home?' he asked. 'With Sissel's father?'

Hammer stepped aside and let him out into the corridor. 'I haven't spoken to them today,' he answered. 'But he's desperate to get back into his house to pick up his belongings.'

'What are the geologists saying?'

'Nothing, as long as it's still raining. But the weather's set to improve from tomorrow. Maybe he'll get a chance later in the week.'

Wisting responded with a nod of the head. 'I need something to drink,' he said, excusing himself, and pointing to the break room.

Hammer disappeared in the direction of his office. Wisting filled a glass of water and stood by the sink as he drank. When he had drained the glass, he checked the time. Still more than an hour until seven o'clock.

He refilled the glass and took it with him back to his office. Benjamin Fjeld looked out as he passed his door. He was sitting with headphones on and flipped them off.

'I'm listening to the recording of Nanette Kranz,' he said. 'It's been sent to the sound technicians to try to isolate background noises, but I wanted to listen for myself.'

Wisting went in to see him. 'Can you hear anything?'

Benjamin shook his head. 'There are creaking sounds, but apart from that it seems as if she's sitting in a soundproof room.'

A gust of wind flung a curtain of rain at the window.

'Let me listen,' Wisting said.

Benjamin gave up his seat and Wisting put on the headphones.

The player moved along an onscreen sound graph, making a deflection each time something was said. The first time he listened, he could not turn off Nanette's voice. He asked Benjamin to play it one more time and shut his eyes to concentrate on listening. At one point he thought he could make out paper shuffling, but there was also a creaking sound. It occurred on three separate occasions. It sounded like someone walking across old timber floorboards.

He listened one more time but could make no more of it.

'Do you think they'll get away with it?' Benjamin asked as he resumed his seat.

'What do you mean?' Wisting asked.

'There's nothing in our investigation so far that points to Gillis Haack or Elton Khan,' Benjamin pointed out.

'We're getting there,' Wisting assured him, taking a drink of water. 'Now the focus is on freeing Nanette Kranz, but after that is when our job begins.'

That investigation was one he would not be able to take part in. No matter what happened in the course of the evening or through the night, it was impossible for this to have no repercussions. The police investigation would be one thing, but the media would also dig into it for all it was worth. It made no difference that the central character was a child.

Most likely he would be suspended until his role had been thoroughly investigated. Afterwards, it was far from certain that he would still have a job.

He headed back to his office and unlocked the drawer containing the logbook. All the actions he had taken were listed there. The messages from the kidnappers were quoted word for word and the conversations had been written down as best he could recall. He entered the details of their last contact and put the book back in place.

The next half hour he spent skimming through the case documents added in the course of the day. Benjamin Fjeld was right. Nothing pointed directly at the perpetrators.

When seven o'clock came round, he took out the memory stick, inserted it into the computer and downloaded the updated files. He did this without any sense of anguish – his sole thought was that everything would soon be over.

59

The car headlights swept across the lawn and glistened on the wet grass when he drew up in front of Line's house. Amalie's new bike was still lying in the same place beside a heap of leaves whipped up by the wind. He walked to the old apple tree, righted the bicycle and shook off the wet leaves. Then he wheeled it over to the house and propped it against the wall, sheltered from the rain.

Line was in the kitchen. She had baked some frozen bread rolls. Some of them were buttered and arranged on a plate but looked untouched.

'Did it go OK?' she asked.

Nodding, he put the memory stick down on the table and placed the encrypted phone inside the microwave.

Bantam was in the living room, talking on the phone. It sounded as if the conversation was drawing to a close. He said thank you and assured the person at the other end that he appreciated the assistance.

'I'll have a list in about an hour's time,' he said when he entered the kitchen.

'Is it long?' Line asked.

'That depends on the way it's filtered and sorted,' Bantam told her. 'But we can expect a huge amount of data.'

Wisting took a seat. The laptop he had used to upload the other files was ready with the screen up. The others sat down on either side of him.

'How detrimental is it?' Line asked once he had inserted the memory stick.

'No direct harm done,' Wisting replied. 'It means they know what the police know and can operate on that basis. But to be honest, the police know nothing about them. What they're left with is a feeling of being safe. That's fine as far as we're concerned.'

He logged on to the anonymous webpage.

'What's here is no more or less than what they would be entitled to see via their defence counsel,' he added.

This was true, but the difference was that they would then already have been charged. And it did not change the fact that what he was doing carried a potential sentence of three years' imprisonment.

A fan inside the computer began to whir when he transferred the contents.

'Are you hungry?' Line asked, pushing the plate across to him.

He did not really feel like eating anything, but needed sustenance and selected a bread roll with butter and jam. Line also took one and picked off a chunk from the crust.

'Do you think they'll read it first, before we get any further messages?' she asked.

'Not all of it,' Wisting answered, with food in his mouth. 'Maybe they'll just do a search on their own names.'

'Will they get any hits?' Bantam asked.

'No,' was Wisting's response.

He had tried that himself. The names Gillis Haack and Elton Khan were not mentioned anywhere in the official documents.

Line popped another piece of the roll into her mouth.

'Can't you send a message?' she asked. 'Tell them you've delivered.'

Wisting had jam on his fingers. He finished eating and rinsed his hands at the sink before retrieving the encrypted phone.

Files delivered, he wrote. *Shall we continue from this morning?*

He hovered for a moment or two with the phone in his hand and his thumb over the microphone, but there was no answer.

'How are things in Sweden?' he asked, glancing at Line. 'Did you get anyone to go to Serner's home?'

'Micke's doing that,' Line replied. 'Apparently it's a detached house half an hour from the city centre.'

Wisting helped himself to another bread roll. He had taken only two bites when he heard a message alert.

Another set of coordinates and a rendezvous time: *20.00*.

Line keyed in the coordinates as Wisting read them out. When the map reference appeared on the screen, she stood up abruptly and pushed the laptop across to her father.

'What is it?' Bantam asked, stretching across to see.

'A churchyard,' Wisting told him.

Line stood with her hand on her mouth. 'What does it mean?' she asked.

'Don't read anything into it,' Wisting said. 'It's in an out-of-the-way location, with few people around in the evening and no CCTV cameras. There's no more to it than that.'

'Do you know the place?' Bantam asked.

'Tanum church,' Wisting clarified. 'Line's mother is buried there.'

'Is it far from here?'

'Ten minutes, out towards the coast.'

He checked the time. He had twenty-five minutes before he had to be there.

'Will we proceed in the same way?' Bantam suggested. 'Line and I in a separate car?'

'We have to anticipate a change of location,' Wisting said. 'The church is beside an old traffic intersection with roads leading off in several directions.'

'Do you still have contact with your watch?' Line asked Bantam. He checked the fitness app and nodded. 'Almost eight hours left on it.'

They got ready. Like last time, they mounted Wisting's phone under the headrest and connected the wireless ear buds.

There were no streetlights along the winding road to Tanum. Rain poured down in front of the car, impairing visibility. Yellowish-brown autumn leaves fluttered through the air.

Wisting was familiar with the road but drove carefully. On one stretch a small silver car overtook him. The rear lights disappeared around a corner and were soon gone. He met an oncoming car with a trailer, but apart from that there was no other traffic.

After a section of dense forest flanking the road, he spotted the church spire, floodlit on three sides, looming ahead of him.

'I'm here,' he said aloud.

'We can see next to nothing,' Line spoke into his ear. 'The image on the screen is out of focus.'

'Is anyone else there?' Bantam asked.

'No cars, at least,' Wisting replied.

He swung into the car park on the left, where he was in the habit of leaving his vehicle. Inside the graveyard, candles and lamps were flickering. He had been there at the end of September and planted some heather on Ingrid's grave, but it was a long time since he had lit a candle for her.

'Seven minutes left,' Line told him.

Wisting reversed his car into place to allow him a view of the road. In front of him, the wind dragged a chocolate wrapper across the asphalt. It landed in a puddle before being tossed onwards, over the fence and in between the tombstones.

Time passed slowly. A car drove by on the road.

Wisting leaned back on the headrest and listened to the rain on the roof. He tried to conjure some pleasant memories to displace the fear of everything that could go wrong. Warm summer days, strawberry picking, bare feet on grass, ice cream, laughter, children singing.

'Four minutes,' Line announced. 'Can you see anything?'

It was difficult to make out anything in the darkness. The wind rustled through the bushes and trees, making him think someone was keeping an eye on him.

A bright light appeared at the end of the road. 'There's a car coming,' he said.

It must have extra headlights fitted. Blazing light was cast far out on either side of the road. Driving at top speed, it shot past. Wisting saw that it was a pick-up truck. Not until it approached the bend did it brake and slow down.

The encrypted phone was cradled on his lap. Two minutes to go, but there was no point in waiting.

I'm in position, he wrote, and dispatched the message.

The response was fast. *Place the goods in the blue container.*

Looking around, Wisting recalled seeing rubbish containers at one end of the car park. 'They want me to put the paintings inside a container,' he said.

'Whereabouts?' Line asked.

Wisting turned the steering wheel, switched his headlights to full beam and turned up towards the far end of the car park, where he saw two metal containers, one green and one blue.

'Here,' he said, assuming they could see them.

'Was that the whole message?' Line asked.

Wisting read it out. 'Do that, then,' Line said.

Leaving the engine running, he stepped out of the car and collected the three cardboard cylinders from the back seat.

The green container was for garden waste, while the blue container was marked *General Waste*. It had a large hatch on the front and smaller hatches on the sides. Wisting opened one of the side openings, keeping the cardboard tubes tucked under his arm. A foul smell wafted out. The car headlights did not reach this far, but he could see that it was three-quarters full.

It did not seem right to simply dump the paintings, even though the cardboard sleeves would protect them. He returned to his car and picked up the blanket from the rear seat, one Line usually kept folded on the settee armrest. He wrapped it around the cardboard tubes, carried them back to the rubbish container and set them down carefully. Then he closed the hatch and retraced his steps back to his car.

Done, he reported to the kidnappers.

The answer was swift: *Leave the location.*

60

Line and Bantam sat in the hire car at the car park beside the golf course. Wisting drove up beside them and wound down the window.

'Any movement?' he asked.

Bantam shook his head. Line leaned forward in the passenger seat and looked out at him. 'We've fulfilled our side of the bargain,' she said. 'Write to them!'

Wisting appreciated that she was impatient, but they probably would not hear anything until the kidnappers had also received the ransom for Nanette Kranz. All the same, it could be advantageous to go on the offensive.

All demands fulfilled from my side, he wrote. *Now our deal has to be finalized.*

He did not expect any response. It was chiefly meant as a marker, but the phone soon sounded a message alert.

Thanks for cooperation.

Wisting snorted.

'What is it?' Line asked.

Another message followed before he had a chance to reply.

Message will come before midnight.

Then one more: *Further messages will not be answered.*

He read them aloud, reaching over the steering wheel as he looked out. 'I ought to go back to the police station,' he said. 'Everything depends on how fast the gold is delivered.'

'What do we do if the paintings are moved?' Bantam asked.

345

'Let me know and follow at a distance,' Wisting told him.

He rolled up the side window and turned around. The gravel crunched under the wheels and spat at the wheel arches as he picked up speed.

The police chief's car was parked in the back yard when he got back. Rain had formed beads on its bonnet.

Wisting let himself in. Following the corridor along to the cloakroom, he found a towel to dry himself a little and tidy his hair before going up to the department.

The lights were dimmed in the conference room to make it easier to see the TV screen and the transmission from Kranz's living room.

Hammer had just finished briefing the chief of police. She looked up at Wisting when he entered the room.

'Are you feeling better now?' she asked.

Wisting pulled out a chair and sat a short distance from the others. 'It'll probably pass, I'm sure,' he replied. 'I thought it was a cold, but now it's affected my stomach. I'm a bit out of sorts, so Hammer has taken over responsibility for the case.'

'All the same, it's reassuring to have you here,' the police chief said.

'Thanks.'

He surveyed the room and noticed that none of the Swedes was present. 'Where are Serner and Falk?' he asked. 'And Walin?'

'Serner has driven to Grenland,' Hammer answered. 'To follow at closer quarters.'

Wisting sat bolt upright. 'We can't have anyone operating solo,' he said.

'Serner knows what he's doing,' Helland assured him. 'He's taken a radio set with him.'

'What about Falk and Walin?'

No one seemed to know exactly. 'Well, Falk is around here somewhere,' Hammer said. 'We still have some time yet.'

Wisting gazed up at the transmission from Kranz's living room, where Kranz and his lawyer were sitting in the same places as before. The two investigators in the house moved in and out at the margins of the picture.

Two bulky bags sat on the floor. 'Is that the gold?' Wisting asked.

Hammer nodded. 'He insisted on Henden being present at the handover,' he replied. 'He felt he wouldn't be able to drive himself. That's very likely true.'

'What do we think about that?'

'That the kidnappers should be informed in advance,' Hammer said. 'The investigators in Grenland have been most preoccupied with obtaining permission to equip his car with a camera.'

'Can we watch from here, then?'

'If the technology works, you can even watch it on your mobile if you like.'

Hammer tucked a wad of snuff under his cheek and leaned back, tight-lipped.

The already oppressive atmosphere in the room grew more paralysing as nine o'clock approached. A kind of expectant hush descended.

Still no sign of Ralf Falk or Ann-Mari Walin.

The restlessness was also obvious on the big screen. Niklas Kranz sat with his hands clasped behind his head, revealing dark rings of perspiration in his armpits. Sigurd Henden had taken off his jacket and kept reaching forward to check the encrypted phone on the table.

There were still a few minutes left when it suddenly emitted a sound.

Wisting leaned forward, noting that everyone around him did the same.

Kranz signalled to his lawyer to read the message. 'It's coordinates,' he said. 'And a specific time. We have twenty minutes.'

An investigator entered the picture. 'What are the co-ordinates?' he asked, preparing to key them into his mobile. Wisting took out his own phone to follow suit.

The lawyer read the series of numbers aloud. 'It's a Kiwi supermarket in Porsgrunn,' the detective announced.

For a second or two, confusion reigned, both in Kranz's home and the room where Wisting sat. Henden was the one who assumed command, shrugging on his jacket and producing his car keys.

Wisting received a message, this time from Line. *On the move*, she wrote.

61

On the large screen, one of the investigators received some final instructions on an earbud before giving the all-clear. Sigurd Henden grabbed the bags of gold, ten kilos in each hand.

Wisting, having downloaded John Bantam's fitness app, now linked up to it. The paintings were moving along the main highway.

On the move here too, he texted back, mainly to let her know he could not call them.

Kranz and Henden disappeared from the onscreen image. Somewhere a technician switched the transmission to the vehicle outside. The picture was split in two, with one camera filming out through the front windscreen and the other a wide-angle lens capturing the driver and passenger seats. In addition, a small map segment in the corner showed their position.

The rear doors were flung open and the bags of gold stowed inside. Hammer cranked up the volume.

Henden settled behind the steering wheel and abruptly pulled the seatbelt across his chest. He was champing at the bit, as if about to board a thrilling ride in an amusement park. Kranz, on the other hand, seemed troubled and clearly exhausted. He sat with slouched shoulders, a look of resignation on his face.

Unnoticed, Falk had returned to the room and gone to the empty chair beside Helland. His hair and shoulders were wet.

The car turned into a residential street. The front headlights shone on the wet asphalt. Henden's phone provided directions.

'How far is it?' the police chief asked.

'Nine kilometres,' Hammer told her. 'Thirteen minutes.'

Wisting checked the time. They would reach their destination within the deadline only if nothing untoward happened en route.

The car carrying the paintings was moving at a steady rate. The app told him the average speed was sixty-three kilometres per hour as it approached the motorway. Wisting followed its movements until it turned on to the E18, driving on the southbound carriageway towards Grenland.

He texted Line, asking if they had any chance of catching up with it to see what type of car it was.

The TV footage from Kranz's car turned white. Kranz raised his right hand to shield himself from the bright headlights of an oncoming vehicle.

'What happens when we get there?' he asked once the car had passed.

'There will probably be another message,' Henden told him. 'It could be we get a message telling us to place the bags in the boot of a car parked there, or something like that.'

Wisting received a reply from Line. *We're one kilometre behind and can't take any risks*, she wrote.

On the screen, Kranz twisted round and looked back. 'Are the police following us?' he asked.

Henden shook his head. 'But they're in the vicinity,' he assured him.

Wisting got to his feet, stretching halfway across the table to pick up the jug of water. Tiny air bubbles were visible through the glass.

'Where's Walin?' he asked, directing the question to Ralf Falk as he filled his tumbler.

'At the hotel, I think,' he replied.

'Shouldn't she be here?' Wisting asked, putting down the jug. 'She's been at all our previous meetings, and now we're on the brink of a breakthrough.'

Falk shrugged. 'Maybe she went out with Serner,' he said.

Wisting sat down and gazed up again at the big screen. The water was stale and lukewarm. Henden stopped for a red light at a pedestrian crossing. A man with an umbrella crossed the road. There was silence inside the car, apart from the noise of the rain. When the light changed, they could hear the wheels spin and grip.

Two minutes before the deadline, the car swung into the car park outside the Kiwi store. No more than ten or twelve vehicles were parked. Henden drove to the perimeter for a good view of the other cars and the store entrance.

The car park was well lit. A mother of small children strapped her kids into the back seat of an estate car before getting in and driving off, leaving the supermarket trolley behind. A black BMW drove into the car park and parked right beside the entrance. The driver dashed inside. Several vehicles arrived, but none of the parked cars stood out in any way.

Wisting checked the movements of the car carrying the paintings. It had passed the Langangen Bridge and was approaching an exit road off the E18.

A message alert broke the silence.

Henden read out: *Buy some bin bags. Divide the goods into four separate bags. Double-packed. Ten minutes.*

Hammer dropped his pen on the notepad in front of him. 'They want us to rewrap the gold,' he said with a sigh.

'Does that mean we'll lose the opportunity to track it?' the police chief asked.

Hammer nodded. 'The transmitter is sewn into one of the bags.'

It had also dawned on the two men in the car what this instruction meant. Henden stepped out and walked with his head bowed through the rain. A couple of minutes later, he was back with a roll of black plastic bin bags. Kranz helped him divide up the gold. From the TV loudspeaker, Wisting and his colleagues could hear the clinking of the gold bars.

Wisting received another message from Line: *Stopped*.

He checked the app. The paintings were on the outskirts of Porsgrunn, the nearest of the six Grenland districts. No movement.

Henden and Kranz were now ready. They sat in the front seats of the car again, waiting for another instruction.

Hammer checked the time and leaned across the table. Wisting could hear his breath quiver as he drew it in and let it out again.

Another message.

A taxi has been booked for Niklas Kranz alone, Henden read out. *Make yourselves known to the driver. Bring the goods.*

Hammer swore. Ralf Falk had not caught the instruction. 'What did he say?'

'They've to change vehicle,' Helland replied. 'A taxi. We'll lose sound and image.'

'And tracking,' Hammer added.

Henden's personal phone rang. He answered and left the car to speak. Kranz remained seated inside.

Hammer received a call on his own phone, answering in monosyllables while making notes.

On the big screen, a taxi swung into the car park. H249

from Grenland Taxis, a silver Mercedes with a star on the bonnet.

Henden raised his hand and waved to it while continuing to talk on his phone. By the time he hung up, his hair was soaked. He returned to the car and opened the door on Kranz's side.

'Come on,' he said. 'This is the final stage.'

They carried the bags across to the taxi. Kranz got into the back seat. Henden spoke to the driver through the window before saying a few last words to his client.

Hammer rang off, looking around for a moment, before making eye contact with Wisting.

'We have sound and location,' he said. 'Henden has left his own phone on the back seat of the taxi, with an open line to the operations room in Grenland. They'll use that for tailing it but have requested more vehicles out there.'

On the big screen, the taxi was driving off, leaving Henden standing alone in the rain.

Wisting rose to his feet. 'I'm driving out there,' he said.

Several chairs scraped on the floor. Ralf Falk was also making an exit. 'I can give you a lift,' Wisting told him as he headed for the door.

There was no time for discussion. 'Sign in on channel two,' Hammer shouted after them.

62

Wisting put his arm in the wrong sleeve as he struggled into his jacket. When he looked up, Ann-Mari Walin was on her way out of the lift, a dripping umbrella in her hand.

She began to apologize for arriving so late but failed to complete her sentence when she realized they were dealing with an urgent situation.

'Nils Hammer will bring you up to speed,' Falk said as he barged past her into the lift.

Wisting finally managed to get his jacket on, patting it to make sure his pistol was still in the pocket.

The doors slid shut and the lift moved slowly downwards. It would have been quicker to take the stairs. There were only two flights.

The cramped space in the lift meant they stood close to each other. Falk drew back to the wall and stared at the puddle on the floor left by Walin's umbrella.

'Maybe you should phone Serner,' Wisting said.

The lift was down by now and Falk took out his mobile to call his colleague. Wisting heard him explain developments while he checked his own phone. No new messages. No movement on the paintings, at least not registered on John Bantam's watch.

Once they were seated in the car, Wisting started the engine and reversed out. Falk put away his mobile.

'Where was he?' Wisting asked.

'In Skien,' Falk replied. 'He wanted to see the location

where Nanette Kranz was abducted. Now he's on his way to Porsgrunn. We can meet up over there.'

Wisting switched to channel two on the closed circuit and reported in to the operator as he drove.

'*Roger*,' was the response, a female voice. '*Your assigned call signal is 4-11.*'

'4-11, got that,' Wisting confirmed.

This meant there were ten other unmarked cars out there in addition to Jan Serner's.

'*For your attention and that of other new units,*' the operator continued. '*Instructions have been issued to drive to Schøningsveg 17. That is Eidanger church. The subject is now driving through Vallermyrene in a southerly direction. Estimated arrival in five minutes. All units stay at a safe distance.*'

'Do you know where that is?' Falk asked.

'I know where Eidanger is, but not that particular church,' Wisting answered. 'It's half an hour from here.'

He cut a corner and accelerated.

On the radio they heard the operator position units on all sides of the church but at a distance of a kilometre or so.

It was easy to envisage the next few minutes. Kranz would receive a message instructing him to leave the gold in a rubbish container in the churchyard. The kidnappers would be waiting in a car nearby. They already had the paintings and were only waiting to pick up the gold as well. The only person who could warn them that the area was surrounded by plain-clothes police officers was the Swedish traitor, or himself. Before Nanette Kranz was released, however, the police would take no action to intervene.

'*The subject is approaching,*' the operator relayed. '*Estimated arrival in one minute.*'

Wisting picked up speed on the motorway and forced his

way past a minibus. The accumulated water on the uneven road surface made the steering wheel judder in his hands.

Falk sat with his mobile on his knee. He sent a text message but did not reveal who he was communicating with or what he had written.

Another kilometre was put behind them in silence.

'*The subject has arrived*,' they heard on the radio.

From habit, Wisting glanced at the dashboard clock as it flipped precisely over to 21.51.

His own mobile vibrated and he took it from his pocket, but waited until he had overtaken a lorry before he increased speed and read the message.

It was from Line, a picture of a woman and a girl of about ten getting into a Swedish-registered car. The child's head was thrown back and she was laughing with her mouth wide open.

Johanne and Isabelle Serner, she wrote. *Photographed half an hour ago.*

Wisting looked at the image again. The scenario seemed fairly light-hearted.

He used his thumb to text a brief reply as he drove: *Understood.*

Then he gripped his phone between his thighs and glanced across at Falk. His jaw muscles were working, as if he were chewing on something.

Yet another kilometre passed in silence. Wisting was casting about for the right wording, a sentence or two with some kind of double meaning that Falk would understand if he were the traitor. Extending a hand, so to speak, to get him to open up.

'This case has become personal for me,' he began, gazing straight ahead. 'What about you?'

Falk looked obliquely across at him, as if he did not understand the question.

'Have you ever had cases before where you've been as personally involved as this one?' Wisting ploughed on.

'Never,' Falk replied.

The radio operator broke in: '*9-8 to all units on channel two. Fresh instructions have been issued. The handover location is a bus terminal at Farriseidet in Larvik. The subject is already on the move.*'

Falk glanced across at Wisting. He nodded, as if to confirm that he was familiar with the location of the new handover site.

'We're going to meet them on the road,' he said.

The operator directed the unmarked units into optimal positions. They were going to end up in a long tail behind Kranz's taxi.

Wisting slowed down but remained in the left lane. Double crash barriers protected the north- and southbound carriageways from each other. In some places there were openings in the centre to allow traffic to be directed into the opposite lane in case of an accident or roadworks.

The traffic began to queue up behind him. The nearest vehicle flashed its lights and followed close on his bumper.

A few hundred metres further ahead, Wisting spotted the opening he was looking for. He switched on his hazard lights and dropped his speed even more. The car behind him swung out into the right-hand lane, its horn sounding as he drove past. Several others did likewise. Falk realized what the driver intended to do and grabbed the handhold above the door. Wisting judged the oncoming traffic, adjusted his speed accordingly and wrenched the car round 180 degrees. Passing cars tooted angrily.

Releasing the handhold, Falk twisted round in his seat and looked back.

Wisting snatched up the two-way radio and reported his position.

'*Roger that*,' was the operator's response. The reply was left hanging in the air for a moment before she followed up: '*Then you're situated about two kilometres in front.*'

Wisting kept slightly below the speed limit. In the mirror he saw a vehicle gain on him, pull out and drive past.

His mobile pulsed between his thighs and he picked it up. New message from Line. The paintings were on the move, en route back to Larvik.

We're following at a safe distance.

Unable to answer in any substantive way, he merely fired off an *OK* before checking his mirror again. The road was well lit, but he could not yet see any sign of the procession he was anticipating: the taxi with Kranz and the gold, followed by the kidnappers with the paintings, then Line and John, along with an assortment of unmarked police cars.

They were approaching the Larvik exit road. Wisting slowed down and turned off. Falk twisted round in his seat and watched the traffic behind them. Two cars passed while they were on the slip road. In the mirror, Wisting spotted a third vehicle with a flashing light.

'I think that's it,' Falk commented. 'Looks like it has a taxi sign on the roof.'

There was a short delay before confirmation came over the radio: '*The subject has turned off towards Larvik. Estimated arrival in one minute and forty seconds.*'

Wisting continued to hold his speed under the limit. The road ahead curved slightly and sloped downwards. A bus was waiting at one of the stops.

Falk looked back again. 'You're just going to drive past?' he asked, seeking confirmation.

Lifting one finger from the wheel, Wisting pointed right, out of the roundabout in front of them. 'I'm driving down towards the town,' he replied.

Just in front of the roundabout, he had to brake and stop for a lorry making its way round. In his mirror, he spotted that the car behind him was a grey taxi, the distance no more than a hundred metres. Behind the taxi, there were two other vehicles, but Wisting could not see if either of these was Bantam's hire car.

He signalled to leave the roundabout, watching carefully in his mirror.

His mobile vibrated and buzzed between his legs, but Wisting did not take the call. Something was wrong.

The lorry circumnavigated the roundabout one more time. The taxi stopped for it, just as Wisting had done. Then the lorry swerved off the roundabout and bumped across the central reservation, smashing into the side of the taxi and forcing it viciously off the road.

Wisting stamped on the brake. His mobile slid off the seat and landed between the pedals. Falk grabbed the seatbelt and used the dash for support. Wisting thumped the steering wheel, wrenched the car into reverse and swung round.

The powder from the taxi's airbags billowed like a cloud around them. Wisting forced his car on to the foot and cycle path. The undercarriage scraped on the ground as he struck the ditch.

'Weapon!' Falk shouted.

Wisting slanted the car across the road, twenty metres from the site of the accident.

A man in a balaclava, toting a sub-machine gun, had jumped out of the lorry. The driver's cabin behind him was ablaze. He positioned himself, feet straddling the road, his weapon across his chest.

A black Audi had moved up from behind. The masked driver rushed across to the damaged taxi. With a struggle, he tore open the back door and hauled out the four bags of gold. The lorry driver moved towards him, guarding the surrounding area while the bags were transferred to the Audi.

People were scrambling from the vehicles behind them. Jan Serner stood at the door of the one nearest. He placed his gun on the car roof and tilted his head to take aim.

The man with the sub-machine gun turned to face him. Wisting saw a flash of fire from the Swedish investigator's weapon. Two rapid shots before the kidnapper fell to the ground.

The other kidnapper dived down and crawled under cover round the bonnet as he pulled out a pistol. Three of the bags were already in the car and the fourth lay beside it.

Serner was on his way round his own car. 'No, for God's sake!' Wisting yelled.

When his foot hit the accelerator, clumps of earth and tufts of grass sprayed around the car. The front wheels struck a kerb and the car veered off course. Wisting wrestled with the steering wheel but managed to right it and cut Serner off.

With two dead kidnappers, no one would be able to tell him where Amalie was being held captive.

Faint explosions came from the blazing lorry as the second kidnapper slithered along the ground, dragging the last bag of gold as he clambered into the Audi. The tyres fought to grip the wet asphalt before the car streaked away.

A barrage of messages exploded on the radio.

Wisting threw open the car door. Falk was out ahead of him. He punched Serner on the chest with both hands, roaring at him and pressing him up against the car – giving vent to the same frustration and rage that Wisting felt.

Plain-clothes police officers came running. Niklas Kranz was helped out of the taxi. The driver was bleeding from a gash on his forehead. Wisting stood hunched over, hands on knees for support. He felt ill. Sick. His mind was in turmoil, thoughts churning.

Line raced along the line of cars and Wisting straightened up, holding out his arms to embrace her.

She had no time for that. 'John's had an answer,' she panted. 'A Mastercard . . . I know where Amalie is.'

63

The dead kidnapper's blood combined with the rainwater and washed across the asphalt. His balaclava was tugged off to reveal Elton Khan.

Wisting led Line away. She was talking in fits and starts, incoherently. He put his hands on her shoulders, looked her in the eye and persuaded her to calm down.

'There's a Mastercard that's been used in Ankara, Amsterdam, Gothenburg and here in Nevlunghavn,' she said.

'Where in Nevlunghavn?' Wisting asked.

'I don't know yet,' Line said. 'But in Gothenburg it was used at a bunkering facility at the harbour.'

Her breath caught in her throat and she had to swallow to continue. 'They filled up with nearly 10,000 kroners' worth of diesel,' she said. 'They came here by boat.'

She swallowed again. 'Amalie's in a boat at Nevlunghavn.'

Still gripping her shoulders, Wisting took a second or two to absorb the logic of this. Gillis Haack had smuggled hash in his uncle's fishing boat from the Netherlands. He should have thought of that before. They called him the Skipper.

'You're right,' he said, letting her go.

Smoke from the burning lorry stung his eyes. A man darted past them with a fire extinguisher.

John Bantam had wound his way through the traffic and drew up beside them. Wisting pointed at him.

'Drive there!' he said.

Answering with a nod, Line jumped into the car. Wisting leapt into his own car – the side panel scraped on a road sign as he rushed to turn around.

Gillis Haack had a two-minute head start, maybe even three. Wisting swerved out of the roundabout. The car skidded, but he managed to right it again as he accelerated out on to the coast road.

Terse messages zipped back and forth on the radio, about ambulances, fire engines and a waiting helicopter hovering in the air above them. Grabbing the microphone, Wisting raised it to his mouth but ended by throwing it aside. Instead he concentrated on his driving. He knew this stretch of road well and cut corners where possible, speeding up on the straight sections.

In the mirror he saw that the distance between him and Bantam had increased and soon his headlights had disappeared.

Nevlunghavn lay on the southernmost point of the municipality, like an outpost facing the Skagerrak. The locals called it simply 'the harbour'.

A patchwork of fields and woods rushed by in the darkness before buildings began to appear. Narrow streets of old timber houses on either side. Quiet and deserted. He knew several people who lived here. Laberg, Thorsen and Semann.

Amalie had been here the whole time.

A man trundled his bicycle uphill from the harbour.

Wisting did not slow down.

The rain slanted across the light cast by the streetlamps around the harbour basin. The wheelhouse windows on an old fishing boat glowed at the far-off jetty. Puffs of grey smoke rose from the exhaust pipe on the roof.

The black Audi was parked there. A man was untying the mooring rope. He turned towards the car as it approached.

Gillis Haack.

He dropped the hawser in the sea and leapt aboard.

Wisting accelerated across the quayside, along past the summer restaurants. He snagged a wooden bench, toppling it over, driving as far forward as he could before jumping out of the car.

The boat was already moving, the engine revving. The smoke turned black and began belching out.

Wisting took a run at it. The gap between the jetty and the boat was now one metre. He got ready to jump and took off, landing on the deck and sliding on the wet timbers.

Another car travelling at top speed arrived in the harbour and drove out on to the pier. John Bantam dashed out and ran up along the jetty, with Line hard on his heels.

Haack pushed up the side window on the wheelhouse, looked out and watched Bantam closely. Wisting crept behind a net drum at the stern, unsure whether Haack had noticed that he had come aboard.

The boat turned to starboard, rounding the pier, and set course for open waters.

Bantam took a leap, waving his arms in the air and grabbing at the handrails, but he could not catch hold. Ashore, Line was shrieking at the top of her voice as he splashed into the water.

Gillis Haack pulled his head back into the wheelhouse and shut the window.

Wisting hauled himself up and peered over the gunwale. Bantam, hanging on to a large, round fender, was being dragged along with the boat. He spat out water and turned his head away from the sea spray. If he lost his grip, he would disappear into the choppy foam of the wake.

The distance down to him was a metre and a half. Wisting looked around for a rope ladder or something similar. The closest thing he found was a thick rope, on which he tied a few knots, making it easier to climb up it. He tethered it to a bollard and cast the other end out. Bantam caught hold of it, heaved himself up and managed to grip with his feet. He angled his head back and gathered his strength before starting to ascend.

The harbour lights soon faded as the large boat rolled on the steadily increasing swell, but it seemed to be holding a fixed course. Haack was nowhere to be seen.

Wisting leaned over the gunwale, waiting for Bantam to reach high enough for him to grab one of his arms and haul him up the final stretch.

Water poured off the American's tall frame. Rolling on to his back, he pulled himself up on to his elbows and gazed straight ahead at the wheelhouse.

'Are you carrying?' he asked.

'What do you mean?'

'Are you armed?' Bantam demanded.

Nodding, Wisting patted his jacket pocket. Bantam sat up and held out his hand.

'Allow me,' he said, with another glance at the wheelhouse before fixing his eye on the afterdeck hatch. 'Amalie must be down below. I can secure things up here.'

The boat heeled to one side, causing Wisting to lurch and stagger as he fished out his gun and handed it over.

Bantam loaded the gun, ready to fire. Wisting flipped up the hatch, drawing in damp sea air as he descended the ladder.

64

The fishing boat pitched in the waves. Wisting was forced to use the hatch frame for support to keep his balance on the way down. The precipitous ladder led to a grimy machine room spattered with oil stains and filled with the miasma of rank diesel fumes. An engine, painted green, filled most of the space, and the clunking noise it made reverberated through the hull.

Below deck, he was even more aware of the heavy motion of the sea. He had to duck to avoid a light bulb swinging from side to side and used any handhold he could find as he staggered towards the door at the opposite end.

The room beyond was a combined galley and saloon, with a cooking area on one side and a table with corner seating on the other. Two swivel chairs, fixed to the floor, spun back and forth with the movements of the boat.

Further forward, he saw a staircase leading to the upper deck and three doors, two of them fitted with shiny metal fixtures, a sliding bolt and padlock. Wisting scouted around for any tools he could find. He pulled out a drawer but saw nothing suitable and went on to open a cupboard filled with pots and pans. A cast-iron pot with a long steel handle would suffice. He weighed it in his hand as he moved towards the doors, looking from one to the other before choosing the one on the left.

He had raised the pot to strike the lock when the third door slid open. Gillis Haack ducked below the doorframe and stepped forward, dressed in a red survival suit. He froze when he caught sight of Wisting.

Wisting swung the pot at him, but hit the ceiling, deflecting all the strength in the blow. Haack lunged forward and charged at him before Wisting was able to strike again. They ended up on the floor and the pot disappeared under the table. Haack lifted his right arm to deliver a punch, but Wisting fended him off with his left, rolling on to his side and avoiding the next swipe. He rolled back again, using the momentum to drive his elbow into Haack's ribs.

The bulky survival suit hampered Haack's mobility. Wisting managed to inflict another couple of blows and a hefty kick that toppled the kidnapper on to his side.

Haack pushed himself back, gaining some distance from Wisting, and pulled out a pistol from inside the suit. Wisting reacted by drawing one foot up and pushing off, launching a brutal kick at Haack's arm. The weapon slipped out of his hands and the steep dip of a wave caused it to slide out of reach. Haack stretched out for it as Wisting scuttled backwards, finding his feet and scrambling into the engine room, anticipating the gunfire that would follow.

John Bantam was halfway down the ladder, blocking his retreat. Wisting flung himself behind the bulky engine.

'In there,' he warned Bantam, pointing.

The door had not clicked shut. It slid open and closed with the movements of the boat. They saw Haack's feet on the stairs, on the way up to the top deck.

'Amalie!' Bantam shouted.

Wisting grabbed a hammer and hurtled back, out into the galley again. Bantam took up position with his gun aimed at the stairs while Wisting tackled the door.

The shackle on the first padlock sprang open after only

two strikes. The second one was more robust but finally also gave way.

He pushed the bolts aside and opened the door.

Nanette Kranz sat hunched at the very back of one of the bunks. She looked overcome with anxiety and confusion. No sign of Amalie.

'We're from the police,' Wisting explained. 'Just wait here.'

He strode across to the second door.

The motion of the boat altered, as if it had changed course and was ploughing through heavier seas. Suddenly it heeled, making Wisting miss with his first blow.

'Water!' Bantam yelled.

Wisting felt it at once. Seawater was washing around his feet, gushing out from the bow bulkhead in front of him and already reaching up to his ankles. He stood, legs straddled, hammering away.

John Bantam swore. 'He's going to sink the boat and abandon ship,' he shouted. 'There's another boat waiting out there – I caught a glimpse of it.'

Wisting managed to hack open the first lock. The water was rising fast around him. Gillis Haack must have gouged a hole in the bow, and the surging sea was steadily enlarging it.

The second lock also gave way. Bantam watched as he yanked the door open.

Amalie was perched on the edge of the bunk. She seemed drowsy and fell back when she tried to stand up.

Swallowing down a sob, Wisting was at her side in two paces. He lifted her, hugged her to him and spoke softly in her ear. 'Grandpa's here . . . you're going home to Mummy.'

The boat pitched violently again.

'We need to go up,' Bantam yelled.

Tucking the quilt around Amalie, Wisting carried her aloft. The water was now lapping in mid-calf and the ceiling light was flashing intermittently.

Bantam stood at the top of the stairs, pushing at the hatch. 'He's bolted it from the outside,' he said. 'We'll have to try the back way.'

Nanette Kranz had left the cabin. Wisting could see the disorientation in her eyes. She collapsed in a heap and began to wail, whimpering softly.

The light flashed again. Wisting grabbed a torch from a charger on the wall and, holding it, carried Amalie through to the engine room.

Bantam clambered to the top of the ladder. 'That's shut too,' he called out, pressing his back to the hatch. 'Do you have that hammer?'

It lay somewhere under the water.

Wisting set Amalie down on one of the swivel chairs and felt his way forward. He managed to find it and hurried back.

Bantam swung out at the hatch timbers and Wisting heard it splinter after a few blows. Slivers of wood drizzled down.

He went back to Amalie and hoisted her up again, the water now up to his knees.

The diesel engine spluttered a couple of times before running smoothly again. Nanette Kranz had crept up on to the bench behind the dining table. Her whimpering had stopped. She followed hesitantly when Wisting shouted her name.

The gash in the hatch above the engine room was now large enough for Bantam to put his arm through. He fumbled his way forward, managing to open the catch on the outside and flip the hatch open.

Before he climbed out, he took hold of the gun he had tucked in at the back of his waistband.

Wisting sent Amalie up after him, followed by Nanette.

The driving rain was cold and relentless. Wisting positioned Amalie behind the drums where he had hidden earlier and asked Nanette Kranz to look after her. At first she seemed apathetic, but then the task seemed to kindle a spark of interest within her. She nodded and tucked the quilt around them both.

Bantam was inching his way forward, walking with his back pressed to the wheelhouse wall, gun raised. Wisting grabbed a boat hook and skirted around to the other side.

Gillis Haack was standing at the handrail near the prow. He tossed a line out to a rib that had steered alongside, but missed and had to drag it back again. Two large waterproof bags sat on the deck beside him, the pistol lying on top of one.

Haack had hauled in the casting line. He stood, legs astraddle, back turned, holding the coil of rope in one hand and preparing to cast off with the other.

Using both hands, Wisting held the boat hook lengthwise in front of him. As Haack swivelled his hand back to hurl the line, Wisting barrelled forward and mowed him down. Haack landed on one of the bags and lay sprawled, back buckled. Wisting sat astride him and glared into his eyes. He held his gaze long enough to watch his self-confidence and arrogance evaporate. Then he grabbed him by the shoulder and swung him violently around. He drew his arms behind his back and forced them upwards with one hand, grabbing the casting rope with the other.

John Bantam came up behind him and put his hand on Wisting's shoulder.

'I'll take care of him,' he said through the raging wind and rain. 'You get Amalie and the woman into the wheelhouse.'

Wisting moved back, making room for Bantam and handing Haack over.

The boat was toiling in the rough seas. Wisting trudged back to Amalie and lifted her up.

The engine beneath them stuttered and ran fitfully before the engine noise stopped completely. Through the din of the waves, rain and wind, Wisting could make out something else – the rhythmic sound of a helicopter's rotor blades. He wheeled around and saw the searchlight approach from behind.

'Come on,' he said, ushering Nanette Kranz into the wheelhouse.

The wheel was tied firmly, but without engine power they were no longer able to maintain their course. The boat was rotating, smashing side on into the waves.

Ahead of them, on deck, Gillis Haack had staggered to his feet. Wisting had trouble seeing clearly through the rain-speckled window, but it looked as if the casting line still lay on the deck.

The boat lurched dramatically but managed to right itself. Wisting laid Amalie on the deck and again asked Nanette to take care of her. A VHF radio was mounted on the instrument panel, but there was no response when he tried to switch it on.

He pulled out various drawers and found what he was looking for: a pack of distress signal flares.

He snatched them up. Although they were old, they should still work.

The overhead light grew fainter and flickered twice. Wisting peered out on to the deck. Gillis Haack was gone, and John Bantam was trudging alone towards the wheelhouse. Swaying and clutching the handrail as he went, he used both hands to hold himself upright in the wheelhouse doorway.

'Where's Haack?' Wisting asked.

Bantam stared past him, down at Amalie.

'I had to let him go,' he replied, wiping rainwater from his face.

'Go?'

'He jumped,' Bantam replied, returning Wisting's service pistol.

The light flickered again and then expired.

Amalie began to sob in the darkness.

'You take her,' Wisting said, carrying the distress flares out on deck.

The helicopter noise still sounded distant, the searchlight moving south-west. He twisted off the rocket tube's plastic cap and tugged at the release cord. It ignited with a sizzle and the signal flare shot up into the dark clouds to hang in the sky above them. The sea glowed red. To the south he spotted the rib that had been alongside them, only one solitary man aboard as it travelled at speed and vanished into the darkness.

The helicopter appeared to be following the same course before changing tack and heading in their direction.

He stuck his head round the wheelhouse door. 'They're coming!' he called.

The distress flare sank and faded. Wisting sent up another one that was still alight when the helicopter hovered above them.

A rescue worker was lowered down. He landed on deck and barked instructions.

Amalie and Nanette Kranz were tied to rescue harnesses and hoisted into the murk. The rotor blades whipped up a mixture of saltwater and rain. Using his hand to shield his face, Wisting watched them ascend and felt a huge weight lift from his shoulders.

The boat was listing badly in the water as waves swept over the prow. The water was splashing around his feet when it was Wisting's turn to don the harness.

'Wait!' Bantam yelled.

He lifted the two heavy bags and placed one on Wisting's lap. He clasped it tightly and felt that it must contain more than just the gold bars.

The rescue worker tilted his head back, squinting up to give the all-clear signal. Wisting took off with a jerk, swinging to and fro for a few seconds before he too reached safety.

Allocated a window seat, he pulled Amalie towards him. Bantam came aboard with the second bag of gold. Wisting stroked Amalie's hair as he looked out, watching the rescue worker on his way up. The boat was listing badly and being tossed around on the waves that crested over the keel. Then it disappeared into the surging foam.

65

Amalie rested her head on his chest. The engine roar prevented him from talking to her. Wisting simply held her close and stroked her hair from time to time.

Although the helicopter circled the wreck site, homing in with the searchlight for almost quarter of an hour, there was no sign of the missing kidnapper. The rescue worker approached now and again to attend to Amalie and Nanette. Then it seemed that some sort of message had been received and they turned towards the shore.

As Wisting leaned his head on the helicopter window, he felt the vibration travel through his body. They were flying at low altitude. He could make out the lights of buildings and moving vehicles.

'Where are we headed?' he shouted to the front of the cabin.

The nearest pilot turned to face him and pushed his headphones off one ear. 'The hospital in Vestfold,' he replied. 'They're standing by to receive you. Ten minutes.'

Wisting turned back again. He glanced down at the bag between his legs, too small to contain the paintings. He angled towards it and drew back the zip. There was a laptop computer inside, as well as some junction boxes, cables and a mobile phone like the one he himself had used to communicate with the kidnappers. Underneath were the plastic bags filled with gold.

The pilot turned to him again. 'Her mother's been informed,' he said, his eyes on Amalie. 'She's on her way.'

Wisting nodded as he zipped up the bag.

Line must have been the one to sound the alert when she was marooned on the quay at Nevlunghavn. His own phone had been left behind in the car. Bantam's had not survived its immersion in the sea.

Amalie looked up at him. Smiling, he found her hand and held it until the helicopter had landed.

A crew member opened the sliding door and helped them out. Paramedics rushed forward carrying stretchers between them, heads lowered in the wind.

'I can carry her,' Wisting told them.

He followed close behind them. Doctors and nurses peered out from lunch rooms and duty rooms as they moved through the building. Two double doors leading into Accident and Emergency were flung open. Line stood in the corridor a short distance inside.

Holding out her arms to them, she opened her mouth in a silent scream.

Wisting was battling his own feelings. His jaw muscles were trembling uncontrollably. He dumped the bag of gold and handed Amalie to his daughter.

'Here's Mum,' he whispered, and heard how thick with emotion his voice was.

Amalie clung tightly to her mother. Line was unable to say anything before a nurse led them into the emergency room.

Wisting and John Bantam were left in the corridor. They sat down to wait, though they were still chilled in their wet, cold clothes.

A nurse arrived with coffee in paper cups. Wisting put both hands around his. He should have borrowed a phone to call Hammer but felt the need to collect his thoughts first. There were so many things he simply could not get to add up.

'Where are the paintings?' he asked, gazing up at Bantam. 'I didn't see them on board.'

Bantam looked up at the corridor clock. It was past 2 a.m.

'The last time I checked, they were still in the car,' he answered. 'Now the GPS signal has probably stopped.'

Wisting took a couple of gulps of coffee. A nurse came out. 'You can go in now,' she said.

Bantam stood up first, but stopped at the door to let Wisting move ahead.

Amalie was sitting on Line's lap, on the verge of falling asleep. She stole a glance at them before her eyes slid shut.

Wisting stepped forward and ran his fingers over her cheek.

Bantam had brought the bags of gold. He set them on the floor, but stood at close range, as if he did not want to intrude.

'What did the doctor say?' Wisting asked.

'No physical injuries,' Line whispered in response. 'We'll stay here until morning and speak to a trauma psychologist before we go home.'

She lifted her daughter across to the bed and covered her with the quilt.

Wisting perched on the edge of the bed beside her.

'They've offered that to the whole family,' Line went on. She approached and threw her arms around him. 'Thanks,' she whispered.

Wisting closed his eyes. Line lingered and did not move.

'You should go and lie down for a bit,' she said, before

turning to Bantam. 'You too,' she added in English. 'Get some rest.'

Wisting peeked at Amalie in the bed. Nothing was urgent any longer, he thought, as he lay down beside her.

66

A nurse woke him gently. Blinking, Wisting noticed that the light in the room was dimmed as the nurse spoke to him in a whisper.

'Phone call for you,' she said, holding out a cordless internal phone.

Muffled noises reached them from the corridor outside. The clock above the door showed the time as half past five. Line and Amalie were lying asleep in the adjacent bed. Bantam glanced up from a nearby chair.

Wisting sat up. 'Thanks,' he replied in an undertone as he grasped the phone.

It was Hammer. 'How's it going?' he asked.

The nurse left, closing the door carefully behind her. Wisting cleared his throat but could not muster a response.

'What about Amalie?' Hammer insisted.

'She's OK,' Wisting finally managed to say, looking across at her. 'She's doing fine now.'

'What exactly has happened?' Hammer demanded.

Scrambling out of bed, Wisting caught a glimpse of the bags of gold stowed at the foot.

'They took her,' he replied.

Hammer seemed afraid to ask anything more. 'There's a press conference at 9 a.m.,' he said. 'The police chief wants a briefing from you first.'

Wisting ran his hand through his hair, which was sticky with saltwater.

'Are the Swedes still there?' he asked.

'Walin will join the press conference,' Hammer answered. 'They'll leave after that.'

Wisting gazed across at his grandchild again. The thought of her had overshadowed everything else. Now that her safety was assured, he began to see everything else more clearly.

'The man in the rib was arrested when he berthed in Jutland,' Hammer continued, it seemed mostly to have something to say. 'He was alone, probably just hired for a transport assignment,' he went on when Wisting had still failed to say anything. 'They're still searching for Haack.'

Wisting coughed. He felt he owed Hammer an explanation but did not really know where to begin. 'There's a notepad in the top drawer of my office desk,' he said. 'It's locked, but you'll manage to get it open. Everything's written down there.'

'I see,' was Hammer's terse response. He still sounded hesitant when he added: 'The chief has alerted Internal Affairs. They're on their way here now. You're to be suspended.'

Wisting had not expected anything else. He hunkered down beside the bags of gold and unzipped one of them.

'I've a couple of things I need to sort out,' he said. 'But you can tell the chief that I'm on my way.'

'Is there anything I can help with?' Hammer asked.

Wisting gave this some thought. 'Meet me in the rear car park of the hotel at eight o'clock,' he said, before setting aside the phone.

Line and Amalie were still sleeping. John Bantam had got to his feet. Wisting took out Haack's encrypted phone and closed the bag again.

It took a while for the phone to switch on. The battery

capacity was good, but it needed a six-digit PIN code or facial recognition.

Wisting shot a glance at Bantam. 'Come with me,' he said.

He headed to the duty room, addressing himself to the same nurse who had brought him the cordless phone.

'A man from Larvik was admitted yesterday with gunshot injuries,' he said. 'Is he still here?'

The nurse's face took on a sorrowful expression. 'He was declared dead at the scene,' she replied.

'But is he here?' Wisting asked.

Her computer screen confirmed this. 'I have to see him,' Wisting said.

'Wait a moment,' the nurse answered, 'and I'll get the duty doctor to accompany you.'

It took no more than five minutes. An older, bald man took them down two floors without asking any questions.

'He's going for post-mortem later this morning,' he commented as he wheeled out the stretcher trolley.

Wisting looked around before helping himself to latex gloves from a box. One tore at the wrist when he tugged them on, but he ignored that. He opened the body bag and folded it to one side. Elton Khan lay there with his mouth half open. Although he had a few scratches on his cheek, there were no visible signs of decomposition.

Wisting produced the encrypted phone and held it above him. 'I assume you know what you're doing,' the doctor remarked.

'I'll be quick,' Wisting said.

He checked the screen, but the phone was still requesting a PIN number. He tried a couple more times without success.

'Maybe only Haack has access,' Bantam suggested.

'Maybe so,' Wisting said. 'You hold it.'

He passed the phone to Bantam and walked around to the head of the corpse. All moral scruples had been jettisoned long ago. He placed his thumbs on the body's eyelids and drew them back to reveal the pupils.

Bantam guided the phone across the face. Wisting could see in the reflection on the eyeball that the screen had opened.

He pulled off the gloves and took charge of the phone.

'I presume you're finished,' the doctor said. Without waiting for a response, he zipped the bag shut and trundled the trolley away.

Wisting headed for the door. The menu choices on the phone were in English and he took a few seconds to locate the security settings, but he managed to add his own face and have it accepted. Then he began to browse through the contents, reading as he moved up the floors again and returned to Amalie's room.

Line had got up. Amalie was still in bed.

'Everything OK?' he asked. Line nodded. He did not wait for her to add anything further. 'Do you have a car here?' he asked.

'Your car,' she replied.

Wisting put the encrypted phone back in the bag. 'I need to use it,' he said. 'This isn't over yet.'

67

Hammer was standing in the back car park of the hotel in Storgata when Wisting turned in. Once parked, he stepped out of the car and opened the rear door.

'What's going on?' Hammer asked, opening out his arms in a gesture of bewilderment.

Wisting did not answer. Hauling out one bag, he carried it across and placed it on the bonnet. The contents rattled.

'The gold?' Hammer asked.

'Among other things,' Wisting replied. He unzipped the bag and took out the encrypted phone.

'Their comms equipment,' he explained, weighing the mobile phone in his hand. 'The kidnappers have been in touch with a third party,' he said, opening the message log.

'What do you mean?' Hammer asked.

Wisting gave him the phone and Hammer began to read. 'Your name's listed here,' he exclaimed. 'Line and Amalie . . .'

As he scrolled on, it dawned on him what this was really all about. 'This is sensitive information from the investigation,' he said. 'It goes far back in time.'

He looked up. 'It's all in Swedish,' he added.

Wisting nodded. 'I thought that one of the Swedes had fallen victim to the same stunt as me, with Amalie,' he said. 'But there were only two hostages on board the boat.'

Hammer waved the hand that held the encrypted phone. 'This isn't about blackmail,' he said. 'It's the answer to all the rumours of corruption and suspicions about leaks the Swedes have had.'

He was spitting with fury as he spoke. 'Who is it?' he demanded.

Wisting gazed up at the hotel. 'Jan Serner,' he said.

'Serner?' Hammer queried. 'Do you have proof?'

Wisting returned the bag of gold to the rear seat of the car. 'We'll go in and get some now,' he said, setting off towards the hotel entrance.

There was a queue at the reception desk. Wisting wanted to walk past, but Hammer held him back. 'You have to tell me more first,' he insisted.

Wisting took Hammer aside and explained how he had tried to obtain an exchange deal for the paintings from Gunnar Helner's basement.

Hammer nodded. He had read Wisting's log and knew about the pictures.

'When the taxi was rammed, I thought Haack had been at the churchyard and picked up the paintings, and that they were in the back of the car he made off in,' Wisting said. 'But they were in the car behind. In Jan Serner's hire car.'

Hammer swallowed so hard he had to clear his throat.

'He's not just a traitor,' he said. 'That also makes him a murderer. He shot Elton Khan. He would have shot Haack too if you hadn't blocked him.'

'He must have spotted the opportunity to get the six-million-pound reward for the paintings all on his own,' Wisting pointed out. 'But then he would have to eliminate Elton Khan and Gillis Haack. At the same time, it was a way of getting rid of the accomplices who could expose him later.'

The reception was no longer busy. Wisting stepped forward to the counter and showed his service badge. The man at the desk nodded, as if he already knew who Wisting was.

'I need to know what room Jan Serner's staying in,' he said.

The receptionist had to check the guest list. 'Two one eight,' he answered, looking up from the computer screen. 'Checking out today.'

Leaning forward, Wisting snatched the master key card. They took the stairs and let themselves into the room. 'He's packed,' Hammer commented.

A travel bag lay on the bed, the same one that Serner had brought when they had arrived by helicopter four days earlier. An open soap bag lay beside it.

Wisting looked through the bag but realized there was insufficient space for the paintings. He lifted the quilt, squinted underneath the bed and opened the wardrobe. There were no other hiding places. The paintings were not in the room.

'Maybe they're still in the car,' Hammer suggested.

Wisting shook his head. 'I think we're too late,' he said.

They let themselves out of the room and handed back the card at reception. 'Is there anything I can do for you?' the receptionist asked.

Wisting looked up at the CCTV dome on the ceiling.

'Are you looking for something?' the receptionist asked when he received no reply.

Something in his voice caused Wisting to stare at him rather than brush off the question.

'There's a package here for Jan Serner,' the man behind the desk went on, indicating an adjacent sideboard. 'He asked the night porter if we could mail it for him.'

Wisting followed his gaze to a cardboard box, big enough to contain at least one of the stolen paintings.

'You said it was *for* Jan Serner?' Hammer asked.

The receptionist fetched the parcel. 'I expect it's something he wants posted to himself,' he said.

Wisting picked up the package. It was to be sent to a care-of address in Stockholm.

He began to tear off the tape. The receptionist brought him a pair of scissors.

'Careful,' Hammer warned. Wisting managed to make an opening large enough to catch sight of the three rolled-up canvases.

68

The assembled press corps stood in the pale early light outside the police station's main entrance, waiting to be ushered in. Wisting looked up at the building's rain-spattered facade as he drove past, uncertain of how to present his revelations.

The paintings lay on the back seat along with the gold. Hammer was following in the vehicle behind.

A cat ran across the road just as they turned into the back yard and, all of a sudden, he was standing in front of them.

Jan Serner.

He took a drag of his cigarette and stepped aside to let the car pass.

Wisting felt hot and uncomfortable at the spectacle. As the car glided slowly past, his eyes watched him in the mirror as he passed. A build-up of anger and frustration made him start to shake and he had to steel himself in order to park the car safely.

Hammer drove into an empty space behind him. The car door slammed loudly as he got out. Wisting leaned forward, opened the glove compartment and brought a pair of handcuffs with him as he left the car.

Serner took another drag of his cigarette.

Wisting could not wait to confront him. 'You . . .' he began, but his voice gave way.

Blowing out smoke, Serner looked from Wisting to

Hammer and stood his ground. 'What fucking awful guys,' he said, referring to the men who had held Amalie captive.

Hammer took a step forward before Wisting had a chance to say anything. He swung his arm in an arc and punched Serner right under his eye. The Swedish policeman staggered back, stumbling into a car.

Wisting felt a surge of rage he was not sure he would be able to control. He made a fist with his hand, but stood watching as Hammer knocked their Swedish colleague about, spread-eagling him across the bonnet and twisting his right hand all the way up to his shoulder blades.

Serner screamed with pain and tried to push himself off with his free hand. Hammer pressed all his weight down, produced handcuffs from his belt and clicked one shackle into place before unhooking the other arm.

Faces appeared at the windows above them.

'What the fuck are you doing?' Serner yelled.

Hammer hauled him up with no explanation and dragged him across the yard to the entrance. He fumbled with the door, using one hand, as he forced Serner against the wall with the other.

Wisting wanted to help. 'I think you should stay well back,' Hammer said, lugging Serner inside.

The man's cries of protest echoed through the basement corridors. Wisting stood in the rain in front of the doorway until the shouts subsided in the custody suite, before entering. A sense of relief flooded through him with each step he took on the way up to his office.

He opened the door and stood just inside, taking in the familiar space, contemplating that it might be a long time before he would be able to return.

He had spent a lot of time there. The seat of the office

chair was well worn and the fabric on the back was torn. The keyboard was grubby. There were fingerprints on the computer screen and rings on the desk left by coffee cups.

The desk drawer was open after Hammer's search. Some of the wood was splintered, but the lock did not appear damaged.

He slid it back in again.

The withered bouquet of flowers still lay on the shelf. He tossed it into the waste bucket and wiped the residue with his hands before opening the door and walking out.

69

They were on the settee. Amalie spelled her way through the first few sentences on each page before Wisting read out the rest to her.

There was a little improvement every day. She was finding it easier to recognize the letters and join them up into words. Progress was slow, but she was reading correctly and not being impatient.

He turned the page. Amalie let her finger slide along the first line. Her hair fell in front of her face and Wisting tucked it behind her ear.

She was going to read many books, he mused, growing a bit wiser with each one and understanding a little more of the world around her each time.

A noise at the door made them look up – Line called out to announce her presence.

Amalie sprang up from the settee, ran out into the hallway and returned with her mother.

'Have you had a nice time?' Line asked.

'Very,' Wisting assured her, glancing down at Amalie.

Almost three weeks had gone by. There was nothing to suggest that she had been adversely affected by her experience.

'We've already eaten,' he added. 'There are some leftovers.'

'It's OK,' Line said.

Amalie climbed back up on the settee and continued reading. Line sat down on the armrest.

'They said on the news that a man's body has been found in the Naver fjord,' she told him.

Wisting nodded. 'Hammer phoned,' he said. 'Gillis Haack.'

'Is there any other news?' Line asked.

'The green container has been returned to Gunnar Helner,' Wisting replied. 'I'm going to meet him this evening. I owe him a dinner.'

'And an explanation, perhaps,' Line said. She began to gather up Amalie's belongings and asked her to get ready to leave.

Amalie put her book back on the shelf. Wisting escorted them to the door and helped her on with her wellingtons and rain jacket.

'When are you returning to work?' Line asked.

'Soon,' Wisting said.

Amalie gave him a long hug before taking her mother's hand as they set off. Wisting stood in the doorway, watching them. It was cold outside, but it had stopped raining.